TIWELNS REDEEMER

To a fellow writer,
Rebekah Arman

Tiweln's Redeemer

Nature's Lady

REBEKAH AMAN

TATE PUBLISHING
AND ENTERPRISES, LLC

Tiweln's Redeemer
Copyright © 2011 by Rebekah Aman. All rights reserved.

No part of this publication may be reproduced, stored in a retrieval system or transmitted in any way by any means, electronic, mechanical, photocopy, recording or otherwise without the prior permission of the author except as provided by USA copyright law.

This novel is a work of fiction. Names, descriptions, entities, and incidents included in the story are products of the author's imagination. Any resemblance to actual persons, events, and entities is entirely coincidental.

The opinions expressed by the author are not necessarily those of Tate Publishing, LLC.

Published by Tate Publishing & Enterprises, LLC
127 E. Trade Center Terrace | Mustang, Oklahoma 73064 USA
1.888.361.9473 | www.tatepublishing.com

Tate Publishing is committed to excellence in the publishing industry. The company reflects the philosophy established by the founders, based on Psalm 68:11,
"The Lord gave the word and great was the company of those who published it."

Book design copyright © 2011 by Tate Publishing, LLC. All rights reserved.
Cover design by Kristen Verser
Interior design by April Marciszewski

Published in the United States of America

ISBN: 978-1-61777-956-5
1. Fiction / Fantasy / Epic
2. Juvenile Fiction / Fantasy & Magic
11.12.06

To TLOML
Without your support,
I'd be a mere shadow.

Wefleca
Azol
Suta
Suta
Lonyi
Reyulicos
Cinnaca
Yima Olem
Yappés
Rom
Wilksom Olem
Meufa
Socuma
Omhemalem
Omhemalem

Prologue

Into the dark, deserted landscape fled two figures. Silent as the slow-coming sunrise, the two ran side by side, fearing not for their own lives, but for the young life between them, embraced within her mother's arms. Fear was a tangible force as the fleet-footed escapees swiftly maneuvered between the silent trees, the crashing sound of soldiers in pursuit ringing in their ears. As long as they remained within the forest's cover, it would be nearly impossible for the human eye to spot them in the darkness, but the wood ended abruptly, and the couple found themselves running across a field, an open space that could provide no cover and instead an end to the chase.

Escaping from the guards by cover of night with a suspiciously absent moon, they searched desperately for a safe and secret haven for Alernoa. Yet now, as they left the shelter of the tall, wooden sentinels, it was easy to see that the chase was almost over, that the King and Queen would yet again be captured, but if they could save their child, everything else from that moment forward would be bearable.

In a wild panic, Lenaia hid her baby girl in some bushes beside a roaring waterfall, uttering a silent prayer that someone would find and save her child. With a last caress, she covered the infant more securely within her tiny, blue blanket and ensured that the locket around the girl's neck was safely hidden. With her last glance, she wished with all her heart to see her again, and with her last taste of freedom, she whispered, "Sleep well, my dear baby, and grow in strength. Find your gift and be happy. I love you, Alernoa."

She stood quickly and joined her husband as he stood lookout a short way from their child. It was only a moment before men burst from the wood, preceded by war cries. With tearful eyes, she looked up to see her beloved's steady gaze as he looked to the horizon. As the sun rose, the two shared one last embrace before the men seized them and dragged them toward their uncertain destiny.

Just before leaving the field, Lenaia chanced one quick, last glimpse at the bushes behind which Alernoa lay, not realizing the girl had found her gift as flowers began to grow round her in the morning sunlight.

Chapter One

"Tell me again, Papa," the girl said thoughtfully, fingering the chain around her neck. "Tell me again how you found me."

"I've told you a thousand times. Don't you ever get tired of it?" the old man asked, rubbing his head. It always worried him when she brought up the subject. The fear of losing his daughter was an ever-present stone in his gut.

The girl gasped. "Never! How could I ever tire of hearing it? Maybe if you repeat it enough, I'll find some clue to my past. Please tell me again. Please!"

"All right." The man forced a chuckle, readying himself to make the story sound wonderful. "There was morning dew on the ground, and I was going to fetch some water. For some reason, I decided to cut across my field and walk through the woods toward the waterfall. I looked down when I exited the wood and saw marks that led me to believe that there had been a scuffle of some sort the night before, and as I followed the tracks, I noticed that some small footprints, probably those of a woman, led away to a clump of bushes. When I walked over, I noticed multicolored flowers growing together, forming a bubble of some sort, like they covered something. Oddest thing I've ever encountered, let me tell you. I shrugged it off, scooped up my water, but as I turned to go, I heard a giggle coming from those flowers. Rushing over, I spread them and saw a beautiful baby girl!"

"Me," the girl said, smiling.

"Exactly, but I didn't know where you'd come from, what your name was, or how you got there, so…"

"So you took me here and named me Genevia…but didn't you find out anything about my parents?"

The old man sighed. Yes, he had a good idea about that. When he had asked around the small town that lay several miles from his own backwoods cottage, he had discovered that Fezam's soldiers had come through dragging elfin prisoners with them—the last free elves, he had heard. By now, they must all be dead; everyone was beginning to consider them myth anyway. The elves had been disappearing years before that night; and even before that odd man who called himself Fezam had appeared, the elves had kept to themselves.

Drisgal knew that Genevia must have come with them—if nothing else, her pointed ears, an elf's defining feature, gave that away—but he was scared for her to ever find out. He had lived as an unhappy hermit before her sudden appearance had brought joy into his life, and the thought of returning to that reclusive existence without her terrified him. What if she left to find her own kind and was captured because of her race? She could be rotting in a tiny prison, crying for his help, and he would be unable to save her. He had to keep her in the dark, enforcing the idea that elves and even dwarves—for who ever saw dwarves anymore these days?—were all fantasy. It was all for her own protection. Even the small town on the coast was rife with potential danger, which was precisely why she had never been allowed to travel with him for supplies.

But she continued to ask this same question, and no matter how often it was uttered, he never got use to lying to the girl. "Don't you know I would have told you had I known?"

"Yes," Genevia stated sadly, eyes downcast. "But I just can't help wishing you knew something."

"I'm sorry," Drisgal said compassionately, truly meaning the words but unwilling to risk the possibility of losing his precious daughter. With a sad smile, he leaned in to give Genevia a kiss on the forehead. "I know how much this means to you."

There was silence in the kitchen, and Drisgal could not handle it. He needed her out of the house so he could compose himself. Lying certainly took a toll on a body. "Now, why don't you go make yourself useful? That firewood needs restocking, and maybe you could go pick us some flowers, hmm?"

Genevia smiled. "Fine, but the flowers I picked last week are still in full bloom."

As she walked out the front door of the little cabin, Drisgal went to examine the flowers. He shook his head in confusion. Flowers weren't supposed to live this long after they'd been picked, not that he had ever let Genevia know that. It was just more proof that she was not human, although he wasn't certain how she kept the blossoms alive so long. He didn't know much about elves.

Genevia was different from those of his race in many ways, though most would overlook the presence of it in her appearance. She was beautiful, as all elves were said to be, with long, dark brown hair and flashing green eyes, but the majority of humans would just grant her as being an exceptionally beautiful person, unless they saw her pointed ears. No human Drisgal had ever seen sported ears like that, and he was certain it would be a dead giveaway.

She was graceful and tall with small feet, and one had to wonder how she managed to keep her balance. Genevia had always been slim, despite what she ate, and she had an air of authority about her, though she was kind and thoughtful. Drisgal liked to attribute most of that to her upbringing and general personality, but he could never get rid of that pesky feeling that it had something to do with her bloodline.

Nature seemed to call to her, and it always appeared that wherever she walked flowers would perk up, but maybe he was just imagining it. Animals never ran from her, and when she climbed trees, the branches seemed to move to accommodate her height.

She was wise beyond her years, though books were her only schooling, and this kept Drisgal wondering. Would she figure it out on her own? He was worried about his girl, all right, because he loved her greatly and would never give her up—if he was given the choice.

After climbing high up a brimblewood tree, Genevia fluttered down gracefully, a smile of contentment stretching across her face. This was where she loved to be, surrounded by nature.

"Maybe my parents were royalty, running from a madman bent on taking over the world," Genevia said to herself with a smile, picking up a stick. This was her favorite game, imagining the infinite possibilities of how she came to be here. So she might be a little old for this indulgence, but who was there to see her? "My father fought to save me and my mother—'Get back, I tell you, or I'll run you through!' And my mother hid me in the bushes and picked up a sword of her own to fight off two men." She laughed. "You'll never take me alive!"

Genevia fought against imaginary soldiers with her stick. "You think you can defeat me?"

She could practically see the scene unfolding before her eyes. "Back, I say! Take this, and that, and this!"

Genevia parried and stabbed, blocked and dodged as imaginary soldiers attacked. Finally, she stopped for breath, still imagining the scene. After the image was spent, she looked down at her weapon, but instead of the ordinary stick she had picked up, she saw a wooden sword. "Oh! I don't remember picking up a stick that looks like this!"

"That's because you didn't," came a deep, rich voice from behind her.

Startled, she spun around. A tall man was leaning against a tree, arms crossed, staring at her. He was very handsome, with a square jaw sprinkled with beard scruff, and he looked to be in his early twenties. His blue eyes were intense, almost cold; his hair was dark and wild, looking as if he had cut it blindfolded, but somehow it still managed to suit him perfectly, giving him an almost mischievous air; and he was tan, but not too much so. Had he even bothered to relax his mouth from that straight, no-nonsense almost-scowl, he would have been devastatingly gorgeous, but as it was, Genevia had to wonder if he had ever learned to smile.

"Who are you?" Genevia demanded, clutching her sword tighter and pointing it at him—as if that would do any good.

Surprisingly, the man bowed slightly, never taking his eyes off her. "I am Frelati. I'm sorry if I startled you, but I heard noise and decided to investigate."

"Oh, well, it isn't nice to sneak up on someone," Genevia scolded, using her stick for emphasis.

"May I have your name?" Frelati asked in a voice neither kind nor cold but chillingly neutral.

Genevia eyed him suspiciously. "Genevia."

"Well, I'm glad to make your acquaintance, Genevia," Frelati said, although his unsmiling face didn't appear glad as he looked her over. "Correct me if I'm wrong, but are you an elf?"

"What?" Genevia asked in surprise.

Frelati's expression softened a bit. "Your ears, they're pointed like mine."

Genevia felt her left ear, unconscious of the motion as her brows scrunched together. She had noticed that her ears were pointed before, but she hadn't seen that many other people for comparison. Although all of them she had seen had rounded ears, she hadn't thought a thing of it. As she examined the man before her, she noticed their similarity, but still…

"There is no such thing as elves." She decided. "They are a myth. And besides, my papa would have told me that I was an elf, if there really were elves."

Frelati smiled then, proving Genevia's impression that a smile would do wonders for his appearance, and he laughed a deep, pleasant rumble of a laugh. It didn't last long, almost as if he was not used to giving in to mirth. "Then what do you think I am? I'm clearly here, and I'm certainly not a dwarf…and, although we resemble them the most, I am not human."

"Well, of course you're human!" Genevia exclaimed, eyes flashing dangerously. "I don't know what game you're playing, but dwarves and elves are myths."

Frelati held up his hands, watching her in confusion.

"Calm down, will you? I'm not playing tricks." He paused. "I'm not sure what sheltered life you've been living, but dwarves and, yes, elves exist. You have undeniable proof right here, standing before you. And you…you have all the characteristics of an elf: pointed ears, small feet, perfect features and build, natural grace. Just by what I've seen, I could not mistake your race."

Genevia felt the blood rushing to her cheeks and focused on tossing away her stick-sword to avoid looking at him. "I'm not perfect."

Frelati shook his head. "Well, maybe not inside, but outside… yes, you are. I'm staring right at you, and there is no other explanation. You have to be an elf, and your father would know that because either he or your mother is one."

"I don't have a mother, and my father doesn't have pointed ears. He's just an ordinary human…like I am."

Genevia stated the last sentence emphatically as if to convince herself because, despite her efforts to ignore him, Frelati's words were worming their way into her mind, and she was finding that a lot of facts were beginning to come together.

"Well, you have some elf blood in you," Frelati forged on. "Maybe a grandmother on your mother's side, though you look more elfin than that blood line would give."

Genevia considered explaining her background, but this stranger didn't need to know a thing about her. Besides, he didn't need any more ammunition with which to argue his case. Before Frelati got too far in the conversation, though, she decided to change it. She didn't relish the idea of having to flat-out lie.

"Well, what brings you here?" she asked.

Frelati considered before answering. It took a while, but finally he cleared his throat and responded. "Two things, actually. First, I was sent here to find someone. Second, I'm on the run. As I said, I'm an elf, and Fezam doesn't like my race too much. That could be the reason your father never told you who you are."

Genevia was confused. "Who's Fezam?"

Frelati stared at her, once again in shock.

"You don't know of Fezam," Frelati stated slowly. "How could you live…what, fourteen years?…without knowing about Fezam?"

Genevia was indignant. "First, I'm sixteen, and second, I'm not an idiot, so stop looking at me like that. I may not know much of the world, but I refuse to be verbally harassed and looked down upon by a know-it-all elf!"

Her face went completely red with anger, and she had to take several breaths to cool herself down. Frelati just watched her with his cool, steady gaze, not the least disturbed by her outburst.

"I didn't mean to insult you. Forgive me." He bowed his head slightly. "Fezam has ruled the land completely for sixteen years, spreading his insanity, cruelty, sorrow, and all other despicable attributes upon the world. The last land given to him, or taken by him I should say, was owned by the Elfin King and Queen of Meufa. Where we stand now is his land, although because it is such a small island his influence here is minimal, as is readily apparent by your ignorance. The King and Queen of Meufa are held captive by Fezam on Azol; they were among the last holdouts. Once they were captured, everything went downhill. The only hope for Tiweln lies in the hands of the one I must find. They have to end this terrible rule, or our world will be controlled by that madman forever."

All of this was stated matter-of-factly, in a cool, calm manner with only a slight darkening of the eyes or tightening of the lips. It sounded to Genevia much like one commenting on the weather. She let it all sink in slowly, wondering how her father could have failed to mention all of this before. On the other hand, the story did seem fanciful, like one you'd find in a story book, and she had a hard time believing it to be true.

She looked at him skeptically. "You expect me to believe all this?"

He turned his gaze from his surroundings to her face. She seemed so young and vulnerable, but it was better for her to know than to go around thinking the world was filled only with butterflies and happy endings.

"Yes."

His voice was hard, flat, challenging, and one to be believed. Genevia stood quietly, staring at him and trying to decide what could make a man so detached and cool.

"So...let me see if I've got this straight. There's a madman running around trying to take over everything and eventually destroy all happiness in the world," she said slowly with more than a bit of sarcasm in her voice, looking nowhere in particular but still testing him by her stance and words.

"If you choose to simplify it in those terms, then yes," Frelati answered, but clearly his mind was elsewhere because he changed his tone to a more pleasant one in an instant. "By the way, do you know of a place where I can stay? I'm planning to look around a bit, explore if you will, and I would prefer to go to bed with a roof over my head as opposed to open sky. It will rain tonight…well, actually, it will begin to rain soon, and I really don't want to get wet."

"Oh, I'm sure you can stay with my papa and me, or at least in the barn. He shouldn't mind, and I…wait, how do you know it's going to rain? The sky is clear, barely any clouds, and the ones there are aren't storm clouds." Genevia looked up at the canopy above them as if she could see through the leaves. She couldn't, but she did remember the look of the sky before she entered the forest.

Frelati's lip quirked wryly. "I can predict the weather—not change it, but predict it. That's my gift."

"You can tell the weather?" Genevia looked at him, eyes full of wonder and excitement despite her initial response to disbelieve him. "Can you tell me the weather of next week?"

Frelati gave her another true smile. "I can only tell a day in advance, unless a terrible storm is coming. Then I can tell a week or so ahead."

"How did you get your gift? And how did you find out you had a gift?" Genevia asked, mentally kicking herself for being so gullible.

"All elves are bestowed with a gift. Some are harder to discover than others. Ordinarily, though, your gift is a mixture of your parent's gifts. My mother could direct sunlight. My father could cause rain. I can tell you the weather as a result." Frelati shrugged.

"Really? That's interesting," Genevia pondered that tidbit. "I wish I had a gift."

"Well, you should. You're an elf, right?" Frelati shot her a look out of the corner of his eye.

Genevia was beginning to warm up to that idea, and her imagination was beginning to run on overdrive, though her rationale was screaming at her to give it up and tell this Frelati to go back to wherever he came from. "Yeah, yeah, maybe so, maybe I am an elf. Maybe I can read people's minds or call objects to me."

She stretched her hand out in front of her and tried to call a stick into her outstretched fingers. When it didn't come, she started dreaming up more ideas.

"Maybe I can call down lightning! Or…or, maybe, I can cause fire to shoot out of my eyes!"

Frelati stood with an amused smile on his face, watching the excited figure flit about. "Have you ever done any of those things before?" Genevia shook her head, and he continued. "I thought not. You will have been showing signs of your gift since you were a child."

"I haven't done anything though," Genevia said, shaking her head and thinking back. She shrugged and shot him a smug smile. "Guess that proves I'm not an elf."

Frelati sighed and rolled his eyes heavenward. "You aren't thinking hard enough. You see that stick?"

He pointed over to where her stick-sword had fallen.

"Yes," Genevia said slowly, her brows drawing together in thought.

"Maybe you control wood or can transform things. That's all I saw, so I can't be certain, but it would have to be something along those lines."

"Oh," Genevia said distractedly, remembering times throughout her childhood when things seemed different from normal. He couldn't be right, could he?

"A lot of the time, the weaker the elfin blood line, the smaller the gift, but not always. If the elfin line comes from your grandmother, your gift is probably weaker." Frelati paused, closing his eyes and tipping his face skyward. He stood silent for a moment before turning his direct gaze on Genevia. "If we start for your home now, we might miss the rain. It all depends on how far you live from here."

Genevia snapped to reality. "Oh, not far, about a quarter of a mile away. Come on. It's this way."

The two swerved in and out of the trees. The crunching sound of crisp pine needles in desperate need of moisture complained at each footfall. The few words that passed between them echoed softly through the trees until the wind snapped them up and pulled them elsewhere along its path. Eventually, all communication ceased as each admired the beauty around them and submerged into their own thoughts, unaware of one another.

After breaking through the forest, they saw the cabin. The firewood had been completely forgotten in the excitement of the day. One lone figure stood silhouetted before the cabin as the day's sunlight began to fade. Genevia smiled with pride as she saw her father the way this stranger must. He was an older man with graying hair, but he was clearly still well fit and muscular from work on his small farm. However, instead of the smile of greeting Genevia would have preferred to see on his face, she found him watching warily as his daughter entered the yard with a new guest.

"Papa, look who I found!" Genevia said with a smile, rushing forward to stop before her father. She wanted to see his face when Frelati came close enough for him to see his pointed ears.

Drisgal looked at her and frowned, noticing her scrutiny and wondering at the cause. "You know, it isn't always good to bring home complete strangers."

Genevia nodded. "True, but I spoke with him in the woods, and he's a special sort of stranger that we really should get to know."

Genevia watched her father closely as Frelati stopped before him. His face went pale, and his body stiffened. That was all the proof she needed. Disappointment flooded through her, but she knew he must have a reason for keeping such a secret, a good one, and she would find out what it was. She just wished she knew what was going on in his head.

Chapter Two

"Papa, this is Frelati," Genevia said, her voice holding anger just barely in check. "I believe you are aware he's an elf."

Drisgal glanced at her. So she knew, and he could guess who had told her. This was why Drisgal had warned her to avoid strangers, but he understood her disregard of that rule upon meeting this elf. He looked just as the stories described male elves to look, and all females—human and elf alike—couldn't ignore their charms. But there was something about this one, about his stance and the set of his jaw, maybe, that led one to believe that this young man had seen hardship. Anyone could read it in his eyes. There was a hardness in them and cynicism. Charm seemed to have bypassed this elf, or maybe it was beaten out of him. Regardless, Drisgal was going to be watchful of this stranger, especially when it came to his daughter, who was currently sending visual daggers in his direction.

"I'm sorry," he sighed softly, purposely ignoring Frelati.

Genevia's lips tightened. "We'll talk about it later. Aren't you going to speak to Frelati?"

Drisgal turned to face this man who had just altered his world. His expression was not one of welcome, and his voice was gruff as he spoke. "Pleased to meet you."

Frelati bowed courteously, though his expression was just as hostile. "Likewise."

Silence descended, which Genevia jumped in to break. "Frelati needs a place to stay for a while, Papa. He's looking for someone."

"Hmm?" Drisgal asked, his gaze still riveted on Frelati and his mind miles away.

Frelati reiterated. "I was hoping that I might find shelter in your barn. As payment, I will help you with your work until I've found the friend I'm looking for."

Drisgal sniffed and eyed his daughter and Frelati in turn, pondering whether or not to allow this stranger to stay with them.

"Please, Papa, it's what we always do. You wouldn't have us be inhospitable, would you?" It wasn't a question. Drisgal clearly heard the warning laced within her words. "Besides, he just promised to help you with the work around here, and you have been mentioning, just recently, the possibility of hiring an extra hand."

He couldn't argue with that logic and come out the victor. Drisgal nodded sharply. "Fine, but if I am displeased with the arrangement, you must leave at once."

Nodding in consent, Frelati assured him, "As you wish."

Drisgal turned toward the house, leading his daughter before him.

"Sir," Frelati spoke, halting his retreat. "May I have your name?"

Drisgal grunted and sent a glare his way. "Drisgal."

Propelling Genevia ahead of him, they disappeared into the house, probably to have that discussion into which Drisgal was so loathe to enter. Frelati nodded in satisfaction and headed for the barn, making it through the door just as the first drops of rain began their descent.

The next morning Genevia was up early, just as the sun began to show its splendid array of colors in the sky. She dressed quickly and began making breakfast, a special breakfast this morning for the new guest. She was determined to make him feel welcome, despite her father, who was treading a very thin rope right now.

She hummed as she cooked, hoping to dispel the gloom in the kitchen and in herself, and pretty soon the smells of sausage and hotcakes spread to fill every corner in the cabin.

The cause of the delicious aromas was quickly transferred to three plates, one of which she left on the table for her father, and then Genevia left to eat breakfast with Frelati. He was still asleep, so after setting the plates down on a nearby bale of hay, she gently tapped him on the shoulder. Frelati opened his eyes to see a curious face peeping at him, just inches from his own. Genevia's hair was tickling his cheek, and he shot up quickly, the anger that seemed always to reside within his being just about to spill over. He had never liked being startled, and prison had taught Frelati that being woken suddenly was never a good thing.

He glanced at her with narrowed eyes, still very tired, which frustrated him all the more. He never seemed to get enough sleep. "Was it truly necessary for such close proximity, or were you simply testing me for my reaction? Because you must know how unpleasant it is to wake and discover a face inches from your own."

"Sorry." Genevia shrugged as she moved to shield the plates from his view, not sounding the least apologetic. "I was curious. I don't know much about elves."

"Well, the next time you decide to study me, tell me about it. And waiting until I'm awake wouldn't be such a bad idea either," Frelati said crossly. Then he noticed the way she was standing. She was hiding something. Instant alarm rose within him. He hid it well, but his next question was a bark. "What are you hiding?"

"Something," Genevia said elusively with a mischievous smile, not the least rattled by his tone.

"That's obvious. What kind of something?" Frelati demanded as his fists tightened. He had to force himself to remain seated and not jump to discover whatever it was she had. If she was planning to harm him, she would have done so by now.

Genevia shrugged and looked at him with feigned innocence. "My, aren't we jumpy? No need to worry; it's just food. I thought you might be hungry."

She stepped aside with a flourish to show him her creation. Frelati saw hotcakes with butter and syrup dripping over the side to fill the whole plate with its sweetness. The sausage couldn't escape and was completely covered. He relaxed instantly, and his stomach grumbled at the sight of the feast.

Genevia chuckled, a smile spreading across her face. "Doesn't it look good? I made it myself."

"It does look good," Frelati said grudgingly, taking his plate from her. "Thanks. I haven't had a decent meal in...well, years."

Genevia puzzled over that as she cut her hotcakes into small pieces. "So elves can't cook?"

"I didn't say that," Frelati said shortly before stuffing a bite in his mouth. "I said that I haven't had good food in years. Elves can cook just as well or just as terribly as any other race."

"Oh." Genevia felt that the subject was closed, regardless of her confusion over his statement. "So, tell me about yourself."

Frelati glanced at her before his eyes moved back to his rapidly disappearing food. "I don't talk about myself."

Genevia scowled. "Well, that's your payment for the food. No story, no food."

She made a grab for his half-empty plate, and Frelati made an instant protest.

"Hey! You could have qualified that before giving it to me." He glared at her, but she made no move to budge on the point. His lips tightened in a grimace before he gave in, speaking flatly, and Genevia released the plate. Manipulative girl. "I grew up on Meufa as a servant to the King and Queen of the elves. I traveled around, and then eventually I came here."

Genevia scoffed. "You are telling me absolutely nothing. Elaborate just a little, will you? Surely that won't kill your gruff personality too much." Frelati smirked quickly before pulling his mask back down again. Genevia continued. "Where's Meufa? Who are the King and Queen? Where did you travel? How old are you? Tell me something."

Genevia sat down on a bale of hay, preparing herself to listen. It was apparent that he wasn't getting rid of her until she was satisfied.

"Meufa is a small island not too far from here. Few elves live there, actually, because it belongs to the Elfin King and Queen and their court. Well, now it belongs to Fezam, but it did belong to them." Frelati took a bite of food before continuing, his voice slightly wistful as he described his childhood home. "Meufa is beautiful. It has rivers and waterfalls, beaches and a jungle. It has many exotic animals, found nowhere else in the world. Some of the more common animals, though, are the pink and blue dolphins that swim around the island, the lefnodes and the zarpinks, and, of course, the flifnimps. The place is almost magical."

Frelati paused, collecting his thoughts and taking a bite of sausage. "The only reason I lived there was because I was born to servants of the King. They were trusted servants, and the King and Queen were always kind to me." A slight smile played around Frelati's lips as he remembered. "While I grew up, I stayed at the waterfall. There was a small cave behind it that led to passageways, and I explored them all. Of course, I was really young, so once the adults found out what I was doing they told me not to go there anymore. I had to travel with the King and Queen at age seven and stayed with them until recently. I'm on my own now, until I find the friend I was sent to find."

Genevia had sat transfixed while listening to Frelati's story, but she still had unanswered questions that bubbled up from inside her. "What are all of those animals you mentioned? Not the dolphins, I've read about them, but those others. What are they?"

Frelati smiled, remembering the creatures. It had been a long time since he'd thought about them. "A lefnode is a curious little creature. They have long snouts, more like trunks, and a tiny nub of a tail. They're pretty small, about the size of three hands in length, I guess, and they're really fluffy and friendly, but they're useful too. They can find just about anything by smell. They come in any color, but if you're lucky you can get one in all colors. They're really rare and almost impossible to find.

"A zarpink is very different. They're a reddish color, sometimes bright pink. They stand upright with a long tail for balance, and they grow to about four feet tall. They hop instead of walk, and they tend to follow you around, grunting for food. Their snouts are almost flat with a large nose smack in the middle, and they have huge eyes with ears like a coyote. They're interesting but don't seem to have much purpose, unless being annoying counts."

Frelati paused then to clear his throat and take a swig of some milk Genevia had brought with her. He hadn't talked this much since...ever. He set his empty plate aside and started describing the last creature. "Flifnimps are camouflaging animals. They're a lot like regular birds, I guess. No one really knows what color they are. They can swim on water, but their nests are on land. They can fly, but they rarely do. I like to think it's because there's no challenge in their camouflaging up there with all that blue. They have huge wings and beady eyes and stick legs, but they don't have any feathers. They're more leathery. They eat berries and nuts, so their beaks tend to be small to accommodate that. Overall, they aren't that big either.

"The other animals on the island are common, but the whole place is remarkable. Plenty of flowers and exotic plants grow there of all colors, and many diseases have been cured by the nectar of those plants. It was a wonderful place to live." Frelati paused and looked down at his hands. "I hope I'll be able to go back, just see it one more time."

Genevia quietly reflected on all he had described in his wonderfully deep voice before she spoke softly. "That sounds…absolutely perfect. I would love to see it."

"Maybe you can one day," Frelati said with a shrug. "So, what do you do around here? I'd like to get started on my work."

"You could get the eggs from the chickens," Genevia suggested.

Frelati eyed the pen warily through the open barn door. "I'm not certain about that."

"Come on, you chicken," Genevia taunted with a grin. "All you do is grab the eggs; the birds won't attack."

He glanced her way and nodded, not at all sure it was as easy as she said, and walked over to the pen with Genevia right on his heels, waiting to see if she would find any amusement after all. Frelati managed to gather the eggs and hand them to a disappointed Genevia before her wish of amusement was granted. A chicken escaped, and Frelati took up the chase. Genevia tried to hold it back, but a burst of laughter slipped through her lips at the sight of serious, no-nonsense Frelati trying to herd the chicken back into her pen.

"Haven't you ever caught a chicken before?" Genevia managed to ask through her laughter. The chicken was valiantly dodging every one of Frelati's attempts to guide her in the right direction.

Frelati stopped, putting his hands on his hips and glaring at the stubborn creature. He didn't need this, and he didn't enjoy being laughed at. He took one more lunge toward the animal, which darted off in the opposite of the intended direction, and tripped over a bucket that had no business lying where it was lying.

"Oof," Frelati huffed as he caught himself with his hands just before landing face first on the ground. He turned annoyed eyes on Genevia. "No, I have never done this before; what was your first clue?"

He pushed himself to a sitting position and glared at the chicken as she strutted around just feet from him. "You annoying little beast!"

His scowl, his unconcealed disgust at the creature, the fact that he was covered in dirt, and his muttered comment, combined to make Genevia laugh all the more. It was nice to see the man act like a normal person for once.

It was to this scene—Frelati on the ground, a chicken strutting around, and Genevia clinging to a post to keep upright through her laughter—that Drisgal entered.

"Well, aren't we having fun," Drisgal commented dryly, his eyes branding Frelati with his dislike.

Genevia stifled a laugh and straightened while Frelati lifted himself from the ground, dusting the dirt from his clothes. After seeing her father eyeing the escaped chicken with disapproval, Genevia hurriedly scooped up the mischief-maker and put her safely in the pen with the others. She glanced at Frelati and saw his annoyed look deepen after she had so easily and quickly deposited the chicken in the pen.

"Did you like your breakfast, Papa?" Genevia asked.

"It was very enjoyable; however, those dishes won't wash themselves." His eyes never left Frelati.

Genevia was still unhappy with him and didn't particularly like his reaction to Frelati, but she recognized her cue to leave. She didn't want to go inside because, although Drisgal had always been a passive man, she worried an argument might follow in her absence. That was almost enough to make her stay, but there was enough stress between her and her father without her disobeying him now, so she nodded and left to grab the plates from the barn before heading inside.

Frelati felt uncomfortable under Drisgal's unwavering and distrustful gaze, not that his countenance showed that, and hurried to fill the silence. "What exactly was the job you wanted me to do?"

"Can you work a garden?" Drisgal asked gruffly.

"I haven't done it before, but I'm a fast learner."

"Good. The garden's over there." Drisgal nodded to the far left. "And the forest is opposite that. You will be in the garden, and Genevia will be in the woods. I will be in the house between them. The tools are in the shed. Follow me."

Frelati accepted his words in silence. He knew he was a hard, cynical man while Genevia was sweet and naïve. Frelati had no desire to corrupt her, so distance was for the best, a fact Drisgal was smart enough not to overlook. His daughter would not be talking to a stranger on his watch, especially not with this stranger. Of course, Frelati reflected, if Genevia wanted to see him, he could picture her devising a way and carrying it out successfully. She wouldn't go against her own wishes.

After giving Frelati his instructions, Drisgal went inside and sat down at the kitchen table, unused to the silence that seemed to envelope them now. Secrets were dangerous things. Genevia, not knowing what to say, kept quiet and continued washing dishes.

Drisgal finally started the conversation for her. "I would like you to stay in the forest today. You can take a picnic, and we need some firewood, seeing as you didn't gather any yesterday."

He shot his daughter a glance, which she ignored.

"You want me to stay away from Frelati," she said matter-of-factly, putting away a freshly dried dish.

"Well…" Drisgal had always been proud of his daughter's intelligence, but now he wished she could have been a bit less intuitive.

"I understand. He's a stranger, and you don't trust him." Genevia paused. "You're also uncomfortable because he's an elf…like I am."

Drisgal moved uncomfortably, staring at the table. "I'm just unsure of him. We really don't know him or his background, and he seems…different."

Genevia said nothing.

Drisgal looked around the kitchen aimlessly before standing to leave with a sigh. Before entering his room, he turned around and pleaded with her. "You will go to the forest, right?"

Genevia spun around and sighed, hating to see that worried look on his face. "Sure, Papa, I love the woods, and I love you. It should be enjoyable."

Drisgal nodded, stepping into his room and closing the door. A determined expression crossed her face as the door slapped closed. The need for adventure and answers was rushing with her blood to course through her veins, making her heart want to fly. She had to know about elves; didn't he understand that?

"I'll go for a little while, but I might make a detour," she finished softly, staring at the wooden door. "I'm sorry."

Hanging up her towel, she hurriedly packed a picnic basket and headed out the door in the direction of the woods, but she had no intention of eating lunch alone.

Chapter Three

After entertaining herself for a few hours, Genevia decided it was time to eat, even if it was still a bit early, and it was always better to eat with someone. Looking toward the house, she tried to formulate a plan to get to the other side without attracting the attention of her father's searching gaze.

She spotted the tree that grew at the side of the house and decided that climbing over the roof would definitely work if she was quiet. At a distance, it looked impossible for her to even reach the first branch, but on closer inspection, she realized that it was just her height. She slung the picnic basket over her shoulder and climbed up onto the roof.

Carefully, she inched her way silently across the rough, prickly surface. When she got to the other side, though, she saw no way down. That was definitely an unforeseen glitch in her plan. A stump that had once been her gorgeous weeping willow was directly below her, and she couldn't help rolling her eyes yet again at the stupidity her father had shown by cutting it down. Maybe she could reach it and not have quite so far to drop, but she didn't need the basket to hinder her. She leaned over the edge of the roof, closed her eyes, held her breath, and dropped her lunch. She waited as the thump resonated through the air around her. Nothing. Grasping the slight handhold at the edge, she lowered herself, but the stump was too short. Figured.

"Curses," she said under her breath.

Dangling over the side of the roof, her little feet swinging back and forth, she desperately clung with the very tips of her fingers to keep a hold on the edge. Then a thought struck her. She was an elf, and Frelati believed she could alter wood. It couldn't hurt to try it on the stump. Thinking hard, she forgot everything except the lump of wood below her. Time seemed to slow as she waited for her mental urgings to take effect, not truly expecting results, when, to her great astonishment, she felt firm wood beneath her.

"Ha!" she yelled in triumph and awe before clapping her hand across her mouth and looking in all directions.

"Quiet, Genevia!" she scolded under her breath as she scooped up the basket.

She crept silently through the sparse trees that separated their house from the garden, blending in with the shadows that filled the landscape, hiding behind tree trunks, and snatching her breath in as she heard the sound of a broken and dead leaf release its last hold on life and drift slowly to the ground to rest. Every sound seemed treacherous, though if she were caught it wouldn't really matter. This was simply a great adventure that played out in the confines of her imagination, which she knew would probably never reach out and grasp reality as she so hoped it would.

Eventually, though, she was on the other side of the wood, facing the garden and its one lone gardener. She smiled to herself over her success and ambled over, her basket swinging from her hands behind her back. When she reached the fence, she called out.

"I see you're hard at work."

Frelati paused with his hoeing and turned to look at her over his shoulder. The sun was high overhead, beating mercilessly down, and he brought an arm across his forehead to remove the sweat hanging there.

"Why am I not surprised?" he asked.

She merely grinned with a shrug. "I come bearing food, so you had better be nice to me. It is noon after all, and with this hard work you must be hungry."

Frelati glanced toward her house as if expecting to see Drisgal standing there. "I really don't think your father would be too pleased to see you here. You'd better go…"

He eyed the food hungrily. "However, if you wanted to leave a little of that here for me, I wouldn't object."

"Oh, no." Genevia shook her head. "If you get food, you have to eat it with me. I climbed a roof to have company while I ate."

A laugh escaped Frelati's lips. "You climbed over the roof?"

Genevia clamped her lips shut and gave him a mischievous look. Then she held out the basket enticingly and nodded her head toward an oak tree to her right.

Frelati walked over to the fence and propped his hoe against it. "So you're not going to tell me anything until I agree to eat with you? Is that what I'm supposed to get from all this?"

Genevia smiled and nodded, turning to make her way over to the tree. Frelati watched her as she spread out a blanket in the shade and began setting out the food. At the urging of his grumbling stomach, he went over to join her.

"This all looks really good," he praised as he saw the spread before him: roasted potatoes, green beans, and a huge slab of beef, not to mention the loaf of bread and peach pie that looked mouthwatering. "I appreciate your sharing with me, but I do hope you weren't serious about climbing over the roof."

Genevia smiled sheepishly. "Well, I did actually, and it wasn't all that easy with a basket."

"Why didn't you just go around back? Surely your father can't monitor every angle of the house at once."

"Well…." She paused. "I didn't think of that."

Frelati laughed. "Of course you would overlook the simplest solution."

Genevia sat up straight in indignation. "Well, there was a tree growing right at the side of the house that was easy enough to climb, and crossing the roof was no problem at all. It would have been fine if there'd been a way down the other side."

Frelati raised a brow. "So if there was no way down, how is it that you made it here?"

"Oh," Genevia brightened. "Well, you see we used to have a tree growing there, and its stump was just below. I remembered you saying that I could conform wood…"

"I didn't actually say you could," Frelati interrupted. "Just that it was a possibility."

Genevia waved a hand dismissively. "So anyway, I dropped down over the edge so that I was hanging onto the edge of roof, and I concentrated on the stump. And you know what? It actually grew!"

Frelati's eyes widened in surprise. "I guess that proves my theory."

"It definitely does. So now, you have to tell me all about elves because I have a lot to learn."

Frelati grimaced as he looked out toward the garden still in need of a lot of work. "Well, since I'm finished eating, I really should start hoeing again. Maybe another time?"

Genevia's shoulders slumped. Then she brightened. "Fine, I guess I'll just have to bring you lunch every day; then you can tell me a little bit at a time."

She popped up and began gathering everything back into the basket, leaving Frelati unsure of what to say. Before he had made a decision as to whether or not to tell her she should stay away from him, she had given him a wave and was walking away.

Just as promised, she came every day exactly at noon with a basketful of wonderful food and her chipper company, and Frelati was obliged to tell her whatever she wanted. He found himself looking forward to her appearance, and it grew less difficult to talk to her with each passing meeting.

One day when she came, she had a specific question for him. "So who exactly is it that you are looking for?"

He paused with food on the way to his mouth and glanced her way. "I'm really not certain I should tell you that."

"Oh, come on," she insisted with an encouraging smile. "Who am I gonna tell?"

After a few moments, he relented. She was right; they were completely isolated out here.

"I'm looking for the Elfin princess, Alernoa." Frelati shifted uncomfortably. "She's missing."

"Did someone take her?"

"In a sense, maybe." He avoided her gaze. "I really need to get back to work."

With that, he shot up from his seat and walked back toward the field, leaving a confused Genevia behind him.

Genevia was running late the next day by about an hour. She hoped Frelati wasn't absolutely starving, but it just couldn't be helped. Drisgal had started getting suspicious of her since she hadn't argued with him at all about staying away from Frelati and she was always packing so much food in her lunch basket. Today he had insisted she stay in the house with him. She kept putting off lunch, even while he ate, saying she just wasn't hungry. Fortunately, he accepted the statement and her stomach stayed quiet. Then she had waited until he laid down for his mid-day nap before sneaking out to see Frelati.

Frelati, for his part, had been aware of Drisgal's intent to keep Genevia in the house, and when she didn't arrive at noon or soon after, he assumed he'd be going hungry. Since he saw no reason in having both a grumbling stomach and an overheated body, he pulled his shirt off, hanging it on a fence post. Drisgal was keeping a close eye on his daughter today, so there was no chance he'd be seeing her.

However, no sooner had he begun working again than Genevia crept out of the trees, hoping to startle him with her sudden presence. Color rose to her cheeks when she saw his shirt on the post, but she couldn't bring herself to do the proper thing and leave. Her curiosity overcame her, and she simply had to take a peek.

However, the sight she expected was not to be found, and instead she was surprised and troubled. The man was indeed Frelati, but he didn't look as she had pictured.

He was slightly tanned, but the color did not come from the sun. It was more like that shade was his skin tone. He was strong and confident as he worked. His arms were masterfully carved and hard, and the muscles in his back were impressive, but that wasn't what immediately caught her attention.

Where she had expected to see the smooth back of a man with no troubles, she saw instead the scarred, red back of a man recently whipped and still healing. Beyond that, though, and even more disturbing, were the odd black markings. They looked like tentacles stretching out from several pinpoints on his back, almost as if something had touched him repeatedly, and at each point of contact a black poison had spread. The troublesome sight arrested her attention until Frelati felt her strong gaze and turned around, staring at her intently but not overly startled.

Although she was impressed by the sight of him as he turned, and she most definitely couldn't deny that fact, Genevia couldn't tear her mind away from the thought of the abuse he must have endured. She even noticed a few stripes across his chest and one very pronounced black mark over his left shoulder, but his chest was nowhere near as mottled as his back.

"I thought I told you to warn me the next time you decided to study me," Frelati said coldly before running a large, calloused hand through his wavy, brown hair to push it out of his eyes. "I assumed you wouldn't be coming today."

He walked over to his shirt calmly, quickly pulling it on without looking at her. After getting his anger in check, he turned to see Genevia's troubled expression. He knew the cause, but he didn't want to bring up the conversation that would surely follow, so he went back to work. It wasn't any of her business anyway.

After a few minutes, Genevia got up the courage to satisfy her curiosity, as Frelati knew she would.

Clearing her throat, she started slowly. "Where, um, where did you get all those…scars and…things? They look fairly fresh."

Slowly, Frelati turned and examined her for a minute before walking over to the fence that separated them, propping the hoe against a rail, and folding his forearms on the wood to look her straight in the eye. "They're six days old. Any more questions?"

His tone was anger in its fullest form, and his eyes dared her to take up his offer. It was very unnerving, but Genevia had never backed down from a challenge before, and she wasn't about to start now.

She spoke with more confidence than she felt as she answered. "You didn't actually answer my first question, so until you do there's no need for any more, is there?"

He stared at her long and hard, finding a stubborn determination in her eyes. Too much determination.

"I don't want to talk about it," he said coldly, pushing off the railing, picking up the hoe, and turning away.

Genevia could tell force wouldn't work and pleading probably wouldn't be much better, so she tried bribing.

"I brought you some lunch," she said, swinging the basket as he turned to look at her again. "Aren't you hungry? It'll be really good. Ham and boiled potatoes and apple cider and watermelon and an absolutely wonderful dessert…apple pie. I made it all myself. Doesn't it sound good?"

It did, and Frelati could almost taste the food he was so hungry, but he wasn't going to let her tempt him.

He set his face to be impassive. "Actually, I think I'll work some more. You go ahead and eat though."

He turned abruptly and started digging the hoe in the earth again, knowing that Genevia would eventually give in.

"But I waited to eat this whole time until I could eat with you."

Frelati stopped yet again, leaning against the hoe, and looked at her saddened face. "I suppose I can join you, but I want to hear no questions."

"Fine," Genevia said with a small smile of triumph.

They spread out the food and began eating under the shade of the oak's protecting branches. It was pleasant in the shade, and the food was wonderful. Unfortunately, Frelati stayed on edge, just waiting for Genevia to pick up their original conversation again. She wasn't satisfied, and it didn't take long before his prediction came true.

"So," Genevia began in a conversational tone. "Those scars that are six days old…they look painful."

"I said no questions," Frelati reminded her gruffly.

She huffed. "I'm just curious, that's all. I thought we were getting to be friends. Why won't you tell me?"

"Because it's my business," Frelati said sharply, looking her in the eye. "Not yours."

Genevia studied him for a minute and finally decided on a nice give-and-take tactic. "If you tell me what I want to know, I'll tell you something about me."

Frelati snorted derisively. "What could you possibly tell me that I'd want to know?"

"Lots of things," Genevia said hotly, angry that his words upset her as much as they did. "My life may not be as exciting as yours, but it has its high points, and I don't appreciate your laughing at it."

Frelati studied her for a moment and sighed. "Sorry; I behaved badly. Forgive me?"

He waited for her nod, which she reluctantly gave. Then he grimaced and looked away. "Well, it seems like you know more about me than anyone else in the world, so I guess it won't matter if I tell you, but it isn't pleasant."

Genevia nodded eagerly. "I promise I won't tell anyone. It'll be our secret…between friends."

Frelati looked at her a moment longer, already regretting his decision, then his face clouded over, his features growing dark and tight. Genevia may not have ever witnessed such a look before, but she recognized the cold hatred that he could not suppress. He began slowly, haltingly, which might have made the tale all the worse, if that was possible. "When Fezam took Meufa, he enslaved the King and Queen and all the other elves living there, myself included. Everyone was frightened, but there wasn't a thing we could do. We all tried to free the King and Queen, and we succeeded for a short while once, but Fezam's troops overtook them and brought them back, watching them like a hawk so that any attempt we might have made afterward would have been futile.

"We were brought to an old stone building, placed in cells in the dungeon, six per cell, and we were fed once a day, sometimes twice, if the guards remembered. I was lucky. Since I was favored and young—I was seven—the Queen begged for me to be placed in her cell. I had no family; my mother and father had died years before all of that—I never really knew them. So, I stayed in the royal cell, which was better than the others, but still terrible. We were to be held there until Fezam called for us to travel to Azol. We stayed there six years; some died, and a very few others came.

"Fezam finally summoned us, but it turned out worse with him than where we were before. It took a year for us to get to his barracks because of all the security to keep anyone from escaping. The barracks were right next to the palace. They were cold, dirty, and very dark. At the Queen's pleading, I yet again was able to stay in their cell. Every day Fezam came to visit. He would pick people, and they would be dragged out of the cell to be questioned. He wanted to find runaways or anyone who might go against him. We were never quite sure what he wanted.

"I started being picked after two years. They decided I was finally old enough and wouldn't listen to the Queen's begging anymore. I remember I was walked along a corridor and into the sunshine. It had been a while since I'd last seen the sun, and it hurt my eyes. There was a clay wall set up in an open area with no grass, and I could see bloodstains everywhere, twisting in all directions. They took off my shirt and chained me to the wall, my back toward them, and they asked me question after question, but I didn't know any of it. Every time they didn't like my answer, they took up their whips. I remember hearing a whir of air and a crack, really loud, just before someone started screaming, and I finally realized it was my screams that I heard echoing, reverberating around the clearing. I felt my blood drain and saw it mixing with the bloodstains of all the others before me. After that first day, I tried to get tougher while I was in my cell, so that I could stand those interrogations better, and they started taking me out from time to time to do some menial labor in one place or another—build up a castle wall or carry water from a river nearby. Just simple stuff, but it got me outside.

"They waited longer intervals between my questionings, since I was still young, but once I turned eighteen it didn't bother them anymore. Each time I heard the click of the bolt, I felt my back cringe. I never knew if it was my turn or not, but usually when it was my door that opened, they wanted me." Frelati paused, a humorless smile crossing his face as he saw in his mind's eye the passing of years in prison. "I didn't realize until I was eighteen that the whip was nothing compared to the other interrogation technique. Fezam has these…creatures under his command. They're called shadow beings, and apparently they can turn anyone into them. I'm not sure if that's true or not because I never saw it, but I believe they can. The black marks you saw…that's their mark. One touch, for just a second, is all it takes. The world goes dark, and you feel cold, so very cold. All your deepest fears rush at you in your mind, mocking you. It's a feeling I'll never forget, and had I known anything, I know I would have told them just to make it stop."

He turned to look at her. "It stayed like that until six days ago."

"What happened?" Genevia managed to ask in a voice barely above a whisper.

She wasn't really sure if she wanted to know or not. It was absolutely horrible, but her curiosity forced her to ask.

"I got angry," Frelati said with an eerie smile still on his face, the food completely ignored. "My last questioning, I decided to do something. I was tired of it, and there were no shadow beings there that time. So I punched the guard, grabbed the whip, and started fighting off everyone else. It worked for a while, but someone jumped me. I got a wicked beating, much worse than the others, and was sent back to the cell, looking forward to death in the morning.

"I told the King and Queen what happened and instantly regretted what I'd done; the Queen was…inconsolable. She's like a mother to me. But they came up with a plan for me to escape. They'd had it mapped out earlier, maybe even years before, but hadn't said anything because they were waiting for the right time. After my idiotic stunt, they knew there wasn't going to be a better time, and they told me information that I hadn't known before. They told me I had to go to Wilksom Olem to find the princess." He blinked, and then his fierce eyes locked onto hers. "I need to find her."

It was quiet for a few moments before Genevia broke the silence. "How did you get away?"

Frelati pulled himself back into control, but he surprised her by smiling conspiratorially. "The building was really old, and so while I slept each night, the King and Queen would bang at the wall with a knife they had taken. There was this huge hole that I went through, and they covered it up after I left. Guess they didn't tell me because they were afraid the guards would beat the secret out of me."

"Then why didn't they escape with you?"

"It's easier to travel alone without getting caught. With three people, we probably wouldn't have made it. Besides, they are the most important elves in all of Tiweln; they have the connections to start a war. If they left, a full-fledged search would have begun," Frelati explained. "With me facing death anyway, what did it really matter that I was gone?"

"Oh," Genevia said softly, feeling sorry for the King and Queen, whom she now felt she knew.

"So what are you going to tell me?" Frelati asked lightheartedly, trying to pull the girl from out of her gloom.

Genevia was suddenly embarrassed. "It isn't anything like your story. Like you said earlier, you probably don't care to hear it."

"I told you my story, and we made an agreement. You need to hold up your end of the bargain," Frelati chastised.

"Fine, but you'll get really bored," Genevia warned, crossing her arms. She looked away from him before speaking. "Drisgal isn't my real father. I don't know who my real parents are and neither does he."

"What?" Frelati asked. "You said…"

"I know," Genevia interrupted with a shrug. "I didn't feel like it was your business when we first met. Now…I had to tell you something, and that was the best thing I could come up with."

"So, you're not related to Drisgal?"

"Well, no," Genevia said. "But he's still my papa."

"But you're not related, and you don't know where you came from?" Frelati questioned.

"No… Why does that matter?" Genevia asked.

Frelati's lips tightened in annoyance. "Because this is really important, trust me. What did you mean by not knowing where you came from?"

"Drisgal found me," Genevia stated briskly.

"Where?"

"Will you tell me why this matters to you?" Genevia asked wide-eyed and confused.

"I want all the information first. Just answer the question," Frelati said hotly.

"In a bush beside a waterfall," Genevia answered impatiently.

"When?" Frelati was staring at her in a manner beyond intense. "Did you have a blue blanket around you?"

"I don't know when exactly. It was around sixteen years ago; I was really little," Genevia said exasperated. "I think Drisgal mentioned a blanket…yes, but it was burned when I was three."

"A locket…do you have a locket?" Frelati demanded.

Of its own volition, Genevia's hand flew to her neck. "How do you know about my locket?"

Her question went unheard.

"I did it," he whispered disbelievingly, gradually getting excited and standing up to release his pent-up energy. "I actually did it!"

Genevia got to her feet as well, watching Frelati in confusion. She didn't understand what was going on, but Frelati's unusual euphoria was getting a grip on Genevia, and she found herself smiling.

"What are you so happy about?" she asked. "I didn't think you had this kind of reaction in you…and, is that a smile?"

Frelati turned and grasped her arms, looking intently at her as if he were a child with a new toy. The smile was still spread widely across his face, making him look incredibly handsome.

"I did it!" He was shaking his head, still not quite able to believe it. "I found you! I didn't think I would, but I did!"

"What are you talking about?" Genevia asked. "You aren't making any sense."

He froze suddenly, looking into the distance without seeing anything, lost in thought. Genevia turned, a sliver of alarm shivering through her. Had Drisgal seen them? But there was nothing there, and Genevia turned back to Frelati with a frown.

Before she could speak, he clapped a hand to his forehead and ran his fingers through his hair. "What am I doing?"

In an instant, his bearing was back, his aloof mask was in place, and he fell to one knee, bowing his head, before Genevia. "I am at your service. Anything you wish I shall try to do, Your Highness, Princess Alernoa."

Chapter Four

Genevia couldn't suppress her laughter, for the humor of the act was overwhelming despite the sincere manner in which it was given. "What are you doing? You think I'm the princess you're looking for?"

Frelati stood gracefully but kept his head bowed. "Yes, Your Highness."

"Stop calling me that," Genevia ordered with a frown. "What's going on?"

Frelati spoke solemnly, finally lifting his eyes to meet hers. "You're the one I've been looking for," Frelati said. "What you thought was just a story was my only clue to find you. I had my suspicions when we first met, when I saw that you were an elf, but once you told me you had a father…"

"You do realize you're confusing more than explaining. Start from the beginning," Genevia said.

Frelati sighed in frustration and scowled but did as she said. "When Fezam first captured us and was leading us away, the King and Queen had a small daughter born just months before the attack. The reason we all tried so hard to free them was partially for their daughter's sake. If Alernoa lived away from Fezam, she could grow in power against him, or at the very least, he wouldn't have her as a weapon to use against us. With Fezam, she would grow up on his side. You would have grown up on his side."

Genevia stopped him. "You're saying I'm Alernoa?"

Frelati nodded and continued. "As I said before, the King and Queen escaped, so did Alernoa—you—but when they came back, she wasn't with them. We all thought you were dead. They wanted us to think you were dead. I thought that until six days ago.

"Just before I escaped, the Queen told me you were still alive and that I had to find you. She told me that you would be sixteen, that you would have been found by a waterfall in some bushes. She told me you had been wrapped in a blue blanket and had a locket around your neck. That was how I was to know you were Alernoa. The King and Queen came back absolutely distraught after their escape, and it apparently convinced the soldiers. At least, they didn't start looking for you. Your story matches what happened. You are Princess Alernoa."

"So my parents are royalty?" Genevia asked, shocked. "I am royalty?"

"Yes. Your parents are the Elfin King and Queen of Meufa, Nalofré and Lenaia. And now that I've found you, you can help me free them," Frelati said with a lopsided smile.

"Me?" Genevia said skeptically. "I don't believe you."

Although Genevia had always dreamed that something grand would happen, now that it was happening, it just didn't seem true. Things like this only happened in dreams or to other people. It was just too farfetched to be real.

"You don't believe me," Frelati repeated in disbelief, the smile gone. "You think I made it up? Do I really seem capable of weaving a fictitious story like this? And hasn't everything else I've told you turned out to be true? You thought there weren't elves; your father told you that I was right. You didn't believe I could predict the weather, but that rainstorm definitely came when I said it would. If you ask Drisgal, he'll tell you Fezam is real, and he probably knows about the Elfin King and Queen too."

Genevia eyed him thoughtfully. "Yes, everything you've said up until now has been right, I guess. But still…it's ridiculous. How can I believe it?"

Frelati glared at her in annoyance. "I'm not lying, but you can believe whatever it is you want. I'm not going to waste my time trying to convince you."

"But you have to be lying!" Genevia exclaimed. "I don't know why, but it's just not possible. I'm me."

"Well, you believed the rest of it, so why not this? It shouldn't be that difficult to grasp," Frelati scoffed.

Genevia's brows came together as she looked at him in disbelief. "So you made up the whole prison thing to make me feel sorry for you and more likely to believe this second ridiculous story? Why would you…? Hey!"

Frelati grabbed her forearms roughly, a fierce fire in his eyes.

"I have absolutely no reason to lie to you," he growled in a soft voice made all the more menacing for the low volume and seemingly controlled calm. "Everything I have ever said to you is true. I have given you no reason to disbelieve me now. And don't forget, it was you who started all this with your incessant questions. I certainly wouldn't have gotten someone to whip me simply to get some country girl to believe a story I made up. There is no point to it, and trust me, my imagination is not so great as to enable me to think up the kind of torture I described. I almost died both in prison and coming out here to this wilderness you call a home. By some miracle, I made it, but so help me, I am not going to stand by while a little waif like you accuses me of lying about the horrors that have made up my life for the last sixteen years."

Where most other people would have been frightened by his fury, Genevia remained outwardly serene, even if her heart was determined to beat faster.

Genevia kept direct eye contact with him and spoke softly but firmly. "You made your point. I'm sorry. I should have believed you because as you said, you had no reason to lie, but you need to see my side of it too. You have to admit that it seems just a little incredible."

Frelati searched her eyes for a moment then nodded.

"Feel better now?" Genevia asked with a small smile.

Frelati scowled and bit out an apology he knew he needed to make. "I apologize for my outburst."

Genevia nodded and started packing up the food. "This is a lot to take in. Me…an Elfin princess?" She shook her head. "It really doesn't seem possible, you know."

Frelati's scowl deepened.

"Well, you either believe me or not. Pick one; otherwise I'll never figure you out."

Genevia tossed him an impish grin over her shoulder. "Now why would I want you to figure me out? Once you do, I've lost your interest."

Frelati said nothing, and Genevia continued.

"So, what exactly do you expect me to do?" Genevia asked.

"Do?" Frelati repeated with a shake of his head.

"About this…" Genevia scrunched her nose and waved a hand. "…princess thing."

Frelati nodded his comprehension. "Travel with me to Azol to release the elves."

Genevia laughed. "I don't think so."

"Why?" Frelati asked shortly.

"I'm not leaving my father to go traipsing around the country."

Frelati stared at her. "You're going to release your real parents from prison. Somehow, I don't think that qualifies as 'traipsing around the country.'"

Genevia shrugged. "Minor detail, but that doesn't change the fact that I can't leave my father." Genevia held up a hand as Frelati opened his mouth to protest. "Yeah, they're my real parents, but I know nothing about them, and they know nothing about me. I'd like to help them, but I won't leave my father to do that, not right now anyway."

"You have a duty to the elves," Frelati objected through gritted teeth.

"A duty that I found out about just five minutes ago. They don't even know Alernoa exists, so why can't I just stay Genevia until my father decides I'm old enough to marry someone I don't like? Then I can run away and save the elves without feeling guilty." Genevia shot him a huge smile. "It'll only take a year or so."

Frelati sighed and looked up at the sky, his control working overtime to keep his anger in check while he talked to this girl. "You aren't just Genevia, and we may not have 'a year or so.' You aren't just an ordinary woods girl, much as you may look and act like one right now. You're a princess, like it or not, and you have a responsibility."

"Well, I don't think I'm ready for that responsibility right now," Genevia argued. "This is…so much bigger than my small little home in the woods. I don't know anything about the world. I can't leave."

Frelati narrowed his eyes and turned away. He needed to put some distance between them before he gave in to the impulse to shake her to her senses. "Fine, be your woods girl and abandon everyone who needs you. I'll just do it myself. I'll fail, probably die, but I'm long overdue for death anyway, right? If you need me before I leave in the morning, you know where to find me."

Frelati left her standing there, watching his back as he walked away with his natural grace. She was not remorseful of her actions, she was right after all, but she did feel a slight twinge of guilt as she saw him walk off. His life had always been difficult, and she had just added more disappointment to a steadily growing and already large pile in his heart.

He was furious. When he first put it all together and realized who she was, he thought she might help, and after he had explained everything and seen understanding in her eyes, he was certain she would help. But of course, she had to go and be a selfish little girl. He knew she was capable of acting mature, but she apparently didn't enjoy that side of her personality. He made it to the barn and started packing the little sack of things that he had managed to acquire after leaving prison. It didn't take long and he was left with time to lie on his back in the hay and stare up at the barn roof while terrible memories bombarded his mind.

Genevia grew as annoyed as Frelati. Just because she was a princess for five minutes, he thought she should be responsible for killing herself on an impossible quest to save some elves she just found out existed? And of course she had to feel guilty about letting him down. So unfair! She stormed back to the house, still determined to follow her decision, but the twang of guilt stayed with her.

Once inside, she saw Drisgal working to reattach the leg to a chair that had broken a month ago. She was about to tell him what she had just learned because they had always shared everything, but now things were different—she was different—so she continued on to her room without saying a word. The moment her door closed, she felt all the strain that had been pushed to the back of her mind rush forward, and she could hold it in no longer. She flew across the room, throwing herself on her bed face down. She didn't know how long she stayed there before she was calm again, but after her crash, she had to move; she had to do something. Sitting around had never been encouraged in her childhood, and the habit had stuck with her.

After looking around and finding nothing of particular interest to occupy her, she decided to pack a few things just on the off-chance her guilt won out and she did decide to go with Frelati.

While she doubted that outcome, it would keep her mind busy, and that was just what she needed—an idle mind was a dangerous thing. She grabbed a medium-sized handbag out of her closet and put some older clothes in it, nice and sturdy daily wear. A money pouch followed. She had been saving since she was five, when Drisgal started giving her small amounts for chores well done during the week. After that, she packed her small stash of food, which she retrieved from under her bed. The food was for emergencies; who knew when she might need a midnight snack? An old pair of shoes was put in next, then a warm blanket. With some room still left, she decided to put in her small collection of jewelry—that could be as good as money—and some keepsakes, one of which was a painting of her father and herself.

The painting had been done six years before by a professional that had stayed at their house during his travels. It was his way of repaying their kindness and hospitality. Drisgal had seen how much she loved it and had told her she could keep it in her room. This was the one possession she loved the most, aside from the locket she always wore.

All of the packing passed the time until she was to begin her preparation of dinner. After she and Drisgal finished eating, Drisgal grudgingly told her to take a plate to Frelati. She would have refused, but then Drisgal would have known something was amiss and having that conversation tonight was not a high priority. So she went without a word.

"Here's your dinner. Enjoy," she said as she walked toward Frelati, forcing mock happiness into her voice and expression as she held out the plate.

Frelati turned with a raised brow. "So you're actually speaking to me? I'm surprised."

"You have to eat," she said with a shrug. "I may not be too pleased with you right now, but I don't want you to starve."

"Don't make me feel too loved; I may never leave," Frelati said sarcastically, although his anger had greatly subsided.

Genevia's lips tightened. "There's no need for you to be nasty. A thank you would be nice, though, if you feel up to it."

Frelati was quiet for a moment. He had thought over everything in the time that had passed since their last meeting, and he knew he had behaved badly. However, admitting his mistakes was not his forte. He cleared his throat. "Listen. I shouldn't have jumped on you with this…whole new responsibility. I shouldn't have done a lot of things I did this afternoon. It wasn't right. Forgive me?"

Funny how difficult it could be to choke out words that in any other form wouldn't be so hard to say, but to put aside pride and ask forgiveness, that was not an easy task. So why did it seem to be even harder for him to leave knowing Genevia was angry with him? It made no sense, not that much of what he had done lately made any sense, but he refused to leave in the morning with regrets.

Genevia looked him over, giving special scrutiny to his eyes. "Fine, I suppose I forgive you, but that doesn't mean I'll do what you want."

"As you wish," Frelati said, bowing his head.

With that she left and prepared for an early bedtime, stopping for a moment in the kitchen to gather a few more food items to stick in her bag. Why she felt such an urge, she didn't know, but past experience had taught her that her sleep would be a lot better if she went ahead and followed her gut.

When her head hit the pillow, she was instantly asleep. She dreamed about the books she had read with the added bonus of those fairytales coming alive. The one difference between the books and her dreams, though, was that she was no longer the reader but the princess. As she dreamed, her wonderful wish became a terrible nightmare. Three loud bangs, running feet, shouts, orders—all ran through her head.

Genevia shot up in bed, sweating and gasping for breath, thankful that everything was just a dream. Then she realized that all the noise had followed her into her wakefulness.

"Where is she?" a loud, coarse voice ordered.

Genevia heard a resonating thud, a cry of pain, and then a soft answer. "Who are you talking about?"

Genevia recognized Drisgal's voice. Though she was terrified, she knew what they wanted and what she had to do. Those men would kill her father if she was found, but if they were wrong, the chances of Drisgal staying alive might be a little better. Regardless, there was nothing she could do now to help him except get away.

Glad now of her earlier boredom, Genevia grabbed her handbag and shoved it through her open window. Quickly, she stowed away everything that made the room look lived in. She made the bed and climbed out of the window after her bag, closing it just before two large soldiers barged into the room.

Grabbing her bag, Genevia ran swiftly and quietly toward the woods. She was glad of the darkness surrounding her, thankful that the moon was hiding behind the clouds, even if it did make it harder on herself. She took one last look at her once peaceful little home before disappearing into the woods.

She ran quickly and silently, nearly hitting a tree here, almost tripping over a root there, but everything seemed to get out of her way at the last minute. When her breath got shorter and her legs began to give out, she leaned against a tree to catch her breath, listening for even a hint of pursuit. There was still a lot of noise coming from her home, but it was fainter due to the distance it had to cover to land upon her ears.

Then she started hearing steps, cracks of twigs, and rustling leaves. It was more than one person, and they were coming straight for her. Panic rushed through her body, making her heart beat wildly, and she clutched her bag tighter wondering what to do.

Just then, she felt a firm tug, and a large hand clapped across her mouth, silencing the scream that was about to surface. She was pulled behind the tree against which she had been leaning and into a hollow that the very same dead tree had formed. Scared out of her mind, she struggled ferociously, but the firm hold around her midriff only tightened to pull her closer to a hard, broad chest.

"Stay quiet; it's me," a voice whispered softly in her ear. "Be still and the guards won't find us."

She slumped in relief as she recognized Frelati's voice, and he slowly lowered his hand from her mouth. The men in the woods weren't trying to be quiet, shouting back and forth and stomping around like they owned the place.

"I don't see a sign of her," one voice yelled.

Another answered, "I bet it was just another hoax. I'm getting tired of it."

"Yeah," yet another yelled in agreement with a chuckle to follow. "I bet that princess isn't even alive. It's probably just another trick to get out of punishments."

The first man shouted his agreement. "You're probably right. Let's head back and report. There's no sign of her, and we can always wait until morning."

The second man yelled his reply. "We could try, but you know the captain's going to make us look all night."

"Probably, but if we accidentally forget to tell him we've stopped looking, he won't be the wiser," the third man said as they all started crashing through the woods back the way they had come.

The noise gradually receded, and Frelati released his tight hold on Genevia.

"Didn't mean to scare you, but I was watching them and saw them heading straight for you," Frelati explained, looking around. "We need to move on. They'll come back, even if they hope they won't. You know the woods better than I do, go ahead and find some place to hide."

"I don't know any places," Genevia whimpered, scared out of her mind.

Frelati shook her gently to get her attention. "Listen, I realize you're scared, but now is not the time to give in to it. You have to try to think of something. Our lives depend on this."

Genevia took a deep breath and nodded. "Okay."

She thought a bit before offering a suggestion. "We could hide behind the waterfall. There's a cave behind it. It's that way."

"Good girl," Frelati praised absentmindedly, looking in the appointed direction. "I knew you'd think of something. Come on."

He grabbed her hand, and they ran stealthily through the woods to the waterfall. Genevia showed him the way behind it, and, after careful inspection, Frelati decided no one would possibly think to look there. He took the time to wipe out their tracks and scout around a bit before returning to the cave.

When he reentered the alcove, he noticed that Genevia had brought a bag with her, but while he was glad of that forethought, the sight of Genevia made the provisions seem inconsequential. She was sitting against the wall, her knees hugged to her chest, her locket in the death grip of her left hand, and tears were almost ready to make their descent. Frelati sat down next to her, hoping his vicinity would calm her.

"It's going to be okay," he said in an attempt at comfort, patting her shoulder awkwardly.

She looked at him with tear-filled eyes that were surprisingly full of trust. What had he ever done to give this girl the impression that he was trustworthy? But his presence did reassure her, and she nodded slightly at his words, then leaned against him and lost complete control, crying steadily.

"What if they hurt my papa?" she whispered.

Frelati hugged her to him, not sure what to say and feeling her sorrow reach out to touch the place within him that others claimed held a heart. He said no words; just let her cry, until her tears subsided and she fell asleep in his arms just a few hours before daybreak was to begin. Frelati was uneasy, and it wasn't just because soldiers were everywhere searching for them. No, Frelati was uneasy because of what he was feeling inside that no external force could rival. This wasn't supposed to happen, but somehow having Genevia in his arms just felt right.

Chapter Five

The sun smiled down through the clouds from its high perch in the sky. Its rays glittered beautifully on the waterfall as it splashed onto the rocks below and gathered in a pool to lap against the bank. It was a glorious day. Birds chatted and jumped from branch to branch as squirrels quarreled and played around the tree trunks.

It would have been a perfect day if not for the soldiers running around and shouting orders. However, they didn't come near the waterfall. It didn't seem to the naked eye as if anyone could possibly get behind it to hide. But the two people hidden there were not disturbed by the noise for it was destroyed by the roar of the falls; they were enveloped in their own private bubble of peace.

A few streaks of sunlight pierced the cascade of water to fall upon the sleeping figure of Genevia. She awakened to this soft touch of light and to the melodious sound of falling water. It took a while for her to realize where she was. Startled by the unfamiliar surroundings, she snuggled closer to Frelati before realizing that it was his arms wrapped around her.

She looked up into his face with a sleepy smile. He had finally fallen asleep after hours of watchfulness from that night, his breathing deep and even, a steady, heartening presence for Genevia in this topsy-turvy world she had entered. The light was gently prickling his tan skin and revealed him to Genevia in a new and special way.

He had a strong jaw line and a very firm mouth, but a trace of laugh lines could be seen etched at the edges of his lips. Genevia couldn't help but wonder if those lines had only appeared after he stumbled across her in the woods, but perhaps they had always been there, just beneath the surface, hiding since his childhood and simply awaiting an invitation to appear from some joyful individual. His dark brown, erratic hair complimented his chiseled face perfectly, and she remembered the deep blue of his eyes that held sorrow and occasional laughter. They were a deep abyss of untold memories, some pleasant, some horrible, and even some he might not be able to recall from the years of early childhood, all of which had shaped him into the man that held Genevia close just now, comforting her even in sleep.

This handsome elf, with his pointy elfin ears, was someone Genevia trusted whole-heartedly, though she had only known him a few days. She rested her head against his chest once more, not wanting to wake him from his slumber. Strangely, she found that she needed still more rest, probably because of all the anxiety and stress she had endured the night before. With the sun still peeping at her and the waterfall's roaring yet soothing music, she fell asleep until dusk crept up upon the day and forced it to flee until the sun came to reign over the land once again.

Frelati woke first. He felt rejuvenated and ready for anything, but he worried about Genevia. She was used to the security of her home, not the uncertainty of travel. He was tempted to let her sleep a little longer, but judging by the slight light coming through the waterfall, Frelati judged it to be dusk, nearly time for them to make an escape, and gently shook Genevia awake.

After blinking a few times to adjust to the light, she shifted but kept her head resting on Frelati. "What is it?"

"It's almost dark. We need to leave while no one can see us," Frelati said, his voice gruffer than usual from sleep. "What do you have in your bag?"

Genevia finally pulled herself out of his grasp and walked over to her pack, pulling a few items out as she spoke.

"I've got food, money, clothes and shoes, a picture, some jewelry, ummm…a blanket. That's about it."

"Well, at least it's all useful," Frelati said, running a hand through his hair. "How did you have time to pack it all?"

Genevia blushed and looked away, answering defensively. "I packed yesterday afternoon. I wasn't going to go with you or anything, but I was very bored. It gave me something to do."

A smirk tweaked the corner of Frelati's mouth. "Right."

"It's true." Genevia persisted with a frown.

Frelati still smirked, but he backed off. "I'm glad you were bored then, even if it had nothing whatsoever to do with my offer."

He looked at the water and the weak light that filtered through. "We need to eat something before we leave. We might not have a chance later. What do you have?"

Genevia pulled out the food. "I've got regular bread, cornbread, stuff for porridge, pickled okra, pickled eggs, pickled cucumbers, and some fruit. I also grabbed some milk and cheese from last night, but not much since it'll go bad really quick. And I have some canteens for water."

Frelati was impressed despite himself. "That sounds good. We need to pace ourselves, though, so the food will last longer. It might be all we have for two weeks for all we know. My bag is empty of food."

"Fine," Genevia agreed. "I'll take cheese, an apple, and a slice of bread."

"Give me some cornbread."

"Nothing else?" Genevia asked with some concern. "That's not much. Why don't you…"

"I'm used to hunger." Frelati cut her off. "I'm sure you're not, so just give me the cornbread."

"I can…," Genevia began, starting to put the apple back with the other food, but Frelati stopped her.

"No," he said firmly. "I'll do the rationing. What you have is fine; don't worry about it. Just give me some cornbread."

Genevia nodded and handed it to him. "Would you like milk or water?"

Frelati considered a moment before answering. "We should both drink the milk. It will go bad soon if not."

"Fine by me."

By the time they finished eating, the darkness had swept across the land and settled on the ground, the day's creatures all nestled in their beds. The two slipped past the waterfall and into the woods on the other side, hearing the crickets' merry chirping all around them.

"Which way is closer to the coast?" Frelati asked, his voice barely loud enough to hear. "We need to get off this island."

"I don't know. Papa never let me wander off too far, and I wasn't allowed to go with him to town."

Frelati sighed and muttered something that sounded suspiciously like "mental, overprotective tyrant" before speaking aloud. "Not good. Do you know which way Drisgal went when he left for town?"

"No, but the river probably gets there fast," Genevia suggested.

"I'm sure it does, but we don't have a boat," Frelati pointed out.

"Yes, we do. Papa has one hidden for fishing," Genevia said, grinning. "Actually, he probably used it to go to town too. Follow me. It's this way."

They walked along the river's edge until they came to a tangle of bushes. Genevia pushed them aside, revealing a barely distinguishable path.

"Follow me," she said again and led the way down.

They slipped down the steep incline, where they came to a small wooden boat waiting for them just beside the river.

Genevia pointed to it proudly. "Here it is."

"Nice job. Let's get it in the water," Frelati said as he examined the boat. Then he looked over at Genevia. "We should probably put you in first."

He extended his hand and helped her into the boat, quickly releasing her from his touch and loading the bags. Then he shoved off and began paddling down river. The only sounds heard were the gentle drips as Frelati lifted the paddles from the water and the slight whoosh as they slipped back beneath the dark, rippling surface of the river.

It was a beautiful ride. The dark, sleepy trees bent their branches over the water, blinding the sky from a glimpse of the river below. Genevia couldn't help but dip her fingers into the cool, rippling surface, leaving a small trail behind her as the boat pushed forward.

The night was cool, and though the thick canopy of foliage hid the twinkling stars above, Genevia knew they were there. She could feel them shining and hear their slight flutter as they winked at the earth. At this time, when naught was seen, but all was heard, Genevia felt the most oneness with the life surrounding her. Nature called her, and she became the river, stars, and trees, the animals, insects, and flowers.

Her soul went out to touch everything, and she left herself to be with nature. She swayed with the trees, twinkled with the stars, and blossomed with the flowers. She scurried with night's creatures and sang with the insects while the river rushed forward to meet the sea. This night, the river seemed to run more swiftly than ever before; it had never had a greater purpose.

By the time the sun began stretching its rays after it awoke from its slumber beyond the horizon, Frelati and Genevia had reached the small town bordering the coast. They pulled the boat ashore, hid it, and sat beneath the branches of an oak to eat breakfast.

"We need to go into town to hire a ship that will take us to Azol," Frelati said after they had finished eating. "You'll be my sister. We're traveling to find a doctor for our mother. My name needs to be changed. I'll be…"

"How about Fredish?" Genevia suggested.

Frelati looked at her and raised an eyebrow. "That's pathetic, but seeing as you're the only one with any imagination, I suppose it'll work. You can keep your name, but we need a name for our mother."

"Kauli," Genevia said with a smile.

"That should do. I'll quiz you," Frelati said, giving her a sly grin.

Genevia situated herself. "Okay, shoot."

"What are our names?"

"Genevia and Fredish."

"Why are we traveling together?"

Genevia looked up, trying to make her eyes misty. "We are trying to find a good doctor that will help our mother. She's very sick. We are so worried."

"What illness?"

Genevia made her lip quiver and pretended to stifle a sob. "We don't know. She says she's always cold, and she's so pale. Her coughing just seems to get worse and worse, and she won't eat anything because of a terrible stomach pain. I'm so scared she's gonna die."

Frelati couldn't hide a smile. "Nice, but can you remember all that?"

Genevia grinned arrogantly and started to repeat her long speech. "We aren't sure. She's always so col—"

"Okay, I get it. You can remember," Frelati interrupted her. "What's our mother's name?"

"Kauli."

"Where are we from?"

"On an island far away from here. We've been traveling for weeks."

Frelati nodded. "Which island?"

"Meufa?"

"That won't work," Frelati replied. "Everyone knows that's the Elfin King and Queen's island. They would have a good doctor or send for one."

Genevia pushed back her hair impatiently. "Well, not *everyone* knows; I didn't. And can it still be considered the King and Queen's island if they're in prison?" Frelati shot her a look of annoyance, and she lifted her hands in surrender. "Fine. Then how about this? I don't have time for all of these questions, and why should you know every aspect of my life? My mother's sick, and I need to get help."

Frelati was amused, but his lips barely twitched. "If that works, you will have my undying respect as a consummate actress, but we'll leave that as an answer for now. What doctor are we looking for?"

"Any doctor that will help."

Frelati continued, trying to trip her. "Well, we have a wonderful doctor here in town. I'm sure he would be glad to help you."

"We live too far away for him to help."

"Well, then, why did you travel this far to find a doctor?"

Genevia paused a bit too long. "Oh, I don't know. I got all the other questions right. You answer that one."

"Well, that answer will definitely throw the questioner off track; might even buy us enough time to run away." Frelati smirked.

"No, I was talking to you," Genevia said. "And if you know so much, you can answer it."

"Fine." Frelati stepped in solemnly. "My sister and I were hoping to find Doctor Steinbackle, a dwarf with much knowledge and many medications. We are certain that he'll know exactly what ails our mother."

"Well, you're in luck! He happens to be in town too. Follow me," Genevia said excitedly, standing up to try to lead him to the imaginary doctor.

Frelati just watched her with a raised brow. "That won't happen, and you know it."

"So, you won't follow me to find the doctor?" she asked innocently, but Frelati's rolling eyes made her break out in a grin. "It could happen, you know."

"You're right, it could, but it's safe to assume that it won't." Frelati stood and walked over to their packs. "Come on. Let's put your acting skills to the test."

They walked into a town full of people, and Genevia's eyes widened in excitement and trepidation as she watched all the bustle. Some went in shops, others came out. It was like looking at an ant hill; hundreds of little ants just milling about the town. They were all so fast and certain of their movements, and suddenly Genevia just wanted to get away from it all. This wasn't the simple life of the cabin.

"Where do we go now?" Genevia asked, growing more and more uncomfortable as she watched the townspeople and inched closer to Frelati.

"Now, we go to the docks to find a ship," Frelati said simply, looking around him before descending the hill to enter the town. "This way."

It took five minutes for them to reach the center of the activity and cross over to the docks. When they arrived, they found it very dirty but full of ships.

Frelati took Genevia by the hand. "Stay close. This isn't exactly the safest place for you to be. We just need to find a ship that can hold us, that's cheap, and that also happens to be going our way."

"Di' I jus' hear ye say tha' ye nee' a ship?" a deep sailor's voice said behind them.

They both spun around, Genevia in surprise and Frelati in defense, his hand tightening his grip on hers.

"Why, yes," Genevia said with a smile. "We did. Can you help us?"

The sailor was a dirty man in great need of both a bath and a shave. He was huge and looked as if he could break in two anyone who dared challenge him. A wad of gyssep, the most addictive herb sold in Tiweln, was held in his jaw, and he reeked worse than the piles of garbage Frelati and Genevia had passed earlier.

The sailor looked Genevia up and down with a greedy gleam in his eye. "Why, sure I ca' lass. Ye ca' jus' leave i' all ta me. I'll take care o' ye."

Frelati recognized their cue to leave and hurriedly broke into the conversation.

"We have a prior engagement with a shipmaster, if you will excuse us," Frelati said coldly, his eyes, twin beads of hatred and challenge, never leaving the sailor as he began tugging Genevia to follow him. "Come on."

Genevia wasn't ready to leave just yet, and she completely missed out on the tension in the air. She turned to Frelati and whispered urgently. "Well, maybe he can help. He said he has a ship, and he did offer assistance, so maybe we should take him up on it."

She turned back around to face the sailor before Frelati could get two words in, her hand leaving his as she walked toward the menace. "Hi, I'm Genevia, and this is my brother, Fredish. We need a boat. Can you help us?"

"Well, now, ye're brother an' sister are ye?" the sailor said, looking at both of them in turn with a smirk that Frelati was certain was caused by some seedy thought. "Me name's Sallus. I ca' give ye boar' on me ship, grub, all ye'll nee'."

Frelati eyed him suspiciously with a hard gaze. "What do you want for payment?"

"Well, now, le's see," Sallus said, scratching his chin and looking Genevia over once more. It was clear he required no thought; he already knew what he wanted, but like Frelati, he was playing the game. Finally, Sallus answered. "For a reg'lar lass, i' be two nigh's, weekly min' you, bu', I seen them ears an' me offer for an elf'n lass, well, I'm bein' very gen'rous. I'll take on'y one nigh' by week."

Frelati had been prepared for the answer, but he was bowled over by the surge of fury that came with it. His gaze became even more frosty, his lips turned into a fiercer scowl, and his jaw hardened painfully from his gritted teeth. Reaching out, he snatched Genevia's hand and pulled her next to him. "I don't think your ship is what we're looking for. We'll be going now."

Frelati turned with Genevia to leave but stopped at the sight of three huge, burly men that blocked their way. Genevia turned toward Sallus with astonishment etched across her face, and Frelati balanced on the balls of his feet, preparing himself for the most difficult fight of his life.

"Ye see, I always ge' wha' I wan'," Sallus said to Genevia with a glitter in his eye and a malicious smile on his face.

She backed up against Frelati, who was still facing the three men behind her. This was not good. One of the three that formed the barricade took a step closer, and Genevia had to take several deep breaths to keep the panic at bay. Frelati might be a good fighter—and really, she had no clue whether he was or not—but three against one was definitely not a fair fight. Genevia looked all around her: in front, Sallus, who now had two more men as backup; behind, three huge, fighting machines that looked just as unscrupulous as Sallus; to the left, water; and to the right, a patch of grass that looked pretty dead, with a tall, stone wall behind it. Genevia felt the futility of it, and it was her fault. Why couldn't she have just left when Frelati first pulled her away? Unconsciously, her left hand flew to her locket as her right hand clenched into a fist. She looked to the ground and closed her eyes, blocking out everything for a moment in a vain attempt to calm herself.

Slowly, in the patch of now-healthy grass beside her, a tree began to grow. It grew taller and wider, finally becoming large enough to hold someone in its branches and allow passage to the other side of the wall. Everyone, save an oblivious Genevia, looked up at the full-grown tree in amazement, then their attention turned to her. Sallus and his men regarded her with bewilderment and fear; Frelati was frozen with incomprehension and disbelief. Frelati recovered first, nudged Genevia to gain her attention, and climbed onto the first branch, reaching down to help Genevia.

"Come on," he urged. "Hurry."

At the sight of their escape, Sallus was shaken from his stupor.

"Ge' 'er!" he yelled to his men as she reached up to Frelati.

They clasped hands, and Frelati began pulling Genevia up to safety, when one of the taller men grasped her ankle. Genevia screamed and tried to loosen his grasp.

"Let go!" she yelled, kicking her feet.

With a last, wild kick, her foot made contact with the side of his head, and his grip loosened. Frelati took his chance, pulling her quickly onto the branch beside him. The tree grew taller, rising high enough to keep the men at bay. Carefully, the two crept to the other side of the tree and walked down a gently sloping branch that took them to the ground beyond the wall that, thankfully, separated them from the docks and Sallus.

Once free and on firm ground, Frelati and Genevia collapsed against the wall.

"The next time I say, 'Let's go,' let's actually do it, okay?" Frelati said gruffly, his anger surfacing to cover the fear of a moment before.

Genevia looked at him pitifully. "I'm sorry. I thought he actually wanted to help."

"Well, he didn't," Frelati barked. "Next time, do as I say, and we won't get into those kinds of messes. I can read people. Unlike you, I've been on my own dealing with people who were trying to kill me. Trust me; I know when to avoid someone."

"I said…" Genevia began to apologize when she caught sight of the tree. "By the way, how did you do that? I thought you said you could only predict weather, but you just made a tree."

Frelati looked at her with a mixture of amazement and confusion. "I didn't do it. You did. How could you not know you made a tree? That takes a lot of power. You would've felt it, or you should have at least."

"I made it!" Genevia said incredulously. "How? I didn't know I could do that."

Frelati studied her for a moment. "You must be more powerful than I thought. In order for you to be able to use that much power without knowing it or even trying to use it…Kiem, you have to be harboring a lot of power in you."

Genevia frowned at his language. "Please refrain from saying that. Kiem created this world, and you should not use his name in that way."

Frelati scowled, not deigning to reply. The little princess had a lot to learn.

"How did I do it though?" Genevia asked, bringing the conversation back.

"I don't know. We're going to have to practice to find out what you can do," Frelati said thoughtfully as he studied her. Then he looked away and came to his feet, offering her a hand up. "First, though, we need to find a ship."

They walked back to the dock, avoiding the men they had first run into. The place smelled strongly of fish and dirty men in need of a bath. Genevia couldn't understand how anyone could work there all day. There were many ships, and Frelati went up to a majority of the shipmasters, but they either had no room or weren't leaving for weeks. The two became very discouraged, but Frelati pushed on.

"How about that ship?" Genevia pointed out.

She wasn't actually looking at the ship, but at the small, elderly man that ran it. If he had a crew, they weren't there to help him, and he struggled to pack up his cargo. Genevia's heart went out to touch him.

Frelati, on the other hand, looked at the battered ship. "It doesn't look steady…or sturdy…or capable of floating beyond the harbor, and it's small. We should…"

He stopped. Genevia had left him to go and help the man lift a crate over the hull of the ship. Frelati released an aggravated growl.

"Of course she ignores me!" he muttered. "Heaven forbid she learn anything from Sallus."

He stalked over to join her, hearing the tail end of her conversation.

"Really! You're leaving tomorrow!" Genevia exclaimed before Frelati pulled her aside rather roughly.

"What are you doing?" he scolded under his breath. "Have you already forgotten what happened the last time you started talking to a complete stranger?"

Genevia placed her hands on her hips, a don't-you-scold-me look on her face. "I'm not eight. You aren't in charge of me, so stop acting like you're my father!"

"I was sent to you by your father with instructions to keep you safe. So yes, I think I am in charge of you, and this will go a whole lot smoother if you start listening to me. Are we clear?"

Genevia squinted at him, a scowl on her face, anger evident in her posture. "Well, I don't think you're in charge of me. I'll only listen to you if you give me good reason to, and seeing as you haven't succeeded in getting us a ship, I decided to try my hand at it. And miracle of miracles, I happen to have found a ship that is run by a very nice man and that meets all of our requirements. Just give this a chance, please."

Frelati was about to argue with her but quickly cooled at the pleading look in Genevia's eyes. How did she do that? Just one little look and he was ready to give her whatever she wanted. She should come with a warning label.

"Have you even looked at the ship?" he asked calmly, trying to reason with her. "It's unsteady, old, and small."

"But it's a 'good ol' ship' in the captain's words. He's taken it on so many voyages," Genevia said with a small smile. "There's room for us, as long as we help him work some, and it's leaving tomorrow. The captain's really nice; he won't give us any trouble, and apparently, he hates Fezam too. We'll be safe."

"How did you manage to find all that out? You only left me for a minute or so," Frelati asked in astonishment.

Genevia shrugged. "I asked point blank, and he answered. Isn't that what you did?"

"How much does it cost?" Frelati asked, looking the ship over again and ignoring her question.

"I don't know. I figured you'd be better at bargaining, so I'll let you figure that one out." She smiled sweetly.

Frelati grimaced. "Well, at least you were going to let me do something."

The old captain and Frelati negotiated for a short while, and once they settled, Frelati seemed satisfied about the price, even if he was still wary about the ship.

"So?" Genevia inquired, bouncing a bit with impatience.

"As long as we work some and pay for one third of the supplies, he'll be happy," Frelati said, looking at the ship while Genevia shouted for joy. "I'm still not sure about this though."

"Oh, come on," Genevia whined, grabbing his hand and swinging it. "We couldn't have gotten a better deal. Please, the captain's really nice, and he likes me. Come on please, please, please? Have a heart."

Frelati looked at Genevia's show of childishness with barely concealed amusement. "Fine, but you have got to start listening to me. If I tell you not to go up to someone, don't. Agreed?"

After his consent, Genevia squealed with delight, throwing her arms around his neck for a hug. "Yes!"

"Did you hear me?" Frelati asked, pushing her away slightly to look her in the eyes.

"Oh, yeah, whatever," Genevia said absently with a huge smile on her face, hugging him tightly one more time before breaking away and looking toward the center of town. "So where do we get supplies?"

Frelati sighed, squeezing the bridge of his nose between thumb and forefinger. This was going to be more difficult than he had first thought.

Chapter Six

Fires blazed. Screams echoed through the cool night air. People scurried everywhere, trying to salvage what they could from burning homes and businesses. Fezam's army was ruthless. If even a child got in the way, he was killed. Once passing through a home, it was burned. It was the only way to keep from wasting time by going through the same home twice.

Mothers clung to crying children, trying themselves to hold everything together and show courage. Men grabbed weapons to protect their household but would usually lose their lives in the utterly futile attempt. Soldiers swarmed everywhere. Their reason for invading was based on the happenings of two days before. Rumor had spread through town after town that there was a girl who could make trees grow from nothing.

"Where is she?" a cruel, heartless soldier yelled as he grabbed a terrified woman by the throat. "Tell me."

He shook her, then threw her aside like a worthless rag when he received no answer except the terrified and confused eyes gazing up at him. The clang of swords rang through the air. Children cried uncontrollably, and all wondered when the torment would end. Finally, as dawn rolled in, all noise ceased. The soldiers had gone to wreak havoc on yet another unsuspecting town.

In their wake, smoke billowed up from the destroyed buildings. Women and children rummaged through the wreck, looking for loved ones, food, and any shelter left standing. The soldiers had been unforgiving, unmerciful, leaving no building untouched. The lives of these simple, clueless people were scarred, never to be mended completely again. They walked as ghosts through the once happy town, not understanding the reason behind the massacre.

Their only knowledge on the matter was the importance of the one the soldiers were after. The torment and misery would continue until she was found.

Laughter drifted through the air.

"I love the ocean!" Genevia said excitedly.

She was leaning against the railing at the bow of the ship. Sea spray splashed against her face as it tilted toward the sun for warmth. The breeze was gentle, the clouds few, and the rolling waves rocked the boat ever so slightly. One could hardly tell where the ocean met the sky, both were so pretty and deep a blue.

Frelati watched Genevia as she spread her arms, laughing. He walked closer, ready to catch her if she were to fall.

"Just wait until you've been here a few weeks. We'll see how you feel about it then," Frelati said, his eyes never leaving her.

Genevia laughed again, turning around. At seeing Frelati's intense gaze as he watched her protectively, she said, "I never would've considered you to be such a worrywart. What? You think I'm gonna fall?"

Her green eyes flashed mischievously, and at the next rock of the boat, she pretended to fall overboard. She screamed, and Frelati rushed to grab her, pulling her roughly against him and far from the bow. Laughter once again bubbled out into the open to play with the wind.

"I'm kidding. Honestly, I'm not that clumsy. But you should have seen your face! Ha! Best thing I've seen today." Genevia wiggled from his grasp and turned back to the water, looking over her shoulder to send him a smirk. "Now, will you please stop fussing over me?"

Frelati's lips tightened. "If you would get down to a safer area, I wouldn't have to worry about you. As it is, you're an accident waiting to happen."

Genevia turned back to him with a scoff and roll of the eyes. "I could fall anywhere, Frelati."

"Yes, but you are more likely to fall up there. Ease my mind a little, will you?" Frelati ordered, watching as she finally relented and stepped down from the bow.

He huffed to hide his sigh of relief and looked away. Undeterred by his gruffness, Genevia came over with a grin and kissed him on the cheek.

"Stop being an overprotective big brother," she said before walking off. She was having entirely too much fun playing her part.

The old captain, Traynord by name, had watched the events silently the whole while. For a sister and brother, they seemed a little too insecure around each other. The majority of the time, Genevia seemed to treat Fredish as a sister would, teasing him and ignoring him, aggravating him and hugging him, but Fredish was too cautious, distanced, and stern to be her brother. Traynord had also heard many a slip of the tongue. Genevia had called Fredish Frelati on too many occasions to count, and she never even realized the slip. Neither did Fredish.

Watching them, he decided that, after being at sea a little longer, he would make them tell their secret. He had a feeling their story would be an interesting one, and he had always loved a good yarn. But for the time being, he would leave them alone and stay quiet.

Genevia popped up, startling Traynord from his reverie. "So how long do you think we'll be at sea? Frel…dish thinks it'll be three weeks, maybe two. Does that sound right?"

Traynord eyed her, there was that slip again, and answered. "Me estima' is bou' two weeks, give er take. The boy's go' goo' sense on 'im."

She nodded and glided over to tell Frelati. She certainly had a grace about her. As he watched the pair, he noticed Fredish's face darken with worry. The boy lifted his eyes to the sky for a moment before heading over to him.

"Is there a port we can get to in eight days?" Frelati asked in a toneless voice.

Traynord grinned. "Wha's the matter? Ye go' a bi' o' sea sickness?"

"No, none of that," he looked toward the sky with a shake of the head. "We'll get into a storm in eight days, and I don't mean a gentle sprinkle. A port is our only hope to get through this."

The old captain's brow crinkled as he looked at the clear, blue sky. Then he turned his gaze back to Frelati and laughed. "Now, where ye ge' nonsense like tha'? No' a clou' in the sky."

"It isn't nonsense." Frelati's deadpan tone abruptly wiped the smile from Traynord's face. "It's a prediction. My gift is to predict weather. Ordinarily, I only know a day ahead. The worse the storm, the farther ahead I see. I see a storm hitting in eight days; in this boat, that's not a good sign. We need to get into a port."

Traynord studied him. "Alrigh', bu' I'll nee' ye're 'elp. There's a por' jus' north of 'ere. If we work 'ard, we migh' make i' 'n time."

"Good," Frelati said, and he couldn't hide his relief as he looked out over the water. "I'll do whatever I can to help."

The old captain nodded. "I'll nee' i'."

Each day after that, Frelati would ask the captain to call him if he needed any help, then he would stand at the bow of the ship, hands clasped behind him, feet apart for balance, and look up at the sky. He stayed like that, still as a statue, until Traynord called him or the sun went down, whichever came first.

Each morning he would give an update on the weather. Most days it was the same, but on the fifth day, Frelati said they had another day to pull into port. Traynord was happy to receive this news, because he had been having serious doubts that they would sail into port before the storm sailed into them.

Genevia made up for Frelati's detached demeanor. When she wasn't trying to annoy Frelati into moving or speaking, she would entertain Traynord. Some days she would talk—tell jokes or talk about her home, though she was very vague on that topic—and sometimes she'd sing. Other days she would sit and listen to Traynord's tales. He enjoyed talking and was thrilled to have an avid listener. She made him laugh, and that was a nice change too.

Finally, on the seventh day, when Genevia was pacing the deck and bored out of her mind, she spotted a green mass in the water.

"Land!" she cried excitedly, grabbing the railing and squinting at the horizon. "I see land!"

Frelati walked over, his eyes looking in the direction her outstretched finger indicated. Then he went to talk with the captain. After a few minutes, Genevia sauntered over.

"Now what are the two of you talking about so intently?" she asked, rocking from toe to heel.

"We should land tonight or early tomorrow morning. The storm should hit tomorrow afternoon," Frelati said, looking toward land, then at the sky. He nodded, a slight smile tugging at the corners of his mouth. "We'll make it."

He was right. They landed before the sun came up and walked ashore, glad to have firm ground beneath their feet.

"Okay," Frelati said, taking charge. "Let's find a place to stay, an inn or something, and then we meet back here in an hour to discuss what's going on."

They agreed. Traynord went off one way, and Genevia was about to walk off on her own when Frelati stopped her and started pulling her off with him.

"You come with me," he said. "I don't need to worry about the trouble you're getting yourself into while also looking out for guards. This way."

The town was very quaint and small. Little houses and businesses lined the street, now empty. Colorful displays were in dark shop windows, and flowers lined the edges of the windows of the houses. It was silent here as all the people slept, and Frelati and Genevia tried to take quiet steps as they walked along.

"Hey," Genevia said suddenly, rushing over to a shop window.

Frelati ignored her, thinking her curiosity was over a cute pair of shoes or some other insignificant trinket. He looked past her and saw a sign advertising an inn.

"There's an inn," he said, indicating the building with a nod of his head and looking toward Genevia. "We can ask...if...they have... What is it?"

Genevia was looking at a sign posted in the window of a weapons shop. Her face had grown pale, and she hadn't heard a word that Frelati had said. He walked over to read the sign.

"Perfect," he muttered sarcastically, his face grim.

The sign was not a pleasant one, and it sent shivers up Genevia's spine.

WANTED

Two criminals on the run,
Frelati and Alernoa wanted alive.
Both young adults. Bring to King if seen.

Beneath was a rough sketch of Frelati and Genevia, but it was a good resemblance. Apparently Sallus and his men had wasted no time in contacting the proper authorities when it came to reporting a girl who could create trees from nothing.

"What do we do?" Genevia asked quietly, grasping Frelati's arm.

"Hide and leave when we can," Frelati replied with an edge to his voice. He grabbed her hand. "Come on, before anyone wakes up."

They ran to the docks and into the cabin of the ship, sitting against the wall behind some crates to catch their breath.

"What do we do if Traynord sees a poster?" Genevia asked.

Frelati glanced at her before his eyes returned to the door. "We hope he doesn't."

"And if he does?" Genevia pushed worriedly.

"We hope he doesn't realize that the pictures are us."

"But what if he does? What do we do then?"

Frelati sighed and slowly turned to look her straight in the eyes. "Hopefully, he won't turn us in, but if he decided to leave us here, that would be just as bad. He's our only way off this coast. We really can't trust anyone else."

Genevia was scared but tried to show courage. "What if he does leave us? What will we do then? I don't think I'd do well in jail."

Frelati's jaw tightened at the last sentence. "I can't answer your questions. I have no idea what will happen anymore than you do. When the time comes, if it comes, we'll figure something out, but there's no need to worry about it now." Frelati made eye contact again, squeezing her hand reassuringly. "I know you're scared. I'm not too happy about this either, but there really isn't much…"

Genevia slapped her hand across Frelati's mouth to shush his last few words as footsteps were heard above them on the ship coming toward the door to the cabin. Both pairs of eyes were drawn to the door as the doorknob slowly turned. The door opened with a slight creaking sound to reveal Traynord. Genevia relaxed a little, but they still weren't sure where Traynord stood—on their side or with the soldiers—so she couldn't completely breathe easy.

"Whachee doin' down 'ere, ay? Hidin' from som'at?" he asked humorously to lighten the atmosphere.

"It was just…" Genevia searched for an excuse, her hand automatically gripping her locket in that nervous gesture of hers. "…just a little warm on deck, so we came down here."

She smiled shakily.

"So i' 'ad nuttin' ta do wi' me, ay lassie? Ye warn' afrai' of me findin' ou' ye're secre', Alernoa an' Frelati?" Traynord smiled at them. "No nee' ta fre'. I alrea'y knew ye 'ad a secre', jus' wasn' sure wha' i' was, an' I'll keep i'."

"How'd you know?" Genevia asked incredulously.

"Ye're slip o' the tongue, Alernoa, callin' Fredish over 'ere Frelati. 'e ne'er slipped, though," Traynord explained, looking curiously at Frelati. "I won'er why tha' is."

"Alernoa grew up with the name Genevia. That's all she knows, and that's the name she gave me when we met," Frelati answered.

"Mmmm, ye wan' ta explain ye're position?" Traynord asked, knowing he would get an explanation. He wasn't disappointed. Genevia explained the highlights, and Traynord listened intently, as a friend would. He didn't condemn the two for being on a wanted poster.

"Well, we'll leave the por' as soon as I ge' me some surplies. I'll be back from town in a bi'," Traynord said.

"They probably already know which ship we're on, since you left after we were spotted. If you hurry, we can leave before they realize you came into port," Frelati said.

Traynord nodded. "Ye two jus' hide down 'ere until we leave."

"But…what will happen when we're at sea?" Genevia asked, her eyes twin pools of uncertainty.

Frelati looked at her in confusion. "The same thing that happened before. The army shouldn't be looking for us yet. We aren't going to be at port that long."

"Yes, but when we were at sea before, there wasn't a huge storm heading our way," Genevia pointed out. "Or, well, there was, but that's why we came here."

Frelati stood with a groan and rubbed a hand over his eyes. "I forgot about the storm. We can't leave until after it hits if we want to live. Not in this boat."

Traynord nodded. "Well, I have ta ge' me some surplies. I s'pose I can see wha' soldiers are abou'."

Frelati's jaw hardened in indecision. He looked over at Genevia, still huddled against the wall. What had he done? She didn't deserve any of this. He ran a hand through his hair roughly as he turned back to Traynord.

"Do that," he said tersely. "We'll plan to stay in port unless it's impossible to do so. Kiem help us if it is."

With that decided, Traynord walked back on deck, staying on board until the town woke enough for him to gather his supplies. He came back an hour later with all they needed, but he came quickly and out of breath with a worried expression on his face.

"Ge' the ship runnin'; the army's a comin'. We have ta ge' ou' ta sea, storm or no storm. They 'ave ships, an' they'll ge' ya if we don' leave," Traynord said hurriedly. "They know ye're 'ere."

Chapter Seven

"What are we going to do?" Genevia threw up her hands in disgust to dig her fingers into her hair, worry finally replaced by a fit of helpless fury.

The sky was dark with thunderclouds, but they all still waited for the first drops of rain to fall. The sea had an eerie calm about it, as it always did before a bad storm. That calm had the opposite effect on the three individuals waiting for the downpour. Genevia had been pacing the deck worriedly for an hour. Frelati just looked up at the sky, giving frequent updates, his back to the others. Traynord was patiently sitting and watching them both. He had always found the reactions of people amusing, and the emotions of these two didn't disappoint.

He already knew there was nothing they could do, and he had accepted it. Of course, he was older and had always wanted to go down with his trusty, old ship. The only thing he regretted now was that the lives of the two youngsters would have to go with him. It was always a shame when a life was blotted out before the story had truly begun to be told.

Frelati's fingers had begun a countdown. His body still as a statue, only his fingers moved.

Five.

"We have to do something!" Genevia shouted.

Four.

She turned to Traynord. "Don't you have an idea? You've been at sea forever!"

He shook his head sadly, and Genevia returned to her pacing. Three.

She looked at the water below. "It looks kinda still, maybe you're wrong, Frelati."

Two.

"Frelati, will you do something other than just stand there?"

One.

"Frelati? I really need a response. Frelati!" Genevia raised her voice.

Frelati's hand closed into a fist as he turned. "It has begun."

Immediately following his words rain splashed down, softly at first, but gradually gaining force. They all watched as the water slowly grew violent. Lightning flashed, thunder sounded, and the rush of the wind blowing straight toward the small boat did not help their predicament. The ship tossed with the growing waves, and Genevia, who had been standing at the railing, almost went overboard but was caught instantly by Frelati.

"I told you to stay away from the railing," he yelled through the wind.

Genevia forced herself not to cry, though there would be no way to tell she was crying through the pelting rain, and she tried to think of a plan. She had to yell to make herself heard to Frelati, who still held her tightly in his grasp.

"What can we do?" she yelled.

Frelati thought a bit before answering. "I can't do anything, but you might."

Genevia was surprised. "Me? How?"

"I don't know; you just have to try."

She nodded and stumbled to the bow of the boat, tightly gripping the railing there. A huge swell could be seen forming a short way off, heading quickly their way.

Genevia hesitantly held out her hand. "Stop! C-cease! Calm! Ummm…. Heel!"

She turned to Frelati in helplessness, and he shouted something that was snatched up by the wind and taken away.

"Get calm! Stop roaring! Do something other than this!"

Genevia was terrified, and the wave was getting closer. She put her hands over her face in frustration. "I don't know what to do!"

She took a deep breath and looked back up at the wave that towered very high above them; just a few yards to go until it reached the boat. Anger and fear welled up within her. With a last determined gesture, she threw her arms toward the oncoming wave with a hard force.

"Listen to me and calm!" she yelled at the top of her lungs.

No one on Cinnaca ever understood the happenings of that day. Some chalked it up to the storm that was coming, even though the two really shouldn't be connected. Some blamed invisible spirits or ancient giants, and yet others worried that Fezam had discovered a new weapon to test or honed a new power. Stories abounded on that gentle day when the entire country rolled like some creature was moving beneath it.

It began simultaneously in the north, east, and west and traveled in one giant wave toward a central point: Ulbig. Everyone rushed under cover, not sure where to take refuge as buildings creaked and groaned with the unaccustomed movement. The people of Ulbig listened for some huge crack as the ripple reached the edge of land, but instead of ending, the wave continued into the sea, rocking boats as it steadily built and raced out to sea.

Some claimed later that it was the herald of the end of the world, but no one on Cinnaca ever knew what truly happened; they just felt the power of nature as it rushed to halt the storm headed their way.

Genevia didn't know what she was trying to prove with her final, uncontrollable outburst, but she definitely didn't figure it would produce any results. Her eyes widened as an even louder roar, loud enough to overpower the voice of the storm, came rushing from behind her. She turned to find the origin of the noise and saw the boat breaking apart as a twin wave of a size to rival the original rushed forward. She saw Frelati and Traynord fall into the ocean just before she felt her own body slip beneath the waves.

She tried to reach the surface, but the current of the storm kept her under until she saw complete calm above her. Then, all turned to darkness as her empty lungs caused her to lose consciousness.

Frelati gulped air as he finally reached the surface, searching frantically for Genevia. After a few frenzied dives, he caught a glimpse of skin in the water and quickly dragged her to the surface, resting her over some boards from the broken ship. Traynord, who had suffered only a cut above the eye, swam over to join him.

"Is she alive?" he asked with a watery cough.

"She'd better be," Frelati said harshly, but his anxiety could not be disguised.

"Is she breathin'?"

"I don't know. Have I killed her?" Frelati panicked before getting himself back under control. "Genevia, Genevia, wake up. Genevia, for once in your life, listen to me!"

He splashed water on her with no response, which made him even more frantic. Eyes wide, he stared at Traynord and muttered, "I've killed her!"

"No, ye haven', la'. Calm yerself," Traynord said firmly. "She's breathin'."

He slapped her smartly across the face, and she came to quickly, sputtering for air and coughing roughly while Frelati supported her.

"What...what...what happened?" she asked after catching her breath.

Frelati closed his eyes and sighed in relief, pulling her into a hug. "Don't ever scare me like that again."

Genevia couldn't hold back her pleasure at Frelati's rather unorthodox show of emotion, and she relaxed in his arms for a minute before pulling back to look around. The sight that met her was not what she expected. "What is this? This isn't good! Did I destroy the ship? How are we going to get to land? How long was I out?"

Traynord decided the last question was the easiest to answer. "Jus' a lil while, lass, an' i' may look ba', bu' we're alive, ain' we? We go' plen'y o' foo' in tha' bag o' yours, an' I foun' this canteen o' water. No' much, bu' we'll make do."

"So, I did stop the storm?"

"Yea, ye di' lass." Traynord grinned and gave her a gentle pat on the back. "Now ye nee' ta res' fer a shor' while, ta ge' ye're stren'th back. We'll talk abou' this mess af'er tha'."

Genevia was drained, so she simply nodded and lay back on the boards, instantly falling asleep as the other two worked to salvage what they could of the boat. Genevia's pack was found floating in a barrel that had managed to stay intact, and surprisingly, it was hardly wet. They fastened together all the boards they found with some of the rope left from the rigging of the ship, and, after a lot of hard work, had a raft big enough to fit the three of them.

By the time they had finished and climbed aboard, fins began to show a short way off. Genevia woke at Frelati's soft touch on her shoulder, and she glanced at the water as the fins drew closer. She was not nearly as wary as Traynord and Frelati.

"They're just dolphins," she said sleepily as she lay back down. "I don't know why you're so worried."

Frelati shot her a look of consternation. "You can't know that. They could be sharks, and you haven't ever been on the ocean to know the difference."

Genevia yawned and answered with her eyes still closed. Why did she feel so…lifeless? "I don't know how I know, but there's three blue, two purple, and four pink. Wake me in an hour."

She was still in a state of half wakefulness when her answer broke through her sleepy haze and she popped up. "How did I know that?"

Frelati raised a brow with a smirk. Traynord was simply confused. Neither of them offered an explanation. About that time, the dolphins had come up to the side of the raft. Three blue fins were seen and two purple, but only three pink.

"I think you need to brush up on your counting," Frelati said.

Genevia shot him a scowl before turning with a grin toward the frolicking, friendly creatures. "She's underwater."

As if it were a summons, the fourth pink dolphin came up to join them.

"Get some rope."

"Alright," Genevia said, grabbing a coil and handing it to Frelati.

He and Traynord both stared at her.

"What's this for?" Frelati asked, setting the rope aside.

"What do you mean?" Genevia asked in confusion. "You just told me to get some rope. Or was that you, Traynord?"

"They didn't say it; I did."

"What?" Genevia was beginning to think the water had gone to her head.

Frelati gave her a funny look. "What do you mean 'what'? No one has said anything. Are you okay?"

"No, I heard it. Someone said something," Genevia said, looking all around.

The pink dolphin lifted her tail and caused a huge splash of water to wash over Genevia. *"Listen to me! Give us the rope and attach one end to the raft."*

Genevia stared at the dolphin. "You can talk?"

"I can talk with dolphins and converse telepathically with you. You carry Kiem, and we are clever. It is no difficulty."

It suddenly clicked. "They can't hear you."

"No."

Genevia sat back, letting it all sink in. "What do you mean I carry Kiem?"

"You carry Kiem."

Genevia nodded but didn't really understand. However, she was talking to a dolphin, so there was bound to be some misunderstandings. This ability probably had something to do with her gift, her attachment to nature. While she pondered this, Frelati was looking at her in alarm.

"Did you bump your head, swallow too much water?" he asked as he scanned her for any sign of injury.

Genevia turned to him. "No, I'm okay. I just…I can hear them."

"You can hear them," Frelati repeated. There was a brief pause before he shook his head. "Well, you seem to be able to do everything else, so why not this."

Genevia studied him for a minute before an impatient chirp from the water reminded her of their predicament. "We need to tie this rope to the raft and give the other end to the dolphins."

"Why?" Frelati asked.

"We'll take you to land."

"They're going to take us to land," Genevia said with a smile.

Frelati stared at her before nodding again. Traynord was baffled, but he helped her with the rope anyway. With the ropes in place, four dolphins began pulling the raft. They were strong and quick, taking rotations with the others to keep from tiring out, and a slight breeze could be felt as the three were pulled along.

As time passed, the sun could be seen playing on the horizon. It peeped up behind the edge of the water that was turning slowly into a deep blue. A cloud would wisp before its shining face, but soon the sun would peek out behind it, as a child would from behind his tiny fingers. The rays stretched high, hoping to reach the rising moon and continue hanging there, just above the horizon, until it was time to rise again, but it steadily sank, unable to reach that pale orb high in the sky.

It was in this sunset, when the water glittered with the multicolored sun, that the dolphins played. Water sprang from their sleek, sparkling bodies as they dove through the air across the distant sun. Silhouetted against the bright light, all that could be seen was the glittering sunlight dancing across their backs until it had to leap off to avoid crashing into the sea below. The sight was one always to be remembered and treasured in Genevia's heart.

Like all things, though, it came to an end, as night came to steal the fun. The only light came from the moon that seemed so forlorn and distant in the black expanse of sky. Then, the stars came out to join him and wink at the three souls on a small raft in a large sea. Their smiling lights and winking glimmers made all the troubles and sorrows of the three seem to melt away.

The night grew silent, with the exception of the gently rolling waves, as they all slept deeply. Comforted by their dreams and rocked by the ocean, they didn't feel the pull of the raft as the dolphins worked to get them to safety. An odd sight it was, but one to bring a smile to any face. The moon and stars saw it all, but never would they tell, for silence was their friend and their mystery.

It continued thus each night that they rested until, on the fourth day, as darkness vanished and the sun began to show its face once again, the three woke to slightly different surroundings. The rays of the sun stretched high and no clouds were in sight when Genevia opened her eyes. She was up first but quickly woke the others after she spotted a green mass in the distance.

"We're not going to die!" she exclaimed, momentarily forgetting she was on a small raft and jumping to her feet in excitement.

The raft tipped, and she fell off, grabbing Frelati in a vain attempt to stay on and instead taking him with her. He was still half-asleep, but at the shock of cold ocean water, he woke instantly.

"Are you insane? You can't stand on a raft!" he sputtered in annoyance.

The spat that might have occurred was broken by laughter. Traynord and the supplies had managed to stay on, mainly because of Traynord's experience at sea. He helped them both up, still chuckling.

"It's not funny," Frelati grumbled as he tried to wring the salty water from his clothes. "I had finally gotten dry from my first dunk, and she has to pull me back in again."

Genevia was wringing out her long hair. "In case you didn't notice, I fell in too. It's not like I did it on purpose. If I had been trying to ruin only your day, I would have done this."

She pushed Frelati backward off the raft and grinned. Frelati came up sputtering.

"What was that for?" he asked angrily as he swam toward the raft.

Genevia reached out to help him up. "I'm sorry." It didn't sound like it. "It was just too tempting. I couldn't resist."

Frelati took her extended hand, but instead of using it to get back on the raft, he gave it a tug, making her fly into the water. After she came up and stopped gasping, he said with a smirk, "Now we're even."

Genevia sighed as she swam over. Frelati climbed onto the raft and turned to help her up.

"Fortunately, the sun's out, and it'll be a warm day," Genevia said to Frelati. "So you can stop pouting about being wet."

She lay out on her back, allowing the sun's warmth to seep into her cool skin. She closed her eyes, just listening to the water.

Frelati said nothing. Instead, he dipped his fingers in the sea before reaching over to spray her with water.

Genevia sat up. "Hey!"

Frelati simply raised a brow, daring her to retaliate.

Genevia narrowed her eyes and grimaced, but lay back down. "I can't wait to be on shore again."

"Really?" Frelati said, stretching out beside her. "What happened to the girl who said she'd never get tired of the ocean?"

Genevia looked over at him with a smile as she tried to cover her blunder. "I'm not tired of it. I just want to have enough space to get away from you. That's all."

"Uh-huh, right," Frelati said.

The day was passing slowly, and it seemed as if the land kept backing up further with each mile they traveled. Genevia was bored but didn't want to say so. The sun was high in the sky, and it was growing hot as they finished eating a meager lunch.

"Will you tell us a story?" Genevia asked Traynord. "I'm sure you've got wonderful tales from your travels at sea."

"Tha' I do, lassie," Traynord said before rubbing his chin in thought. "Le's see. Which one will ye like the mos'?"

He thought a bit before snapping his fingers. "I go' jus' the one. This was twen'y or more years ago. I was on me boa', been travlin' three weeks, I ha'. I ha' me a small crew, five men, I say. A price woul' be given to the ship tha' pulle' in the larges' franick."

"What's a franick?" Genevia asked.

Traynord looked at her in surprise. "Ye ne'er hear' o' a franick?"

Genevia shook her head.

"She hasn't heard of most things," Frelati muttered, though no one paid any attention.

"I' 'as five arms, on'y one gian' eye, an' i's green. Huge, i' is, an' we was goin' ta catch one. We was deep a' sea, no lan' in sigh'. The line was ou', an' we was waitin'. Tug! We all fel' i'; som'at 'ad our line. Two men grabbe' i', bu' i' was too strong. All me men 'ad ta tug ta keep from goin' under."

"What happened?" Genevia asked.

Frelati was only half paying attention, but he had the main idea. "They got the franick, won the prize, parted after a fight over the money, Traynord didn't get much, and here we are."

"Oh, stop messing up the story," Genevia grumbled. "What happened next?"

"Ac-chu-lly, lassie, the la's righ'."

Genevia rolled her eyes with a huge sigh and glared at him. "Thanks a lot."

"Uh-huh, anytime," Frelati said, unperturbed from his relaxed position beside her.

Genevia sighed again. "Okay, I admit it. I'm tired of the sea. I'm ready to be on land. It's just an added bonus that I can get away from you as well as the water."

"At least you admit it now," Frelati muttered before opening his eyes to look at her sternly. "But you won't be able to get away from me on land either."

Genevia looked away, and Frelati sat up to get a look at the green mass ahead. "We don't have much time until we land. I think you can make it."

"Aye, la', ye're righ'," Traynord said. "We're close."

"Finally," Genevia sighed.

"I' will still be a while ye', lassie," Traynord warned. "We migh' lan' tanigh' er early mornin'."

"Uhhh," Genevia groaned as she collapsed back on the raft. Time just couldn't move fast enough. She watched the waves and the dolphins, but mainly made note of the changes in the sun's position. She watched it fall slowly from the top of the sky to touch the horizon gently with just a tip of its glow.

The sunset it created was sprinkled across the ocean and splashed across the sky, the most beautiful array of colors it had ever worn. Enchantment was placed upon the viewers of this magnificent spectacle while the bright light once again danced along the horizon. No words were spoken; all was silent as the light played its grand finale of the day.

That morning the light shined splendidly across the quaint, little town on Rom. Small, stone streets were lined with shops, and the outside landscape was sprinkled with farming homes. It was still early yet, but activity was beginning.

It was to this welcoming sight that the three travelers arrived on shore. They had traveled all night and were thrilled to be on land again. They pulled up to the beach, which was only a short way from the town, and began walking to gather supplies.

"What a cute little place!" Genevia exclaimed as they entered. "It's so orderly and quaint."

"Aye, lassie, bu' ev'ry town 'as i's dir'y corners," Traynord said, winking.

Frelati ignored them, looking around to find the best shops.

"This way," he said, motioning and walking forward.

They entered a bakery at the edge of town. It was filled to the brim with bread, muffins, and any other flour-based product it could hold. The bakery was small but homey, and the woman behind the counter made it seem even more so. She was a plump lady, Jezzie by name, who was prone to gossip but very loving. She had a welcoming smile and a kindly face, and her sweet, rich voice made her the kind of woman you would think of as the perfect mother.

"How can I help y'all?" she asked with the twang of those who lived in the more rural areas. "I got every kind of bread ya need. Just pick one."

Frelati walked right up to the counter. "Which bread will last the longest? We're traveling."

Jezzie looked him up and down. "Now, what ya need is some fattenin' bread. Look at the little, scrawny thing ya are. Skin an' bones, I declare. Who's been starvin' ya?"

Genevia had been examining the bread, deciding on the tastiest and biggest to take with them. On hearing the rather loud woman's remarks, though, she looked toward an astonished Frelati with a smirk. Although he was definitely not what an ordinary person would call "skin and bones," Genevia was not going to pass up this opportunity.

"You're right," she said to Jezzie, walking over to taunt Frelati a bit more. "He's just so picky. I can't get him to eat anything."

Frelati shot her an angry glare before turning back to Jezzie. "Will you just give us the best bread?"

"Oh, now, ya need to be thinkin' on yur little lady's needs. She doesn't need to go hungry, got to build herself up for children," Jezzie said, turning to grab some of the most unhealthy-looking bread, jam, and cakes imaginable.

"What!" they both exclaimed in alarm before glancing at each other and turning away abruptly; Genevia in embarrassment, Frelati in annoyance.

Traynord walked up chuckling. "Ye're righ', miss. They nee' ta buil' up their stren'th. Give us the bes' ye go'."

"Well, finally someone agrees with me," Jezzie said, turning and seeing Traynord for the first time. "My, but you need some weight too. Goodness me! I declare someone's starved the lot of ya! You just leave it to Jezzie; I'll have ya all set in a minute. Here's some extra."

"We can't pay for it though." Frelati tried to push some of the contents back.

Jezzie broke in, drowning out his voice. "Oh, it's on the house. Look at all this bread! Ya think we'll sell it all? And my husband just don't know when to quit makin' all that bread. Here, eat up and gain some pounds."

She handed Frelati a large loaf.

"I wouldn't even see ya if ya stood sideways. I swear ya'd disappear. Eat up."

"We really…" Frelati started in a matter-of-fact tone.

"Eat up. I'll not have ya die of hunger after ya've been in my store," Jezzie interrupted.

Frelati sighed and tightened his lips, but he dutifully took a bite. It was wonderful. He praised her grudgingly. "This is very good. Thank you."

Jezzie shot him a motherly look. "Oh, hush up, now, and eat. I want to see that whole loaf gone. You need something, too, dear."

She turned to find the right bread for Genevia. While her back was turned, Frelati tore off a huge chunk of his loaf and stowed it in his bag. After seeing the admonishing look Genevia gave him, he shrugged and took another bite.

Jezzie had been muttering in the back, never quite deciding on the best bread. "This'll have to do. Here ya go, doll. Eat up. The poppies is s'posed to help with havin' kids, but who really knows in this town. All sorts of hogwash here."

Frelati choked on his bread, bringing Jezzie's attention back to him. "Heavens! You were hungry! I'll get another loaf, darlin'. If I'd only known!"

She hustled back, a bewildered and disbelieving Frelati watching her, mouth agape.

"Is she trying to kill me?" he muttered under his breath.

Genevia grinned. "No, she just wants to fatten you up, stick you in the oven, and have herself a nice midnight snack. Enjoy your bread."

She smiled at him before nibbling at her own. Jezzie came back with her arms full of three more loaves.

"That'll hold ya and ur li'l lady. Go on, now, I've got other customers comin' in."

Jezzie shooed them out and gathered in the other customers. The three just stood on the side of the street looking at their food.

"I like her. You picked a good shop, Frelati," Genevia said.

Frelati stared at all the bread in amazement. "No ordinary person could eat this much bread in two months, much less in the hour she gave me to eat it."

Genevia smirked. "Well, it wouldn't have happened if you hadn't hidden half of it in your bag."

"Yea, yea," Frelati said with frown. "But now we have to find a way to carry it all."

He was juggling the load of bread Jezzie had shoved into his arms, trying desperately not to drop it all. Inevitably, though, one slipped free, and a shower of laughter escaped Genevia's lips. He scowled as he retrieved the loaf.

"Make yourself useful and get a bag for me to put it in," he ordered.

She ran into the bakery and returned with a basket and more bread. "This was all she had to give me, and she told me to make you eat this."

"It'll work," Frelati said as he shoved the loaves into the basket, ignoring Genevia's smirk as she waved the new stick of bread in front of him. He grabbed for it, and she danced away. Setting the basket on the ground to allow for a more effective assault, he took two steps forward before seeing a small child dart out from the shadow of the bakery to steal a piece. "Hey!"

"Hold this," Genevia said, shoving the bread into Frelati's arms and taking off after the child before Frelati could stop her.

"Genevia!" Frelati yelled.

He threw the bread into the basket and ran after her. Foolish girl. Traynord watched them go, shaking his head. He was too old to go running off after two young sprites, so he grabbed the basket, found himself a stone a short way off, and sat down.

"Young'ns," he muttered under his breath with a smile, settling down to wait for their return.

Chapter Eight

Heartbeat pounding, blood rushing, breathing heavy, legs aching, and still pushing onward to avoid the terror behind her. Lela was frightened, her running and actions quick as she darted around buildings and hid in shadows. She stopped to listen and heard no noise but the steady pounding of her own heart. She rushed into an alleyway to hide against the wall and watch the street before her for the figure of her predator.

She looked at the stolen loaf of bread in her hand and sank down to the ground to eat while still keeping a wary eye on the street. Lela had never wanted to hurt people, and she knew stealing was wrong, but her stomach never allowed her to go hungry too long before making her steal again. When she was younger, she used to just ask for food and the kind shopkeepers and farming families would give her some, but after a year of being on her own, she had gained a wild look, and the families would turn her away. It was because of them that she had to steal. She just wasn't going to die.

Her parents had died three years earlier; they both caught pneumentalouse. It took her a year to find out exactly what that was, but after sneaking into a doctor's room and looking at some medical scrolls with lots of pictures, she found out what it did. Her parents had eaten the poison of a small weed that had gotten onto their vegetables. The poison would stick to their lungs and grow. After a while there was no hope for survival. Lela had been lucky; she had been allergic to the poisoned squash, so she hadn't been given any.

When she thought of her parents, she felt sad, but she really couldn't remember them. They were a distant memory in the life of this child, and now she just wanted to survive. Some kind neighbors had taken her in for a year, but they were elderly and died soon after, leaving her alone again. She had been relying on herself now for two years, and she was getting used to it. For her six years, Lela was smart and quick, perfect for snagging meals, but this last masquerade hadn't been thought out as well as the rest.

Lost in what few memories she had, feeling safety creep over her and the tasty morsel of bread filling her more with each bite, Lela didn't hear the soft footsteps of Genevia. The girl's shadow stretched beyond the building, and Genevia knew right where she was hiding. Footsteps thudded behind her, and she rolled her eyes, turning swiftly to stop Frelati. He got the hint and stopped some feet away.

Genevia pressed against the wall, watching the shadow ahead of her intently for any sudden movement. She began inching forward slowly, trying her hardest to make no noise. The brick building was rough, and the edges of the bricks were sharp, pushing into her back as she crept along. She was still a few feet from the end of the building when her sleeve caught on a brick. She turned to release it before it tore and pushed herself against the wall, inhaling quickly to stifle her startled, yet silent yelp.

"Frelati," she mouthed with mad eyes. "You were to stay there."

He shrugged while motioning and mouthing that he wanted to be right where he was. Genevia sighed and turned back to look at the shadow, but it was gone. She whipped around to Frelati.

"Did you see someone run down the alley?" she asked quietly, annoyance in her words.

Frelati shook his head. "No, I was too busy trying to read your lips. Just look in there."

They moved to the mouth of the alley. There were trash bins, trash, and cats, many cats. On sight of their sudden appearance, though, the startled animals ran toward them and away in all directions.

"It's blocked," Frelati said.

"How do you know that?" Genevia put her hands on her hips.

"If there was another way out, I think the cats would have taken it rather than having to face you." He smirked.

Genevia stuck out her tongue.

"Come on," Frelati said, pulling her with him.

The alley was L-shaped, lined by brick. It smelled and looked terrible and made Genevia feel terrible.

"This is disgusting," she complained.

"You're the one that wanted to chase the kid," Frelati pointed out.

"Well, I didn't know I'd have to come here of all places."

Frelati put his finger to his lips to shush her then motioned for her to follow him. They rounded the bend and saw a brick wall at the far end. The alley was mainly empty; only a trash bin was placed against the wall. Frelati scanned the surfaces for climbing access, but it seemed impossible. The trash bin was the only hiding place, and he could see a small foot peeking out from behind it.

"Well, I guess we were wrong," he said loudly, "Come on, let's go back."

Genevia stared at him in astonishment.

"We haven't checked behind the…" Genevia stopped upon seeing Frelati's expression.

"Oh." She breathed before saying loudly, "Well, the trash bin is probably too small for anyone to hide behind."

Frelati stomped on the ground a few times before stepping lightly toward the trash bin. He motioned for Genevia to help him close the child in. Genevia nodded. They crept forward slowly until they were just a few feet from the child's view.

"On three," Frelati mouthed and motioned. "One, two, three."

They rushed around the trash bin, closing Lela in. She stared at them wide-eyed, looking for a way to escape. Genevia and Frelati covered every place before her, and the trash bin behind her took up the only other escape route. She was stuck.

"Ie'n hiff," Lela cried, throwing herself on the ground in front of them. "Safa oh gsa yfaew. Ie'n hiff!"

Genevia's brow bunched in confusion. "What's she saying? Is she insane?"

Frelati ignored Genevia and stared intensely at Lela. "Biu…biu pid Alzam?"

Lela perked up. "Biu umwafgem na? Miima she azaf umwafgiiw na."

"What's going on?" Genevia asked, a little unsettled that Frelati was speaking the same gibberish as the little girl.

Frelati continued staring at the child in amazement while answering Genevia. "She knows Elven, the language of the elves."

Suddenly, he leaned forward and pushed the girl's dirty, blond hair behind her ears—her pointed ears. "Biu'fa em alz."

Shocked, he sat back on his heels and glanced over at Genevia in bewilderment as he repeated, "She's an elf. What is she doing here?"

"What was she saying, though? You understand her. What did you say? What's her name? Can she speak Welnish?"

Distractedly, Frelati translated the previous conversation. "She apologized, several times, about taking the bread, and she offered it back, well, part of it. I just can't believe she speaks Alzam…uh, Elven."

"Can she speak Welnish?"

"I don't know."

"What's her name?"

"Bseg oh biuf mena?"

"Lela," she said. "Bseg oh biufh?"

"Ie en Frelati. Has oh Genevia," Frelati said. "Wi biu haep Welnish…Dalmohs?"

Lela shook her head. "Mi…dall, e loggla."

"Her name is Lela," Frelati interpreted. "She says she knows a little Welnish."

"Why is she out here by herself? Where are her parents?" Genevia asked, looking at Frelati.

"That's what I'd like to know."

Lela rubbed her head. "Slow."

"Huh?" Genevia said in surprise, turning to look at Lela. "Oh, where are your parents?"

She took great care to enunciate each word. Lela looked up at her with startlingly blue eyes, concentrating hard. When she answered, she spoke slowly, but clearly, and her small voice had power behind it, showing a willful and brave heart.

"I…am…" she paused to think. "I am…alone. Parents…parents gone by…by…sick…by sickness. I am…alone."

Genevia gasped. "You're an orphan!"

Lela shook her head before turning to Frelati for understanding. "Dseg?"

"Ifsem."

Lela locked eyes with Genevia. It felt as if Lela knew all Genevia's secrets just by looking into her eyes.

"Yes. I am…orphan?"

"You're an elf," Frelati repeated. "What are you doing here? Elves live on Omhemalem and Meufa…when we're not dragged into prisons…but we don't live near humans." A glance at Genevia revealed her confusion, so he paused to explain. "We live a lot longer than humans. It's easier for us to keep contact to a minimum. For her to be here is…unusual. Although, I suppose it would be a good way for fugitive elves to hide."

Just then, Lela spoke up. She had been trying to decipher what Frelati was saying but hadn't done too well. "I am…um, one…one elf."

Genevia and Frelati turned to look at her, thoroughly confused.

"What?" Genevia asked, kneeling down to be eye level with the small girl. "Can you say that again?"

Lela thought a bit before speaking. "I am…one elf…um, one…human."

Lela saw their blank expressions and sighed. She didn't know the Welnish words.

"Ie wimg pmid gsa dif!" she exclaimed rapidly. "Ie'n ser alz."

"That makes more sense," Frelati said then thought about it. "Wait. Your elfin parent married a human?"

"Mama…elf," Lela said. "Gave her…life…gave her life…for Papa."

Frelati realized what had happened. Although it was uncommon for an elf to give up their life span so they wouldn't outlive their spouse, it did happen on occasion. It was a dangerous procedure, but it could be done with the help of a rare plant, and the child would still be able to have a normal elfin life span. The child was fascinating, but as Frelati spoke with her, he realized the danger he was putting them in. She might inadvertently tell a soldier about them. It was time they left.

"Genevia, we don't need to stay in this town much longer, and Traynord has been waiting a while. We need to head back," Frelati said. Then he squatted down to look at Lela. "Hgeb hera. Yba."

Genevia looked at him for translation. "Stay safe. Bye."

"Can't we take her with us? She has no one. I'll take care of her," Genevia begged suddenly.

Frelati gave her a stern look. "You do remember what we're doing, right? We can't take a child with us. I already have to look after you, and that's not easy with you always asking for trouble. I can't watch a little kid too. We can't take her."

"Frelati, use your heart at least once, will you? We can't leave her here by herself," Genevia said, keeping her voice down and reaching out to touch his forearm.

"She seems to be doing fine now, and she has been for a while. We can't take on this responsibility or put her in the middle of our fight."

Genevia squared her jaw. "I'll take care of her then! You don't have to do a thing!"

"We aren't taking her!" Frelati said firmly, his voice loud.

Genevia took a step closer, determined and angry, pointing a finger at Lela as she argued with him in a slightly higher volume. "I won't leave without her!"

Frelati was about to shout back when he felt a small tug on his pants leg. Lela knew the yelling was about her and wanted it to stop.

He looked down into her childish, crystal blue eyes. He saw sorrow, pain, the need for comfort and love, but he saw courage too. He understood her.

"Please," Lela said in a small, soft voice. "It is...scary."

Genevia knelt to embrace her, and Lela clung to the mother-like love and protection. She wished to never have to let go, just to sink into the comfort of Genevia's arms and stay there, safe and happy. It had been so long since she'd felt this security. Lela knew Genevia was only a stranger, but she felt like she knew her, and she didn't want to lose her.

Though she tried to be strong, Lela felt a tear trickle slowly down her dirty, little cheek to be soaked up in the warm cloth of her comforter's dress. She snuggled closer and silently wept, Genevia holding her tightly and caressing her hair.

Genevia knew what it was like growing up without a mother, and although Drisgal was the best father she could ask for, he couldn't give her the motherly love she needed. Compassion welled up within her heart, and she knew she had to be strong for Lela. She looked up into Frelati's face, startled to find a slight softening of his features as he looked down on them. A faint smile could be seen at the corner of his lips, though he tried to hide it. Frelati straightened his features, once again becoming the emotionless elf she knew, and gave her a short nod. Her face lit up as a slight smile broke the gloom. Lela was small and light, so Genevia scooped her up as she followed Frelati out of the alleyway.

"Do you want to come with us?" she whispered slowly in Lela's ear.

A tearstained face peeked out from the folds of her dress. The awed look in her eyes gave Genevia the answer before a smile spread across Lela's face. She threw her arms around Genevia and nodded enthusiastically. As they caught up to Frelati, Lela looked at him with a smile then leaned over far enough to be caught in his arms. A startled but pleased expression spread across his face before he hid it with a blank look.

"Gsemp biu," Lela said, giving him a big hug before reaching back over to be claimed by Genevia once again.

Frelati gave her a look full of warning about what was to come, but Genevia just smiled. Lela rested her head on Genevia's shoulder.

"I…have…mama, and…I have…papa." She yawned and closed her eyes. It had been awhile since she had slept in peace, and she was happy to at last be able to rest, happy and loved, in Genevia's arms.

Chapter Nine

"Wha' took ya so long?" Traynord grumbled, picking himself up off his stone seat and dusting off before finally making eye contact with Frelati and Genevia in turn.

Genevia smiled sweetly at the sleeping child in her arms. "We picked up a companion."

A startled expression swept across Traynord's face before he chuckled. "Now, I know ye was gone a long time, bu' I din' expec' ta see a chil' from ya."

Genevia smiled and rolled her eyes. Frelati looked at the ground with a scowl.

"Her name's Lela. She's six. We followed her to a back alley—she was the one who took the bread. Her parents died three years ago. We couldn't leave her," Genevia explained.

Frelati looked at the child with a hint of tenderness in his eyes, but he tried to sound frustrated. "Genevia made us bring her. She'll have to travel with us."

"Wha' a tragedy an' burden," Traynord said in mock sincerity with a twinkle in his eye.

"She'll be no trouble at all," Genevia argued, stroking Lela's hair.

"Well, come on," Frelati said. "We still have some supplies to get."

They walked off quickly to get the last of the things they needed. As they turned and left the tree Traynord had been sitting under, a face with an evil sneer could be seen looking from behind it. After checking his surroundings, the soldier stepped from the shadows, snickering cruelly.

"That promotion is mine," he said as he rubbed his greedy hands together.

Then he slithered off in the opposite direction, after hours of careful surveillance, to tell General Slump of the town's two new travelers.

"Frelati, can you hold her?" Genevia asked. "I've been carrying her now for an hour and a half, and my arms need a break."

They had finished shopping an hour ago, entering the woods on the other side of town to set up camp. Frelati was convinced that if they bought a room from the local inn, they would all be turned in. So they had to rough it in the woods, which Genevia didn't mind too much, but she thought it would have been better if Lela could rest in a room. They had been wandering in seeming circles while Frelati tried to find the perfect place.

He stopped to look at Genevia. "I thought you were going to take care of her. I wouldn't have to do a thing."

"When I said that, I didn't know you would make us wander in the woods for an hour," Genevia explained. "Besides, you're her father figure now, so start acting like one and help me out. You know you want to carry her anyway, regardless of whether you'll admit it, because you like her."

Frelati walked over with a scowl, taking the small child in his arms. Lela stirred a bit before settling back into a deep slumber.

"Thank you, Frelati," Genevia said, surprising herself and him by kissing him on the cheek. "It's not that bad, is it? I think you'll make a great father figure."

"Right," he said sarcastically, trying to sound normal despite the increase in his heartbeat after the caress from Genevia. "Come on."

They walked along, twisting through trees, stepping through underbrush, until Frelati found a clearing that suited him. The grass underfoot sparkled as the sun's rays glanced off its back, and a slight rustle in the leaves overhead gave evidence of a breeze as it swept against the canopy of green above them. The chirping of birds welcomed them, and the chittering of squirrels could be heard all through the clearing. It was peaceful, cool, and full of the sounds of nature.

"This should do," Frelati announced.

Traynord and Genevia were pleased with the choice as well.

"Make a pallet, will you? She'll be more comfortable," Frelati said to Genevia.

She put her hands on her hips and smirked. "Getting tired, are you? Is twenty minutes too long for you to carry a light, little girl?"

"She'll be more comfortable on a soft pallet."

Genevia smiled. "Fine. It's time for her to wake up, though, if she's going to sleep tonight. I hear a stream down that way. We'll go there while you two set up camp. You are not to go to the stream, okay? I need to freshen her up and myself as well."

She pushed Lela's hair back and whispered to her gently. "Lela, Lela, honey, wake up now. It's time to wake up."

Lela scrunched her face before opening her eyes and blinking several times. Her tiny arms unwrapped from around Frelati's neck to rub her eyes and reach out to Genevia.

"Did you have a good nap?" Genevia asked.

Lela nodded slowly, the aura of sleep still fogging her brain. She turned and smiled sweetly at Frelati before turning her gaze back to Genevia.

"We're going to go to a stream and clean you up. I got you a pretty dress to wear, but you have to be clean before I let you put it on." Genevia touched the tip of Lela's nose, smiling. The girl scrunched it, a happy smile on her face now. Genevia turned to Frelati. "Will you get the clothes for me, please?"

Frelati retrieved them, and she walked off into the woods, talking with Lela all the way. Frelati's eyes followed her, and though his expression gave nothing away, it was clear he was worried about her walking off alone. Traynord smiled.

"They're fine, la'. Don' worry," he said.

"Huh? Oh." Frelati startled out of deep thought. "I know they're fine."

The words were untrue, and he still stood looking at the place he last saw them.

"Ya migh' wan' ta tell 'er how ya feel. Lassie's like 'earin' i'," Traynord said as he started pitching a tent for the girls.

"What are you talking about?" Frelati whirled to face Traynord. "I have nothing to tell."

Traynord lifted an eyebrow. "Don' go lyin' ta me, la'. I seen i', clear as day, an' I'm sayin' tell 'er or ye'll lose 'er."

Frelati scowled and ran a large, calloused hand through his wavy, brown hair. "You're wrong, but even if you weren't, there are several good reasons why I couldn't do that, the main reason being she's royalty, better than me. I'm just the messed-up guy sent to protect her. So you can knock that thought right out of your head."

Traynord looked at the young man standing in front of him with a wise, old sailor's eye.

"Ye shoul'n think tha', la'. Everbody 'as problems; ye're no' special there." Traynord paused to study Frelati's intense expression. "Don' give up, la'. She coul' do a lo' worse than you. When ye're ready, give i' a sho', I'm sure she feels the same way."

With that he went back to the tent, and Frelati turned away to ponder his words. He walked off into the woods to gather firewood with a slightly lighter step. Traynord chuckled to himself, thinking what his late wife would have said.

"Med'lin' ol' fool," he mimicked as he tied the last knot on the tent and sat on a log to rest.

Laughter sped through the air, skiing on the water's surface and bouncing between trees to rebound back to the ears of the two making the joyous noise. A waterfall sprinkled over the rocks, making a light, roaring melody nearby. Fish swam in the shallow pool and darted every which way to avoid a little girl as she splashed into the water above them, her shrieks of gladness still clinging to the air even as she slipped beneath the cool surface.

Up she popped, spraying water and laughter all around once again. Her toes barely reached the bottom as she stepped up the water's edges to reach Genevia.

"Again!" Lela shouted, jumping into her arms. "Again, again!"

Genevia chuckled, grinning widely. Lela had learned the word quickly. This was her third language. She had grown up with Elven and Sutan—the rural dialect picked up centuries before by nearby villages from wandering nomads leaving Suta. After the deaths of her parents and the elderly couple that had cared for her, she had begun to learn Welnish, which was the primary language in Tiweln. With time, she would be able to master the language. Genevia marveled at the intelligence of the child.

The two were isolated behind bushes in a small inlet and had stripped to their undergarments for a much-needed bath. Genevia had decided to make the time fun for Lela, so she'd thrown her into the deeper water. She hadn't realized she would enjoy the play just as much as Lela. She stood knee deep in the water, listening to Lela's laughter and joining in with her, identical smiles stretched across their faces as Lela waited for another toss.

"Okay." Genevia laughed. "One more time, then we have to clean you up."

Lela nodded, and Genevia squeezed her into a tight hug.

"Ready?" Genevia asked mischievously.

Lela nodded enthusiastically.

"Are you sure?" Genevia said to more nods. "I don't know, maybe I shouldn't. We have been playing too long."

She slowly started inching Lela back into the water.

"No, again!" Lela said, giggling.

Genevia continued, "I don't think I should. You just can't handle any more fun today."

A look of dismay crossed Lela's face. Genevia suddenly smiled, throwing her a few feet forward through the air and into the water. A delighted squeal bounded in the air, ricocheting off every surface. Genevia was showered with droplets as Lela landed in the water. Her head broke the surface, a laugh escaping her.

"Come on, now," Genevia said. "Time to get squeaky clean."

Lela obliged, half-swimming, half-crawling in the water to reach Genevia. She pushed off the soft, squishy sand at the bottom and jumped into Genevia's arms, which embraced her tightly as Genevia smiled before setting her in the water again.

"We don't have soap, but if we scoop up the sand from the bottom and rub it on our skin, it will work just as well," Genevia said, reaching down and grabbing a handful.

She began rubbing it on Lela's arms to get rid of the dirt she had lived in for so long. It took a little while, but eventually Genevia was satisfied.

"There," she said. "You look beautiful. Do you want to put on your new dress now?"

Lela nodded, eyes wide with excitement. They walked up the bank to stand on the thick grass amidst wildflowers. Genevia grabbed the light pink dress. Pink was a rare color for commoners so it had taken a lot of her little amount of money, but she didn't mind spending it on Lela. Lela deserved it, and she looked adorable.

The little girl twirled and smiled up at Genevia. Then she stopped, standing perfectly still.

"What is it?" Genevia asked, suddenly worried. "What's wrong?"

Lela looked up with tears in her eyes. She ran up to Genevia, wrapping her arms around her waist in a hug, her little face hiding in Genevia's skirt. Squatting down, Genevia took Lela's head in her hands.

"What is it, sweetheart?" she asked softly.

Lela looked her in the eyes. "I…no have…any…pretty. Gsemp biu…um, thank you…Mama."

She hugged her again, her head resting on Genevia's shoulder. Genevia was pleased and a bit startled at hearing herself called Mama. It brought a whole new realization. She was actually going to be a mother to this child, and she found herself thrilled with the prospect. Before, when Drisgal had talked about her being ready to marry and have kids, she had shied away from the topic, though she knew he was right. Sixteen was the usual age to get married. She hadn't felt ready then; she wasn't sure why she felt so now.

"Ie liza biu. I…love you," Lela whispered.

"I love you, too," Genevia whispered back, hugging her tighter. "I love you too."

Snap! After the twig broke in half under his weight, the soldier held his breath, frozen to the core like a statue. He knew the general behind him was fuming with rage, for even a small sound could give away their position. A full minute passed before the soldier continued, scouting ahead for the small group following him.

It was his first year as a soldier, and this was his first chance to scout, not that he had ever wanted anything to do with the army. His father had other ideas on the matter, and if not for his sister…but his father wouldn't hurt her now that he had gotten his way. Besides, the army wasn't all bad. Right now his group was looking for two criminal runaways; he wasn't sure what they'd done, but locking very dangerous people away from good townsfolk was enough reward for him. It was a bit unusual though. The local authority was typically in charge of catching runaways, but his group had been shipped over from Wefleca a few weeks ago. That had to mean these fugitives were highly dangerous, which didn't sit too well with him as he was scouting alone.

The general had immediately picked him as scout. He hadn't remembered his name, but his crooked, evil-looking finger had pointed straight at him, so he knew. They had left their quarters so fast, many of the men were still getting ready, so the general ordered him to come back after scouting for ten minutes and show them the way to go.

After two minutes of walking, the soldier, Jackson, had heard wild laughter. It drew him to a waterfall. A young woman was standing knee deep in the water inside an inlet, throwing a small child into the deeper water. It was a touching scene, but Jackson turned away quickly upon realizing he was peeping at a woman in only her undergarments. Embarrassed, Jackson turned and ran in the other direction, careful not to make too much noise.

That was when he stumbled across a camp. An old man was sitting on a log watching a younger man build a fire.

These must be the criminals, he thought to himself before turning and stealthily sneaking back to his group. The general had looked at him expectantly.

"Well?" he commanded in a loud bark.

Jackson was greatly intimidated by this huge man. He swallowed and forced himself to speak. "There…there's a camp."

The general stood looking at him a minute before his fury rose, and he yelled again. "Where, you idiot?"

"Th-that way," Jackson pointed, shaking.

He heard snickers among the group, making his face go red. Then the general turned, glared at them, and turned back to Jackson with silence behind him.

"Lead the way," he ordered with a touch less harshness in his voice, which surprised Jackson.

Now they followed him as he led the way to the camp. They were almost there, so he slowed a bit, watching where his next step would land. When he stopped, the general came up beside him, motioning for the troops to stay back. Both he and Jackson rose up just enough to see over the bush before them to examine the camp. There were the two men with only a fire and a tent for their camp. It would be easy to take.

The general crawled back to give instructions before joining him again and relaying the same message. He gave the signal, and all the men rushed into the clearing.

"How long can a bath take?" Frelati grumbled. "They're not an army, just two people."

Traynord chuckled. "Aye, bu' they're two lassies. Lassies take twice as long."

Frelati mumbled something inaudible, leaning down to poke the fire with a long stick. When he sat up again, he heard the snap of a twig and was immediately on his guard.

"Wha'? Wha' is i', la'?" Traynord asked, sitting up straight.

"I heard a twig snap," Frelati said softly, staring fixedly at the bush in front of where he had heard the sound.

Traynord relaxed again. "I's jus' a bir' or squirrel."

Frelati stayed alert, watching in all directions, but leaned back down to tend the fire. The next moment, a loud shout came from Frelati's left, and men charged into the camp, forming a menacing circle around the pair. Frelati jumped to his feet, grabbing for the lamentably small knife kept in the scabbard at his waist. He felt the futility of fighting off the dozen or so cruel looking men, all armed with polished, sharp swords that would easily skewer him before he got close enough to give them even a nick with his blade. However, he had no inclination of being taken back to prison.

Weighing his chances against the three men closest to him, all of whom were fortunately smaller than the others, which meant they were relatively the same size as Frelati, he lunged toward them, barely missing two swords but dealing a deep gash into the forearm of one of the men. Unfortunately, that was as far as he was going to get with his attack. Two other, huge men joined in the fracas and held a struggling Frelati between them. Traynord, who had scrutinized the group for some weakness while sitting by the fire, stood slowly, weaponless but not outwardly worried. The first unfortunate man to approach him was startled by the sturdy, quick movements of the old man. He went down easily, which brought a scoffing snort from one of Frelati's captors.

Traynord raised a brow, which another man took as a challenge. Up he went, taking big strides. This was a mistake. Midstride, he was twisted, tripped, and laid out on the ground moaning. A quick smile crossed Traynord's face. Three more men tried, with no success, before the general ordered the rest of the group to storm him. Realizing his defeat, Traynord put his hands behind him quietly, allowing the men to take him quickly and without bruises, which were very hard on an old man.

With the two taken, General Slump ordered two men to check the tent. Nothing. The general then ordered two men to check the surrounding woods and send back if they saw anything. He walked up to Frelati, shoving his face right up into the prisoner's so that they were locked eye to eye. Instead of fear, though, General Slump saw anger and a deep coldness toward life; both, at the moment, directed toward him as well. It didn't slow him down any.

"Where is she?" he yelled.

Frelati held his gaze defiantly, giving nothing away. His lips drew tight together, the edges twisting up slightly in a humorless smile. General Slump moved to Traynord. Upon looking in his eyes,

General Slump found humor, a love of life, and wisdom, but, once again, no fear.

"Where is she?" he demanded again.

Traynord chuckled. "Ye'll ge' nothin' from me, Gen'ral."

General Slump turned away sharply in agitation. He walked around the camp in a huff, thinking. He stopped after seeing Jackson walk up slowly, hesitantly.

He stared at him, waiting.

"Excuse me, sir, but aren't these the two runaways?" Jackson asked timidly.

"No, we only have one," he pointed to Frelati. "We are looking for a young woman, an elf like that one. She is the other fugitive. Our spies tell us a child is with her as well."

A shocked expression crossed Jackson's face. Those two couldn't be fugitives. The young girl was no older than his little sister, and surely that tiny child hadn't done anything wrong. He looked away quickly as his lips tightened. Although he knew he shouldn't, he kept the information on their location to himself; somehow, he didn't believe they deserved to be caught. Fortunately, General Slump had taken his surprise as being related to hearing that the fugitives had a child with them, which was, indeed, unusual.

The scouts came back out of breath but excited, bringing news that Jackson knew he wouldn't like. Even if he protected them, the scouts would divulge the whereabouts of the females. He held his breath, hoping, wishing, but his worst fear had come about.

"We found the other fugitive and the child," the first scout reported.

"They're by a waterfall, in an inlet to the east. We can surround them," the other scout explained.

The general smiled. "Take me to them."

Chapter Ten

Genevia had sensed someone's presence immediately after she and Lela had broken from their embrace. She pretended that nothing was wrong, but she knew someone was out there. Her fears were solidified soon after when she heard footsteps running away—two sets. Traynord wouldn't have run that fast.

She looked all around her and found reeds growing around the edges of the water. More were near the waterfall. She searched and quickly found two reeds that were hollow, breaking them off long.

"Lela, honey, don't be scared, but we need to get in the water near those reeds," Genevia explained hurriedly, yet calmly. "We have to be completely underwater, okay? Breathe through your reed. The bubbles and spray of the waterfall will cover us."

Lela was used to hiding, so she obeyed without question, excluding one. "My...dress?"

Genevia saw the pain in the little girl's eyes. "It will be all right. It'll dry after a while. Right now, I just want us to be safe."

Lela nodded, and they sank underwater and out of sight.

After the general shouted orders to five soldiers to take Traynord and Frelati to headquarters and lock them up, he sent two soldiers to give word to Fezam of the captured runaways; he was confident in the capture of one girl and her child. He then directed the remaining men to help him retrieve the last fugitive.

They rushed to the waterfall as quickly as possible. Jackson was among them, close to the front. As the roar of the waterfall grew louder, General Slump's heart soared, while Jackson's heart began to skip beats. The men burst through the bushes, skirting the edge of the inlet. The sunlight dancing off the waterfall's surface showed every eye the emptiness of the place.

"Where are they?" the general shouted at the two scouts who had led the way.

"Sh-she was here. I swear, sir," one scout stammered.

While the general shouted orders, Jackson walked closer to the waterfall. As he looked into the water, he saw beneath the foam and spray a bit of pink. It swayed in and out of his line of sight, but it was no fish. He smiled at the cleverness of the young woman when he saw two reeds bobbing in the water above.

"Jackson!" the general yelled.

He ran over, saluting. "Yes, sir."

"Were you too busy daydreaming to hear my orders?" the general shouted, not expecting an answer. "You are in the third search party with me, heading east."

"Sir," Jackson said slowly, gaining more confidence with each word. "Wouldn't it be good if someone stayed here, just in case they come back through to get to the camp?"

In his anger, the general didn't fully listen to Jackson, instead giving an affirmative to hurry the process along. "Fine; move out."

All the parties obeyed, breaking off in different directions. When they had all disappeared and the clearing once again grew silent, Jackson sat under a tree to wait.

It had been a while since she had heard any noise. All at once people were shouting orders, which sounded garbled under the water and the roar of the waterfall. After several minutes, though, it had quieted down, so Genevia peeped out of the water. Lela came up after her, upset that her new pink dress was soaked.

Genevia leaned down to hug her. "Oh, you did great, wonderfully! I couldn't be prouder."

Just then, as she looked up, she saw a figure sitting under a tree a few feet away. The shadows covered his face, but his uniform told Genevia she was in trouble. The man stood slowly and began walking forward. Genevia grabbed Lela's hand, practically dragging her out of the water on the other side.

"Don't...don't go that way," Jackson said quickly. "I just want to...to talk to you."

Genevia turned around, a suspicious look on her face. She picked up Lela in case she had to run suddenly, her eyes never leaving the soldier's face.

Jackson started slowly, trying to inflict some confidence into his voice. "I'm Jackson. I don't want to hurt you or turn you in, but if you run off, you'll meet a search party. They will capture you."

Genevia's eyes flashed. She still didn't trust the soldier.

"Where's Frelati?" she asked firmly.

"The young one?" She nodded. "Captured. So was the older man."

Genevia let her gaze drop to the ground. She watched as tiny ants crawled among the grasses. She felt the breeze blow her hair; the coolness of the water as it sprayed her face. She was aware of it all. She felt the gaze of the soldier, the dampness of the shade, but she wasn't really there. Captured...they were captured.

"So you were with them?" Jackson asked, breaking into her thoughts.

She looked up, worry replacing the suspicion on her face. "Yes, where are they?"

"They're being taken to headquarters," Jackson paused. "Why are they after you?"

Genevia laughed, but it held no joy. The hollow sound rang around the opening, taunting her.

"I'm a fugitive because I was born. I'm Alernoa, Princess of the Elves, but you can call me Genevia."

Jackson was shocked. He had never even seen an elf before today, and now he was meeting the princess of them.

"Prin...cess?" Lela questioned.

"Do you remember any bedtime stories about a pretty girl being saved?" Genevia asked.

Lela thought a moment and nodded.

"Fagb fomcah…pretty…princess." She paused. "I am…princess…Mama?"

Genevia smiled at the little girl. "You are to me, and a wonderful princess, too."

That pleased Lela greatly.

Upon hearing the child speak, Jackson came back into the conversation. The girl seemed to calm Alernoa, and that's just what he needed. "What's her name?"

"Lela," Genevia said, returning her gaze to meet his. It was still distrustful.

"How old is she?"

"Six."

"You look pretty young to be the mother of a six-year-old."

"I'm not her birth mother. I'm only sixteen."

"So is your husband only a fugitive because you are?" Jackson asked.

Genevia shot him a puzzled look. "I'm not married."

"Oh, I just assumed that…with Frelati…I mean, you're old enough…" Jackson broke off.

"Don't worry, you're not the only one," Genevia muttered.

Suddenly, she remembered where she was and looked around. "I should be going. The other soldiers could come through here any minute."

Jackson snapped back to reality. "Right. Come on, I can hide you. This way."

He waited as Genevia crossed the inlet before going off into the woods to find a place to hide them. Genevia was still unsure of Jackson, but she had no one else to turn to. Besides, what could it hurt? Even if he led her to the soldiers, they would have found her eventually anyway.

After a while, Jackson found a hollow tree large enough to house them. "You can hide up there."

He helped Genevia and Lela up. "Listen. I'll help you get your friends back, but you have to let me travel with you. I'll be killed for insubordination if you don't."

"Why are you helping us?" Genevia asked.

Jackson looked away, his jaw firming in resolution, before answering. "You remind me of my sister. I may not know exactly why they want to capture you, but I do know that I don't want to be part of it. It seems to me that you were just unlucky enough to fall into this; I know a lot about that...my sister knows a lot about that. Besides, I never wanted to be a soldier anyway."

Genevia thought about his proposal before nodding. "Fine, but if we even think you're betraying us, we'll leave you."

"Agreed," Jackson said quickly. "General Slump will probably leave some men to patrol the area. I'll try to be one of them. At dusk, I'll come get you, and we'll walk to headquarters. Once I'm inside, I'll go to the back door and let you in. You go down to the basement, where they hold prisoners, and do your elf thing to let them out."

Genevia pursed her lips. "Two problems: one—how do Traynord, Frelati, Lela, me, and you all get out without anyone noticing? Second—I can't do some 'elf thing.' Each elf has a different gift, and while I'm not completely sure about elf ways yet, I'm pretty sure I can't change my gift so that I can break bars."

Jackson was a bit confused, but now wasn't the time for unnecessary questions. "What is your gift?"

"Well, it has to do with nature. I'm not completely sure what I can do. I mean, I only found out I was an elf a few weeks ago," Genevia said, feeling rather stupid as she said it. "Frelati says I'm powerful, though."

Jackson stared at her moment before moving on.

"What can she do?" Jackson asked, pointing to Lela and ignoring his growing questions.

"I don't know," Genevia said, realizing for the first time that Lela would indeed have a gift. "Do you know what you can do?"

Lela nodded, motioning to be put down. Genevia passed her to Jackson. Once on the ground, Lela stood facing him in deep concentration. After a while, she began to change. Genevia and Jackson watched, astonished. Lela had turned into a mirror image of Jackson.

"Mother...gift...too," she said in Jackson's voice. "I...talk... look...like."

Then Lela turned back into herself, weary from the change. She reached up to Genevia, and Jackson helped her back up.

"We can use that," he said. "Only for a little while, but that'll be enough."

Lela smiled. "I...help Papa."

Then Jackson began planning. Soon they had everything figured out, and Jackson walked back to the inlet to put the first act into play.

The guards had pushed Frelati and Traynord around cruelly for an hour, and they still hadn't reached headquarters. Five guards escorted them around the town and down a dirty lane. They were all huge, probably in their late thirties or early forties, and they were all heartless. All their attention was focused on Frelati. Traynord was apparently too old to be pushed around after the first thirty minutes.

One shoved Frelati to the ground, and Frelati had to grit his teeth to keep from turning around and punching the guy. He knew he was strong enough to take each soldier separately, maybe even up to three, but together...he wouldn't have a chance. He just hoped Genevia and Lela were safe.

The sun was beginning to set in the distance. A beautiful splash of color adorned the sky. Frelati wondered if he would ever be able to see such a beautiful sight again. He figured he would die. Maybe not now or tomorrow, but pretty soon. Soldiers didn't like runaways and hated to keep them alive.

The thought of his death hadn't bothered him when he was in jail in Azol. People were taken randomly out of their cells and weren't ever seen again. So while there, Frelati guessed he would eventually be chosen. It hadn't happened, though. Back then, he sometimes wished they would kill him, take him from his misery and despair, but now he wanted to live.

In the old cell, he had no reason to avoid death, no family, friends...anything. Now, in the new imprisonment he was facing, he had a strong desire to live. He wanted to tell Genevia how he felt, though he still wasn't completely sure what exactly that was. He wanted to see Lela again. They were the family he'd never had, and it took a time like this for him to realize it. He remembered how holding Lela had made him feel, and he wanted that again. He had felt wanted and loved in a way only a child could manage. Most of all, he wanted to just see Genevia one more time, but it was too late. He'd lost his chance, and he felt like a fool for pushing them away with gruff words.

He took one last glance at the sunset before he was shoved inside a dark building. The soldiers walked him along a hall, down some steps, and then threw him in a cell. He heard the door slam and a short click as he was locked in. It was all familiar—the cold, the dark, the hard walls and floor, the dampness—but something was new. This time he was utterly alone. Traynord was in another cell.

That was when despair set in; that was familiar too. All gloomy thoughts that can be hidden and tossed away while the light still shines can attack suddenly and brutally when the darkness comes, and Frelati was swallowed by darkness. He realized that he had no chance with Genevia, regardless of what Traynord said, because she was Alernoa, a princess. He realized Lela didn't love him; it was all an act so he would give his consent for her to stay with Genevia. She would be fine without him. He was truly alone.

"I spy…some…something…um…r-red."

"Hum. Is it that leaf?" Genevia guessed.

Lela laughed softly. "That is…br-brown."

Genevia smiled. "What about…that bush?"

"No, that is…green." Lela giggled.

"How about, hum, that flower?"

"Yes!" Lela said excitedly, hugging her.

Genevia had taught her the game after a slow, boring hour of hiding. It was a good way to teach Lela her colors in Welnish, too, and she was learning quickly. Luckily for them, there were two holes that allowed them to look out together. They had watched as the sun's pattern slowly changed over time. It was getting darker now, and it was harder to play.

"Your…um…your." Lela looked at Genevia, unsure of the word she was looking for.

"Turn?" Genevia offered.

Lela thought, then nodded. "Yes. Your…turn."

"This is the last time. It's getting dark and hard to see. Besides, Jackson will be coming to get us soon."

"I want…Papa," Lela said, crossing her arms.

"Yes, Jackson's helping us to get…um, well, to get your father, so we have to be nice to him."

"He…no…good…like Papa," Lela said matter-of-factly. "You… with Papa."

Lela nodded for emphasis.

Genevia, uncomfortable with the conversation, changed it quickly. "Maybe so. I spy something…Jackson!"

"Mama…no spy…c-color," Lela grumbled.

She was getting tired and a bit irritable.

"Maybe later, honey," Genevia said, handing her down to Jackson.

He set her on the ground and reached up to help Genevia before realizing she was already down.

"I grabbed this from your camp," he said, lifting Genevia's bag.

Genevia stared at it in astonishment. How did it always manage to stay with her?

"Thanks, Jackson," she said. "That was really sweet."

"No problem." Jackson shrugged. "Let's go."

Lela reached up to Genevia, who lifted her into her arms, and they began walking. After five minutes, Lela was asleep. Jackson looked back at them.

"You need a carrier," he said.

Genevia smiled. "It would help."

Jackson stopped. He had a pack with him, which he slung off and emptied. It contained some water, flint rocks, a lantern, some knives, and a map. He transferred everything but the lantern and one of the knives into Genevia's pack.

"What are you doing?" Genevia asked in astonishment as he grabbed the knife and started cutting two semicircles in the bottom of his bag.

"You have a ways to walk, and we need to get there quickly. If you have her in a carrier on your back it'll be easier."

He finished. "There. Now it has two purposes: a carrying case and a travel bag."

Jackson opened the top, put the bag on Genevia's back, and took Lela from her arms.

"Will it hold her?" Genevia asked worriedly.

"This is a soldier's bag," Jackson explained. "It took three months and twenty yards of the sturdiest fabric you can find to make it. It can hold one hundred fifty pounds, and she barely reaches forty."

He gently placed her in the pack so that her head rested against Genevia's back. Grabbing her bag, he began to walk again.

"Let's move."

Chapter Eleven

The darkness seemed to swallow them, invade upon them so much that they would cease to exist and instead become part of it. There was no light, no way to see, and she had to feel her way forward. Genevia would have questioned her existence if not for the steady breathing of Lela on her back. She held Jackson's shoulder as they moved along. Somehow, he knew just where to go.

Night had settled quickly on the land. The darkness had gotten a good grasp before the travelers had even left the woods. The chill it brought with it made Genevia shudder, but she forced herself to stay calm. It seemed as if the light had fled for good, never to return, and all the inhabitants on Tiweln would live forever in darkness.

"Can we light your lamp?" Genevia asked quietly.

Jackson slowed his pace. "We had better not until we get closer to headquarters. We don't want someone to stop us or see you two. When I turn on the lamp, both of you have to be out of sight."

They walked on in silence, their pace quickening. After a while, Genevia could see two pinpricks of light shining through the darkness. Jackson headed toward them. When they were close enough to see the building that the lights illuminated but still far enough not to be heard, Jackson stopped and squatted down. Genevia followed his example.

"Wake her up," Jackson said. "I'm going to sneak inside to get what you need."

With that, he stood and walked off, but he didn't go toward the lights. Instead, he angled off, and Genevia saw a door at the side of the building that was in complete shadow. Jackson went through that door. Genevia took off her pack and gently woke Lela. The little girl opened her eyes and stayed silent.

After a while she leaned forward, cupping her tiny hands at Genevia's ear and whispered, "Where…Jackson?"

Genevia did the same to Lela. "Inside."

Lela nodded. Soon after, Jackson's head popped out of the door; he looked both ways before he exited the building completely. Then he crept toward Genevia and Lela.

"Here. This was the best I could do. You'll have to make it work."

He had an old mop head, a cloak, and a cane.

Genevia looked it over. "Can you cut the mop strands smaller?"

Jackson nodded and began.

"Lela, you have to stay on my back, stay quiet, and stay still. Can you do that?" Genevia asked softly.

Lela's head bobbed up and down.

She climbed up, and Genevia threw the cloak over both of them. It was big and dragged the ground. Then, Genevia grabbed the cane, hunching over.

"Finished," Jackson said, and he placed the mop on her head to cover her hair.

Lastly, Genevia grabbed some clay and rubbed it on her hands, face, and neck to give herself a different complexion.

"Your basket is right inside the side door I used. You need to find the soldier with the keys and somehow get them from him. Then go down to the cells," Jackson explained. "You know what to do from there."

Genevia nodded and whispered to Lela. "You okay?"

She felt Lela nod her head. Then she began to limp to the door without another word. Genevia reached out to open it. It weighed a ton. She threw all her weight against the wood, opening it barely enough to squeeze through.

She looked down and found the basket, just as Jackson had said. Once she had it in her grasp, she looked around. The dimly lit, small room held more shadows than light, and coats were hanging all around the room. It was warm inside, but the lifeless enclosure made Genevia's blood run cold.

As quickly as she could with an elderly lady's limp, she exited the closet, but instead of leaving that ominous feeling behind, she added to it dread and fear. She had entered a slender hallway that was completely dark. At each end she saw one lonely lamp hanging from the ceiling. Shivers ran up and down her spine as she thought of the risk she was taking. But what else could she do?

Before moving, she closed her eyes and took a deep breath. When she opened them again, she was no longer a timid, young girl but a courageous, old woman. She turned to the right and limped down the corridor. It seemed endless, but she made it to the light.

The room at the end of the hall to her left was still a short way from the solitary light, so Genevia took a turn and continued. As she got closer, the hallway grew lighter until she emerged into a large, yet strangely empty, greeting place. A table in the center with a chair behind it was the only furniture.

Genevia stopped, helpless and out of ideas, in the center of the room. She waited but not for long. A tall soldier came walking toward her from a hall to the left. He eyed her suspiciously, taking in her basket and appearance quickly.

"Can I help you?" he asked with a frown.

Genevia cleared her throat and tried to make it sound cracked and weak. "Can I see the gen'ral?"

That got a startled look, followed by another suspicious one. "Why?"

"I need to speak with him, please," Genevia tried to give him an innocent smile.

The soldier looked her over one last time before turning and beginning to walk off. As an afterthought, he threw over his shoulder, "Follow me."

Genevia started limping after him but was quickly falling behind. She needed him to slow his pace.

"Could you slow up a bit, dear? My bad leg keeps me from moving like I used to," Genevia croaked.

The soldier turned and raised an eyebrow but did as she asked, keeping an eye out behind him so he wouldn't leave her behind. They took many twists and turns before stopping in front of a door. The soldier raised a fist to knock and paused.

"Are you sure you want to see him?" he asked.

Genevia nodded slowly. "It's important."

"Okay, but he's not happy right now," the soldier warned. "You don't want to aggravate him."

"Don't worry about me. I'll be all right." Genevia smiled again.

A loud, hollow knock rang throughout the corridor. Another followed shortly after. Genevia could hear the sounds of life slipping under the door from inside. She hoped everything would turn out all right and that she and Lela would remain free. Jackson had warned her that this would be the difficult part, but Lela had to see General Slump for this to work.

"What do you want?" a cross voice yelled from inside.

"Sir, there's someone here to see you," the soldier said.

Nothing was heard for a while before the general spoke again. "Well, send them in! What are you waiting for?"

The soldier quickly opened the door, and Genevia limped in. The door shut loudly behind her, leaving her in a very dark room with an angry stranger. One candle burned on the corner of a desk, throwing an eerie, red glow around the room.

"Who are you? State your business, quickly!" the general ordered.

Genevia swallowed as she remembered what they had practiced earlier as they walked around the town. "I'm Candy, sir. I came to see if I could give the prisoners and guards some food. I saw the hard work put into bringing those fugitives back to headquarters and thought they might be hungry."

Part of the plan was going nicely, but Lela still needed to see the general, not only hear his voice. Genevia thought, trying to come up with some way to get him into the light.

Her thoughts broke apart when he spoke. "You woke me from a pleasant and greatly needed rest because you wanted to feed worthless human scum that pass as soldiers?"

Although his voice was calm, it held much anger, and Genevia knew she had to think fast to get what she needed and get out. This was not a man to tamper with.

The general started rummaging around, and soon a lamp was lit, illuminating the room nicely. Genevia had to hide a smile. He had just given her the last thing she needed. Now, she just had to wait for Lela's signal and she could leave. It didn't come.

Genevia paused in confusion but still felt no tap. She took a breath and opened up part of her basket. There really was food inside, not much but enough.

"I'll give you some food as well," she offered in her cracked voice. "I have enough, and a fine, hard-working gen'ral, such as yourself, deserves good food."

The general had his chin resting on his fingertips. His intense gaze seemed to penetrate into Genevia's brain and read all her secrets. He sat watching her for a minute before answering.

"Flattery will not work on me." He smiled evilly, a cruel plan forming in his mind. "I think you are here for another reason, and I intend to find out what it is. Serve me food."

The general caught a glimpse of the surprised look that crossed Genevia's face, but, like his two prisoners, he saw no intimidation or fear, which confused him.

Genevia began to unpack the food and place it on the desk before him. She had to be careful not to move like herself but to move like Candy; it wasn't as easy as she had thought it would be. It seemed that with each morsel she took out in her slow, slumberous movements another bit of food would appear, but finally, it was all set before him.

"Here you go," she announced kindly.

General Slump sat motionless, scrutinizing her appearance and actions. Silence settled about the room heavily. Genevia was uncomfortable, but she held her ground, locking her deep, green eyes onto his cold, brown ones. Eventually, he dropped his gaze to examine the food in front of him.

He picked up a piece of ham, smelled it, looked it over, and tasted it. Then he looked at Genevia again.

"Is this contaminated?" he asked.

Genevia forced a broken laugh. "Of course not! Why would I try to poison you and your soldiers? You help protect me."

He looked at the meat again and extended his hand. "You eat first."

"You licked it!" Genevia blurted out childishly, but miraculously, her voice still held its fake quality.

General Slump eyed her, pushing the meat forward. "Eat the other end, then."

Genevia reached out a hand, making it shake a little in the process, and took it. Before her hand had moved away, though, General Slump grabbed her wrist.

"What are you doing?" Genevia asked, trying to keep her voice calm.

The general stood and walked around his desk. Now he stood towering above her, Genevia's wrist still in his grasp. Through her fear, Genevia felt Lela's signal but ignored it in the face of this danger.

"This is not the hand of an old lady. There are no wrinkles, no signs of age." He pinched her skin. "And the skin is taut. Who are you, and what do you want?"

Genevia spoke regularly as she answered. "I'm Candy, but I'm not this old. I'm middle aged. My friend's son is a soldier in the king's army, and she hasn't heard from him in two years. She saw one of her son's friends in your group and sent me to get news from him. I'm sorry."

"Why didn't she come?" the general asked.

"She's too sick. She's had to stay in bed for a month now." Genevia thought rapidly, terrified that she wouldn't be able to answer the next question he asked.

"Why did you come disguised?"

There wasn't a good answer for that. The general spotted her hesitation and smiled. He had her. He was about to speak when Genevia broke into the silence.

"I don't know why I chose to. I was frightened, and I feel more confident when I pretend to be someone else. Soldiers frighten me."

"Then why did you come so late? It's after midnight."

Genevia gave a disbelieving laugh. "The townspeople can't see me coming here. They barely tolerate my friend because she's the mother of a soldier. If they saw me, they'd think...not that we don't all respect what you do."

She gave a half-hearted smile, and the general sneered. "You fear us. No need to lie, but I'll help. Which soldier do you need to find?"

Genevia answered this readily, which solidified her story. "Jackson."

The timid boy who had scouted for him? He was getting popular.

"I'm sorry, miss, but he isn't here now. If you come in the morning, he should be back," General Slump said, pushing a gentleman's air into his voice.

"Well, I should go, but I did make this food. Would it be all right if I gave it to your men? It would be like I was doing it for my friend's son," Genevia said softly.

General Slump looked her over one last time. "That'll be fine, but you might want to keep your disguise. My men aren't the most noble of creatures, best not tempt them."

He turned to sit at his desk, and Genevia scooped up most of the food, setting it in her basket, and leaving his office. After limping a short way, she leaned against the wall and sighed. Her wrist was still throbbing from the death grip it had been given, and she rubbed it.

"What took so long, Lela?" she whispered kindly, hiding her aggravation.

"I had...see...legs. No...tall...with...no legs," she whispered back.

Genevia nodded. General Slump had to stand.

"Are you still okay?" Genevia asked.

Lela nodded.

"Onto the second part of the plan."

She started down the hall at her slow pace. Hunched over and walking with a limp, she made quite a picture. After many twists and turns, she began to see light. It stretched out to meet her and caused a long shadow in the hallway.

When she entered the room, a different guard was sitting at the table. He stood up quickly at the sight of her. The light from the lamp in the room glittered off some metal hanging at the soldier's waist—the keys.

"Sonny, could you help me?" Genevia asked in a weak voice. "I've been walking a while and need to rest."

A concerned expression crossed the soldier's face, and he hurried toward her just as she pretended to lose her grip on her cane and sent it falling to the ground.

"Oh!" Genevia fell against the surprised soldier.

He tried to reach the cane, and Genevia started to fall the other way, making the soldier straighten again to help her gain her balance.

"I need my cane, sonny!" she yelled while reaching for his keys.

The soldier tried again, but the cane was out of reach and Genevia started falling again. During all her terrified yelling, Genevia grabbed the keys, put them in a pocket in her cloak, got the extra set Jackson had filched from a coat pocket, and placed them on the soldier's belt. Then she quieted and allowed the soldier to grab her cane. He handed it to her and led her to his chair, which she gratefully sank into. The soldier didn't say anything, just watched her with concern.

Finally, after a few minutes, Genevia spoke. "Can you tell me where the cells are, son? I have food to give the guards there."

She motioned to her basket, and the soldier nodded, gesturing as he gave directions.

"Walk down the hall to my left. It leads to stairs. Go down those and turn to the right. The cells are at the end of that hall," he explained.

"Thank you, son." Genevia got up slowly. "I think I'm okay now. Thank you for your help."

She walked slowly until she was out of sight and then quickened her pace. She descended the stairs, feeling her way down because, once again, there was no light. The stairs seemed to continue forever, but she finally got to the bottom. She followed the hallway, veering to her right for a short distance before it began curving left.

Light began to spread out, though it was dim, and Genevia saw a room with row after row of jail cells. Huge stone doors with padlocks on the outside lined the sides of the room. Genevia backed up into the darkness again, and Lela slipped off her back.

Genevia gave her a smile and nod, and Lela started to change. Soon, General Slump was standing right in front of her. The only difference was the facial expression—it was worried. Lela was scared.

"Harden your face and you'll look just like him," Genevia whispered. "You'll do fine. Do you remember what to say?"

Lela nodded. They had practiced the words over and over again while waiting for Jackson.

"Okay, go ahead and relax." Genevia tried to reassure her, but it didn't work. Lela was still too scared. "Do it for your papa and me, okay? Pretend you're a big cat, and those men are little mice. I'll be right here, so if you get worried, just come back."

Lela's face hardened in determination. "Yes."

She walked off, and Genevia had to shake off the weird feeling she got when she had heard Lela speak like General Slump. It was up to her now. Genevia had done the hardest part, but there was nothing she could do now. She retraced her steps until she came to the stairs and hid in the shadows of a walkway straight in front of them.

If Lela could make this work, everything would be okay. If not, Genevia needed to start getting used to this gloomy darkness, because she would be surrounded by it while locked in a jail cell.

Chapter Twelve

Frelati was lifted from his gloom suddenly when he heard voices outside his cell. It sounded like the general, but he couldn't be sure. He crept to the door to listen.

"Men," a voice yelled. "Go to the…woods, immediately! They need help."

The general didn't sound quite right, but Frelati couldn't be certain. He had only heard the general once, after all.

"Sir?" one of the guards questioned.

"Go!" the general bellowed.

Now that sounds like the general, Frelati thought.

"But, sir," the other soldier stuttered. "What about the prisoners?"

"Go! I'll stay…until…others come. Go!"

Frelati heard the men push back their chairs and run off, before moving back to lean against the wall. If the general opened the door and caught him listening, Frelati might not breathe again. The door never opened though, even after a few minutes had passed.

Frelati had begun to relax when he heard a key slide into the lock. It jiggled a bit before sliding back out. He heard the same sounds over and over again, but the lock never clicked. He knew more than just the general was outside due to a muffled, feminine voice muttering to herself about the number of keys.

The right key was finally chosen, and he heard the lock click back. The keys were then tossed to another person who walked off lightly. Frelati watched the door open to reveal an old lady with only a sliver of light shining behind her.

He stood. "What do you want?"

The lady didn't say anything. Instead, she just ran up to him, folding him in her embrace.

"I'm so glad you're okay! I wasn't sure what I would find," Genevia exclaimed.

At the sound of her voice, Frelati's rigid form relaxed, and he hugged her tightly. "Genevia? I didn't think you'd come. You shouldn't have come."

Genevia pushed back to look at him. "You expected me to leave you here?"

"This is too dangerous," Frelati scolded, but her face made him relent. "I'm glad you came anyway."

Genevia grinned and hugged him again quickly. "We stick together. I'll explain everything later. Come on; Lela's waiting."

Frelati stepped from his prison. Traynord was already out, smiling profusely. The moment Lela saw him a grin broke across her face, and she ran into Frelati's arms.

"Papa!" she yelled happily.

Genevia smiled but issued a warning. "We aren't out yet, so we have to be quiet. Okay, Lela?"

She nodded and snuggled up against Frelati's chest. Genevia looked around her. There was no way out except the way they'd come. She headed back toward the stairs with the others following, but instead of ascending immediately, she motioned for the others to stay back while she checked out the room above. They followed at a distance.

Genevia saw a hallway directly across the room with a door at the end. That was their exit. She stepped from the shadows and immediately saw a soldier. She was still dressed in her old lady garb, but she took it off as an idea formed from the general's warning. If she could distract the guard, everyone could get out safely.

She stepped loudly, and the soldier looked up. He seemed to be in his early thirties, and he also looked in great need of a shower. A smile spread across his face at the sight of her.

"Can I help you?" he asked with a glint in his eye.

"Actually, you can in just a minute." She flashed him a smile. "Clumsy me, I just realized that I dropped something in the hall, and I need to find it. Be right back."

She hurried to the others.

"What are you doing?" Frelati whispered in alarm.

"I'm getting you out of this place. There's a door out straight across the room. You can leave while I distract the guard," Genevia explained quickly.

Frelati looked at her intensely, a worried and funny look on his face. "What are you planning?"

Genevia glanced over her shoulder and grimaced. "Hopefully, only sweet talk him a bit and then leave."

"Genevia, don't do that." Frelati took a step closer. "Let me handle him."

"No, that could alert someone. Just leave it to me," Genevia said and hurried off.

The soldier looked up. "Took you a while."

"I couldn't find it." Genevia shrugged. "It was too dark."

The soldier got up from his seat to stand in front of her. "I can take a lamp and help you find it."

"Oh, no, don't do that," Genevia said, giving the soldier a winning smile. "It was just a small, worthless trinket. I've been meaning to throw it away anyhow."

The soldier smiled. "Well, then, there's no need. How about you take a seat?"

Genevia needed his back to the hallway. The chair would give him a full view.

"I don't really feel like sitting, if that's all right?" Genevia leaned against the wall.

"That's fine," the soldier said, his smile gaining width.

He turned to her, as she hoped he would. She looked toward the hallway and saw Traynord walk out. The soldier saw her glance and began to turn his head, but Genevia hurriedly brought a hand to his cheek to stop him. The soldier was startled but pleased.

Genevia leaned closer to him, looking past him at Lela, who was crossing to the door. "You know, you have beautiful eyes."

Her gaze returned to meet his.

"You're the first to tell me that," the soldier said.

Genevia didn't notice as Frelati began to cross the room. He seemed to simply materialize at the door. Time for her to leave.

"You know, I think I will go look for that trinket," she said.

Frelati stood waiting for her at the exit.

Genevia continued, slipping out of the small space between the soldier and the wall. "I think I dropped it outside. I remember! It was just right outside that door."

"I'll come with you," the soldier said, winking. "To find that trinket."

"You still have a job to do," Genevia pointed out as she inched away.

The soldier stopped. "Then you can stay here and find your doo-dad later."

"I...I just remembered that it's very important to my...um...sister," Genevia stammered. "I really should find it."

Genevia moved a bit farther, realizing now how ill planned her idea had been. She glanced to the door and saw Frelati standing out in the open. His hands were clenched into tight fists and his eyes held a bright, blue blaze that Genevia hadn't seen before. She looked away from him, returning her gaze once again to the soldier.

"I really do need to go anyway," she said.

She motioned to Frelati to get out of sight, smiling at the soldier. Frelati stayed put.

"You aren't going anywhere," the soldier said fiercely, grabbing Genevia tightly by the arm.

She stared up at him in utter shock. This was getting out of hand. She tried to pull away.

"Let me go!" she yelled as she tried to twist her arm from his grasp.

Frelati advanced quickly. He knew this would happen, but Genevia hadn't given him the chance to stop her. He reached the soldier in three long strides. Grabbing him by the shoulder, Frelati spun him around. The soldier, caught offguard, released Genevia, who hurried out of his reach.

"You picked the wrong girl to mess with," Frelati said through gritted teeth, raising his arm back, fist clenched.

He put his weight into the punch that landed square across the soldier's jaw. The man slumped to the ground. Frelati stood over him, fists still tight, and his eyes still full of anger.

"Impudent pig," he muttered, giving him a kick in the leg.

Genevia stared in shock at what Frelati had just done. Never before had she seen someone harm someone else. Frelati turned away, put his arm around a stunned Genevia's waist, and they walked out of the building.

It was still completely dark outside. What had felt like forever to Genevia while inside headquarters had really only taken around forty-five minutes. Once outside, Genevia picked up Lela, still in her stupor. The man had just crumpled, like a rag doll, into a heap on the floor…because of Frelati. She shook her head to clear her thoughts of the fog that had befallen them.

"Traynord? Where are you?" Genevia called quietly.

From her left she heard, "Here, lass."

"Okay, good. We have to meet Jackson," Genevia stated, handing an anxious Lela over to Frelati.

"Who?" Frelati asked in surprise. Anger could still be heard in his words, a pent up frustration that would take some time to fully dissipate.

Genevia turned in the direction of his voice. "Jackson, he helped us get you out."

"Well, le's no' stan' aroun'. We nee' ta ge' ou' o' 'ere," Traynord said.

Genevia heard him start to shuffle off. They walked away from the building just as clouds rolled away to allow the moon a glimpse of Tiweln. Genevia led the way. Eventually, they came to a darker patch of grass, and she stopped.

"We're back," Genevia whispered.

Jackson lifted his head, then his body. He glanced around the group. "All here?"

Frelati saw his uniform, and his jaw tightened. "A soldier? You got help from a soldier?"

He could just make out the sheepish grin on Genevia's face in the moonlight. She had some explaining to do.

"Actually, it's ex-soldier now," Jackson corrected.

Frelati glared at him, causing the man to flinch back. "You've still got the uniform." He looked closer at Jackson's face and recognition flashed across his own. His glare instantly intensified. "You were in the group that captured us."

Frelati turned angrily to Genevia. "How could you trust him? He could have easily turned you in. The blackguard is probably planning something right now."

Genevia was insulted. "Well, I didn't have much choice, now did I? I had to get you out of jail and try to keep Lela safe at the same time. Not an easy task, Frelati, when one is by oneself."

"Look, I'm only here to help," Jackson broke in. "And Genevia made sure I wouldn't double-cross you before she agreed to let me travel with you."

Frelati glared distrustfully at the soldier again. He didn't like this guy and just wanted him to pack up and…wait, what had the soldier just said? He whirled to face Genevia.

"You told him he could travel with us," Frelati exploded.

"You need to keep quiet." Genevia laid a hand on his arm but held her ground. "Of course he's traveling with us, and this is a terrible way for you to treat Jackson. He could have been killed if someone found out he was helping us. Not to mention the fact that I and that sweet child you're holding would have been captured as well. He saved us, helped you escape, and the least you can do in gratitude is treat him kindly."

Frelati clenched his teeth and turned away from her and that soldier, conceding the point with one short word. "Fine."

Genevia nodded. "Good. Thank you. Jackson, I would like you to meet Traynord, and that disagreeable fellow is Frelati."

Jackson smiled in Traynord's direction before turning to Frelati. He found a cold stare that penetrated the darkness, deepening the shadows. Frelati very obviously despised him. That could strain the trip a bit, but Jackson would just avoid Frelati whenever possible. The other three seemed pleasant enough.

Genevia watched Frelati's expression. She hoped his attitude was just left over from the episode in the building. His temper had been hot then, and apparently it still hadn't simmered down.

"Well, le's ge' goin' ya slowpokes," Traynord said with good humor.

Jackson took the lead with Traynord just a step behind him, striking up a quiet conversation. Genevia laid a hand on Frelati's arm again and gave him a warning look.

"Try to be nice, you don't know him yet," she said before turning to follow Jackson and Traynord.

Frelati watched her intently, beginning to feel a little remorse over his outburst but not willing to do anything about it. He truly didn't like the soldier.

"Don't be sad, Papa," Lela said sweetly in Elven. "You are better than Jackson."

Frelati gave her a small smile, and she laid her head on his shoulder. At least he didn't have to worry about losing his little girl to the soldier. He started after the three ahead. He could have caught up with them but decided to stay behind with Lela. The closer he got to Jackson, the less control he seemed to have over his temper.

Sitting by the fire the next evening and listening to Jackson, Frelati just couldn't figure out why he disliked him—if he ignored Jackson's background as a soldier.

However, if he was honest with himself, somewhere in the back of his mind, Frelati knew the cause, but he continued to dismiss the thought each time it began to creep forward. Genevia talked to Jackson a lot. Of course, he was easier to talk to than Frelati was, which was no surprise. While Frelati had worked on blending in to keep away from prison guards, Jackson had been working on social skills.

That couldn't be the reason he disliked Jackson, though. So Genevia was paying more attention to him, Frelati shouldn't care. He was only here to protect her and get her to the prison. Other than that, he would have no dealings with her, and it would be good for him to remember that. As hard as he tried, though, Frelati couldn't run from the truth. Jackson was getting more of Genevia's attention, and Frelati was jealous.

Frelati tuned back into the conversation.

"So la', how di' ye know where Genevia was?" Traynord was asking Jackson.

Color slowly crept up Jackson's neck and onto his cheeks until he was beat red. The tips of his ears turned a pale pink. Frelati was suddenly very glad that he had decided to listen after all. Jackson looked into the fire to avoid the two men's eyes.

"I...um...I..." Jackson swallowed. "I...saw her at the...um...the waterfall before I ran across your camp."

He relaxed a bit after the confession, but he was still tense. Traynord grinned, a mischievous look in his eye.

"So, ye caugh' 'er bathin'," he joked, pretending to scold. "Shameful."

Jackson looked up sharply and stammered a reply. "Sh-she...um...I...I ran the other way real quick. I didn't see nuthin'."

A wild look of panic was in his eyes, and Traynord laughed to calm the boy.

"I'm jus' playin' with ya, la'. No worries." Traynord clapped him on the back.

Frelati watched Jackson closely. The ex-soldier was nineteen, but his maturity level was years below that. Jackson tried to smile at Traynord's joke but was too shaken. Frelati decided to help him out by changing the subject. He didn't particularly enjoy discussing what the boy's eyes had seen either.

"So what made you decide to be a soldier?" he asked, startling both men by joining in the conversation.

Instead of relaxing at the change in subject, Jackson seemed to grow more uncomfortable. "My dad was a soldier, and my grandfather. I'm just following in their footsteps."

"Seems ta me there's a bigger story there than tha'," Traynord prodded.

Jackson looked away, clearly not willing to say more. Frelati shrugged at Traynord and grabbed a stick near his feet, leaving Traynord to pick up the slack.

"So how do ye like our li'l travelin' group, Jackson?" he asked.

"It's comfortable. You're all really nice and welcoming. Genevia makes good food. Lela livens things up running around, and you keep me company," Jackson explained, smiling.

Traynord grinned too and tried to pull Frelati back into the conversation. "I din' 'ear ye mention Frelati."

Jackson's face grew red again.

Frelati looked up, his eyes locking onto Jackson's, but he stayed silent.

"Well, you are..." Jackson glanced at Traynord before looking back at Frelati, thinking quickly. "You are...um, well, quiet support.

You gather wood and pitch the tent. You help out a lot and make things run smoothly."

Frelati's mouth hinted at a scoffing smile, but he went back to his stick, pulling out his knife and shaving it. Traynord thought quickly. Frelati was too quiet for his own good. He'd at least been more talkative before Jackson started traveling with them, but now he seemed to just be there. He was like a turtle. Before, he'd gotten comfortable and was fine showing who he truly was, but now he saw Jackson as a threat, and he had withdrawn back into his protective, silent shell.

"Wha' do ye think o' Genevia, la'?" Traynord asked, glancing in Frelati's direction to check for a response.

Frelati continued shaving his stick, but his eyes were watching Jackson as he formed an answer. Traynord hid a grin.

"She's nice, friendly," Jackson said slowly, weighing each word thoughtfully before speaking. "She's really pretty and laughs a lot."

Traynord eyed Frelati while making his next statement. "She's go' a lo' o' good trai's. Make a goo' wife some day, woul'n' she, la'?"

Jackson smiled. "Yeah, definitely. She can cook and carry on a conversation."

"She's no' much younger than you, la'," Traynord pointed out, still watching Frelati closely.

As interest was seen creeping across Jackson's face, Traynord could see Frelati struggling to remain in control of his tongue and anger.

"She is," Jackson agreed thoughtfully.

Traynord nodded. "Jus' a few years betwinx ye."

Jackson nodded as excitement lit his eyes before it was extinguished by a troubling thought. "But she's an elf, and I'm not."

Traynord saw Frelati relax, a smile hidden beneath his bowed head.

"Well, la', marriage betwinx an elf an' human is possible. I's no' so rare," Traynord explained. "Lela's paren's are an example."

"Yeah?" Jackson exclaimed, excited once again.

"Yeah, so tha' woul'n' stop ye two." Traynord slid a sideways glance at Frelati to measure the effect of his words. Maybe this would provide the little extra nudge Frelati needed when it came to Genevia.

Frelati stood, anger etched across his features. He threw his stick into the fire and walked to the edge of the clearing, stopping only at the sound of Traynord's voice.

"Where ye goin', la'?" he asked, amusement twined in with his words.

Frelati's hands balled into fists, but when he spoke, his voice was calm. "I'm getting firewood."

He kept his back to them as he spoke. Traynord glanced at the large pile of wood stacked near him.

"No nee'. We have plen'y," he said.

"It's better to be sure." An edge of agitation could be heard in his voice.

"Genevia shoul' be back soon, la', an' she'll make dinner, so don' be long."

Frelati jerked his head in the semblance of a nod and walked off. Once enough time had passed so that he was out of earshot, Traynord turned to Jackson.

"'E loves Genevia, the boy does. Jus' won' say so, or maybe i's tha' he don' know hisself ye'," Traynord explained. "He thinks she's be'er than 'im."

"Oh." There was a hint of disappointment in Jackson's voice but also understanding.

"Sorry ta lea' ya on like tha', la', bu' I was tryin' to ge' 'im ta realize he neede' ta tell Genevia 'ow 'e feels."

"What's his story? Why is he traveling with you anyway?" Jackson paused. "He's so quiet and serious; are all elves that way?"

Traynord smiled at the last comment. "Ya hear Genevia talk la'ely? The lass don' stop, an' she's quick with a smile. As ta Frelati's story, ye'll have ta ask him. I don' really know."

Laughter filtered through the trees and entered the small clearing, warning the two companions of Genevia and Lela's return. She broke through the dense woods with Lela on her back.

"Well, let's get dinner started," she said to Lela, and they got out supplies.

Traynord enjoyed watching Lela follow all of Genevia's instructions perfectly, wanting to be just like her. They made a nice team, and soon dinner was bubbling nicely over the fire. As the smells began reaching out to scratch the men's noses and tempt their taste buds, Frelati appeared. Genevia smiled up at him from her seat beside the pot of stew.

"I'm glad you made it back, and just in time for dinner," she greeted him.

His lips quirked up a bit in a small smile that was only ever given to Genevia or Lela, and he went to sit on a log. Soon enough, Genevia gave everyone their portion of the stew. Then she took a seat beside Frelati. Lela sat on his other side, eagerly eating her food and swinging her little legs back and forth. Traynord and Jackson were quietly talking on the other side of the clearing.

Genevia turned to Frelati. "You've been quiet all day…quieter than usual. Why?"

Frelati took a swallow of food. "Nothing to say."

Genevia raised a brow in disbelief.

"I've just been thinking," Frelati answered.

"What about?" Genevia's curiosity could be heard in her words.

"Nothing much," Frelati said, and he saw her begin to slip away from him—not physically but emotionally. He was pushing her away and wasn't that just what he had regretted most as he was led into his most recent cell? Frelati stared at his dinner, deep in thought, before making his decision. He turned to look at Genevia and set down his food. "I have something to tell you."

Genevia glanced back up at him, taking in his serious but uncomfortable expression. Once again, he had her undivided attention. His beautiful, deep blue eyes locked onto her inquisitive, green ones as he tried to build up the courage to say what he knew he needed to say. Just as he was about to speak, two people burst into the clearing.

"Well, I declare! I certainly am glad it's you here, not that we was lookin' for you two darlin's, but now that we have ya, gather ur stuff quickly. The soldier's are comin'!"

Everyone in the clearing, excluding Lela, jumped to their feet. All eyes were on the two weary, travel bag laden travelers. Lela grabbed Frelati's leg for security.

Genevia took a step forward. "Jezzie?"

Chapter Thirteen

"What are you doing here?" Genevia asked Jezzie in confusion.

"We'll explain everything later, hun, but those soldiers are tearing everything apart. We need to get out of here," Jezzie said.

After packing quickly, everyone left the clearing at a brisk pace. Introductions were put off, questions left unanswered until they were safe. Hours had passed, and Lela was asleep in the carrying pack on Frelati's back. Genevia walked at his side, his arm placed securely around her waist. If not for the comfort it gave her, Genevia would have asked what led him to make such a gesture, but she was sure he would draw away if she said anything.

The group of seven walked in silence, darkness surrounding them. They followed Jackson's lamp until daylight began creeping in and the weary travelers could walk no longer. They quickly set up camp and laid down to rest. Everyone except Frelati.

Genevia had helped Lela out of the carrier on his back and laid her on a blanket covering a soft patch of grass. Several times that night she had tried to help Frelati carry her, but he had refused. He sat beside Lela now, clearly tired, and Genevia lay down on the child's other side.

"Aren't you going to sleep?" she asked Frelati.

He turned to her. "Someone has to be lookout."

He glanced over the sleeping figures before turning back to Genevia.

"Seeing as everyone else is asleep, I guess I've been elected," he said with a wry grin.

"Then I'll stay up too, to keep you company," Genevia said after a moment of thought.

"No, you need to sleep." Frelati turned away from her.

Genevia eyed him closely. "I do what I want, and right now, I want to stay up and keep you company. Besides, I believe that you were going to tell me something rather important earlier before we were interrupted. I want to know what it is."

"It...wasn't important," Frelati said without looking at her. "Now, go to sleep for a little while; I'll let you keep me company later."

"You keep avoiding me, except for tonight when you put your arm around me. Since Jackson came, you rarely say two words to anyone, especially me. Why?"

"Maybe I'm just not talkative," Frelati said, his blue eyes flashing.

"You're avoiding my question," Genevia stated, waiting for an answer.

Frelati looked at his hands with a scowl. "I was sent by your parents to find you, protect you, and bring you back to them. That's it, nothing else. I wasn't sent here to talk to you or to keep you company."

"Mm-hmm." Genevia didn't buy it. "You're still avoiding the question. I would like to know what you were really going to say to me earlier."

"You're a princess. I'm a servant. I'm just here on orders," Frelati stated evasively.

Genevia studied his eyes for a long time before speaking. Then, she drew in a deep breath, her eyes wide in astonishment. "You like me, don't you?"

Surprise and guilt registered in his eyes, and Genevia smiled smugly.

"It doesn't matter," Frelati said angrily, confirming Genevia's statement. He stood. "Now will you go to sleep?"

"No, I told you I'd stay up, and I intend to do just that."

"Fine." He stood with his back to her, hands on hips, feet spread, staring out into the dark woods.

They stayed quiet as the sun steadily rose higher and higher in the sky. Finally, Genevia spoke. "What are my parents like?"

Frelati turned to look at her.

She smiled. "Hey, I got you to turn around."

He gave her an annoyed look but moved to sit across from her, gazing down at Lela. "Do you really want to know, or was that just a ploy to get my attention?"

Genevia shrugged. "It'll give us something to talk about."

Frelati looked straight forward, but he wasn't seeing what was in front of him. Instead, he was gazing at a hazy memory of the woman who had become like a mother to him and the king who had worked so hard to protect him.

"Your mother is beautiful. You look like her, I think. The last time I actually got a good look at her was when I was seven. You have her same hair, though. Her gift was new birth. She always seemed to know when babies were ready to be born, for any creature, and she always made it easier on the mother. Lenaia always treated me like her son. She did it for my mother. She was a trusted servant, and your mother loved her," Frelati explained. "I really can't describe your father. I didn't see him that much, so all I remember is his personality. He could be very stubborn, a lot like you, but he was also kind and thoughtful. He helped calm us when we were scared in the cell. His gift had to do with the moon. I'm really not certain what all he could do, but I know that when they escaped with you, no light from the moon could be seen."

"What happened to your mother?" Genevia asked quietly.

"She died giving birth to me. My dad didn't take it well, threw himself over some cliffs a year later. I never knew them obviously, so your parents are the only parents I've ever had."

"I'm sorry." Genevia reached over to pat his arm, not sure what to do.

Frelati stood again. "I'll gather some firewood. They'll all be hungry when they wake up."

Genevia watched him walk off to sit by the fire. He definitely wasn't good at expressing his emotions. She looked down at Lela and smiled. At least he didn't have any trouble showering this little angel with love. Genevia lay down and closed her eyes. It was time to doze.

Bright sunlight filtered through the brilliantly green leaves. Many trees stood tall, creating a canopy above a small clearing. In this clearing, tiny flowers grew amongst the grass, bees and butterflies zigzagged all around, and squirrels fought with birds to be the loudest animals in the forest. Sleeping figures were stretched out in the grass, and their gentle breathing mixed with the other sounds of nature to create a beautiful rhythm and melody.

One figure sat away from the rest. Flashing red, orange, and yellow flames licked at the air near him. It lit up his face and scorched the ground. He was alone. It could be read on his face. Then the female elf awoke and moved from a smaller figure to the one by the fire, making his eyes light with happiness.

The dreamer watched it all from high up in the trees. She was a young dreamer, but she knew more about other races than did many elders. She watched the group silently. Since she had been removed, banished from her family of dreamers, she had tried to find another group to live with. Dreamers weren't meant to be alone, and the group she was watching below her could be just the one to end her solitary existence.

Everyone sat around the fire eating the meal Genevia had prepared. They had all been fairly quiet, eating quickly while trying to shake off any lingering sleepiness. The sun had already begun its descent, and Genevia guessed it to be around five. They would need to hurry into the next town and get on a ship quickly before the soldiers blocked all escape from Rom.

Genevia set down her empty plate. It was one of the few that Jezzie had packed.

"So, Jezzie, will you to tell us how you got here? What happened?" Genevia asked.

"Well, first, this is my husband, Asben. The soldiers woke us up, even though they was on the other side of town," Jezzie explained. "We packed up real quick and escaped just in the nick a time. They burned down our bakery though. Good thing we ran into you, or we mighta been lost in this forest forever. My Asben may be brilliant, but navigating in trees has never been a talent a his."

"In my defense, everything looks the same in here. However, what I would like to know is who the soldiers were searching for. They were yelling, 'Find them.' I can't imagine who would be so dangerous that a whole army would be after them," Asben said absently before stuffing a spoonful of food into his mouth.

Frelati and Genevia exchanged guilty glances, which Jezzie didn't miss.

"Y'all don't know who they was after, do ya?" she asked suspiciously.

Genevia smiled sheepishly while Frelati confessed.

"They're after us."

Jezzie gasped, placing a hand over her heart. "Well, I declare! Whatever did ya do?"

Frelati finished off his last bite before answering. "I escaped from Fezam's prison on Azol, in which I was unjustly placed, and Genevia, well…"

"I was born," Genevia finished for him.

"Well, darlin', people don't go lookin' for ya just 'cause ur born," Jezzie said with a small laugh.

Genevia smiled. "I'm a special case."

"She's an Elfin princess. Fezam needs her either dead or on his side in order for him to fully take control of Tiweln. Her parents have been in his prison with me for sixteen years. I escaped to find her so that we can help free the elves."

Stunned silence and shocked faces followed. Then Jezzie started laughing. "Well, you two do have urselves a story, now, don'cha? That'll entertain ur kids for years. My! We've joined an excitin' group, haven't we, Asben?"

Her laughter rang through the clearing, but the others were still trying to adjust.

"So tha's why ye're so quie', isn' i', la'?" Traynord said, looking at him with great interest and more than a little pity.

"You were in jail! For sixteen years? That means you were in there since you were just a kid!" Jackson looked at him in astonishment. "How'd you do it?"

Asben was looking at Frelati with curiosity, completely missing Jackson's meaning with the question. "Yes, I was wondering how the escape was possible too. The last time there was an escape from the jail in Azol was fifty years ago. They had the place rebuilt immediately and caught the fugitive two weeks later. They haven't had a prisoner escape since then. Security was tightened to four hundred guards, fifty in three-hour intervals on rotation. How did you manage to escape? Logic goes beyond that. You could plan down to the last minute and still be stopped."

"How do you know all that?" Frelati asked.

Asben walked over to one of his bags, bringing out a book. "I've traveled everywhere. To the dwarf undergrounds on Yima Olem, to the pixie islands, to Socuma with the dragons; once I even traveled to the mermaid swamps. I've been to Azol, probably while you were in prison there. I checked out everything, making detailed observations for my research. The only place I've left to visit is Lonyi. Shapeshifters are tricky creatures.

"Anyway," he continued, opening up his book to a page depicting a detailed outline of the prison in Azol. "This is a blueprint I drew while there. As you can see, the only exits are here, here, and here." He pointed to three doorways. "This one leads outside, to where they…well, they interrogate you."

He grew uncomfortable, realizing Frelati had probably made more than one trip there.

"I'm well aware of the activities undertaken outside that door," Frelati said coldly.

"Yes, well, what I was saying is that it only leads to a courtyard where high walls that couldn't be climbed block all exits," Asben continued after clearing his throat.

"I realize." Frelati avoided looking at him, staring instead at the map.

"That leaves only these two exits, which are guarded by four guards. Seems an overkill, I realize, but they explained it was for extra security. You know they pay really extravagant attention to detail, making sure that when guards change out, a number of eight guards stay until an hour has passed. I was actually able to watch firsthand as…"

"Asben," Jezzie said firmly. "Ur runnin' off at the mouth again."

A bit of color crept into the scholarly man's face. "Sorry. As I was saying, it is impossible to leave by any exits. A few of the walls are old but rather sturdy. Guards patrol the outside, so I don't see how you could escape."

Frelati raised his gaze to meet Asben's. "I was with the King and Queen in this cell."

He pointed to the farthest cell, the largest, without looking at the map. It was as if the layout was one he knew well, though he really only knew the short path to the walled courtyard.

Asben's face showed astonishment as he studied his carefully drawn lines. "That's impossible. My calculations were performed perfectly. That cell has its very own captain to guard it at all times, not to mention the additional rotating guards that roam that corridor. There is no way you could have escaped from there."

Frelati's gaze hardened. "I'm here, aren't I?"

"Well…yes." Asben looked at him, incredulous. "How did you do it? Wait, just a minute, let me get something to write it down."

He rushed over to his bag, thoroughly enjoying himself now. Then he hunkered down on a log next to Frelati, waiting for an explanation.

"The back wall, this one, wasn't sturdy. The King and Queen dug a hole in it, told me to squeeze through and go to Wilksom Olem to find Genevia, and I did."

Asben was taking notes rapidly. After he had gotten that down, he stopped, waiting for more. Frelati said nothing, just helped himself to seconds.

"And?" Asben prompted.

Frelati looked at him blankly. "And what?"

Asben's face fell. "That's it?"

Frelati nodded.

"Okay, well, can you tell me how long ago that was?" he asked, grasping at straws.

"Six days before I met Genevia on Wilksom Olem," he said, thinking back.

"You made it to Wilksom Olem from Azol in six days?" Asben asked as his interest sparked yet again.

"Yes." Frelati's eyes dropped to the ground again.

"How? That's at least...um, let's see," he paused to calculate. "It should have taken over two months, depending on the direction of travel. There's no way you could make it in six days. How'd you do it?"

Frelati, to the surprise of everyone in the clearing, looked extremely uncomfortable. "I can't say."

"What?" Asben was completely taken aback. "Why? This would be the ultimate information for my research: a safe and quick way to travel."

"I didn't say it was safe, and I can't tell you," Frelati stated.

"Give me a reason," Asben forced, writing implement poised above his leaflet.

"It's a heavily guarded secret of the elves. Actually, part of it is only known to royal elves, but I'll say no more."

"How do you know about it?" Asben questioned.

"The King and Queen gave me the information so I could find Alernoa faster. It's tricky and, like I said, dangerous, but that's all I'm saying." Frelati dug into his meal.

Asben recognized the end of the conversation and tucked his notes back into his pack. All was quiet for a while as everyone tried to adjust to the odd conversation. Genevia and Jezzie, who were going stir-crazy from sitting, started cleaning and packing up. Finally, Frelati broke the quiet.

"We need to move to the next town, find a ship, and leave before the soldiers reach us or close up port. Let's go."

Chapter Fourteen

People wandered everywhere within the large town. Genevia and her group would easily blend in. Everything was fast paced; no one bothered to notice them as they walked to the boating docks. Now, if they could possibly get a ship, everything would be okay.

Frelati was uneasy. Something was going on in this town. Why else would they be running around in a frenzy? With each step they took toward the docks, Frelati's unease grew. Finally, he pulled the group into a side alley to form a plan.

"Something is going on here," he said, talking louder than normal to be heard above the noise from the street. "This is a town. Granted, it's larger than most, but still, there shouldn't be this much activity. Someone will recognize Genevia and me. We're on every wanted poster from here to Azol, but, Traynord, if you could find a ship, they shouldn't know you. And, Jezzie, they won't know that you and Asben are traveling with us, so you can get any supplies we'll need."

He turned to Traynord. "How long do you think we'll be at sea?"

"Where ye heade'?" he questioned.

"Well, the Pixie islands are the closest. If we go to Yappés, the pixies might not turn us in, but that'll lead to a long trip on the ocean," Frelati said.

"Yea, tha' woul' be long, bu' no' too long. Prolly ten days or so. Can' really say now. All has ta do with the weather, an' the ship, o' course."

"Can you get us a good one?"

"I'll see wha' they go'."

Traynord walked off, leaving the group to finish their discussion. Once again, Frelati was in charge of the situation.

"Jezzie and Asben, you need to get enough supplies to last us a month and a half, just in case. Genevia, Lela, and I will stay here."

After Jezzie and Asben headed out, Jackson spoke up. "What do you want me to do?"

"Oh. You can either stay with us or go shopping for anything you need."

Jackson looked from Genevia to Frelati before speaking. Their faces were completely blank, as if they didn't care what he did, but he knew what Frelati wanted.

"I need some clothes. This is all I have, and everyone is sure to recognize the uniform. I shouldn't be long."

Frelati and Genevia both nodded, and then Jackson left them as well. Lela tugged on Frelati's arm to get him to pick her up. Tenderness crept into his eyes when he looked down at her, and once again Genevia realized that bringing Lela had been her best idea.

"And you said you wouldn't be a good father," she teased.

The corners of his lips lifted in a self-deprecating grin.

"Papa, play." Lela smiled sweetly. "Mama too."

They walked to the back of the alley and sat down.

"What do you want to play?" Frelati asked gently.

Lela grinned up at him. "I spy."

"Foun' a ship," Traynord said half an hour later, but he wasn't smiling.

Frelati stood, depositing Lela in Genevia's lap. "But?"

A wry grin crossed Traynord's face. "Ye're righ', la'. There's a bu'. The ship don' leave 'til nex' week, an' they hear' o' ye two."

Frelati grimaced. "There's absolutely no other ship?"

"Sorry, la'. None tha'll carry the seven o' us."

Frelati paced back and forth in the small confines of the alleyway. "What now?"

Genevia spoke quietly. "We could, um, well...no, we really shouldn't do that. Nevermind."

"What?" Frelati stood in front of her, his eyes coaxing her to speak.

"Well, I...we could cause a distraction of some sort and borrow the ship. After we defeat Fezam, we can give it back...with money and anything else they want," Genevia said, feeling terrible about the suggestion.

Frelati sighed, obviously not pleased but seeing no other way, and spoke. "No choice but that, I guess. Once Jackson, Jezzie, and Asben get back, we'll take suggestions on how we'll get things done."

It hadn't taken much to get everyone's attention away from the ships. Just a little gunpowder, a match, and Asben's ingenuity did the trick. Lighting some rags and walking away quickly got Asben to the boat before the gunpowder blew. Then, with everyone crowding around and the men on the targeted ship running off to view the spectacle, Traynord maneuvered the ship out of port. Now, they just hoped they weren't followed.

Traynord had picked a good ship. Quick, hardy, and spacious, it was just right for their needs. Everyone would pitch in to keep the ship running, and they would make it to the Pixie Islands soon enough.

Jezzie was below deck in the kitchen, putting away their supplies. Asben went into one of the three cabins to store his books and clothing. Jackson did the same in another cabin that he was to share with Traynord. Lela was running around deck, thrilled to be on the water, and Frelati was keeping a watchful eye out for her as well as Genevia, who was leaning over the railing at the bow to catch some sea spray. At the wheel was Traynord, maneuvering the ship with precision.

The day was gorgeous, the wind just right, no ships were following them, and it seemed that they had left all their problems behind.

"It's a nice ship, ain't it?" Jezzie beamed as she came up from the kitchen.

Genevia turned, returning her smile. "It most definitely is."

Jezzie put her hands on her hips. "Now, have ya been below yet, honey?"

"Not yet, I'm enjoying the sea breeze." Genevia threw her arms out, closing her eyes for emphasis.

"Then I'll give ya a layout," she said. "There's three cabins. The farthest is for me an' Asben. The next is for Traynord an' Jackson. Now, that last one is for you, Lela, an' Frelati."

Genevia's eyes snapped open. "What?"

Jezzie frowned. "What do ya mean what?"

"Back up." Genevia wound her fingers backward. "There's only three cabins?"

Jezzie nodded, and Genevia continued, "So Frelati, Traynord, and Jackson can bunk together."

"Well, the beds ain't that big, dear. Lela's small, so you an' Lela an' Frelati can share the last cabin," Jezzie said and crinkled her brow. "I don' know why ya'd expect Frelati to bunk with Traynord an' Jackson anyway."

Genevia stared at the woman. "I don't think you understand, Frelati and I…"

"I'll be staying on deck," Frelati interrupted. He nodded at a far corner with a ledge. "That'll work."

Jezzie huffed. "Well, hun, why would ya stay out here when there's a nice, soft bed in the cabin?"

Frelati nodded in Genevia's direction. "She and Lela need the bed, not me."

"We gave you two the biggest room with the most space. The bed's big enough for all three a ya," Jezzie persisted.

"I won't sleep with them. It's not right."

"Well, why not?" Jezzie's fists were planted firmly on her plump hips. This conversion was making her head reel. *Young'uns these days.* "The both of ya are actin' childish. For a married couple, ya sure don' seem to want a lot to do with each other."

"We're not married," Genevia said in exasperation.

"Well, why not?"

Genevia turned to Frelati, clearly bewildered, so he answered. "I've only known her a little under a month; I'm simply here to protect her."

Jezzie looked them both over for a while, then nodded, her smile returning. "Um-hum."

Then she turned back to the door leading below deck. Genevia and Frelati shared a bemused look, and he shrugged.

"You jus' sleep on that bench a urs," Jezzie said suddenly, startling them both. "Oh, an' did I mention that Asben was a judge when he was younger? I'm sure he's still able to perform a weddin'."

With that, she disappeared downstairs.

Genevia watched her back. "I think she's hinting at something."

"Hinting?" Frelati rolled his eyes and scowled before walking over to sit on "his" bench. Lela quickly settled beside him, wiggling her legs back and forth.

"You…and Mama…married?" Lela asked innocently.

Frelati glanced down at her. "No."

Lela pouted and crossed her arms over her chest. Frelati couldn't help chuckling, and her frown grew.

"Hey, Mama," he teased Genevia. "Your daughter's pouting."

Genevia turned and feigned an accusing expression. "What did you do to my baby?"

"Nothing." Frelati put his hands up in defense. "I did absolutely nothing."

Lela looked up at them before ducking her head again and trying to be upset.

"Oh, come on, you want me to believe Lela would just pout," Genevia said. "Really, what do you take me for?"

Frelati smiled. "Think we can make that pout go away."

"I don't know if that's possible," Genevia said, shaking her head.

Lela took another peek up at them.

Frelati took his chance and tickled her. She emitted several high-pitched giggles. Then Genevia joined in, making the little girl laugh all the more. Jezzie stood watching them from the doorway and smiled. She was right, as usual. Reading people was what she did best. She smiled as she turned to go back down to the kitchen to prepare some lunch.

'Neath stem and petal the baby lies,
Earth and nature are her ties,
She determines if good lives or dies,
After her sacrifice, evil flies.

Near and far, travel shan't end,
Three days after all will mend,
World to world they must defend,
Earth, sea, fire, light, and wind.

After staying up late looking through all his books, Asben had finally found something. Now, he looked around the group. "It was written two hundred years ago by a philosopher, prophet, and elf. He had been in seclusion for many years when he wrote this book, *Kfiks ir Dilwoh*, or Prophecy of Worlds. Everyone raved over the book because at the time we knew only of this world. No one understood what he meant to say by this poem, and he was killed before he could enlighten us. It has remained a mystery. I dug it up last night.

"How he came up with this concept, I'll never know. When I first read this book, I put it aside thinking the guy was crazy. I kept it only because I never throw a book away." He smiled at Jezzie, who rolled her eyes, before continuing. "After hearing Genevia's story, I knew I'd heard something like it. This is what I remembered. Listen, 'Each world possesses a protector. Whether the protector is born of the world is unidentified as of now. This world will create, if indeed this is the order, one of great power in times of trouble. An elf will be born after years of peril and must save Tiweln.'

"The poem follows," Asben said, looking around.

Everyone was quiet for a while. Genevia finally broke the silence with a question on everyone's mind.

"What exactly does that mean? I understand that last part, but the poem, what on Tiweln could have possessed him to write it?"

Asben's face was grim. "Well, best I can surmise is that this is what we're facing. The beginning of the poem is your beginning. The second line is your gift. The third line is up to you basically. Your actions will determine whether or not Tiweln returns to normal, that is without Fezam as its overlord. The last line of the first part has many meanings. There will be some sacrifice. It could be that a member of this party is captured until you win or lose, or perhaps you have to give up something you dearly love, which could mean the death of someone possibly. The most common meaning, though, the one on which most scholars agree, is rather unsettling when one actually knows you."

Asben paused, a look of great of unease creasing his forehead. As he was about to speak, Genevia broke in quietly. "The last is my death, isn't it?"

A pained expression was in his eyes as Asben nodded slowly. "It could mean many things, but that is the most likely outcome."

Silence hung heavy in the air as everyone allowed the recent news to settle in their thoughts. Frelati, unconsciously, reached out to rub Genevia's back. Whether it was for his comfort or hers, Genevia couldn't guess. Lela was hugging her arm tightly. The child knew something bad had just happened, but as to what it was, she was in the dark.

Finally, Asben cleared his throat. "The next section is highly speculated. No one knows for certain what he means by it, well, part of it anyway. They agree that there will be a lot of travel, as it says, and it's possible that it could be world to world. No one knows how that would be achieved, and this is cause for argument. Apparently after the...sacrifice mentioned above, everything will go back to normal. It will be mended, presumably after three days, but, yet again, scholars wonder how that is possible. Because it mentions all the elements and other worlds, apparently each one will confront some threat. It is doubtful they will receive help from the other worlds because if any knew how to travel beyond, we would have discovered the secret. It's rather vague.

"There is a problem, though, in his prophesies, or rather a conflict within his writings. Earlier in the reading, he speaks of six elements, of six worlds. This world with Genevia's gift over earth would be one, obviously, but that is beside the point. What I find interesting is the fact that the sixth element is not mentioned. He does not say what it is, ever, throughout the reading. He mentions earth, sea, fire, light, and wind, but never the sixth element. It's very interesting," he concluded, becoming enraptured within his book again. "Very interesting."

Things were quiet for a while. The ship was kept on course, there were no storms, and no one felt a need for argument. Everyone had entered into a routine. Traynord was the first to wake and the last to sleep, and he was always found at the wheel. Frelati woke next, and he too stayed up late. During the day, he would walk around the deck, helping out here and there where he was needed, but he was quiet. He spoke only rarely in monosyllables, which was strange and disturbing to Genevia.

She woke with the sun and went to bed with Lela because Lela was afraid to be inside the ship alone. She played with the girl, helped cook and clean, and tried to keep everyone in a cheerful mood. Unfortunately, she failed with Frelati, who refused to be amused.

Jezzie cooked the most because she did not want anyone in "her" kitchen. She was always bustling around, working hard at something, no matter how trivial. Asben stayed in the cabin most of the time, reading his books and trying to find some other good explanation for the sacrificial line. Once, he bustled up the stairs exclaiming, "I got it!" However, no one ever learned what he had because he immediately shook his head, muttering under his breath as he returned to his cabin.

Lela was having fun. She would make up games and play with herself, or so it seemed. Everyone was amused at how well she played alone, but they didn't look closely enough. If they had, they might have found it more than a bit unusual.

Chapter Fifteen

"Rium biu, Dayze!" Lela cried as she discovered Dayze in her hiding place, touching the shadowy figure on the shoulder.

The shadow smiled, replying in the language Lela was most comfortable using. That was the way of dreamers; every language was their own. "Yes, you found me. Now, it's my turn!"

Frelati smiled, understanding what was said but not realizing that it was two voices he heard.

Dayze the Dreamer had followed the travelers. She walked behind the ship to avoid discovery by day and slept on board at night. She had done so for three days before she decided to reveal herself to Lela. Dayze was bored and wanted to have fun. Lela was good at coming up with games. The two hit it off immediately, and a quick friendship ensued.

With every game they played, Dayze made Lela see a different place instead of the ship, but, unlike her family, she told her victim what she was doing. When they played hide-and-seek, Dayze made Lela see a jungle, when they played tag, she made Lela see a desert. Every time there was an obstacle, though, Dayze made sure to let her friend know, so that she would not get hurt.

Dayze loved being with Lela; it was like having a sister. She just hoped once the rest of the group discovered their new addition, as they certainly would eventually, that they would accept her. She wanted a family…no, she needed one; dreamers weren't meant to be alone.

"How long until we land?" Genevia asked Traynord for the third time that day.

Traynord sighed, concealing a smile. "Do ye see any lan', lassie?"

"No." Genevia looked around grumpily. "I just want to be around trees and flowers and, well, just land in general."

"Aww, now the sea ain' tha' ba'," Traynord said cheerfully.

Genevia sighed. "I guess."

She walked slowly to the bow of the boat. Leaning against the rail, she stretched out as far as she could and closed her eyes, breathing in the salty, sea air.

"The sea smells nice," Genevia said over her shoulder to Traynord and opened her eyes, quickly sucking in her breath. "Um…uh… there's um…"

She started backing up, and Traynord looked toward the bow to discover the problem. Frelati hopped up from a bench to help her.

"What is it?" he asked quickly.

"This isn't good; this isn't good at all," Genevia muttered, continuing to back up with no thought of the step just behind her.

"Genevia!" Frelati exclaimed, catching her before she hit the deck. "What's the matter?"

Genevia gulped in a deep breath. "Huge fleet of ships, just ahead of us."

Frelati sat her down and rushed to the bow. His hands balled up, and his mouth became a straight line. Before him, stretched out in a line along the horizon, was a fleet of ships larger than he could have imagined. Where Fezam found all the manpower to sail them baffled him, but they clearly weren't going to be able to go around.

"No!" He slammed his fist into the rail beside him. "This can't happen!"

He began pacing, running a hand through his hair every few minutes.

Genevia picked herself up. "What are we going to do?"

"Well, there's not much we can do. There is a line of battleships for at least a mile blocking our path and advancing toward us. Short of turning completely around, we can't get past them, and even if we do that, another fleet will be waiting for us. We're caught, and that's probably just what they had been planning. I knew that town wasn't right."

"What…what about that travel thing you did? Won't that get us away?" Genevia asked desperately.

"It won't work," Frelati said, frustration creeping into his voice.

Genevia put her hands on her hips. "How do you know? You could at least give it a try."

"I can't." Frelati stopped pacing.

Genevia walked over and placed a hand on his arm. "This could save us. You need to try."

"I know that it could, but I can't do it," Frelati said, wrenching away from her and looking out at the endless row of ships before them. They were tiny in the distance now, but all too soon they wouldn't be.

"Why won't you do it?" Genevia walked back over to him.

Frelati's eyes never left the water. "You don't understand; I *can't*."

"You can't." Genevia shook her head.

"We're not near the portal."

"The portal?"

Frelati heaved a breath before explaining. "There are two ways to travel the way I did: a natural portal, which is the one I used on Wefleca, and a necklace, which…"

Frelati broke off when he remembered the necklace, and Genevia's hand went unconsciously to the locket around her neck. Frelati saw her fiddling with it.

"I wonder," he said, reaching out to finger the chain. "The necklace belongs to the royal family; Lenaia didn't have it…this…this might be it."

Genevia looked at her familiar little locket. "My necklace? You think this could transport us? It doesn't even open!"

Frelati examined the necklace closely. It did look like just another necklace, gold with a small emerald embedded in the front; still… the portal hadn't looked like much of anything either. "This could be it. You said you were found with it, which means Lenaia must have given it to you. The necklace has always remained in the royal family for protection, and I know she wasn't wearing a necklace in that prison. This must be it."

Genevia looked at him, startled, pulling the precious necklace from his fingers to wrap within her palm. "That's impossible."

"No, it's very possible," Frelati said. "That's the moving portal."

"Are you sure you don't have this wrong?" Genevia asked.

Frelati shook his head. "I'm right. That can get us out of here."

Genevia started to smile. "So, we can escape. Right?"

Frelati was taking a deep breath in exultation when a thought struck him. He blew out the breath on a word full of disgust, "Wrong."

"What? Why?"

Frelati's jaw clinched in frustration at himself.

Genevia pushed. "Tell me why."

Frelati looked away, but he answered her. "I forgot the words. The necklace only works when you say certain words. The natural portal is simple to travel through; you simply state where you wish to go. So when Lenaia was telling me about the necklace, I didn't pay much attention. I didn't think I'd be using that portal, and I didn't bother to remember the words. I know that sometime back it started being sung as an elfin children's song, but I never really learned those."

"Maybe you can…" she tried, but Frelati interrupted her.

"No, I can't."

"Oh." Genevia's face was the reflection of pure and utter hopelessness. "I guess that's it then."

She walked over to the bench and sat down, propping her chin in her hands. Frelati sighed, yet again running his fingers through his already thoroughly mussed hair, and went to sit down beside her.

He spoke softly. "This isn't over yet; we just have to think. We've been in worse situations than this and come through, haven't we? I was locked in a prison, and you got me out. If you could do that, then there's no way anything can stop us from finding some way out of this."

"It wasn't that great a prison; security was awful," Genevia argued half-heartedly. "Are you sure you don't remember any part of the words?"

"I'll see what I can think of; you go down and talk to the others. Tell them what we're up against and see if they have any ideas."

Genevia nodded and descended to the cabins.

"We're doomed," Frelati declared bitterly to Traynord.

Traynord shook his head. "Well, la', usu'ly I see the brigh' side o' things, bu' I agree with ye. Don' think we have too much o' a chance wi' this un."

Frelati's head sank into his hands. "My thoughts exactly."

Whispers carried on the wind all the way up the steep, rugged cliff side to brush through the grass overlooking the sea. Waves crashed steadily against the rocks below, and the beautiful melody of the sound blending with all of nature was a wonder to hear. Trees bent down to caress the ground's surface, and the flowers pushed their faces to the sun. All on the cliff side was harmony; just twenty miles out to sea, though, a struggle was about to occur.

A small boy lived on this cliff with his mother in a tiny hut that was in need of repair. He enjoyed playing on the cliff, but his mother was always worried for his safety. She was in the woods collecting mushrooms, and any other edible plants she could find, while her son went off to play a short ways away. This woman had always loved to sing. When she was a young girl, she had lived next door to an elfin couple—one of the few hideaways off Omhemalem free after Fezam's scourge—and they knew many unusual songs and rhymes. Her parents had allowed her to visit them often, and she quickly learned the tunes, even though she didn't understand the language.

Now, as she gathered food for her son and herself, she began to hum one of the songs. After a while, she began to sing the words too, gaining volume steadily. Her voice rang through the trees, a beautiful tune that just had to be shared. The trees passed the song to the wind, which carried it along its path out to the sea.

The ships were coming closer, and there wasn't too much time. Genevia was sitting on the bench again after getting no ideas from those below.

"Still nothing?" she tried again.

Frelati sighed and looked at her tiredly. The annoyance he would normally have felt had no place in this high stress situation. "No, I can't remember the words."

Genevia slumped before standing to walk back to the bow. She watched the waves roll and the light play with the water, but it didn't interest her. Instead, her gaze traveled to the long row of ships ahead. It wasn't a very encouraging sight. Then, the wind picked up, blowing her hair every which way, and with it came a beautiful voice.

> Ikam gsa wiif gi fezal juocl,
> Fuhs na gi Ien wagomegoim.
> Rli na gi Ien hera sezam,
> Is, keh na gi Meufa.

"Frelati, come listen to this. It sounds like that Elven language," Genevia said quietly. "I'm not sure where it's coming from though."

Frelati walked up to the bow. "I don't hear anything."

"Shhh, just listen. I think it's being carried by the wind."

Frelati stood quietly and heard a faint whisper of song that steadily grew louder. "Those words sound familiar. 'Open the door to travel quickly, rush me to my destination. Fly me to my safe haven, oh, pass me to Meufa.' Those are the words!"

He grinned in astonishment, not bothering to question the gift, and rushed down to the cabin to gather everyone on deck. In moments, they were all crowded in the middle with their luggage piled around them.

"Okay, now this will only work well if we travel a short distance. There are a lot of people that have to be transported, and it's already dangerous enough. Traynord, is Yappés still the closest land?"

Traynord scratched his chin. "I shoul' think so, la'."

"Okay, that's our destination. The ship can't be transported, so make sure all our supplies are up here and touching, actually touching, the group."

Everyone checked and double checked their belongings.

"Genevia." Frelati grabbed her arm. "I really don't know how that necklace works, so to err on the side of safety, I think it would be best if you said it. You have to be careful though; there can be no mispronunciations. Once it's started, you have to say every word right or, well, we could end up anywhere, if we make it through at all."

"Why should I say it? I don't even know Elven!" Genevia panicked.

"For all I know, that necklace stays with your family because you're the only ones who can operate it. The portal is open game, but the necklace…" He shrugged. "I really just don't want to risk it. I'll say the words, you repeat after me. We'll do a quick practice run first. Just trust yourself, okay? You're Alernoa; Elven is part of who you are."

Chapter Sixteen

Everyone was gathered at the bow of the ship, bags, food, books, and all other possessions surrounding them on all sides. They formed a tight circle, everything and everyone touching in some way. Nervous glances crossed from one to another and shaking hands clasped together for a sense of security.

"Is everyone touching what they want to take?" Frelati asked, looking at everyone in turn.

Each person nodded and dread fell on the small crowd as they awaited the dangerous task they faced.

"All right, Genevia, let's practice before we use the necklace." Frelati waited for her nod. "Repeat after me. Ikam gsa wiif gi fezal juocl."

"Ikam gsa wiif gi fezal juocl," Genevia repeated tentatively.

"Fuhs na gi Ien wagomegoim."

"Fuhs na gi Ien wagamemoig," Genevia stumbled.

"No, the last word is wagomegoim. Say it after me," Frelati prodded. "Wagomegoim."

"Wagomegoim," Genevia said, thinking the word over intently. "Fuhs na gi Ien wagomegoim."

"Good." Frelati smiled. "Rli na gi Ien hera sezam."

"Rli na gi Ien hera sezam."

"This is the last line. Is, keh na gi Yappés."

"Is, keh na gi Yappés."

Frelati drew in a deep breath, clearly anxious about what was to come. "Now, can I see your locket?"

Genevia undid the clasp, handing it over reluctantly. "You know, I still think that you should do it."

Frelati shot her a scowl. "Everyone needs to touch some part of the necklace; it should make the transition easier."

They complied, and Frelati looked to Genevia. Her face was white. "Ready?"

Genevia nodded slightly, and Frelati took one last look at everyone. "Everything you need is with you and touching you, right?"

Silent nods followed the question.

"Good." Frelati breathed deeply and turned to Genevia. "Repeat after me."

"Ikam gsa wiif gi fezal juocl."

The wind picked up as Genevia began, and the locket glowed a bright green.

"Fuhs na gi Ien wagomegoim."

Genevia's silky, brown hair began blowing around wildly with the wind as it rushed around their circle. The roar it caused made it difficult to hear, and the light that flowed from the necklace grew so bright that everyone had to shut their eyes against the glare.

"Rli na gi Ien hera sezam." Frelati had to shout to make himself heard over the wind.

The necklace grew hot to the touch, and Lela pulled her hand away.

"No," Frelati yelled. "You need to hold on, no matter how hot it gets."

Lela nodded slowly and returned her hand carefully. Genevia looked to Frelati expectantly for the last line.

"Is, keh na gi Yappés."

"Is, keh na gi Yappés!" Genevia yelled as the top of the locket that couldn't even open snapped back, releasing a ray of light that spread to surround the small group at the bow of the boat.

Wings, tiny voices, nothing made any sense. A roaring headache and fuzzy vision filled all thought. Then everything began to come into focus. A tree, a huge tree, a huge oak tree was looming high above.

Nothing was broken, just limp. Moans were heard; that couldn't be good. Lela, where was Lela?

Genevia sat up quickly. Too quickly. She gripped her head as a searing pain coursed through and made her temples throb.

"Ugh, what is wrong with me?" She winced.

Looking around, she saw all of her group sprawled haphazardly, none moving. Lela was right at her side. Frelati was on her left. All of her belongings and those of the others were strewn everywhere. The necklace was gripped tightly in her hand.

How did it get there? she wondered.

Then she looked in a wider range. Tiny, winged people were flying around. They were very colorful, tiny, flying people that looked at her with great curiosity but kept their distance. Then Frelati stirred and moaned.

"Oh, thank goodness," Genevia exclaimed, kneeling over him. "Wake up! There are tiny, flying people everywhere, and I need to know I'm not seeing things!"

Frelati sat up slowly and waited for his eyes to adjust before groaning a reply. "They're pixies."

Genevia heard a small whimper and turned to Lela.

"Lela, honey, are you all right?" she asked worriedly.

"Og sufh," Lela whispered. "Hurts."

"It's okay, sweetie," Genevia assured her, "you'll feel better in a bit."

Everyone else started coming to, and Genevia went around checking all of them. They seemed fine, except for throbbing heads. Then she crawled back over to Frelati.

"What do we do?" she whispered.

He rubbed his eyes and stood. He wobbled for a bit, trying to find his balance before sitting back down again with a thump.

"Don't try to stand up yet," he warned as he gripped his head. "It makes things worse, which is surprisingly possible."

"Okay, but what do we do?" Genevia pushed.

Frelati looked at her, not understanding the point of the question. "Talk to them."

He turned to face a tight group of pixies. "Do you have any medicine for headaches?"

The tiny creatures looked at each other before flying off.

Genevia turned to Frelati in astonishment. "You scared them."

"No, I didn't," Frelati grumbled. "They're getting medicine."

He was right. They flew back with four flowers. It took five pixies to carry one. They deposited one flower on Genevia and Frelati, one on Jezzie and Asben, one on Jackson and Traynord, and the last on Lela, who had a peculiar shadow lying beside her.

Genevia looked at the flower in confusion before a pixie flew up to her ear.

The little pixie pushed a strand of hair back from Genevia's ear and spoke. "Drink the nectar, but not all of it. A little goes a long way."

The little pixie had a high pitched but sweet voice. It sounded like small chimes carried on a breeze. Genevia followed her instructions and handed the flower to Frelati.

"It won't kill us, will it?" she asked no one in particular.

The little pixie tinkled a laugh and spoke in Genevia's ear again. "No, it helps. Makes you tingle all over."

Just then, Genevia felt a hot, yet pleasant tingling sensation rise up from her toes to the tip of her head. She turned to look at the pink pixie flying next to her face.

"You're right." She laughed in astonishment.

The little pixie doubled over in tinkling laughter, falling onto Genevia's shoulder.

"You're funny," she said, standing on tiptoe to reach Genevia's ear.

Just then a deep blue, elderly pixie flew up to the pink one.

"Treenix!" the blue pixie commanded. "Get away from the elf."

"Papa," the pink pixie whined. "I'm not doing anything."

"Go!" the blue pixie ordered, pointing toward the oak tree.

Treenix stamped her little foot on Genevia's shoulder and crossed her arms. "You never let me do anything fun!"

Then she flew off with a pink trail burning behind her.

The blue pixie turned to Genevia and placed her under an icy stare. "What are you doing on my island?"

Genevia's startled eyes found Frelati's. "Frelati, where are we, and what did we do?"

"This is Yappés, right?" Frelati asked the blue pixie.

"Yes, now, what are you doing here?" the blue pixie demanded.

"Who are you?" Genevia asked.

The pixie looked at her in astonishment. "You…you do not know who I am? I am King Flix. Who are you, and what do you want with my island?"

"We're travelers trying to reach Azol to defeat Fezam. This is Alernoa, Princess of the Elves, and I am Frelati. We all," Frelati said, motioning to everyone lying in the grass around him. "…need your protection for a little while, if you are willing."

King Flix flew up to Genevia and examined her closely. "I thought you were dead."

"We all did," Frelati cut in. "That was what King Nalofré and Queen Lenaia wanted us to think, for her safety."

"For the moment, I'll pretend to believe you," King Flix said suspiciously. "But how is it that humans, elves, and a dreamer are all traveling together? Isn't it a custom of the elves to stay away from other creatures? And Dreamers do not amicably consort with other races."

Frelati looked around at the group. "A dreamer? We don't…"

He saw Lela speaking with a shadow. A dreamer.

"Lela," he asked gently. "How long has the dreamer been traveling with us?"

Lela crawled to Frelati and plopped into his lap with a smile. "Dayze on…ship."

"Dayze? That's her name?" Frelati asked.

Lela nodded. "We…play."

Frelati looked over to the shadow, which began to shrink. "Dayze, can you come over here, please?"

Dayze drifted over slowly and settled on the ground a short ways from Frelati.

"How long have you been traveling with us?"

"I followed you from the woods," her lullaby voice explained. "I was cut off from my family of dreamers, Doze. I needed another family, and after watching you, I thought you'd be perfect. Please don't make me leave; I need a family. I can stay, can't I?"

Frelati looked uncomfortable with the idea, but Genevia was all for it. "Of course you can, sweetie. Doesn't everyone agree?"

Genevia looked around the group and saw each nod in turn. Jezzie was the most enthusiastic.

"Well, I never thought I'd see the day! A dreamer; right here. Come here darlin' an' let me look atcha."

As Dayze drifted over, the King cleared his throat. "Back to the issue. Explain."

"Well," Frelati began, not entirely certain what he was explaining. "I don't exactly…"

Genevia interrupted him. "It makes sense, doesn't it? We are going to overthrow the evil King and save Tiweln, so isn't it understandable to have a member of each race traveling with us? I mean, I know this isn't every race, but the unity provided reaches out to encompass the whole of Tiweln's creatures."

Frelati looked like he was about to argue with her, but she shot him a look to shut him up. She was not going to leave a child to fend for herself, even if inviting Dayze made it a little more difficult to travel. However, there was no need for the pixie king to see dissension in their group.

King Flix thought this over.

"I suppose that makes sense." King Flix looked at each of them closely before nodding and smiling. "Well, then, it is pixie tradition to throw a welcome party to all newcomers on the island. Tonight, we will feast, and you will be my guests of honor."

King Flix flew up in a burst of blue sparks, and immediately six pixies came to join him.

"I need rooms made ready for the travelers. Give orders to the cooks of the food that must be prepared. Someone, tell my daughter to go to the throne room. I need to speak with her."

The pixies flew off, a different stream of color following each. Genevia watched in awe before making eye contact with Frelati.

"Ummm, what do we do now?" she asked.

"Well, right now, we need to discuss Dayze. After that…we wait until the feast."

"People don't just disappear. They searched the water thoroughly, even beneath the surface?"

"Um...I suppose so, sire," a nervous messenger stuttered, avoiding the red, soulless eyes drilling into him.

He had never been in Fezam's presence before and sincerely hoped he would never have to return. The fury and hatred that radiated from this being in ever-present waves was insufferable, made all the more so by the darkness surrounding his castle and cradled within this very room.

"Are you certain this information is correct? You did not hear wrong?" the slippery voice said with an eerie, deadly calm quality.

"I...um...yes, that's what the captain told me, but I...I don't know for sure, sire." The messenger returned his gaze to the floor.

Immediately following his stumbling answer, the back doors blew open to allow a huge soldier entrance.

"Is there a reason behind your sudden entrance that is important enough to save your life?" he asked softly.

"The interrogation didn't yield any information helpful to discovering the whereabouts of Alernoa," the soldier said. His eyes remained glued to the floor.

"Mmm, that's unfortunate for you," Fezam stated calmly, examining an exquisite onyx ring on his right hand. "Tell me, was the King or Queen in possession of a necklace?"

"Sir?" the soldier asked uncertainly.

Fezam's eyes blazed. "In the future, learn to listen the first time I bless you with my speech. Was Queen Lenaia or King Nalofré in possession of a necklace?"

"I...I don't recall."

"Well, it would be best for you if you did suddenly recall." The red gaze glared at the trembling soldier.

The soldier, though still clearly frightened, turned thoughtful before replying. "Neither was wearing a necklace."

"Are you certain?" Fezam leaned forward, a look of intensity replacing the bored one of a moment before.

The solder nodded. "Yes, sire. I am certain."

Fezam stared forward at nothing in particular as he deliberated this notion, but soon the fidgeting of the messenger caught his attention. He scowled.

"You are useless. What need have we of a messenger who relays incorrect information?" An evil smile crept across Fezam's face as he gave his deadly order. "Kill him."

The pixies played tiny flutes and harps, creating a lovely melody to which many others danced. A large bonfire had been built in a deep pit, and the guests of honor were heating food against it while pixies flew in their wild, yet organized flurry all around the orange, yellow, and red blaze. Colors blended against the night sky and made the stars seem dim in comparison. Blue, purple, pink, green, yellow, orange, and red of all hues and shades and blends meshed together as the pixies welcomed the travelers to their island.

Genevia laughed happily, completely engrossed in the ceremony.

"It's wonderful, isn't it?" she said in a hushed voice to Frelati, who sat beside her.

"Um-hmm, it's nice," he agreed.

Treenix broke from the frolicking pixies to sit upon Genevia's shoulder, her little feet steadily bumping Genevia's shoulder as she swung her legs back and forth. "So how do you like the feast?"

Genevia grinned. "It's more like a dance, isn't it?"

The pixie laughed. "It's a dinner show! We dance in all our color while you eat your food!"

"I hadn't thought of it that way!" Genevia laughed, and Treenix flew off to join the other pixies.

Frelati and Genevia sat in silence for a while, listening to the music and enjoying the dances. It was absolutely beautiful, like a living rainbow gleaming across the night sky.

Genevia turned to smile at Frelati in pure happiness.

Feeling her gaze, he turned to look at her. "What?"

"Have you ever seen anything more beautiful?" she asked, her eyes locking with his.

It took Frelati a moment to find his voice. "No."

Her gaze held his a moment longer before landing on Lela, who had her head cradled in Frelati's lap.

Frelati looked down as well and brushed back some of the girl's hair. "Lela fell asleep. We need to get her to bed. Isn't she sharing a room with you?"

Genevia grimaced in self-admonishment. "I should have thought of that sooner. Will you carry her to our room? I'll get Dayze."

Frelati nodded, gently scooping Lela into his arms, and waited as Dayze glided over to them from Jezzie's side. Then the four of them left the festivities behind them to be enveloped by the darkness separating them from the big oak.

They walked in silence until they came to Genevia's room. Frelati ducked inside after Genevia and laid Lela on the bed beside Dayze, covering both with a blanket. He was quiet for a bit as he looked down on the sleeping girls. Genevia laid a hand on his arm. "They're precious, aren't they?"

Frelati glanced at her hand, then at her face, before looking down at the floor. "Yeah…we should probably let them sleep."

Genevia chuckled softly as she followed him out of the room. "Fine, don't admit it, but you aren't fooling anyone."

Frelati scowled. "Let's just go back to the feast."

With a laugh, Genevia looped her arm through his as they walked back to join the festivities.

Chapter Seventeen

"That was a nice feast last night," Genevia remarked. "I felt really welcome."

"I think that was the goal," Frelati answered.

They were walking in the woods a short way from the large oak. In front of them, intermittently, sparks of color would flash through the trees as pixies flew around to forage. The elves' footsteps were silent as the pine straw and moss cradled their feet, and light filtered through the leaves above to warm their skin and reveal all the wonderful sights on the island.

"It's beautiful here. You know, it's peaceful and quiet and, well, it's just…nice," Genevia finished lamely.

Frelati smothered a smile and kept walking.

"You've been really quiet lately, you know?" Genevia said, trying to pull Frelati into a conversation.

"I suppose." Frelati shrugged.

"Is it something I've done? 'Cause you haven't been talking to me either, and you usually do."

"No, it's not you." Frelati paused before deciding to elaborate. "Large groups of people make me uncomfortable. It's difficult to predict the behavior of one when he's surrounded by many. I don't care for uncertainty."

"Oh." Genevia was quiet for a while.

They walked together in silence. It was afternoon, not too hot, and not too cold. The sun gently glistened through the trees, creating a wild, light and dark mosaic on the forest floor. Genevia was studying this natural art when she saw a multicolored animal running straight toward her. It was small and quick, stopping just before Genevia and jumping against her leg.

Genevia squatted down, allowing the little animal to climb up into her arms. "Hey, little guy!"

The small animal was maybe three hands in size, and it was extremely furry. Its rainbow snout sniffed at Genevia rapidly to take in her scent.

"What is he?" Genevia asked, turning her face up to Frelati.

Frelati was surprised by the sudden occurrence but more so with the animal. "It's a lefnode, but they don't usually run up to other creatures. They're supposed to be smarter than that."

"He's so cute." Genevia picked him up. "Isn't he cute?"

Frelati looked closely at the animal. "He's a rainbow lefnode, very rare. There are only a handful of them, if that."

"Really? Can I keep him?" Genevia asked.

"No," Frelati said firmly, feeling terrible as her face fell but standing firm regardless. "We cannot bring an animal with us. You know that as well as I do."

"But…" Genevia started to protest before common sense replaced her selfish desire. She sighed. "I know."

She set the little lefnode on the ground and gave it a short pat on the head. "Let's go, quickly. I can't bear to see the little thing sitting all by himself."

Frelati put an arm around her, and they walked back toward the large oak. The little lefnode sat on the pine straw, his head cocked, and his little stump of a tail swishing back and forth. He sniffed the air one last time, reminding himself of Genevia's scent. Then he started off at a slow shuffle, sniffing the ground and following Genevia's trail.

"Ready to go?" Frelati asked Genevia the next morning.

"Ready when you are," she answered.

"All right everybody, you have everything you need? We aren't coming back."

Murmured yesses and short nods accompanied his statement.

"Everyone crowd around. We have to get to the dwarf undergrounds on Yima Olem. They can get us a boat so we can continue to Azol. Ready, Genevia?" Frelati asked.

Genevia swallowed. "Yes."

Genevia brought out her necklace, and everyone took hold. She repeated after Frelati, just as before. On the last line, a colorful ball of fur burst across the space separating it from the group. It reached the bags, just barely making contact, as Genevia said her last word. A blinding flash spread out, and as it died, emptiness met all the pixies' eyes.

Moaning sounded throughout the barren landscape.

Frelati sat up slowly, looking around at the group. "Everyone here? Do you have everything?"

After a brief search, his questions were affirmed. Genevia crawled over to her bag and took out the flowers that had brought relief after the first trip. She took a sip and passed it around. Then she went back to her bag.

"Ahh." She jumped back in astonishment. "What are you doing here?"

All eyes were on Genevia and a colorful bundle of fur.

"He followed you?" Frelati exclaimed.

Lela and Dayze moved over to play with the little lefnode, and Genevia laughed happily as the little animal sniffed her all over, its whole body quivering with joy.

Genevia turned to Frelati, grinning from ear to ear. "Isn't he wonderful? He's so clever!"

Frelati sighed, looking to the sky with a shake of the head, but by the time he returned his gaze to Genevia, he was resigned to the inevitable ninth member of their group, if not particularly pleased. "All right, so we have another mouth to feed. What do we call him?"

Genevia picked up the little fellow and examined him minutely.

"Quinsnap," she said nodding. "Yes, that's it. Your name is Quinsnap."

"Quinsnap?" Frelati repeated with a questioning look.

Genevia shrugged and gave a slightly embarrassed laugh. "You know that really colorful flower that you saw around my house? The Kinns Nelap? When I was little, I couldn't say it, so I called it a quinsnap. This little fellow reminds me of that flower."

Frelati looked away to hide a smile.

Lela held out her little arms. "Hold…him, Mama?"

"Be careful," she warned, placing Quinsnap gently in Lela's arms. The girls instantly began fretting over the small creature. Then she turned to Frelati with an apologetic smile. "I suppose, maybe, I shouldn't have loved on him so much. I know you said we didn't need to take him with us."

Frelati grimaced before releasing a frustrated sigh.

"Just what I needed," he muttered before pointing a finger at Genevia and giving her a stern look. "But we are not catering to the animal. It keeps up or it gets left behind."

Genevia grinned. "All right then, let's see if we can find us some dwarves."

"Dayze, stop it. Where are you?"

Whispered laughter flowed through the field of multicolored flowers and giant willow trees. The vines brushed the ground beside Lela's feet, and the wind lifted her hair to dance with its wild, whipping movements. The grass kissed her ankles, and the gently sloping field of flowers brushed the stream's edge for nourishment. The sun shone down upon the dewy surfaces all around Lela, and as the wind played its encore along the grasses' edges, Lela added her voice to the sweet music.

"Dayze, I'm trying to find Quinsnap. Stop it!" she exclaimed in Elven.

Dayze's laughter filtered into the clearing once again. "Oh, but isn't this place so much better than where we are?"

She materialized beside Lela as she answered. "Yes, it's better, but we have to find Quinsnap. That's our job."

"Can't we just stay here for a little longer?" Dayze pouted.

"No, now let me out."

Dayze drifted with the wind along the gentle slope and rested on the water's surface. "Oh, come on, the water's great! Let's stay here until someone calls for us."

"I'm gonna tell Mama if you don't let me out right now!" Lela stomped her foot and put her balled fists on her hips.

Dayze immediately sat upright, and the façade disappeared. Gone were the flowers, replaced by struggling twigs trying vainly to become trees. Gone were the great weeping willows as they formed into bare rock. The water receded into a patch of soft sand among the barren rocky landscape. The cooling wind changed its gentle touch to a piercing cold that played discord music along Yima Olem's surface.

"Don't tell Mama, please," Dayze begged. "I won't do it again, not without you wanting me to, and we can go find Quinsnap right now. Just don't tell Mama."

Lela walked over to Dayze and slung an arm around her shadowy shoulders. "I won't tell. We're sisters, and we have to stick together. Let's find Quinsnap."

Dayze smiled. "Thanks."

Lela cupped her hands around her mouth and yelled. "Quinsnap! Come here, Quinsnap!"

"Quinsnap!" Dayze joined in. "There he is!"

The little rainbow bundle of fur came running for them, practically flying over the dusty ground. He stopped just before the girls and then turned around, rapidly sniffing the air.

"What is it, Quinsnap?" Lela asked, kneeling down to massage his head. "What do you think is wrong?"

Dayze dropped to her knees as well and shook her head. "I don't know."

Lifting her face, Lela gasped as her eyes caught sight of the horizon. "What's that?"

Dayze looked up as well and shivered.

"I don't know, but it doesn't look good. Go tell Mama and Papa," she said worriedly. "They're coming fast. I-I'll make them think they're in a different place until you come back."

Lela hugged Quinsnap against her, tugging on Dayze's arm. "Come with me. I'm scared to go by myself, and I don't want to leave you. Besides, we're supposed to stay together. If they catch up, then you can put them in a different place, okay?"

"Okay," Dayze agreed in relief.

They took off running, a group of unknown horror behind them and a distance that seemed far too long stretching out in front of them.

"I can't do this."

Frelati expelled an exasperated sigh and hung his head before looking back at Genevia. She was standing hands on hips, feet apart, and wearing a look of pure obstinacy. Frelati rubbed his forehead with a hand.

"You made a tree spring up from nothing when you weren't even trying. Clearly you are capable of growing a flower when you do try." Frelati's frustration mixed with his words, despite his efforts to calm himself.

"Frelati, I can not—and I stress *not*—do this. I don't even know how I made that tree, so how am I supposed to do this?" Genevia gave an exaggerated huff. Hours of practice with no results were quite trying.

"Okay then." Frelati took in a deep breath and counted to ten. "What do I have to do to get you to try again?"

Genevia's face transformed instantly from full stubbornness to complete mischief. She grinned, and Frelati angled a glance her way warily.

"What?"

Genevia looked at the ground with an air of innocence. "What are you so worried about? I'm not gonna ask you to do anything difficult. I will try my hardest to make a flower grow if you will just admit that you like me. That's all I want."

Frelati threw his head back and released a moan. "Will you just give it up? You have been at this for two days, Alernoa, and I think it's time that you grow up and stop."

"Well, you see, I would, but there's this word that keeps popping up every time I mention it. Let's see if I can remember what it was. Hmmm…" Genevia tapped her chin and looked to the sky in mock thought. "I think it starts with an A and has something to do with a princess. Oh, I know what it is!"

She stopped and looked Frelati straight in the eye, her humor gone. "Alernoa. Every single time I mention anything about you and me, you always throw that name out. It's like a shield to you, like you have to remind yourself who you think I really am."

"Genevia…" Frelati sighed.

"See," she interrupted him. "That's my name. That's what you call me, not Alernoa. I am Genevia."

"No," Frelati cut in. "You grew up thinking you were Genevia, but you aren't. You are Alernoa, an Elfin princess. It's time you understood that, and high time I remembered it."

Genevia growled in frustration. "I am who I grew up being. I know no differently. To me, I'm Genevia, and that's who I'll always really be. You grew up without parents, so you grew up thinking you were an orphan. If all of a sudden you're parents popped up and claimed you, it wouldn't change that. You still would have grown up an orphan, and you would still think of yourself as one. You can't change who you were. It will always be a part of you, and quite frankly, I like who I am and who I was, and I plan to stay that way."

Frelati looked at her long and hard before he spoke up. "You might not be able to change the way you grew up or who you were, but you also can't change your responsibilities and your position in life now. You are an Elfin princess, and that won't change, no matter how hard you try to act otherwise."

"That doesn't matter. I still feel the same about everything. I'm not all high and mighty. I don't look down on you because you're not a prince, so why do you have to plant this huge chasm between us?"

Frelati turned away from her. "It may not matter to you, but it matters to me, and it will matter to your parents. I'm…it just wouldn't be good for you."

Genevia let out her exasperation in a huff and threw up her hands. She paced a bit before speaking, mostly to herself but loud enough for Frelati to hear.

"All I asked was that you say you liked me; just admit the truth. That's all I wanted." She turned to look at him and punctuate her point by holding her hands out to the side. "Not that hard."

"It's not the truth," Frelati argued.

"Yeah, you just keep trying to convince yourself of that. I know it's true because if it wasn't you wouldn't remind yourself who I am every time I broach the subject," Genevia said.

"Why are you still pursuing this? It just complicates things," Frelati accused.

Genevia took a step closer to him. "The only one complicating things is you. Lies always complicate things."

Frelati crossed his arms, shooting an annoyed and very stubborn look her way. Genevia's lips tightened.

"Fine, don't admit it. Keep lying to yourself because, I can assure you, you're the only one that believes it." Genevia knelt down to touch the parched earth with her forefinger before looking up at Frelati. "If a flower grows right here in this spot, you owe me a declaration. I deserve that at the very least."

Frelati snorted in disbelief. "*You* don't even believe you can do it, so why should *I*?"

Genevia smiled and lifted her finger. "Because I now have motivation, and apparently it works."

Frelati looked to the ground. As Genevia slowly lifted her finger from the parched earth, grass began to grow in the place she had once touched, and nestled within the grass was a single red rose. Frelati couldn't stop the grin spreading across his face.

"I told you you could do it," he said smugly.

Genevia looked at her fingernails in a flippant manner. "So, what was it you wanted to tell me?"

Frelati glanced at her in suspicion. "You knew all along that you could do it; you just wanted to try to get a confession out of me."

"So you admit you have something to confess?" Genevia flashed him a triumphant grin.

"I admit nothing. I just know you're convinced there is."

"Ah, sad, sad, sad." Genevia shook her head. "Still in denial, and after I worked so hard to grow you a flower…in a desert, no less."

"Fine." Frelati huffed, taking an obnoxiously long time before he muttered something unintelligible under his breath.

"I'm sorry, could you speak up? I didn't quite catch that."

Frelati looked up in aggravation, but then his expression changed to one of concern as he looked past Genevia. She turned slowly.

"Mama! Papa! Mama, Mama!" Lela and Dayze were hurtling toward them, yelling at the top of their lungs.

Lela jumped into Frelati's arms instantly, and Frelati held her close after feeling her frightened shivers, the little lefnode sniffing his neck between them. Dayze hugged Genevia's legs in a death grip and shoveled her face into her skirt. Genevia squatted down beside her and brushed back her shadowed wisps of hair, barely able to make out the tears that streaked down her cheeks.

"What's the matter, baby? What is it?" she asked soothingly despite her sudden alarm.

Dayze just hid her face in Genevia's shoulder and burst into tears, so Lela began to explain.

"Hinasomt oh cinomt. Gsab'fa ergaf uh."

Frelati translated for Genevia. "She said, 'Something is coming. They're after us.'"

"Who's they?"

"I…" Frelati turned to the hysterical child in his arms, "Dsi'h gsab, daagsaef?"

Lela leaned back before speaking rapidly. "Ligh ir nam, yot emw im sifhah, efa cinomt rehg. Ligh ir wuhg emw ballomt. Wewwa, Ie'n hacefaw."

Lela buried her face in his shoulder, and he rubbed her back reassuringly. "Genevia, we need to get to camp, now. There's a troop of men coming. I don't know if we can hold them off, but we need some type of defense. Come on."

Genevia scooped Dayze into her arms as she and Frelati ran into camp.

"We have to get everything together as quickly as possible. Find whatever weapons we have. We may be facing a fight. There are men coming this way on horseback, fast."

The quiet camp burst into activity. Genevia and Frelati set Dayze and Lela at the center of the whirlwind with Quinsnap still held securely in Lela's arms.

"Lela, Dayze, be good and keep Quinsnap with you at all times." Genevia turned and yelled for Jezzie, who rushed over with a worried expression. "Jezzie, keep an eye on the girls and Quinsnap. Girls, listen to Jezzie, and do exactly as anyone tells you, okay?"

They both nodded solemnly.

"Good girls." Genevia swiped a kiss across each cheek and smiled before turning to meet Frelati.

"Genevia, I'm about to ask a huge favor." Frelati grasped her forearms tightly to get her full attention. "I need you to build high earthen walls around our camp, okay?"

"Frelati," Genevia cried, worry heightened in her eyes. "I can't do that."

"Genevia, you can. I know you can." Frelati paused momentarily in indecision before finally saying, "I may like you."

He released her and turned to jog over to Traynord but spun around quickly. "Is that enough motivation?"

Genevia smiled, nodded, and closed her eyes. When she opened them, Frelati could see a set determination in her eyes. He smiled encouragingly as his gaze locked with hers. "You can do it."

Genevia tossed her hair over her shoulder. "Of course I can."

As she turned to stare at the flat, barren ground in front of her, Frelati made plans with Traynord.

"Are these all the weapons?" Frelati motioned to the small mound in dismay.

"Aye." Traynord chuckled, a look of complete ease on his face.

Frelati stared at him in bewilderment. "There are men riding toward us, and we have absolutely no defense against them. How can you not be worried?"

"Nah, with you an' Genevia, we'll ge' through." Traynord waved off Frelati's understandable unease. "I'm jus' expectan', la', jus' expectan'."

"Expectant for what exactly? Total annihilation or capture?"

Traynord guffawed. "The two a ye have ye' ta le' me down, la'. I have faith in ya. Coul' be a couple scrapes, but i's gonna be a fun ride, la', with ye an' yer li'l lassie as companions, a fun ride. Tha' is."

Chapter Eighteen

"Get up!" a burly soldier yelled in disgust as two other men in uniform dragged Lenaia and Nalofré to their feet unceremoniously. "Follow me."

The royal couple was paraded down the aisle, watching as door after door filled with more of their people slid past them. Although more light permeated this part of the dungeon, it was nothing compared to the shock of light that hit King Nalofré and Queen Lenaia as the door opened to the outside world.

They had not been led this way since they first arrived, and the fact that they were now increased their sense of dread. The castle rose before them, five stories high, completely made of dark stone and mortar. It was a terrifying sight to behold; the volcano that rose behind it saying more clearly than words ever could that this was a place of evil.

"What do you think they will do?" Lenaia whispered to Nalofré in Elven.

He gripped her hand tighter. "I don't know."

The lead guard turned abruptly. "Stop muttering that gibberish. No speaking until you're before Fezam."

Lenaia lifted her worried eyes to meet her husband's. Although his tense body revealed his anxiety, his eyes held hers with warmth and reassurance. *It will be all right*, they seemed to tell her, and she smiled weakly in return.

They were pushed along the castle's wide hallway and shoved into a small room with only a table and three chairs standing in the middle.

"Stay put; Fezam will grace you with his presence in a moment." The soldier looked at them in disgust before leaving.

The door slammed shut, a hollow ring sounding throughout the room. Lenaia flinched at the loud sound and shrank further into Nalofré's embrace as he settled them both into two chairs. He whispered lovingly to calm her until her shaking began to stop. Then she lifted her head from his shoulder, her vivid green eyes filled with sorrow as she discovered what prison had done to his once athletic frame and smiling face.

He was filled with just as much sorrow as he took in her appearance. Her face was gaunt, her skin—once a beautiful, golden hue—was pale, and she was much too thin. Tears pooled in her eyes, and Nalofré wished he could put the once mischievous gleam back into them.

"What do you think he wants? Do you think he's found Alernoa?" she asked, her voice just barely short of hysterical.

"No, darling," Nalofré said calmly, smoothing back her hair. "This is probably just another of his tactics to get us to disclose her location."

"What if he has found her, though? What would he do?"

"We don't need to worry about that. Our little girl can handle herself, and she has Frelati with her. It will be all right."

"What if Frelati didn't find her?"

Nalofré smiled. "You are not putting enough faith in that boy."

"I suppose." Lenaia's face softened as she thought of him before worry clouded her eyes again. "But, what if Alernoa will have absolutely nothing to do with him?"

"Then I suppose she'll be in for a big surprise when she finds out she's betrothed to him." Nalofré chuckled.

That brought a smile to Lenaia's face, but she had no time to respond as the door flew open to reveal a ghastly figure. The room grew cold, and a sense of self-consciousness descended upon the King and Queen as red eyes scanned them both. Nalofré's stature straightened and his arm tightened about his wife. His eyes grew hard, and all sense of humor fled.

"Forgive me if I don't stand. My recent accommodations took the strength right out of me," he said with cold sarcasm.

Fezam sneered and proceeded into the room, sitting before them and motioning for the door to close. After the hinges stopped singing their creaky music, silence descended, and he sat immobile for an interminable amount of time as he attempted to stare down each in turn.

Although Lenaia refused to meet his unearthly gaze, she admired her husband for meeting those piercing eyes head on. And even though Nalofré was sorely tempted to lower his lashes and inquire as to this sudden summons, he refrained and earned a flash of admiration from Fezam before it was smothered.

"I suppose you are wondering why you are here." Fezam eased out his oily words.

Nalofré examined his hand before speaking. "The thought had crossed my mind."

Fezam's eyes flashed danger and anger. "Respect is something I demand, not suggest."

Nalofré feigned innocence. "Of course you do, why ever would you think you would need to inform me of this?"

"Your wife looks as if she needs your strength. It would be a shame to leave her alone, don't you think?" Fezam reached out to trace a finger down Lenaia's cheek before turning evil eyes upon Nalofré.

The Queen recoiled from his frigid touch. Nalofré suddenly grew silent and meek, worry for his wife surpassing anger at this unwelcome interrogator. Fezam smiled in triumph as he spied a weakness in the Elfin King. This he could use to his advantage.

Genevia took a deep breath, closing her eyes to the world around her. "I can do this. I can do this."

After another deep breath, Genevia opened her eyes and lifted her arms, focusing all her energy on building an earthen wall.

"Okay, now, lift," she muttered to herself. "Move."

The earth shifted beneath her. "Okay, wrong part. Let's try again."

She dropped her hands before lifting them with more pointed focus on her task. Soon a wave of earth began to roll toward her.

"Yes, keep coming, keep coming."

In little time, she had a waist high mound. "All right, now, maybe if I could lift it from underneath...maybe?"

She sat contemplating for a bit before lifting her arms slowly. The mound grew, following her hands until it towered above her head.

"Yes! I did it!" she cried, jumping excitedly.

Jackson walked up behind her. "That's great!"

Genevia whirled around. "Isn't it? It took me a little while, but I got it!"

"Yeah, really, that's good work," Jackson said with a smile before looking around at all the open space surrounding the rather slender mound. "But I don't think that'll stop them much."

Genevia turned in a circle, realizing the ineffectiveness of her mound. It still left their sides and back fully open to attack. Her face fell before she turned back to Jackson.

"Joy kill," she muttered to him, her eyes holding a teasing glint. "Go work on whatever it is your supposed to be doing and let me finish."

Jackson grinned and walked off. Surprisingly, everything came together quickly after that; it took only ten minutes for the entire camp to be surrounded. She was exhausted though.

Frelati came up behind her after she finished the last stretch, and she leaned against him, her legs growing weaker.

"You did a nice job," Frelati commented.

Genevia nodded, her eyelids fluttering closed. "Are they here yet?"

Her weak voice caught Frelati's attention. He spun her around to face him. "Are you all right?"

She nodded, her eyes still closed.

"I'm just a bit tired is all." She stifled a yawn.

Frelati sighed, examining her closely as she leaned more and more heavily against him.

"Great, I overworked you." He groaned. "How could I not think of that?"

Genevia's knees buckled, and Frelati swung her up into his arms before she could hit the ground.

"I'm going to lay you down in the tent. You need to sleep, okay? Don't worry about the riders." His only response was a light nod and half-hearted mumble.

He carried her back to the tent and lowered her onto a blanket inside. "I'm going to get Lela and Dayze to stay in here with you, okay?"

This time he got no reaction. Genevia had already descended into a deep sleep. Frelati ran a hand through his hair.

"Perfect." His worry bled through with his words. "Please don't die on me."

He walked out of the tent and gathered Lela and Dayze. "I need you girls to watch your mama. She's really tired from making the walls, so don't wake her. If she does anything unusual, or if you get scared, just come get me, okay? Keep Quinsnap in the tent with you."

Both girls nodded and ducked into the tent. Frelati took one last look at Genevia before joining Traynord to discuss the coming confrontation.

"Why would I do anything for you, much less something that would harm my daughter?" King Nalofré demanded with a disgusted look.

Fezam was not in the least perturbed. "I just thought that the safety of your wife was important to you."

King Nalofré's gaze had been narrowed, but at the threat, his eyes widened, revealing panic, which he quickly replaced with an unreadable expression. The flicker of distress did not elude Fezam's observant scrutiny, though.

"I see you recognize the value of persuasion. I also assume that you understand the consequences if you choose to defy my order," Fezam stated calmly, a sinister ring in his voice. Although Fezam's amusement in his trap was enough to send the elf's blood to boiling, he contained his anger for fear his wife would ultimately pay the price. She had been removed from the room by two huge soldiers just moments before Fezam issued his bargain.

"I would like to learn the location of your daughter. Miraculously, she has been successful in eluding me, but I grow tired of the chase. I need you to enter her dreams and learn her location, or, failing that, send her to a new location of my choice."

Fezam had said this behind steepled fingers, his eyes captivating and calculating. Nalofré had flatly refused, but that was before he had learned of the danger facing Lenaia should he proceed in that frame of mind.

King Nalofré lowered his angry gaze and sighed. Unbeknownst to him, Fezam allowed the flicker of a triumphant smile to grace his twisted features before it returned to its neutral norm.

"I am glad you see things my way," Fezam said softly. "This will be quite simple really, but I must warn you not to pull any trickery. Do this quickly but efficiently. Do we have an understanding?"

Nalofré nodded. Fezam bowed his head and reached out a hand. The air before it turned black as night as shadow spilled from his palm.

"Alernoa," Fezam muttered, and the dark air swirled like a raincloud in the sky.

Once again, Fezam muttered Alernoa's name. Immediately following, the black cloud began to writhe, a window opening at its center and beginning to widen. Soon the darkness had withdrawn to form a thin, oval ring around a looking glass that revealed a sleeping young elf. Nalofré sucked in his breathe quickly at the sight of her.

"Is that...?" His voice failed him.

Fezam's curious gaze watched the play of emotions running across his face. "That would be your daughter, Alernoa."

Nalofré reached tentative fingers out to touch the hazy surface that revealed his child's sleeping figure. He said nothing, not trusting his voice were he to speak. He felt the prick of tears as he gazed upon the beauty that his infant daughter had grown into.

"She looks so like her mother," he finally whispered. "I had wondered if ever I was to see who she would become."

Fezam, impatient for his task to be completed, cleared his throat. "Now you have seen her; get on with your task."

Nalofré looked up suddenly, surprised to hear annoyance flavoring Fezam's words. Then his gaze returned to his precious daughter.

He could not give her over to Fezam. With a new determination in his eyes, Nalofré met the expectant gaze of his tormentor.

"No."

Not a muscle moved in Fezam's face, and even his eyes were shuttered from emotion. "Guards, bring Lenaia."

Worry flitted in Nalofré's eyes, but he remained firm. Once his wife entered the room, though, his resolve began to disappear. He watched as the guard roughly jerked his wife around and sprang to his feet in outrage, his chair falling to the floor with a loud smack, at a soft, protesting cry from Lenaia at the cruel treatment.

"Return to your seat," Fezam ordered, and Nalofré slowly righted the chair and sat down. "Good. Now, I ask again for you to perform your task."

Chapter Nineteen

As she was led inside, Lenaia glanced about the room, pausing only momentarily on the odd, dark-rimmed oval before focusing on her husband's face. He was distressed, but it seemed different, more intense now. White-hot anger burned in his eyes—an anger she had never seen mar his peaceful face.

The soldier jerked her to the center of the room, jarring her bones and causing a cry to escape her lips. She heard chair legs scraping against the cold, stone floor before the smack that signaled its collapse and glanced up to see Nalofré. His hands were fisted at his sides, his mouth stretched in a grim line, and a wish of death blazed toward the soldier.

"Return to your seat," the cold, calculating voice at the other side of the table ordered. After Nalofré released his tense muscles enough to pick up the chair and settle into it, Fezam continued. "Good. Now, I ask again for you to perform your task."

Nalofré hung his head, heated anger still radiating from his whole being. Then he lifted his head to the smoky oval hovering before him. She watched as his anger changed to sorrow, and a softness spread across his features as he beheld the image revealed by the shadow-ringed orb.

Lenaia craned her neck far enough to catch a glimpse of that impacting image. A girl slept within the oval. Lenaia looked closer and gasped. The girl had hair just as her own had been before prison, and her features matched Lenaia's as if she was looking into a mirror.

She could see traces of Nalofré in the young, innocent face as well. There was no mistaking her identity.

At the sound of her gasp, Nalofré had whirled around. She met his gaze a moment after the realization. Pain was in his eyes as his gaze locked with hers, and his nod of confirmation left no doubt that the young woman she saw was their only child. Tears spilled over in her eyes, and a sob caught in her throat.

Nalofré broke eye contact and turned back toward Fezam. One more glance at the young woman, and then he spoke. "I can't do it."

A smile spread across Fezam's face. "I had guessed that the love of a father for a daughter, regardless of the many years since your last limited time with her, would be too strong for you to save your wife."

He turned his red eyes on the Elfin Queen. "I'm sorry, Lenaia, but your husband has made his choice."

He gave a nod to the soldier, who brought his arm back and whipped a hand across Lenaia's cheek. She felt the sting and brought a cold hand to caress the burning, red mark left upon her skin. She closed her eyes against the tears.

Nalofré once again burst to his feet, crossing the room quickly to kneel beside his wife. He brushed back her hair and moved her hand to take a look at her cheek. He placed a kiss over the offensive mark and hugged her to his chest. Over her shoulder, he glared at the soldier then looked toward Fezam.

"You must promise me that you will leave my wife alone if I do your bidding."

Fezam bowed his head with a smirk. "I am not certain that is a deal I can adhere to. What I will promise, though, is to allow your wife and yourself to return to your cell after you fulfill my assignment, and once Alernoa is in my care, I will allow you to see her one last time."

Sorrow and anguish filled Nalofré's eyes, and once again, he looked toward the oval, clouded frame. He swallowed, closing his eyes against the decision he had been forced to make, and finally met Fezam's gaze. His voice was pain as he gave his answer.

"Tell me what to do."

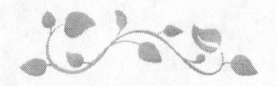

Genevia moaned in her sleep, but it did not wake her. She was aware of being asleep but could not shake its enveloping fog. She wasn't sure if she was having a pleasant dream or a nightmare. She had the feeling of being watched, but by whom, she could not determine. Her mind screamed out for answers but was answered only by silence.

Then she saw a face. It swam into focus, forming into an elf. She saw herself standing beside this vaguely familiar figure, and happiness threatened to overwhelm her. She felt as if she had been waiting all her life to meet this man. It wasn't that she could place him in her memory, he actually looked quite haggard, but his air was one used to power.

Then he spoke to her, his smile genuinely happy, welcoming her into his embrace, but when she looked into his eyes, she saw a sadness that she couldn't begin to decipher.

"Who are you?" she asked tentatively.

He brushed her hair back from her face, a crooked grin on his own. "I'm your father, Alernoa. You don't remember me, and I don't expect you to, but I've been longing to see you for sixteen years."

He took a shuddering breath, his eyes tearful. "You are so beautiful, just like your mother."

A sad smile replaced the warm one of a moment before as he looked down upon her. "I want you to remember, no matter what, that I love you. Promise me you'll remember that."

The desperation in his voice alerted her instantly. "Why is it so important?"

He worked hard to paste a cheerful expression on his face. "I just want to make sure that you don't think I abandoned you."

She scanned his face carefully, hoping to find some answer behind his behavior. "Of course I know you love me. You didn't abandon me; you saved me."

Once again came the flicker of sadness in his eyes, followed by anger, before Nalofré got control of his emotions. He smiled down at her.

"Good. Now, I have some instructions that will help you avoid Fezam." His eyes glazed with hatred, and he shook it off. "You need to travel to the shore of Yima Olem, immediately."

"But…" She stifled the protest, a look of unease in her eyes. When she looked back up at her father, though, she felt an urge to agree. "Okay, sure. Will I see you again?"

He nodded as grief flooded his features. "Follow my instructions, Alernoa. You need to so that…everyone can be safe."

He had paused and avoided her gaze as he said everyone, returning it back to her face only to receive an affirmative. She nodded, and he began to recede.

"No," she cried out, reaching for him.

His melancholy smile was his only answer to her cry as he disappeared.

Genevia jolted awake. Her heart was beating rapidly, and she was gasping for breath. She went back over the conversation with her father. Was it all in her imagination? Did she want to meet her father so badly that she resorted to false conversations in her dreams?

She shook her head. No. That was real, very real. She knew it, just as she knew that her father had been trying to warn her while giving his instructions. There was no need for him to look at her in despair if he was saving her from trouble. All the signs were there; Fezam was trying to set her up.

She finally grew aware enough of her surroundings to notice that Lela, Dayze, and Quinsnap were occupants with her in the tent.

"Are you…okay, Mama?" Lela asked tentatively, moving closer for a hug.

Genevia smiled. "Yes, I just took a little while to get fully awake."

Just then she heard the clash of blades. She sat up a little straighter. "What's going on?"

Dayze moved closer to her as she explained, nervously looking all around her as if she could see beyond the tent walls. "Those riders came. The walls you built held them out for a little while, but they're in now."

Genevia's hand flew to her mouth. "Oh, no. I have to go help."

She hurried out of the tent, whirling around quickly to speak to the girls. "Stay here."

Genevia ran to the source of the sound and stopped in her tracks when she saw the battle surrounding her. Jackson and Traynord were fighting side by side, Jackson with his military-grade sword and Traynord with a heavy, twisted wooden staff. There were several men surrounding them armed with wicked scimitars. All of the invading men in the camp were swathed in colorful robes, and they outnumbered Genevia's small band of fighters three to one. Asben was awkwardly swinging a small sword back and forth to avoid the nomad that had taken an interest in him. It was clear that the nomad was toying with him, but while focusing on Asben's meager attempts with the borrowed sword, Jezzie snuck up behind him and struck him over the head with a heavy skillet. Genevia was about to try to help them dispatch the second nomad heading toward them when her attention was arrested by the fight closest to her.

Frelati had just narrowly missed a swing aimed for his sword arm. After his dodge, he had moved in quickly to jab at the man's side with the dagger held in his left hand. Fortunately, he moved back in time to avoid the brunt of his attacker's retaliation, but blood from the jagged cut received across his shoulder bubbled forth. Fear gripped Genevia as she watched Frelati fight the tall, rugged man, and their scuffle was bringing them closer and closer to her while she stood rooted to the spot. Frelati turned yet again to avoid a blow but this time caught sight of her.

"Genevia," he yelled, anger flashing across his face and darkening his features. "Get back in the tent, now!"

"I...I..." Genevia shook her head.

"Genevia!" Frelati shouted, dodging the sword's tip by barely an inch.

The fighting was all around her now, and Frelati dragged her behind him.

She tried not to hinder him, which was not easy the way they were dancing around, and gasped at each dodge, thrust, and slash. Frelati moved with an athletic grace, but it was clear that although he was good with his sword-dagger combination, he hadn't had much practice fighting. He moved solely with an instinct for survival.

"Frelati, look out!" Genevia exclaimed. "Frelati! Oh, watch it! Frelati!"

Frelati gritted his teeth. "Cut the commentary."

He took one last thrust, disarming his opponent, who ran off to retrieve his weapon. With this brief respite, Frelati whirled toward Genevia. "What are you doing out here? Have you lost your mind? Go back into the tent now!"

He was incensed and looked more than a little dangerous. "Sorry, I...I thought I could help."

Just before entering the fray again, Frelati shoved her in the direction of the tent, and she ducked inside. Lela and Dayze hurried over to sit by her sides.

"Is everyone okay?" Dayze whispered.

"I don't know, sweetheart. They were fighting everywhere, and I couldn't keep track of everyone."

"Are you...scared?" Lela asked.

Genevia nodded and kissed the girl on top of her head. "A bit."

Lela leaned over to look at Dayze and nodded her head. Genevia didn't miss the exchange.

"What's going on, girls?"

Both had guilty looks and wouldn't make eye contact.

"Girls?" Genevia asked a little more forcefully.

"I want to put an illusion around the men, confusing them and making them ride off."

Genevia pondered the idea. "Could you do that, Dayze?"

She nodded.

"Then do it."

Dayze stood and glided to the opening of the tent. She surveyed her surroundings, took in the people and their ever-changing positions. Then, for the members of the attacking party, the scene began to change. They weren't fighting against a small band of travelers but against a host of armed men. Everywhere they turned, more and more people were standing, ready for a fight.

Fear chased them from the camp, leaving the members of Genevia's group standing bewildered. Frelati was the first to recover, and he immediately looked toward the tent. At the sight of Dayze, he realized what had happened. He shook his head, half in annoyance, half in amazement and admiration.

Then he walked over to the tent and leaned in. "Come on out; Dayze has scared off the opposition."

He ruffled her gray, wisp-like hair. "Good job."

She smiled up at him and hugged his knees before running off to meet Lela and Quinsnap. Genevia remained in the tent.

"Are you coming out?" Frelati asked.

Genevia looked up at him, defiance and hurt spreading through her eyes. "Are you going to yell at me?"

"Genevia," Frelati sighed and went to sit beside her.

"I was just going to see if I could do anything. I woke up in a haze. It was a strange dream that wasn't really a dream." Genevia shook her head. "If I had been thinking, I wouldn't have gone out, but you didn't need to get that mad at me. I did nothing wrong. I had just as much right to be out there as you did."

"Genevia, I was scared you were going to get hurt. We were both so wild in our swings one could have easily hit you. I wasn't thinking, I was reacting, and you wouldn't listen."

Genevia searched his eyes and found the remains of worry still lurking in them. "I'm sorry. I just...*froze*. I kept thinking that someone was going to die."

As if the words were a summons, Jezzie came running in. "Frelati, Genevia, Jackson's hurt. Come quickly."

They followed Jezzie to the middle of the campsite, where Jackson lay gasping for breath and clutching the six-inch blade protruding from his chest.

Genevia's hand flew to cover her mouth, her breathing coming in short spurts. Then she saw the girls, and her eyes widened.

"Jezzie..." She couldn't finish the sentence, but she didn't have to. Jezzie quickly rushed to where the girls were curiously peering their way, as yet unaware of what had happened, and urged them into a tent.

Genevia turned back to Jackson, and she collapsed on her knees beside him.

"Jack-son," she said softly, her breath catching as she tried unsuccessfully to hold back her tears. "Jackson, you stay with us. We're going to help you."

She looked up at Frelati, who had just returned with a shirt that he was ripping into strips.

"What do we do?" she sobbed before looking back down at the knife. It was just below his heart, and it had gone in deep.

Her hands fluttered around it helplessly as she tried to decide whether it was best to leave it in or pull it out. Jackson coughed forcefully, blood leaking from his mouth. Genevia heard Traynord return and announce that he had brought his whiskey, and Asben was rapidly flipping through a book and telling someone to look for a needle and thread. All the activity around her did not penetrate Genevia's brain. She grabbed Jackson's face in her hands and tried to will his eyes into focus.

"Jackson...Jackson," she sobbed, her tears falling freely now. "Can you hear me? Jackson. Come on, you know we need you."

For a minute, his eyes locked with hers. They were full of fear. It looked as if he wanted to speak, but before he had the chance, he went into a coughing spasm. His eyes closed, and Genevia felt him try to catch a few more breaths of air before growing deadly quiet.

"Jackson?" Genevia said urgently, shaking him a little. "Jackson!"

Asben pushed forward. "Let me see what I can do."

Genevia collapsed backward, her arms barely keeping her seated upright as she stared at Jackson in utter shock. She was hardly aware of Traynord and Asben working diligently to bring him back. All she remembered was the fear in his eyes as he looked at her and his body's futile efforts to force air into blood-filled lungs.

Frelati knelt down beside her, shielding her from the sight of Jackson's lifeless body. His jaw was firm, his eyes full of pity as he gently lifted her to her feet and urged her away. They had not even taken ten steps when Genevia's sobs overcame her and her legs gave way. Frelati caught her, lifted her in his arms, and simply continued to walk. She cried against his shoulder as he cradled her, carried her away from the site of the pain. He walked in silence until his wounded shoulder could take no more, and he settled them down behind some boulders.

Minutes passed without a word spoken before Genevia finally looked up at him.

"What are we supposed to do now?" she asked softly, her voice still broken by sobs.

"We keep going," Frelati said without looking at her. His voice was gruff.

Genevia shook her head. "How can we? After this?"

Frelati gave her a look full of compassion and some other emotion she couldn't name. "People die, Genevia. We can't stop living because they aren't there to move forward with us. I know this will be hard, but we started this for a reason. Jackson knew the risks when he came with us, and he wouldn't want us to stop because things got difficult."

Genevia sniffed and looked down.

"Genevia," Frelati urged her head up with a finger beneath her chin. He gave her a small, sad smile and brushed a tear off her cheek. "I'll be right here. We can get through this. Together."

She gave a small nod and nestled down to rest against him, taking comfort in his strong arm around her and the kiss he placed on the top of her head. There they sat in silence as the sun slowly joined the horizon, watching as the barren landscape changed minutely under the wind's brutal beating.

Chapter Twenty

Frelati leaned his head back to look up the sheer rock cliff. When he leveled his gaze to the hard rock dead in front of him, he shook his head in irony. After several days' travel, they had finally found the entrance to the dwarf undergrounds; they just had no way to get inside.

"Are you sure this is the *only* entrance?" Frelati asked Asben.

Asben looked over his maps again. He had spread them out earlier to get his bearings. "This is it. I'm sure of it. Besides, look at this pictograph."

He walked over to the base of the cliff and brushed his fingers across a small carving. It was two axes crossed in the middle and was barely discernable against the rocky background. Frelati nodded in resignation.

"So there's no way to get inside."

Asben consulted one of his books. "When I came last, I had a guide that was quite careful. There is some trigger, I know, maybe a password, that will open the entrance, but I'm just not positive what."

Frelati sighed in agitation and looked away.

"I'm sure I can figure it out given a few hours," Asben rushed on.

"Well, time's all we have right now, so you can take all you need," Frelati said as he glared at the cliff face again. "Just find some way to get us inside."

Frelati walked toward the camp, leaving Asben to immerse himself in his books and suppositions. As he neared the campsite, the smell of delicious food assaulted his senses and Lela ran up to attack his knees. He swung her up into his arms.

"And what have you been up to today?" he asked with a small smile.

"Ie salkaw Jezzie dogs gsa riiw," Lela explained with pride.

Frelati nodded. "You helped Jezzie with the food? So you're the mastermind behind all the delicious smells."

Lela nodded and wiggled to get down. Frelati complied, and she ran off, shouting Dayze's name. Genevia walked over to him.

"I do believe it's time for my lesson," she said with a huge grin.

Frelati couldn't help but respond to her. "All right, lead the way."

Asben rushed from his books to his maps and back to the sheer cliff, muttering nearly incoherent things all along the way. He was fascinated by the intricate pictographs he kept finding hidden in the stone. They depicted a time in the past when all the creatures were peaceful, and the elves were the dominant race. Beneath the pictures were words written in an ancient language that he suspected of being Elven, and Asben searched the entire cliff face to find all of the paired, illusive marks. They were spaced at random intervals it seemed, but each picture, which he managed to decipher with the help of his faithful books, uncovered an illuminating past. He had yet to attempt a translation of the language beneath.

Throughout the day, Asben made notes in his scrolls and watched as a picture story began to form. He discovered that the different pictographs stood for nations, and Asben assumed the ancient markings in Elven found beneath each picture simply described what the pictures meant. It would take further study and a translation he wasn't certain he could procure to understand the true meaning behind them.

Asben noted each of these details and recorded them in his scrolls to root out the secret of them later. He worked at this task until the light faded into night and the sun melted into the horizon. Still he worked on, pulling out a torch to study even more. It wasn't until Jezzie dragged him away from "that old pile of rubbish" that he finally came to a stop.

"Ur workin' too hard, honey. Ya need ur sleep. Those rocks'll be there tamarra," Jezzie said considerately after hearing several protests from Asben.

He had been trying to crack the ancient writings in the waning firelight. "I just need to look at this a little closer. I know there's a pattern here, if I could just find it."

"Honey." Jezzie came up behind him and stroked his hair. "Dahlin', just come in the tent and go ta sleep. Ur tireder than an old dog on a long trip under a hot sun. Maybe the others can help ya ta crack tha' ol' code if ya just give em the chance. Come on to bed, now."

Asben finally relented and safely tucked his scrolls in his pack. He lay down on a thin pallet and closed his eyes, muttering about all the work he still had to do. Jezzie was used to this preoccupation when Asben worked on a difficult project, and she wasn't surprised when Asben fell asleep midword. In the morning, he would start that grueling study again, and by nightfall she knew he'd have it solved.

Genevia and Frelati had been working on perfecting her gift all morning, and Genevia was ready for a break.

"Let's see if Asben is any closer to solving that puzzle," she suggested, and Frelati nodded reluctantly.

They joined him at the cliff's base and watched his hurried movements from one place to another. Asben had told them a bit about what he was working on at breakfast, but he hadn't stayed in camp long enough to explain exactly what it was he was trying to uncover.

Genevia broke into his self-induced trance. "So what can we do to help?"

He looked up from the scroll he was studying with dazed eyes, shaking his head to clear a path into reality. "Oh, I, um, well, that would be difficult to say."

He looked around him at the clutter. "I don't really know myself quite what I'm looking for, but if I peruse this information with a systematic method, the probability that I will unearth a very pertinent element from within this data that could direct me to the ultimate genius in this creation is significantly higher if I do it myself. Please do not be offended, but if I can't fathom what it is that I myself am supposed to accomplish, how can I even entertain the notion of directing you in this unenlightened course?"

Genevia smiled at his hurried and intellectual answer before replying. "I suppose I can see exactly what you mean, but don't you suppose that by your relaying the information you have gathered to an interested second party, you could suddenly hit upon your own enlightenment? Perhaps all you need is for another person to listen to your ideas, so that in hearing yourself speak you will say something that will spark in your mind the answer and cause that illusive puzzle piece to fall into place."

Asben rolled the thought around a bit before speaking, and once he delved into his exhaustive explanation, a gleam crept into his eyes.

"All right, well I began to puzzle over the entrance after finding this pictograph." He walked over to the cliff and pointed to his first find. "Do you see the crossed axes? Well, that is symbolic of the dwarf nation because they chisel out their living. I continued to scout the rest of the rock face and found other images. This is where I found my second symbol."

He moved a few feet to the left and pointed out another image. "This one is a two-sided picture. Do you see the line drawn down the middle of the tree? On the right is a twig, struggling for life, but on the left is a full, thriving tree. This is symbolic of the Dreamers, how they make others see what isn't truly there.

"Next, I found this marking." He indicated yet another carving, this one higher up than the others. "This is one with a hut in the background, and at the forefront a small fire burning. I'm sure you've heard of the ever present idea that man made fire?" He barely paused before continuing. "Now, we move to this picture.

"This one took me a little longer to figure out. I thought that the carving had eroded and the picture was forever lost. Come look at it."

He motioned to them, and Frelati and Genevia stepped up to examine the picture.

"What is it?" Genevia asked, bewildered.

"That was exactly my thought. My next was the erosion theory. I wrote down these findings and moved on to the next picture, but this morning I found the sequence and inspected this picture minutely." Asben paused. "What do you think this is a picture of?"

Frelati stared at the picture a little while before answering. "It looks almost human, but at the same time it could be a zarpink."

"I think it looks like a chair made of vines, maybe? But all the lines are running together. It's a huge mesh of things," Genevia said, tilting her head.

"Exactly, it's all of those things, and anything else we can see in the picture. That was the purpose of this pictograph. For the shape to shift into anything we can see." Asben's excitement was flowing through his words.

Light dawned for Frelati. "The shapeshifters."

"Precisely. This carving is symbolic of the nation of shapeshifters." Asben rushed to his next picture in excitement. It was located to the far left between the highest and middle carvings. "And this one has a fish tail out of the water, and on the shore you see the upper torso of a human, a really simple engraving, just like the one for the dwarves. It is the mermaid nation that is symbolized here.

"This next one takes some background knowledge." He moved over to the far right and down between the middle and lowest carvings. "These pictographs have no color, so that makes it more difficult to carve this particular nation. Instead, they carved a ritual. Notice the seven separate spirals at the bottom? They begin to intertwine with each other as they move up. Finally, at the very top, it is just a swirl of lines. This is a ritual of the pixies.

"They break off into their seven colors: pink, purple, blue, green, red, orange, and yellow. Then they fly upward, and the colors begin to mingle. Once they reach the top, the colors fly in and around one another, forming a rainbow of color. This ritual is to signify union amongst all pixies of every color. It's done in the dead of night during the new moon, when only the stars are visible. It is the perfect contrast to their sparks of color as they fly among each other. It's difficult to tell in this depiction, but the carving here most definitely symbolizes the pixie nation."

Genevia and Frelati swapped glances of amusement and admiration before they were drawn back to the rock. The picture just looked like a bunch of lines to them.

"This one here," Asben motioned to a carving dead in the center of all the images, "was another simple one to decipher. The wriggling line twining around the edge leads to an oval that is tilted upward at the bottom of the carving, and you can see that the fire in the center stems from that oval. To the casual observer, it would seem to be only fire framed by a twisting line, but upon closer observation, as I have given this intricate work and all the others, you can see that this symbolizes a dragon.

"Now, as the pictures are going, there should be one more." Asben motioned to each picture in turn. "We have found dwarf, dreamer, human, shapeshifter, mermaid, pixie, and dragon. What is the one nation that's missing?"

Frelati spoke up. "Us. Elves."

"Exactly, but I have searched this entire cliffside without finding a trace of another pictograph. If these carvings have survived, then the one for the elves should have survived as well, which means that it is either hidden very well or it was never carved."

"I see the problem," Genevia said with a thoughtful expression.

She walked along the side of the cliff, her fingers brushing against its rough surface. She looked up and down the wall of rock but saw nothing. Then she stopped and turned abruptly to face Frelati and Asben.

"So, what connects these pictures? What is the common factor? Why are they spaced as they are? Can they be pushed or turned like doorknobs so that a secret opening can appear? Is there a sequence that will unlock an entrance?" Genevia stopped with a half grin playing on her face. "It's a puzzle, Asben. Frelati and I will look for the hidden pictograph while you piece it together."

Chapter Twenty-One

"So, we can't find the last picture on the rock face. Where does that leave us to look?" Genevia paced before the wall, speaking her thoughts to give them order.

Frelati had knelt down and was sifting through some sand by his feet, listening to Genevia's prattle without actually hearing it. He rubbed the sand from side to side, brushing it back and forth idly. Then, he began to make wider sweeps, pausing immediately as they passed across hard ridges. Puzzled, he brushed the sand aside and uncovered a circular marking, similar to the images on the rock face.

"On the ground?" he muttered in surprise.

Genevia spun around, taking his comment as the unexpected answer to her ponderings. "Why would they put a pictograph on the ground? Honestly, Frelati."

She began pacing again, not expecting an answer to her second rhetorical question of the day.

She got one anyway. "Because it's the last place anyone would look. Come here."

Genevia frowned, but she crouched across from him, gasping at the discovery and then frowning again in confusion. "What is it?"

Frelati turned eyes full of amusement on her. "You might be able to tell if you weren't looking at it upside down."

Pink crept up Genevia's neck as she glared at him.

She crawled around to see it properly and brushed more dust from its surface. This pictograph was much larger than the others and the grooves went deeper, but that wasn't what arrested their attention when they looked closely at the marking. It held a figure, its back toward the observers, with its head turned to see what was looking at its form. It was a woman with pointed ears and a half smile on her face. Her long hair coiled down her back; her dress brushed her ankles.

The purpose of the picture had to be pointing out the ears, which a casual observer might overlook, as Asben would have explained, and while Frelati and Genevia recognized this feature, that wasn't what grabbed their attention. The face of the carving was familiar, the expression commonplace.

"It's you," Frelati whispered.

"That's not possible. They didn't know me when they carved this. It's just someone that looks very similar," Genevia argued, but she was still disturbed.

Frelati shook his head. Everything was beginning to fall into place. "No, it's you. They must have known, somehow. They were closer to the beginning of the creation of Imaemaroza. The ancient secrets wouldn't have been lost yet. They knew and tried to pass them on, leaving this to ensure the secrets were never fully forgotten. The dwarves and elves hold the oldest and most sacred knowledge from Kiem. This picture isn't coincidence or a look-alike; it's you."

Frelati turned wide eyes on her; it was as if he had never seen her before. A mixture of awe and something akin to fear was in his gaze and expression.

"I'll...go get Asben," he said quickly and hurried over to the scholar.

Genevia's sigh was full of anguish as she looked down at the picture, running her fingers over its surface. She felt no different, but everyone would treat her like she was. "Why did you have to be here? Don't you know that some secrets are meant to stay hidden?"

She hit the ground with a fist and ran off, trying to hold the tears at bay. Why did she have to carry this huge burden? She ran until grief overcame her and she collapsed beside a rocky outcropping, lying on the barren ground and wishing for the comfort of trees and grass and flowers.

Through her tears, she saw her wish come to life. Small green sprouts quickly became lush vegetation in this harsh wasteland. A protective haven of nature grew around her comfortingly as she buried her head in her arms and wept.

Frelati was having trouble grasping his new revelation. Genevia wasn't just an elfin princess that was going to help them out. She didn't just have a powerful gift. She was part of Kiem. Genevia was one of the six; the one they had grown up learning about. Now he wondered how he had missed it. Asben had practically shouted it at him, but he hadn't wanted to believe it. Maybe it wasn't true… but how could it be anything different? It didn't matter how much he might wish it to be otherwise, she was well and truly out of his reach now.

Through his own turmoil, he ran to Asben, and he didn't turn back until he reached him. That's when he realized the affect the picture had on her. He watched her stroke it in an almost pleading gesture before her fist pounded down and she ran, just ran with no destination, and he wanted to comfort her, but how could he? Frelati's guilt almost overwhelmed him; she had no one else. As he started to go after her, Asben laid a hand on his arm.

"She needs to be alone," he said quietly.

Frelati turned to look at him, confused and a bit angry.

Asben continued before he had a chance to respond. "Everyone needs time alone to cope. You can go to her, but give her some time to herself first. Now, you need to tell me what you've found, what has caused this upset."

Frelati turned to look in the direction Genevia had run and stared into the distance before returning his gaze to Asben and replying.

"We found the last pictograph. It was…you need to see it for yourself."

Frelati walked off, assuming Asben would follow. Frelati led him to their find but refused to look down at it himself. Asben knelt beside it and sighed, reaching out to touch the ridges gently.

"I was afraid something like this would show up." Asben shook his head.

Frelati started. "What?"

Asben met his eyes. "Had you not guessed who she was? The poem, my books, this present world of turmoil...how could she be anyone else?"

Frelati nodded but didn't speak.

"This is hard on you, though," Asben continued. "You're emotionally involved."

"I'm not emotionally involved," Frelati argued.

Asben persisted. "You must feel empty, overwhelmed, unsure of your path."

"No, I'm fine," Frelati argued. "Why should it matter to me?"

Asben clearly didn't believe him but tried a different tactic anyway. "You do care, as we all do, so try to imagine how she feels." Asben saw Frelati glance once again in the direction Genevia had run before turning back to listen. "Imagine being at war with yourself, hating yourself because you're different and can never do all the things others take for granted. This is new and foreign; you want to rebel but don't know how. Your dreams of marriage, children, a nice home seem lost. You love someone who's terrified of getting close, more so now, and that chasm seems impossible to overcome."

Frelati couldn't speak, couldn't think, not about anything but that instant realization, and he couldn't handle it.

"No," he said through gritted teeth, clenching his fists as anger surfaced to assuage his guilt. "That's not true. She's not in love with me. She knows that nothing can work out between us. I told her time after time, even before all this. She just...she's confused. She'll get used to it."

Pity and frustration filled Asben's face, and he shook his head. "You should open your eyes, son. I'm nearly blind when it comes to reading people, but I can see this. It's clearly written in everything Genevia does. She saw the possibility that you were too stubborn to see."

"It wasn't ever possible, not then, not now. Maybe Genevia will finally realize that."

Asben stood with a firm, new determination to protect Genevia. He shook a finger at Frelati, his voice full of soft anger. "Your pessimism will be your undoing if you let it, and I won't let it corrupt Genevia now. Stay here and do something, anything, but you aren't going to destroy what little hope and happiness that poor girl has left. She may very well die saving us, and the least we can do is keep her away from misery in the present."

Frelati wanted to argue, but something told him that when Asben's anger showed everyone should listen. However, he wasn't completely ready to relent. "Well, someone needs to go talk to her."

"I'll go," Asben said emphatically.

"You need to find a way to get us inside," Frelati argued hotly.

"It'll be here when I get back. Genevia needs someone right now, and you will only make matters worse."

"But..." Frelati began his protest.

"It will wait," Asben hissed before walking off.

Asben found Genevia's enclosure in no time. Of course, in a land of sand and rock, a spray of vegetation stuck out like a sore thumb, even if it was slightly hidden behind huge boulders. He pushed aside the vines and walked into the beautiful, green enclosure.

"Genevia?" he called tentatively.

"Go away," she mumbled through her arms.

She was lying on her stomach in the grass, her trembling shoulders the only proof that she was crying.

"Do you really want me to go away?" he asked softly.

Genevia looked up in surprise after recognizing Asben's voice. She brushed a hand across her wet cheeks and sat up. "What are you doing here?"

"Do you want to talk?" Asben asked. "I've been told I'm a good listener."

Genevia shook her head and sniffed. "There isn't anything to tell. I'm just being overemotional. You don't want to listen to me."

Asben spoke softly. "What makes you think that?"

Genevia's lip quivered, and she wiped away a stray tear before answering. "Because even Frelati doesn't want to talk to me, and I thought he cared. So why should you?"

"Genevia," Asben began slowly, sinking down to sit beside her. "Frelati's not here because I wouldn't allow it. He wanted to come, but I was afraid he would make matters worse."

Genevia shook her head, not sure what to say.

Asben filled the silence with his explanation. "Everyone can feel the underlying current between you two. I have a feeling one of the main reasons for this outburst stems from the realization that any possible relationship has been compromised?"

Genevia hesitantly nodded. "I suppose."

Asben gave her a small smile. "Yes, and I also assume that you need understanding and someone to listen right now, rather than hearing an 'I told you so.' Am I right there as well?"

Genevia nodded again, and her face fell. "It's just hard. I don't want this."

"Yes, I can understand a bit, I suppose. Perhaps it would help to talk?" Asben cajoled.

Genevia sat quietly for a while before she could hold it in no longer. "I just knew it was going to work out. It was. Frelati was going to come around, and I think he was beginning to, but now it doesn't matter. It doesn't matter at all, and I have no one."

Genevia hid her face in her hands, her shoulders heaving with sobs.

Asben patted her shoulder awkwardly, wondering if there was a way he could help.

"Well, you know the old adage." Asben tried to put some light-heartedness into his words. "Love finds a way."

"What could love do about this?" Genevia quipped, sorrow coloring her words. "I'm different; that can't change."

"Yes, you are different, I won't argue with you there, but that doesn't mean nothing can be done to change your position," Asben started slowly. "I can research all the ancient scrolls and writings to see if there is any way out of it…after the defeating that is."

Genevia lifted her tear-stained face, hope filling her eyes. "You would do that?"

Asben smiled. "Of course. As Jezzie says, you're like family. Each and every one of you is family now, and family looks out for each other. We'll find some way out of this, and then we'll work on Frelati."

Genevia saw his resolve on the matter and knew he would do everything in his power to follow through with his promise. Genevia sincerely hoped he would be successful; she needed something to believe in, even if only for a little while.

Genevia smiled, though it was still tinged with sadness. "Thanks."

Asben patted her hand. "You just continue being a wonderful girl, and I'll do the hard stuff. Agreed?"

Genevia nodded, and Asben stood to leave.

"I'll just stay here a bit longer, if you don't mind," Genevia said.

"Take all the time you need."

Asben left the comfortable little enclosure and shook his head. Poor girl. He would break into every library and tear into every book he could get his hands on to help her and put a genuine smile back on her face and in her eyes. And whether or not Frelati realized it, despite him in fact, Asben would be helping him too and making sure that he didn't lose the pure love of Genevia's that was so hard to find.

Chapter Twenty-Two

Asben cleared more of the dirt from a wide circle around the last pictograph. Just as he had expected, he found more words from the ancient language and cleared the dirt off that too. There were a lot more words here than under the others.

"I think these words are instructions. At first, I thought they were meant to explain the pictures, but…there has to be some explanation behind the process, and these words just might be it. I recognize it as the ancient language, but I haven't yet found a book that can help me translate it."

Frelati walked over to kneel by Asben. "Isn't the ancient language Alzam?"

Asben glanced at Frelati. "Yes, that's right. That was the language when Kiem split into six, but it was forgotten by most, excluding his chosen people, the elves. However, it has been years since then, and languages alter over time. Besides, this is the entrance to the dwarf undergrounds; it may be some older form of their ancient language, not *the* ancient language."

"Maybe, but the elves on Meufa thrive on tradition. Maybe I can read it," Frelati said as he knelt down. One glance at the familiar characters and he knew they were going to get inside. He looked up at Asben. "I can decipher this."

Asben grinned. "Truly! What a break! What does it say?"

"What does what say?" Genevia asked as she walked up. Her steps were slow, and her shoulders slumped, but there was a slight hint of interest in her eyes that belied her deep sigh as she stopped beside them.

"The words beneath the pictograph are Elven. They should give the instructions to open the door," Asben explained, his excitement too much to hide.

Frelati had taken Asben's place in front of the writing and began to read. "I don't think it's instructions; it seems more like a bad poem."

"But what does it say?" Asben asked impatiently.

"Dreams shift as the waters and fly o'er the deep chasms; normal though they be, each is unique and as different as red fire gems. Yet when all return to the source; they push open the door to the soul," Frelati read.

"At least the first two lines rhyme, kind of, if you force it," Genevia said. "The poem could be worse."

Asben had been quiet, contemplating the writing. "It's not supposed to be a poem. It's a clue, just like everything else. Here, Frelati, write it down on this scroll."

Frelati complied, and Asben read over the poem. "This tells us the sequence. 'Dreams shift as the waters,' just that one line tells us the first three: dreamer, shapeshifter, then mermaid."

"Okay, I get the dreamer and the shapeshifter, but how did you get mermaid?" Genevia asked. "I know that they live in water, but couldn't it be one of the others, or nothing at all?"

"It could be nothing, as you said, but after perusing the rest of the poem, there is nothing else that could allude to mermaids, so it must be that one word," Asben explained.

Genevia shrugged.

Asben continued. "The red fire could be humans or dragons, and the fly could be pixies or dragons. Either for both would work. Red fire…I think that's supposed to represent dragon, which would leave the fly to pixies. Nothing else refers to them, so that assumption seems accurate. The deep chasms must be dwarves because of their trenches.

"So now we have dreamer, shapeshifter, mermaid, pixie, and dwarf. I think human must be tied with the normal because we have no special abilities really. So that would make the next two human and dragon. That's all seven, and I suppose after that sequence, we return here and push this picture down."

"Well, that makes the awkwardness of the poem less awkward," Frelati said as he stood.

They walked over to the cliff face, and Asben moved to the pictograph for the dreamers.

"What does this say?" Asben asked, pointing to the markings underneath the picture.

Frelati leaned closer and dusted off the words. "Left turn."

"Well, that's self-explanatory," Genevia said.

Asben followed Frelati with scroll and quill in hand, taking notes as to what was to be done with each image.

"We should wait to open it until we have all of our gear packed and everyone is ready to go," Frelati said after they had finished.

"Yes," Asben agreed. "But I don't want to wait too long. Let's go prepare everyone and try to get inside before dark."

Fezam viewed his former palace overseer with distaste. He had sent him to Yima Olem for one simple task, and he couldn't even fulfill that. How hard could it possibly be to find the entrance to a huge underground city that housed thousands of dwarves? He rubbed his temples. No, the real question was why he put up with so many incompetent creatures.

"So, let me get this straight," Fezam said in exasperation, emphasizing his words with hand motions and rolled eyes. "You came all this way to tell me you didn't find the dwarf undergrounds. Do I have that right?"

A look of discomfort crossed the captain's face. This wasn't the welcome he had expected. "That wasn't exactly what I came here for."

Fezam sighed and motioned for him to continue.

"Well, I...found out some information about Alernoa." The captain cleared his throat.

With raised eyebrows Fezam counted the wasted seconds as he waited for an explanation, wishing humans were more straightforward. Why were these beings so incapable of being direct?

"Okay." The captain took Fezam's silence as encouragement to move on. "Well, she apparently has an army, a large one. It's unusual; at least, that's what the marauder said."

Silence again. This time, though, it was a silence that would not be broken without encouragement, regardless of the many questions that his explanation had just brought to the surface.

"All right, I'll ask." Fezam sighed. "What marauder?"

The captain nodded. "While at Yima Olem, some marauders came upon our camp, and I had an interesting discussion with their leader. He was actually afraid of Alernoa's group, and when he described it, he was almost quivering. He said that one minute it looked like you could beat the group and the next there were people everywhere."

"Just like that?" Fezam was skeptical.

"Yes." The captain nodded vigorously. "It sounds crazy, I know, but that was what he said, and from his reaction it has to be true."

Fezam thought this over. "There must be an explanation."

Silence filled the room for a third time before Fezam spoke. "You haven't found the dwarf undergrounds?"

The captain was confused by the repeated question. "No, sire."

"So you're still here because…?" Fezam prodded.

"Yes, sire." The captain bowed. "I'll find the undergrounds."

"That would be wise." Fezam's eyes narrowed. "Now, go."

The captain bowed one more time before exiting the room.

Fezam rubbed his temples and closed his eyes. "If I didn't know better, I'd say they get dumber every day, and more useless with each world."

"All right, Genevia, follow this sequence and do as I say," Asben said.

Genevia nodded and readied herself.

"Dreamer, left turn."

Genevia twisted the pictograph, which was an accomplishment because it really didn't want to move.

"Shapeshifter, push."

That one was easier.

"Mermaid, right turn."

Genevia grimaced as she complied. The pictographs were very stiff from disuse. There had to be another entrance that the dwarves used.

"Pixie, slide up."

She hadn't thought it was possible, but this instruction was the most difficult to achieve. It was like she was lifting the whole cliff.

"Dwarf, slide down."

Finally another easy one.

"Human, left turn."

Genevia rolled her eyes, preparing herself for another fight with the earthen picture, but she was pleasantly surprised. It moved smoothly.

"Dragon, right turn."

The ease of the last movement was equaled by the difficulty of this one, but once again, Genevia pulled through.

"All right," Asben continued. "Now, come back here and push the elf pictograph."

It took several steps for Genevia to reach the last image from her place at the cliff face. The others were already crowded behind it. She looked down at the picture of herself before leaning forward to push it. Anger and fear threatened to spill out, but she tamped the feelings down before they could escape.

"Okay," Genevia said. "Let's hope this works."

She pushed, and everyone held their breath. Silence. Finally, a hissing sound reached their ears, and they watched in amazement as a huge slab of stone shifted and began to fall toward them. It lowered slowly, and once it reached eye level, everyone could see it was lowered by chains. It settled softly on the ground at their feet but still sent up a spray of dust, sending the group into a coughing fit. They waved at the air before them to clear their vision and found themselves staring at a gaping, pitch-black hole where once gray stone had been.

Lela grabbed Genevia's hand, and Dayze did the same with Frelati. Cool air filtered from the opening to hit their anxious faces.

"Well, come on, then, lassies an' la's. We go' a dwarf colony ta fin'," Traynord said, breaking the silence and walking to the entrance. He turned back. "Are ya comin'?"

Frelati began walking first, Dayze at his side, and Genevia followed him with Lela in tow. Lela hid her face in Genevia's skirts, and Genevia scooped her up into her arms for both their sakes. No one spoke as they entered the cave; it just didn't seem like something they should do. The darkness was heavy and stifling. The cold made everyone feel as if they were dead. The uneven floor caused each to stumble occasionally, and when they reached out to the wall to steady themselves, the moist surface startled them into snatching their hands back quickly.

The sun outside only penetrated a few feet into the cavern, leaving their eyes to search for some other source of light in the gloom. Frelati grabbed a lantern and lit it, but even that illumination only made a pinprick of difference to the imposing wall of black. Slowly, their eyes began to adjust, and they moved forward into the cave-dark night. No sooner had they all moved several feet inside than the door began to close. It crept up inch by inch, taking the sun's light away and enclosing them in its cruel tomb.

After a slight hiss and much scraping, the door had returned itself once again to its camouflaged position, sealing away their escape. Now the only way to move was forward. Everyone was glad for the lantern light, even if it didn't really help much. The silence was deafening, but no one could bring himself to say anything and slice the thick veil with his voice. They stayed close together, reminding themselves that they weren't alone and, at the same time, making sure that they were still alive.

The place had a deathlike and dreamlike quality, although the dream was much more nightmare. No one would touch the walls for fear of what they might encounter and not really wishing to feel the murky, slimy moisture that clung there. The floor was at a slight incline, but no one noticed. They were too busy finding their footing on the uneven pathway.

There was an eerie feeling in the cool air, and the darkness allowed their imaginations free reign. Small noises would become poisonous snakes and monsters; the swish of hair against an arm was most definitely a spider. What was that brushing against their foot? It wasn't the hem of someone's dress, no, no that would be too ordinary, too sensible. In the darkness, imagination says that the brush was caused by a rat's tail. And that slow dripping, could that be water? No, definitely not, that is what common sense would say, not wild imagination. That steady dripping was the blood of those who came before them, or perhaps the saliva of a dragon waiting for his next meal.

Eventually, though, as all tunnels go, they came to an area with light. Unfortunately, what that light illuminated was two paths.

"Which one should we take?" Frelati asked no one in particular, waving his lantern in front of both.

Asben studied each to spark an old memory, while Traynord walked over to the torch on the wall that provided the added light and removed it from its stand.

"The left one will lead to a larger room with more paths; we'll need to take the right one there. That path should lead us to the heart of the dwarf undergrounds. Thank goodness they didn't blindfold me the first time I came here, eh? Although, it would have been nice if they'd shown that same courtesy while I was still outside the tunnels. Then all the frustration I went through to get us in could have been avoided."

Frelati nodded and led the way. Sure enough, they came to another room and took the path on the right. This path was quite wide, and it was longer than the other. The main difference, though, between this walkway and the first, was that this particular walkway was lined with torches.

They had all expected to meet someone along this last stretch but were disappointed. They had also expected to hear some noise, but even that small supposition was to be denied. When they reached the end of the tunnel, they found themselves looking down upon a large city. It descended deeper and deeper into the ground. Mound after mound of huge earthen structures that could have been homes or businesses were carved within Tiweln's belly. As far as the eye could see were dwellings and at the very center was the largest building of all.

"That's the king's palace," Asben declared, but no one was really listening.

"Where is everyone?" Genevia asked, setting Lela on the ground.

Nothing stirred. Silence reigned

"Well, I declare," Jezzie exclaimed. "Did they just up an' move, ya wonder?"

"This can't be right," Asben exclaimed in dismay. "It just can't be. We would have heard if they changed location. There's thousands of them."

"Look," Dayze said and pointed at the door to the palace. "Someone's coming."

And sure enough, someone was. It took him a little while, but soon the dwarf was standing right before them, hands on hips, his small stature not taking anything away from his angry glare.

"Why have you come here? What is the point of your destroying our perfect peace?" he demanded.

No one spoke for a moment, astounded by his loud, gruff voice and pointed questions.

Finally, Genevia's curiosity made her speak up. "Where is everyone?"

The dwarf moved his gaze to her and instantly did a double-take. "You're…you're her. You're here. You have finally come!"

He stared at Genevia a moment longer before turning to face the underground city. "Everyone, it's okay; you can come out! The chosen one has finally come to redeem this world of terror!"

Instantly, the city was swarmed with dwarves, all crying out in joy. As for the travelers, they were taken aback by the sudden turn of events.

"What?" Genevia cried out as the dwarf turned again to face her, a huge grin beaming from within his beard.

"You have come to save Tiweln. Come and meet our king."

Chapter Twenty-Three

Dwarves watched from windows, doorways, and pathways as the unusual group walked up to the palace. Faces lined the sides of the street. Each person in the group felt uncomfortable under the intense scrutiny, and while previously they did not really want to be trapped inside the palace, after just a few steps under the crowd's watchful gaze, they suddenly didn't mind being hidden inside four walls.

Even their guide turned back periodically to look at them. Whether it was to make sure they were still following or to get yet another glimpse at Genevia was anyone's guess. He was a stout little man, but he possessed great strength, both in physique and in character. He had long, dark brown hair and a braided beard that covered half of his naturally tan face.

Eventually, they made it to the palace doors. They held jewels in abundance—rubies, diamonds, amethysts, and sapphires. Their design was beautiful and intricate, clearly carved by skillful hands, and the pattern was so intertwined between the two doors that the crease between them seemed nonexistent. Then the large double doors opened to reveal a long hall lined by lit torches. It was relatively dark, but what else could be expected of an underground city? Shadows danced along the walls as the fire flickered on the torches in a vain attempt to escape from its bond and to roam and consume all that was susceptible to its heated touch.

This eerie, living light caressed the travelers' faces as they continued, but upon reaching another large set of doors, these less ornate and of smaller stature than the first, this dim light altered into a strange glow coming from stones interspersed in the walls. Along the floor of the new chamber ran a maroon rug with gold fringes and tassels. It led to the base of a throne, which held a cushion of the same colors, and upon this cushion, a small, old dwarf sat. The dwarf king watched as they entered; his face inscrutable and as blank as an unwritten page.

Each in the small party showed respect to the king, after which an awkward silence followed. Genevia looked to Frelati, who stared at the king as he waited for him to speak. Eventually, he did.

"How many of my people do you want?" he asked suddenly.

His voice was strong for his frail body, and it resonated throughout the large stone room. Genevia was surprised by the question, but Frelati seemed to be expecting it.

"If we could have one dwarf to guide us through the tunnels to the ocean, we would greatly appreciate it," Frelati said without breaking eye contact. "And a ship."

The king nodded. "Tell no one of the secret to this place."

He waited for signs of confirmation from each of them before turning to his advisor. "Fetch Pilloop."

The dwarf hurried off, and the king turned back to his guests. "Pilloop is our best guide. He knows these tunnels backward and forward. He could navigate them blindfolded, not that we've tried, but…he's the best we have. You'll be in good hands."

A side door opened, and two dwarves entered the room. The first was the king's advisor, and the other was Pilloop. He was as wide as he was tall, but that width would by no means be described as fat; it was pure muscle. He had a long brown beard and small, dark eyes. His face was blank, as if he were neutral to everything. No smile, no frown, nothing to reflect his feelings on the assignment laid before him.

Pilloop took in everything, though. His eyes imperceptibly scanned the room and the people that occupied it. He wasn't too happy about traveling with complete strangers. Who knew what they might do to him? Besides, this trip would set him back two days in his work, something he would never have considered if not commanded by the king.

However, no one knew his thoughts because Pilloop worked hard to keep others guessing, no matter what situation presented itself. He walked over to the small group after bowing to his king and examined each one without being obvious.

"I expect you are in a hurry to move on," the king said, interrupting Pilloop's reverie. "We will give you a place to stay the night, and you may continue on your journey in the morning."

The king dismissed them all, and Pilloop led them to the guests' quarters. He had already been told where they would stay. At each door, he pointed and grunted, smiling to himself when uncomfortable looks passed between the travelers and a few broke off to claim the room indicated.

"So, you're Pilloop?" Genevia asked after clearing her throat. She, Frelati, Lela with Quinsnap, and Dayze still trailed along behind him in the corridor.

Pilloop grunted, hoping that the young elf would take the hint and stay quiet, but he had no such luck.

"I'm Genevia…or Alernoa, I guess," she continued.

That surprised Pilloop. She *guessed* she was Alernoa? What exactly did that mean?

"This is Frelati, Lela, and Dayze. The others are Jezzie, Asben, and Traynord. And this little lefnode is Quinsnap." Genevia's voice was dripping with affection and happiness.

Once again, Pilloop grunted.

Genevia stared at his back before turning to Frelati for conversation, but he didn't seem to want to talk either. Fortunately, Lela filled the silence.

"Why don't…you talk?" she asked curiously.

Pilloop turned and raised one bushy eyebrow, not replying as he again faced forward and continued.

Lela was unperturbed, stepping up her pace to draw even with the dwarf. They were the same height. "Can you talk?"

Pilloop grunted again.

Lela looked back at Genevia in a silent question. Genevia shrugged, so Lela turned to Dayze.

"Was that a yes or a no?" Dayze asked as she caught up with the two leaders.

"I can talk; I just don't," Pilloop said gruffly with a fierce look that should have scared them off. He thought it had worked until Lela piped up again.

"Why?"

"He just prefers silence, Lela," Frelati reproved gently.

"Oh," Lela said, nodding her head in understanding. "That…is okay, Pilloop. You…can be my…friend. Me and Dayze will…tell…stories, and you…don't have…to talk if you don't…want to."

That startled Pilloop, but he quickly recovered. That child would either drive him crazy or touch his heart. Either way, Pilloop had a feeling he wouldn't like the result. Fortunately, the next door they came to dropped off both children, the animal, and the girl elf who was causing so much turmoil in the underground city. That only left the young male elf who had come to his rescue with the never-ending questions.

"I apologize for the interrogation," Frelati said. "Lela is very friendly and expects others to be so as well, which is surprising, quite frankly."

Pilloop wondered about that last bit, and his curiosity got the best of him.

"Why?" he asked grudgingly.

Frelati took a bit of time to answer, probably because he was gauging Pilloop's actual interest. He must have realized that Pilloop wasn't the sort who chatted unnecessarily because his reply came a moment later.

"She had a rough childhood before Genevia and I found her. She ran the streets, an orphan. She was very shy and knew a lot less Welnish when we first happened upon her." Frelati's love for the little girl entwined with his words, creating a nice melody to carry the story along. Pilloop had the stray thought that he would make a good storyteller, but it was knocked aside when Frelati continued. "Genevia made me take Lela with us. At the time, I thought that it was a terrible idea, just another child to look after…"

"Another child? You mean the dreamer?" Pilloop asked suddenly, unable to help himself.

Frelati smiled and chuckled a bit. "No, not the dreamer. We hadn't met her yet. Genevia…Alernoa grew up sheltered…*very* sheltered. I felt, and still feel that I need to look after her closely. It's my charge by the royal Elfin family."

"A difficult task for one as young as yourself," Pilloop observed.

Frelati shrugged. "I grew up in a prison. I may look young, but inside I'm not."

Pilloop nodded. They stood before the last door of the offered guest rooms.

"Your room," Pilloop said shortly with a nod at the door.

"Thank you," Frelati said, moving to disappear inside.

In spite of himself, Pilloop could not hold back the words that were fighting to be released. Perhaps it was because he felt an odd sort of kinship with this quiet, solitary elf, but for some reason, he felt an overwhelming urge to share some wisdom. He cleared his throat. "It's hard to get words from me, but you need to know this: treasure what you have right now with your friends. They seem a good bunch. Treasure yourself too. Don't sell yourself short, and don't be too quick to leave your childish tendencies behind. Staying young on the inside is good medicine to the soul and brings a glow to your life. You say you feel older on the inside, but, boy, hear this. Try to find a bit of the young man that's buried. It can help, in everyday tasks and in battle. You'll find enjoyment and extra strength, giving aid when it seems you should give up. The young wish to live. Mark my words, boy, everyone, even those with many years, can live longer, happier lives if they keep a bit of youth in their souls. Don't give up on that."

Frelati stared at the little man in curiosity, and Pilloop couldn't blame him. This was out of character, way out of character. He hadn't spoken that many words in years, and even a few moments in his presence had alerted Frelati to that fact. True, he had just dished out a huge bowl of wisdom, but that was not his way. Never had been, and he hoped would never be again. He stared into Frelati's eyes intently, assuring himself that the boy would think on his words. There was no need to waste them. Then he turned to walk down the hall without looking back.

"See you in the morning," Frelati said as a goodnight before shutting the door.

"Not another word from you, not another word," Pilloop muttered to himself. It was all that little girl's fault; that it was. Before that little chatterbox had come along, he'd been doing just fine. He needed to stick with silence, and if anyone persisted in trying to talk with him, mean glares should shut them up. "Just don't say another word. I'll just not say another word."

With that decided, Pilloop felt a bit better, and with a grunt he shuffled on his way.

Tunnels were a lot like life, Genevia decided. Only one part could be seen at any given time because all else was hidden in the darkness beyond the torchlight. This was like the past, present, and future. She could remember some of what she had already been through, was experiencing the rather dull part of the tunnel she could see now, and had absolutely no idea what horrors awaited her in the darkness ahead. They went down deeper into the earth, where it was colder and damper and more frightening. Then they went back up closer to the surface, where it was more pleasant, a bit warmer, and comfortable. This was like the ups and downs of life's tumultuous sea. And all of that wasn't even bringing in the twists and turns, the widening and thinning, and the taller and shorter openings that they encountered periodically. She supposed these inconsistencies were a lot like those faced every day. There were good days and bad days, surprises and mysteries waiting around each bend. These thoughts helped pass the time. It also kept her mind from wandering to all the creepy-crawling things that probably inhabited the tunnels.

The travelers didn't speak much; they simply followed Pilloop and his torch. He, for one, enjoyed the relative silence, but Genevia was having trouble dealing with it, as was Lela, she was sure.

"Mama," Lela whispered after several hours had passed. "How much...long...in dark?"

Genevia looked down at her and squeezed her hand. "I don't know, baby, but it can't be too long."

"How long?" Dayze asked from her left.

Genevia turned. "I'm not sure."

"Oh," the girls sighed in unison.

Faced with their disappointment, Genevia decided to get the answer from Pilloop, even if he was surly.

"Pilloop," she called to the front.

He stopped and whirled around. "We stop in an hour for lunch. Now, we must move on."

"Oh, well, that wasn't what I was asking," Genevia said as he began walking again.

"Then what were you asking?" Pilloop asked gruffly over his shoulder.

"How long will it be until we can travel above ground?"

"We should reach the surface at sunset, but that is only if we continue with minimal stops."

Genevia nodded. "Thank you."

They continued at the same pace. Few words were spoken and only the shuffling of feet was heard. There was no sense of time, except the rumbling of stomachs at noon, when Jezzie insisted all the "dahlin's" eat something to put some meat on their bones. She still wasn't happy with the size of Genevia, thinking that she needed to gain at least twenty pounds, and she never could give Frelati enough to eat, which was a great source of amusement to Traynord.

They moved through the tunnels at a steady but quick pace, the scenery remaining the same—bleak and dark—and the end of the tunnel seeming entirely too far away.

"My men have been waiting patiently on the shore of Yima Olem, but unfortunately, despite this great patience, your daughter has yet to appear. Do you have a valid reason for this unforeseen complication in my plans?"

King Nalofré sighed in relief. Since entering Alernoa's dream, he had been worried sick that she would follow his instructions. He tried to hide his reaction from Fezam though, knowing that this response could easily break that barrier holding in his almost uncontrollable fury.

Fezam's eyes flashed red flames. "Well, do you?"

King Nalofré met his angry gaze defiantly. "I can only assume that she took my order as what it was: a dream. If my daughter is anything like her mother and myself, as I am fairly certain she is, she would not think twice about following orders that she remembers from her sleep. It would not seem logical to her."

"So now I suppose you are thinking that my plan was useless and should not have been implemented?" The question was bait. Fezam had murder in his eyes and was just bursting to prove his authority.

King Nalofré knew he had to tread very carefully now. "Of course not; for anyone besides my stubborn and strong willed daughter, it probably would have worked. I only know that Lenaia never changes her course once she's decided upon it, and more than likely Alernoa received that occasionally annoying trait from her.

"Aside from that, Alernoa was traveling with many other people who might not have agreed with her. She would have been forced to do as the majority wished. So no, that was not at all what I was implying. Rather, what I was hoping you would see is that your next plan needs to cater to her weaknesses. I'm sure that you have already figured that part out yourself, but I wanted to make certain you had thought this through."

"Why should I believe your rubbish?" Fezam chuckled and raised a brow. "You don't want your daughter captured, of that I am certain."

Nalofré hung his head wearily. "True, I love my daughter, but I have my wife to consider. I haven't seen my daughter since she was six months old. My attachment to her, while strong, is not nearly that shared with my wife, whom I need to keep my sanity. I know that if I do not help you to capture Alernoa, you will see no reason to keep my wife alive and with me. My daughter is not worth that."

Fezam nodded, and an evil smile twisted up the corners of his mouth. "Yes, self-preservation I understand. The quality of your life is dependent upon hers. This is a wonderful arrangement for me. I am so glad you deigned to show me this weakness and to provide me with your valuable services. Now, go."

Nalofré bowed and was taken by the guards back to his cell, where Lenaia waited impatiently. As soon as the guards' footsteps receded, she spoke.

"Did he accept it?" she asked quietly.

Nalofré smiled. "Of course he did; Fezam knows nothing of love. He now thinks that I will do anything to keep you alive, which I will with exception to our daughter as I'm sure you'll agree…"

"Yes, of course, Nalofré," Lenaia said hurriedly, reaching out to caress his cheek. "You must keep Alernoa safe. Don't even consider placing her in danger…for any reason."

Nalofré nodded. "I want you to know that if there is any way for me to keep you both alive I will take it, even if it means my life."

"Oh." Lenaia buried her face in his shoulder. "Please don't talk like that!"

Nalofré rubbed her back. "Well, I am in with Fezam now. He won't suspect me of sabotaging his plans. Apparently, self-preservation is my motive. The man, if you can even call him that, can't even equate my wish to keep you alive as love, rather as some indirect way to save myself."

"Just be careful. We may have him fooled now, but he isn't stupid. I don't want to lose you." Lenaia gripped his shirt tightly.

"I'll be careful," Nalofré said, pulling her close. "Don't you worry, I'll be careful, and we'll all get out of this."

Frelati and Traynord were the stragglers of the group. It wasn't too much farther until they reached the sea, but Frelati was tired of listening to talking and laughing, so he had fallen behind. Traynord decided to join him, which disappointed Frelati's hopes of avoiding chatter. What was worse, though, was the topic Traynord was determined to discuss, regardless of Frelati's numerous distraction tactics.

"I notice ye, la'," Traynord said grinning. "I notice all a yas, an' wha' ye do an' don' do."

"Well, it's great to be noticed," Frelati said sarcastically without turning to look at him.

"Ah, now, I know ye're tryin' ta stop me from talkin'. Tha's yer way, bu' I have me some questions, la', an' I wan' you ta answer 'em."

Frelati sighed inaudibly. "And what might these questions be?"

"Well, la', fer sure ye know wha' I'm talkin' 'bout. Tha' lil lass ain' gonna wai' forever. Ye nee' ta snatch 'er up."

"Traynord, stop playing matchmaker. We've been through this before, and you know I don't play that game." Frelati was barely containing his annoyance.

"Come now. On this voyage, ye know som'at coul' happen ta'er, so's ye nee' ta talk ta 'er, tell 'er how ye feel."

Frelati shot Traynord a quick look from the side of his eye. "I don't think she would appreciate my saying that it wouldn't work out and that she needs to give up. Anyone but a masochist would resent that."

"La'." Traynord sighed. "Stop lyin' ta yerself. Yer drivin' us all ma', I tell ye."

"I'm not doing anything," Frelati argued.

"Exac'ly, la', yer no' doin' a thin'. Tha's wha's drivin' us all crazy. Ye're stubborn, pessimistic, blin', an' ye're scared."

"Right," Frelati said.

Traynord shook his head and tried for another tactic. "When ye firs' me' 'er, wha' di' ye think? Was she outta yer league then?"

"I don't have to talk about this."

"Then don', jus' listen," Traynord persisted. "I be' ye though' ye ha' a chance, an' ye woul' 'ave taken i', wouldn' ye, la'? Yeah, ye woul' 'ave, bu' now ye're jus' bein' stubborn an' hurtin' tha' poor girl. Jus' look a' i' from 'er view, la', an' think abou' i'."

"Why do you even care?" Frelati asked in annoyance.

Traynord chuckled. "I'm meddlesome. Besides, ye two are perfec' tagether, an' I'm a sucker fer romance."

Frelati was saved from answering by the sight of the sea. It had been hidden from view just behind a rise and had finally made its debut.

"Tha's wha' I miss. The sea nee's me, an' I nee' the sea," Traynord said, breathing deeply of the salty sea air. "Le's catch up, la'. We nee' ta se' sail, soon as possible."

"Why as soon as possible?" Frelati asked.

Traynord pouted. "Well, maybe *we* don', bu' I do. I nee' the sea, an' I imagine tha' Genevia's parents wouldn' hur' none if we go' there a bi' early."

Frelati smiled. Traynord may get under his skin on occasion, but the man was certainly good at cheering him up right after his taxing conversations.

"Then let's get going. Lead the way."

It took an hour for them to set sail, but they were on the water soon enough. After riding the waves for three hours, when they were just a speck from the shore, Fezam's men rode up. Any place but there would have been preferable when the men realized how close they had come to catching Alernoa. Their lives had hinged on a three-hour difference, and unfortunately, they had been given the losing hand.

Chapter Twenty-Four

"I'm gonna miss the sea," Traynord moped, looking back at the lonely boat.

"Ah, Traynord, you'll be all right. The sea isn't going anywhere, and you'll be back riding it soon," Genevia said with a pat on his back.

"Tha's all tha' comforts me," Traynord said after one last glimpse at the boat. "I'll be all righ'. Don' worry 'bou' me, I'll be alrigh'. Jus' hate ta leave the sea is all."

Genevia smiled. "Well, what kind of seaman would you be if you didn't hate to leave the sea?"

"I s'pose ye go' a poin' there." Traynord chuckled. "Ye're a goo' lassie; none be'er."

"Thanks, Traynord."

They walked in silence for a short while. Genevia kept an eye on Lela and Dayze ahead of them as they ran around with Quinsnap. If they kept that up, none of them would last past noon. Genevia jogged over to them.

"Girls, why don't you take a break for a little while, okay?" Genevia said. "If you keep this up, Frelati and I will have to carry you for hours while you store up more energy."

Lela smiled and nodded. "Yes, Mama."

Genevia smiled with a shake of her head as she watched the girls just barely arrest their energy as they continued with their game. Her gaze was pulled away from them as Asben walked up.

"I've been researching your predicament," he said as he drew up beside her. "As of this particular moment, nothing has been enlightening, but I'm sure that something will reveal itself presently, especially since I gathered several more books from the dwarves' library."

Genevia laughed. "Why am I not surprised? But, tell me, how exactly do you plan to return these books?"

Asben waved a hand in dismissal. "That will be no problem. I've already arranged for my next visit. I hope to learn all about their political history. Do you realize that the dwarf hierarchy is extremely intricate? Even a small misstep within each class could be reason for expulsion, and their punitary system is—"

"That sounds…fascinating," Genevia interrupted. "I just hope you have luck with all those books you brought."

"Not to worry, I'll find some answers. There's not any question yet asked of me that I have not had the ability to answer."

"Then I'm very glad you've decided to help me."

"It is an honor and privilege," Asben said, his voice declaring his words as truth, even if he was being a bit dramatic.

Genevia smiled to herself before changing the subject. "So, this is Suta. It's sort of…dry."

"Well, yes. This is desert country. The land of the nomads, as it's called by the few who dare to travel here," Asben explained.

"Do you know a little bit about everything?" Genevia asked.

"Well, I do try to stay informed," Asben said, smiling.

"A good pastime. So, do you think we'll see any nomads?"

Asben thought a bit. "The odds for it are about as good as the odds against it. Nomads travel all over the country. They don't stay in one area for long, so if we're traveling where they just were, then we won't see them. If the case is vice-versa, then we will probably meet up with them. I wouldn't want to run into any, though. They enjoy sport with those unfortunate enough to meet them."

"What do you mean by sport?" Genevia asked when he paused, not sure if she really wanted to know the answer.

"They test each person's limits. Put one of their men against one of the strangers' group. If the stranger loses, part of the travelers' money goes to the nomads and a new sport begins. If the travelers win, usually, there are no more sports, and they are free to go, but there have been exceptions."

"Wait, the travelers don't get anything if they win?"

"Well, they had lost their freedom, so in essence they get something they didn't have, but the nomads are fair people, relatively. They won't give up their gold, but they allow the strangers to ask one thing of them…within reason that is."

"Well, that's better than nothing."

"Most certainly. They know Suta well, better than anyone. No maps have been drawn accurately. Of course, it is my belief that the reason for this lies solely with the nomads. I think they alter the land to keep the world confused about not only their whereabouts but water locations. That keeps travelers away and gives the nomads the upper hand when it comes to those few brave enough to travel through these parts."

"So, if we don't know where water is, why did we stop here? Couldn't we have passed this land by and gone on to another place?"

Traynord broke in to answer that question. "Well, lassie, the reason for tha' is the flee' o' the Dark King's boa's sailin' behin' us."

"What!" Genevia exclaimed. "How long were they there? Why did no one tell me?"

Traynord shrugged. "Sorry, lassie, Frelati sai' no' ta tell ye. No nee' ta worry ye, he sai'. They weren' behin' us lon'. Jus' saw 'em meself two days before."

With that, he hurried to catch up with Frelati; there was no need for the boy to walk alone. Genevia turned back to Asben.

"Why did we stop *here*, though? Isn't this worse than riding ahead of a huge fleet of ships?"

"I'm afraid not. Based on the quality of Fezam's fleet, they would have caught up in a few days' time. On foot, though, given the size of the army, we will outdistance them. Also, accounting for the rumors spread about this place, many will move slowly and cautiously. Besides, as I said before, no one knows the layout, so they won't make it through."

"Um…neither will we," Genevia said, trying to keep panic out of her voice.

"Exactly, but that is why we are looking for the nomads. They know how to get through, and since we landed first, we have a head start in finding them. Once we do, the soldiers won't be able to find the nomads or us and will be forced to stop following," Asben said with a proud grin.

"But you just said we don't want to meet any nomads because they always make sport," Genevia said in confusion.

"Yes, but the nomads don't like Fezam because he has been sending troops into Suta to find them. Once we tell them that we plan to overthrow Fezam, they will choose to help us without their sports."

Genevia was skeptical. "How can we be sure of this?"

At that, Asben grew a bit uncomfortable. "Well...we can't, but the probability that everything will work out as planned is high, much higher than that stating the plan will end in catastrophe."

"Okay, so how do we find the nomads?" Genevia asked.

"We...well...we don't."

"What?" Genevia asked in exasperation. "You just said that the nomads were the only way we could get through Suta."

"Right, but we can't find the nomads unless they choose to be found. So, in reality, it is they who find us."

"What if they don't want to be found?"

"Then...we'll perish." Asben paused. "But they will want to be found."

"Why?"

"Because we will entice them."

"How?"

Asben chuckled. "What do nomads like best?"

Genevia's brows drew together in thought.

"Gold?" Hadn't he mentioned that earlier?

Asben nodded.

Genevia's brow crinkled even more. "We don't have much."

"They don't know that, and we won't let them realize it. Instead, we are going to make them think the opposite."

"And how are we supposed to do that? I mean, look at us. Our group doesn't exactly scream rich. We're two kids, a lefnode, an old sailor, a middle-aged married couple, and two young elves. Why would our unusual group be carrying huge riches with us?"

"Exactly, no one would suspect us of transporting gold."

Genevia shot him an odd look. "You are going in circles."

"All right, follow me now," Asben said as he readied himself for what Genevia knew was going to be a very involved explanation. "We need to pretend to be a normal traveling group…"

Genevia interrupted in exasperation. "Why do we have to pretend? We already are that!"

"Just listen," Asben said quickly. "We need to pretend to be a normal traveling group, but do it in an obvious manner, too obvious a manner for the nomads to overlook. In addition, all the men, and yourself as well, I guess, need to constantly look around, as if protecting something. We have a trunk full of clothing and cooking implements, right? Well, that is to be our chest of gold. Someone is to be guarding that trunk at all times."

"That won't necessarily get their attention," Genevia pointed out.

"You're right, which is why I am going to drop a few pieces of gold to get them interested. After they have observed our unusual behavior, they will come to the conclusion that we are trying not to be suspected of carrying gold, and then they will approach us."

Genevia wasn't at all sure of the plan. "I suppose that might work, but it is a bit farfetched, don't you think?"

"Precisely," Asben said. "No one travels through Suta without a reason. The nomads know this, so we are automatically suspects. We need a farfetched plan because our situation is sort of…farfetched."

"If we're really lucky, it'll work," Genevia said. "And I hope it does because dying of thirst here is not a top priority."

"I suppose, in hindsight, I should have calculated every option and consequence before we conducted our experiment." Asben sighed wearily.

He was swinging upside-down by his ankles. Jezzie was tied to a rock beside him.

"Hun, even you couldn'ta seen this," Jezzie said. "Although, it woulda been nice if ya had."

"I should have predicted this outcome, though," Asben said emphatically. "If I had just thought the plan through, this would have been one of the options. Of course, I probably would have considered it quite improbable."

Jezzie sighed. "Stop beatin' urself up, dahlin'. We'll get outta this, just you watch."

"It would help if they would turn me right-side-up. The pressure in my head is building to an excruciating climax," he said before calling out to a nomad. "Excuse me, sir, is there any chance you could cut me down and tie me back in an upright position?"

The nomad stopped to look at Asben's beat red face. "I'll see if you have been punished enough. Don't move."

"I'll try not to," Asben said sarcastically.

He was bound so tight, only his head was mobile.

"See, dahlin', things are already lookin' up," Jezzie said encouragingly.

Asben didn't reply. Soon the nomad returned. He looked intently at Asben's face before nodding.

"You're red enough. I'll cut you down."

The huge nomad slid out a wicked looking blade and sliced through Asben's bonds before pulling out fresh rope and retying him beside Jezzie.

"Thank you, kind sir," Asben said with a bow of his head.

The nomad smirked and walked off.

"I only hope the others are faring as well," Asben said with a sigh. "Who would have thought that the nomads would act as barbaric as they have, just over a slight misunderstanding?"

"Maybe it's just a misunderstanding," Genevia said weakly.

Frelati was sitting with his back against the rock wall. They were trapped in a cave with bars covering the only opening and guards barring the way beyond that. Genevia was going to try moving the ground, but Frelati had advised against it. They still needed the nomads' help to get off Suta, and if Genevia started breaking everyone out, the nomads might take offense.

With raised eyebrows, Frelati looked up at Genevia, who was standing at the bars looking out. "No, I think they know exactly what they're doing."

Genevia turned back to look at Frelati. "What do you think they're going to do?"

"No clue."

"Do you think the girls are okay?" she asked worriedly.

"'Course they are. The nomads wouldn't hurt children. They're fine; trust me," Frelati said reassuringly with a smile.

Genevia nodded. "Why do you think they separated us from everyone else?"

Frelati had been wondering the same thing and had come up with some possible answers. "Two possible reasons. One, if we were all together it would be easier to break out together. Two, since we're elves, they know we have gifts; since they don't know what the gifts are, they're taking no chances."

Genevia turned again to look outside. "Someone's coming."

Frelati stood and dusted himself off. Genevia backed up to stand by him, and he put a protective arm about her shoulders. The nomad unlocked the door.

"I'm just here to tell you what to expect tomorrow," he said.

He was young and seemed nice, if a bit uncomfortable. Frelati and Genevia said nothing. The nomad shuffled from one foot to the other.

"Well, one from your group is going to participate in a sport," the nomad said. "I can't tell you which sport it is, but I can tell you three of our common sports. There's a fight with knives, short knives, to the death."

Genevia gasped and gripped Frelati's shirt. "You're kidding, right?"

The nomad's brow creased in confusion. "No, why would I kid? All of our sports are to the death."

"That's barbaric," Genevia exclaimed. "What is wrong with you people?"

"Genevia," Frelati said quietly to silence her, pulling her closer to him and rubbing her back before speaking to their visitor. "What are the other two sports?"

"Plateau wrestling and a battle of wits."

"Who is participating?" Frelati asked, hoping against hope that Genevia was not chosen.

"The thin human that wears lenses."

Frelati breathed a sigh of relief. "Thank you."

"Good luck," the nomad said as he left.

There was a moment of silence before Genevia spoke. "Frelati, what if Asben dies?"

"He doesn't have the choice to decline," he said softly. "Don't worry; everything will work out."

"I just hope he doesn't get hurt," Genevia mumbled.

"He'll be fine," Frelati said.

Now if only he could believe those words.

"They went into Suta? They traveled into the place I would have control over if not for my army's incompetence? Am I hearing this correctly? My men, my new recruits, the replacements for the last incompetent group, managed to botch this assignment by allowing that annoying little girl into Suta?"

The messenger didn't say a word. He stood there shaking and looking at the ground. After word had spread throughout the army that Fezam killed messengers that delivered bad news, they had started recruiting peasants to deliver the messages. This man had been unlucky enough to be chosen. Of course, after the way his luck had been going, he should have expected it. Now, he was feeling the King's eyes as they drilled into him. Yep, his luck was still on the same rutty track, and it was a truly bad track to be on.

"Why do I put up with all the incompetence?" Fezam muttered. "The people in this world can't do anything right!"

"Sire," one of his men spoke up suddenly. "This might not be a bad thing. The nomads must be a difficult bunch to deal with if the soldiers couldn't get them to cooperate, so why would it be any different with Alernoa? She will probably have just as much difficulty with them as anyone else has over the years."

Bless him, the messenger thought in relief as he glanced over at the speaker.

Fezam turned to look at the soldier. "Your point?"

"Well, if you send your men to guard the sea at key inlets, then you could simply wait until Alernoa leaves; that is, if she manages to do so."

"I suppose that could work." Fezam thought a moment. "But are you saying none of my men should follow them into Suta?"

The soldier shook his head. "Not necessarily. Some could, but Suta is such a large continent it would be difficult for them to find Alernoa's small group. It would probably be best to put all of your men in the water, but it's your choice."

Fezam nodded. "That does sound like the best plan…"

The messenger was feeling a little bit better. The man that had just spoken had gotten Fezam's mind off him, so maybe he could leave this awful place alive. He cringed as he felt Fezam's eyes return to him.

"Give me one good reason why you should live," he commanded.

The peasant stood there shaking, unsure of what to say.

Fezam scrutinized him. "If you say nothing, I'll just assume you have no reason to live and relieve you of the tremendous burden of keeping yourself alive day after excruciating day."

"I…I have a family, ch-ch-children. I…I'm not p-part of your army," the messenger stammered.

Fezam smirked. "Not part of my army? Well, that decides it."

The messenger hung his head. He had said the wrong thing.

"Let him go," Fezam ordered, causing the messenger's head to snap back up to look at him. "Actually, escort him home and make sure nothing happens to him."

The messenger stared at this supposedly evil king. "Wh-what?"

Fezam only spared him a brief glance. "You aren't part of the imbeciles that make up my army. You should be rewarded for that. My wrath is not for you; you have done nothing against me. Because of that, and that only, I am going to allow you to live."

The messenger gaped. "Th-th-thank you so much."

Fezam grimaced. "I would advise you to keep your mouth shut and say nothing of this. I am not being kind to you, just relieving myself of another responsibility. Just go, now, before I change my mind."

The messenger left as another person. His luck had changed. His life was going to be worth living. He was a new man. He could do anything, and he was going to ensure that his family had a better life.

As the man left, Fezam leaned back in his chair.

"Retrieve the royal prisoners and bring them to me. Quickly," he ordered.

Two men rushed from the room, and within ten minutes, Lenaia and Nalofré knelt before him.

"Men," Fezam yelled, spreading his arms wide. "We can at least be hospitable enough to give the king and queen chairs, can we not?"

Seconds later, Lenaia and Nalofré found themselves seated in chairs, and Fezam nodded in satisfaction.

"Now, I'll go over this one more time, just to make sure you know exactly what to do and don't 'accidentally' make a mistake. You will enter her dreams and find out where she is. If she can't tell you, you are going to tell her to take her group to Callum Cove, which is the largest cove on Suta's eastern coast, in case she and her companions don't know that. You are not to give her any signals; I want no code words, no facial expressions, and no gestures that might give me away. Do you understand?"

Nalofré nodded. "I understand."

"Good. Now do it. And remember," Fezam gave him a threatening smile, "if I catch even the hint of a warning throughout your chat, your beautiful Lenaia dies."

He nodded to the guard standing behind her, who produced a knife and held it to her throat. Lenaia showed no fear, just radiated fury and hostility.

Fezam sat forward in his throne and held out a hand, closing his eyes and murmuring Alernoa's name softly. Again, the odd gray smoke appeared, slowly swirling before him as it waited to allow passage into Alernoa's dreams.

"Alernoa will be asleep soon, and you can begin."

Nalofré nodded slowly as a plan formed to buy some time. Feigning hesitance, he asked, "Could you...explain to me how you do this?"

Fezam was not usually one to explain anything, but this elf could be cocky, and it might benefit him to be a bit frightened by the Dark King's power. "You know of Kiem, of his creation of the worlds and his split into six."

Although certain this was the case, Fezam waited on Nalofré's nod before continuing. "I am not from here, as you may have surmised. My world is Ashneer, and the part of Kiem it houses is darkness, the ability to allow rest, produce creativity or solve problems while asleep…if used positively. However, it can easily be altered for simple manipulation, even while awake at times, but that is more difficult."

He stopped to gauge the Elfin King's response. Not surprisingly, Nalofré had paled as the enormity of Fezam's power was finally revealed.

"You…you house Kiem."

The Dark King sneered. "Yes, just as your daughter does."

Nalofré's eyes widened and darted to the still swirling gray matter. "My daughter?"

Fezam huffed in annoyance. "Surely you knew this. Why else would I care to possess her? But enough of this. You will speak to your daughter and relay my instructions, nothing more. We will monitor her movements periodically. If I don't like her course, you will change it. You are to be firm but…loving." He seemed to almost gag on the word. "She isn't to suspect a thing."

Nalofré nodded.

"Then let's begin."

He muttered Alermoa's name a last time, and the cloud cleared, allowing Nalofré a glimpse of his daughter, his beautiful daughter, but he saw another face as well. The one that owned the shoulder his daughter rested upon.

"Frelati," he whispered, overwhelmed with relief at knowing the boy had safely found Alernoa and was watching over her.

"What was that?" Fezam snapped.

"I'm ready," Nalofré covered.

"Then begin."

Chapter Twenty-Five

Genevia paced back and forth in their cell; her worry for Asben, who was at this moment facing death, forced her into movement. Frelati tried several times to get her to sit, but he hadn't succeeded.

"Why won't they let us watch?" she said in aggravation yet again. "I mean it's a mind game. We have no control over that."

She started walking faster. "What if he dies? Why couldn't they just let us...ooo, Frelati..."

"What? Genevia?"

She rubbed her eyes and yawned. "It's nothing; I just feel really... tired."

"Then come sit down," Frelati ordered in alarm.

"Yeah, I'll..."

She collapsed to the ground.

"Genevia!" Frelati crawled over to her, scooping her into his arms and shaking her. "Genevia...come on..."

He was somewhat comforted when he realized she was still breathing, but alarm kept his heart beating wildly. Realizing there wasn't much he could do, he settled them both comfortably as he prepared to wait...for her to wake up or for Asben, if he made it through this test, to find a way to make her better.

Genevia was surrounded by white. There were no walls, no ceiling, no floor. It was just like the time before when she spoke with her father. This time, though, he wasn't there. She looked all around her and saw continuing white. It was a bit frightening. She took a few steps, but there was no sound. She called his name and heard it echo all around her, sometimes loud, sometimes soft, sometimes shrill, sometimes deep.

Then she saw a door begin to appear, seeming to grow from nothing. As she watched, the door opened to reveal a familiar figure.

"You're back!" she exclaimed, but this time there was no echo. She rushed over and stopped before him, glad that she could hear her footsteps. Everything seemed to be made right now that her father had arrived.

He smothered her in a tight hug, kissing the top of her head. "Oh, I've missed you, sweetheart."

"I missed you too," Genevia said. "It was a bit frightening here by myself."

Nalofré chuckled. "I can understand that. I saw the boy with you. Your mother and I are glad you are not traveling alone, that you have his protection."

"Yes, he's really nice; I like him a lot," Genevia admitted with a smile, but she was slightly confused. Her father spoke warmly of "the boy," but it was as if he was speaking of a stranger. She wanted to question him, wanted to ask why Frelati's name was not mentioned, but surely he had a good reason. She would follow his lead. "I'm not sure what he thinks of me. Sometimes I think he likes me, but other times, he seems afraid. I don't know what to do."

Nalofré smiled. "It will all work out. Sweetheart, I need to tell you something important, and we don't have much time."

He paused and looked away before he continued. "Right now, you're on Suta, right?"

Genevia nodded. "Yeah, but the nomads captured us. We were actually trying to get captured so we could get through, but it backfired. It was Asben's plan. He…"

"Alernoa, honey, you can explain later. Our time is limited," Nalofré said softly. "So you are on Suta. Do you know exactly where you are? Have you heard a name?"

"No, we're just surrounded by rock and sand."

"All right, well, I know Fezam's plan. He's hoping to capture you while you leave Suta. You have to avoid him, so listen very carefully." He looked straight into her eyes before continuing. Something was wrong; she could sense it...unless she was imagining things. "Go to Callum Cove, the largest cove on Suta's coast. Repeat that."

"I need to go to Callum Cove, which is the largest one on Suta's coast."

"Good. You also need to pay attention to anyone who says anything about your location. I'll be checking in, making sure you're staying safe, and I want you to be able to tell me where you're headed. Then I can warn you if it isn't...safe. All right?"

Genevia nodded. "All right, I'll try."

"That's my girl." Nalofré ran his figures through her hair. "You have your mother's hair, Alernoa. You're beautiful."

He smiled sadly, and it felt and looked so real. Surely this wasn't a dream.

"I need you to do this, sweetheart. It's important."

Genevia nodded. "I'll do my best."

Nalofré studied her for a short while. "When you were a little girl...were you taken care of?"

Genevia smiled. "Very well. My papa told me the story of how he found me almost every night. He loved me very much." Her smile faded. "But I think he...he may have been killed when the...the soldiers came."

Genevia tried not to cry as Nalofré hugged her again. "I'm sorry, so sorry. You didn't need that."

"The soldiers were looking for me. They burned down the cabin, and I just ran. It's my fault."

"No, no, sweetheart, you are not to blame. You had no control over this, my sweet girl. Promise me you won't think that; we'll be together soon and put all of this behind us. I want you to tell me all about your...father when I see you in person."

Genevia nodded and stepped back.

"I love you, sweetheart. I want you to know that."

"I..." Genevia started. "I've always wanted to meet you and my mother, always. That's why I got Papa to tell me the story of how he found me again and again. I loved hearing about you both, even though he knew nothing of you."

Nalofré smiled. "I'm sorry I wasn't there for you, and I'm sorry I have to leave you now."

Genevia watched him walk toward the door through the tears held captive in her eyes.

"He's my father," she whispered, so softly he could not hear. "My father."

She looked up as he opened the door and shouted after him. "Father, don't leave!"

He turned, and she saw great sadness in his eyes, but he didn't say a word. He gave a shaky smile and stepped through the door. As it began to close, he turned to say a parting word.

"Remember Callum Cove, Alernoa, and be careful."

"Father, don't go! I need you with me! Father!"

The door shut and white invaded again. A tear slid down Genevia's cheek. "Father, don't leave me here! Father!"

Her world began to shake, and a voice came to her from far away.

"Genevia, Genevia, wake up. Genevia."

She sat bolt upright.

Frelati looked at her in concern. "Genevia, you were calling out for your father. What were you dreaming about?"

Genevia was in her own world. She felt out of sorts and didn't even hear Frelati's question.

"Genevia, are you okay?" Frelati asked again.

"I'm...I'm fine," Genevia answered absently.

"What were you dreaming about?"

Genevia looked at him intently, trying to grasp reality, before she looked into the darkness surrounding her. Night had fallen over Suta, but it barely registered. When she spoke, Frelati had to strain to hear her words.

"Callum Cove, the largest cove on Suta's shores."

"I'm a bit nervous about this challenge, Jezzie," Asben confided quietly as he waited for the nomads to arrive. They hadn't bothered to tell him how late into the morning it would be until he was called, so his nerves had steadily been building since he woke three hours earlier.

"Well, what do ya have to worry about, dear? Ur smarter than the whole lot of nomads," Jezzie encouraged. Trust his wife to put too much faith in him.

"This isn't a simple equation or puzzle. There aren't going to be symbols to decipher or numbers to balance or a language to translate. This is a battle of the wits. For all I know, the answer will be so simple I'll overthink it and get it wrong."

Jezzie hadn't considered that. Asben did tend to overthink things, but since he had pointed it out, he would be on his guard against it.

"Besides," he continued. "You heard what they said. This is going to involve poison. I have to answer five riddles or questions correctly to avoid drinking something, and then if I get one wrong, I have to hope I'm lucky enough to pick one of the five vials that doesn't contain poison."

"But hun," Jezzie interrupted. "The man said the vials didn't just hold poison. Two have an antidote for the poison, and one is water. And they said they'd tell ya which one ya chose after ya drank it, an' ya get a chance to choose the antidote if ya happened to drink poison and get the next question right."

Asben sighed in frustration. "But the vials are constantly switched, so I'll be picking from five each time, which means I could simply double up on the poison in my system as opposed to stopping it with the antidote."

"Asben, stop fretting, just as long as ya think through the questions and answer 'em carefully, you'll get 'em right, so you won't even have ta worry about the poison," Jezzie consoled him. "And, if it's any help, I believe ya can do it."

Jezzie smiled, and Asben couldn't help but return it. That was one of the many things he loved about his wife. She always knew exactly what to say.

He looked up as several nomads approached.

"It is time to win your way to freedom," the largest nomad said before untying him and Jezzie and leading them to a small table with a chair on either side. On the table were brown goblets filled with either dark red or clear liquid. Asben was pushed down into a chair. He looked around him.

"Where is the rest of my group?" he asked.

"The children and the old man are on their way," the nomad replied. "The elves are staying in their cell. We don't want any trouble."

"I understand completely," Asben said with a nod.

The leader of the nomads walked up with the others from Asben's group trailing behind him amidst a crowd of nomads.

"Are you ready to begin?" the leader asked.

Asben swallowed and nodded. "As ready as I'll ever be."

"Then let's begin."

He sat in the chair across from Asben and stared at him.

"I'll explain a bit about each riddle before it is given. It will be repeated once again at your direction. You will be given enough information to successfully discover the answer, but you will have to think outside the box to get the answer correct. Do you understand?"

"Yes."

"Do you also understand the rules? You know what happens if you get the answer wrong or right at any given time during the game?"

"I do."

"All right, then I will now give you the first riddle." The leader grinned in anticipation. "Let's see how smart you really are. Here is the information you will need. There is a one-word answer. Each line, excluding the last, yields an important piece of that word. Are you ready to hear the riddle?"

Asben shook his head. "Not yet. I have a question first. Is there any chance I could have some parchment, a quill, and ink?"

The leader smiled and motioned to his people with two fingers, his gaze never leaving Asben's. Two women rushed forward and placed the appropriate items before him.

"Thank you," Asben said. "Now you can recite the riddle."

The leader nodded and cleared his throat.

> Marriage is a holy, blissful thing,
> All hope that health continually reigns,
> Add the places that rest for travelers bring,
> Correctly answer, and you'll have no poisonous pains.

Asben wrote it down word for word. "I can talk out loud to figure this out?"

The leader nodded.

"Marriage has to do with a man and a woman. Vows are taken. So it could be man or vow, not woman—that would be too long. Man and vow."

He wrote those two words on his parchment.

"Health continually reigns," he muttered. "Okay, that could be to be well. Someone's well, healthy, showered with good fortune, lucky, luck, good. All right, it could be well, luck, or good, those are short enough."

He added those three words in a separate column on the parchment.

"A place where travelers can rest...that's simple. An inn."

He wrote that last word in yet another column and studied what he had.

"So my choices are man-well-inn, man-luck-inn, man-good-inn, vow-well-inn, vow-luck-inn, and vow-good-inn. I can take out good. That doesn't sound right at all. So now I have man-well-inn, man-luck-inn, vow-luck-inn, and vow-well-inn."

He said the last combination quickly, giving the *inn* more of an *n* sound. He said it again, pondering.

"That *inn* isn't literally *inn*. It's the letter *n*. Man-welln, man-luckn, vow-luckn, vow-welln. Luck doesn't sound right either. Vow-welln and man-welln."

He thought about the words, rolling them around on his tongue. He glanced at the nomad leader to see if he was on the right track, but the nomad's face was inscrutable.

"You know, these words sound a lot like Tiweln," he joked, trying to see even a hint of emotion on the man's face. He got nothing. "Tiweln. It has the well in it and the inn in it. All that's left is the ti, like tying a knot."

Asben had started to laugh, but then he snapped to silence as he thought about what he had just said. "Tying a knot. Matrimony is referred to as tying the knot. Breaking that up, it would be tie. Tie-well-inn. Tiweln. That's the answer! Tiweln."

The leader finally spoke up. "Are you sure you want to give me an answer? Or would you prefer to think about it a bit longer?"

Asben shook his head, despite the warning look on the nomad's face. "No, that's my answer; it's not going to change. Tiweln is the answer."

The leader nodded. "The next riddle requires answering a question. Once again it's a one-word answer. You must think outside the usual thought processes to avoid a drink. Are you ready to hear the riddle?"

"Wait, did I get the first one right?" Asben asked.

The nomad raised his eyebrows. "Did you avoid drinking from a flask?"

"Yes."

"You just answered your question. Are you ready for the next riddle?"

Asben grinned excitedly. "Yes."

The leader took a large swig from his own flask before reciting the riddle. "What is one short of left, occurs in the middle of lunch, and is only as good as a poet's word?"

Asben wrote it down and stared at it, shaking his head. He blew out a puff of air. "One short of left, that could be a path that isn't like another one because it's one short of a left turn. Or it could be degrees. Ninety degrees to the left would be a complete left turn. One short of that would be eighty-nine degrees. Unless you turn the other way, then it would be two hundred sixty-nine degrees. So it could be a degree."

He wrote degree down and moved on.

"Occurs in the middle of lunch, that would be eating, talking, food, drink, digestion, the sun is at its highest. It's at the highest degree, directly overhead. So degree would work for that too."

He got excited as he wrote degree down one more time on the parchment. "All right, only as good as a poet's word. That could be the degree to which people enjoy a poem. The answer has to be degree!"

"Are you sure you wish to answer the question now, or would you prefer to think about it a bit longer?" the nomad asked again.

"I don't need to think about it. The answer has to be..."

"Asben," Jezzie yelled. "Look for another answer."

A large nomad rushed over to silence her, but it was too late. Asben glanced over at his wife; it always paid to listen to her. He made eye contact and nodded before turning back to the nomad leader.

"I would like to think about it a bit more, thanks," Asben said and was rewarded to see dismay cross the nomad's face before it was smothered. Jezzie had just saved him from making a grave error.

He looked at the question again. "I'll deal with the poet's word. That is a poem or an ode, or it could be a song."

He wrote those three words down.

"All right, one short of left," he mumbled softly. "Short is small, or smaller. So, one smaller than left. One smaller than a number is one number subtracted or cut off from the previous number. One cut off left could be one letter cut off of left. That leaves me with lef, eft, and let; taking out the e wouldn't make any sense."

After writing that down, he went to the next group of words. "Occurs in the middle of lunch could be along the same lines as one short of left. If that's the case, then n is what I'm looking for. It's the middle letter in lunch."

He looked at his paper and saw the words lined up.

Lef		poem
Eft	n	song
Let		ode

"Lefnpoem, that's not a word. Eftnpoem, not a word. Letnpoem, once again, not a word."

He crossed poem off the list. "Lefnsong, Eftnsong, Letnsong, none of them are words."

Song was crossed off as well. "Lefnode, wait, lefnode, that's an animal. One short of left is lef; the *t* is removed, making left one short of *t*. *N* is in the middle of lunch, *l* and *u* on one side, *c* and *h* on the other. A poet's word would be an ode. Together it makes lefnode. That's the answer. It's not degree; it's lefnode."

Asben saw that the nomad was about to ask the inevitable question, and he cut him off. "Yes, that is my final answer, and I don't want to think about it any more. Lefnode is the answer."

"Then we will move forward. This next riddle is a game. I will be playing with you. The challenge requires the speed of wit." With two fingers, he signaled to a man, who stepped forward and placed three hourglasses on the table. "We each have until the sand runs out in our hourglass to respond. The object of the game is this: we begin with one animal, weapon, or disease—it has been predetermined—I will say something that can defeat it or repel an attack, then you will, in turn, say something that can defeat or repel what I mentioned. The game continues until one or the other can think of nothing to defeat or repel the last thing mentioned. In other words, the game ends when the sand runs out on one of us without a response. After the first animal, weapon, or disease has been given, an hourglass is turned and my time has begun. After I answer, another hourglass is turned for you. We get one minute per turn, and we cannot repeat an answer. Do you understand?"

"I'm pretty sure I get it."

"All right, now, after answering, the time is paused with this." The leader motioned to a small metal protrusion located just at the center of the hourglass. The nomad in charge of keeping time did a demonstration, and sure enough, the sand could be stopped. Asben would have to ask for one of these contraptions. The leader continued. "We have to explain how our answer either defeats or repels the previous item. If the announcer"—the nomad motioned to a nomad standing a bit apart from the group of bystanders around them—"thinks the explanation is sufficient, we will move forward. If it is not, you will be given the remaining time to come up with another answer."

Asben nodded and took a deep breath. "All right, I'm ready to start."

The leader nodded, and a nomad that stood slightly in front of the group walked up to the table.

"Quiz will start," he said, motioning to the leader with a nod of his head. "The word is lefnode. Begin."

The hourglass was turned.

Quiz thought only fifteen seconds before answering. "Hawk. A hawk can capture and eat a lefnode."

The announcer nodded, and another hourglass was turned.

Asben took thirty seconds before thinking of something. "An egg. A hawk doesn't eat eggs."

Right after the announcer nodded and before the hourglass could be turned, Quiz countered. "A snake. Snakes eat eggs."

It took Asben quite a bit longer. He still had some sand left before he answered but not much. "A snail. Snakes don't eat snails."

The announcer nodded.

This time it took Quiz a bit of time before he thought of something. "A crab. Some crabs eat snails."

Another nod.

"A fish. Some fish eat crabs."

It was accepted.

"A cat. Cats eat fish."

"A dog. Dogs scare cats."

"A zarpink. Dogs stay away from them because they don't want to be kicked by their powerful legs."

"A mouse. Everyone knows zarpinks are afraid of mice. The reason has never been determined, but it is a proven fact," Asben clarified.

The announcer gave a nod.

"A horse. It can step on a mouse."

"A dolsiyot. Horses are afraid of them and for good reason."

The announcer stopped him, and the time nomad slipped the metal piece into place. "We have read about many animals, but this is one I have not heard of. Please explain what it is, and we will decide whether or not it's real."

"Oh, it's real," Jezzie spoke up loudly. "One tore inta our shop one time and ate most of our bread. Ugly critters, they are, and I don't care ta ever see one again."

"Please, tell us about a dolsiyot," the announcer said to Asben, ignoring Jezzie's outburst.

"A dolsiyot is like a boar, but it's a bit smaller. It has four, very sharp tusks, and it has spikes along its back. Its tail is long and thick with a stinger on the end, somewhat like a scorpion. The venom from the tail is very poisonous. Anyone stung has an hour to get an antidote before they die. You can't get close to them. They're very dangerous. When the dolsiyot broke into our shop, we had to get the best shot in town to take it down. He obviously used a bow and arrow, but he had to be precise."

The announcer nodded, and Quiz grinned.

"Thanks for the wonderful description," he said. "I want a bow and arrow, which is the only way to kill a dolsiyot."

Asben grimaced. One of these days he was going to learn to keep his mouth shut.

The announcer grinned and nodded for Asben to take his turn.

It took him a short while. "A fire. It can burn the bow and arrows."

"Water," Quiz said after the announcer nodded. "It puts out a fire."

"Dirt, it turns water into mud."

"Pigs wallow in mud."

"Frying pan to fry up some bacon, which is made from pigs."

That brought a chuckle from the announcer as he nodded.

"Human, to use the frying pan and eat the bacon."

The announcer nodded.

Asben thought a minute then smiled. "Leprosy. It infects the human and kills him. There is no known cure."

Quiz thought until the sand reached the bottom, and Asben was declared the winner. The nomad leader was not a very gracious loser.

"You won't get the next two challenges. You will drink from one of these flasks."

Asben smiled. "I look forward to your tests. Let's see what you have that can stump me."

Chapter Twenty-Six

Quiz looked Asben in the eye. "Your next challenge is a memory game. I will only say this once. You may write down what you can on the parchment and hope it helps, but don't count on it. Are you ready to begin?"

"Yes."

Quiz smiled and began to rapidly relay the information. "I am on a ship. The captain's name is Lernix. He has one hundred oarsmen aboard his ship. They will be traveling five months. Each oarsman shares his name with someone else on board. The first oarsman's name is Albo. He shares a name with the twenty-seventh oarsman and the twelfth oarsman. The fiftieth, forty-second, and thirty-first oarsmen share a name with the captain. After three months of travel, they encounter a storm and half the oarsmen are lost at sea. Among those lost is the oarsman who shares his name with the sixteenth oarsman. The sixteenth oarsman's name is Nefla, which is one letter off of the seventeenth oarsman's name, Neflo, which is also the second oarsman's name. Because of the storm, the traveling time extended an extra month and a half, and many supplies were lost. There was a food shortage, and one oarsman died every three days. Now I would ask how many oarsmen will be left by the time they land, but instead, I want to know what the forty-second oarsman's name is."

Asben stared at Quiz completely overwhelmed. He dropped his quill and looked unbelievingly at the nomad leader, who grinned maliciously. Asben had disregarded the names, focusing on the numbers. That was the mathematician in him. He figured the names were thrown in there to distract him. Apparently, he was wrong.

Jezzie knew Asben would miss this answer. He had always been terrible with names. If she were the one sitting at the table, she would have rattled off all the names in order: Lernix, Albo, Nefla, and Neflo. Then she just would have said the first as her answer. But poor Asben, she knew, had to have been focusing on the numbers.

Asben looked at his parchment. Numbers, of course. He sighed.

"Alflo?" he said with a shrug.

Jezzie shook her head. Poor man couldn't even remember one name.

Quiz smiled. "Take a drink."

"Hey," Jezzie yelled. "On all the other riddles, ya asked if that was his final answer. You should do the same this time."

Quiz shot a look at the plump, annoying woman. If she said one more thing, he was locking her up.

"Is that your final answer? Good. Now, drink."

Asben looked at the cups before him. "So, I just pick whichever flask on the table I want and drink it?"

"That's the idea," Quiz said.

"All right." Asben smiled. He reached over to Quiz's side of the table and picked up the flask the leader had previously taken a sip from. "I choose this one."

He took a swig.

"That isn't one of your choices," Quiz said angrily, snatching his flask from Asben's hand.

"Let's recap," Asben explained. "I asked if I could pick any drink on the table. You said yes. Now, this flask was on the table, so technically, it was one of my choices."

"You were to pick from these five." Quiz pointed out the five lined up in the middle of the table.

"You're right, that was your idea, but when you said any drink would work, you included that one." Asben pointed to the leader's flask. "Now, seeing as this is a battle of the wits game, I think you should give me credit for outwitting you."

Quiz was angry, but he was also impressed. "I will give it to you. No need to punish a man for using his mind to its fullest extent."

"Thank you," Asben answered with a smile, very relieved that the nomad hadn't made him pick another flask.

"We will move on to the last riddle. Once again, it is a memory game. The context from which you will find the answer has already been given. You took notes on it. The question has two parts. The first is the following: how long was the trip supposed to originally take? The second question is how many men are left when the ship arrives at its destination? That is assuming each month contained thirty days and that the ship traveled at the same speed until reaching land."

Asben can answer this one, Jezzie thought. *He knows numbers.*

I can answer this, Asben thought happily as he looked at his notes.

"The first answer is five months," Asben said triumphantly. "The second answer...let's see. Two months were left after the storm hit, and then I need to add a month and a half, so three and a half months of travel. Thirty days each, that's one hundred and five. One oarsman dies every three days, so three into one hundred five days is thirty-five, so thirty-five of the fifty oarsmen left after the storm hit are dead. That leaves fifteen oarsmen. The second answer is fifteen."

Quiz grinned and opened his mouth to reply when Asben glanced to the top of his notes. "Wait..."

At the top, he had scribbled "on ship." Asben chuckled and shook his head as he looked up at Quiz. "Tricky. I give you credit; you almost had me. You are onboard that ship as well as the captain. Only the oarsmen died. Adding two to my calculation, the second answer is seventeen."

Quiz gave a half-smile of reluctant respect. "We will choose a guide to lead you through Suta. Congratulations on winning the battle of wits challenge. You are the first."

Jezzie broke away from the group and ran to Asben. "Oh, my smart, smart husband! I knew ya could do it."

She showered his face in kisses and hugged him tightly. She smoothed back his hair and straightened his lenses. Then she stepped back and unrumpled his clothes as best she could.

"That's my smart, brilliant man," she said sweetly. "Honey, I am so glad I married ya."

Asben smiled. "And you didn't even get the best out of the deal. I, however, have a lovely wife with the culinary skills of a king's chef."

"Aww, ur sweet, but I don't believe ya," she drawled, patting him on the cheek. "Come on, let's get our stuff, get Frelati an' Genevia out of that cell, an' get a move on."

"Don't make me do this!"

Quiz frowned. "Dreda, for months now you have given us trouble, more trouble than we need. You stir it up and cause overall chaos. I have tried to get everyone to understand that you just need time to adjust to our tribe, but the truth is, I no longer think you will."

"Please, please, Quiz, I'll do better, I promise!"

"Dreda, you know as well as I do that you won't change." He held up a hand as she began to protest. "I know you will do better for a few weeks, but then you'll slip back into old habits. That's what happened when we met the Dolwa tribe just a few months ago."

That episode was a disaster, and it had taken Quiz entirely too long to calm both his camp and the other nomad tribe. It had also cost him quite a bit of gold, for which Dreda had worked five weeks to pay off. It was clear by her guilty flush that Dreda remembered her terrible sabotage of the other tribe's supplies, all because of her trust issues.

"Please, Quiz, just one more chance."

Quiz shook his head. "I can't do it. I know that you had trouble in the past, but that is no excuse for your actions while you have been a member of this tribe. Your punishment is to be a guide for the travelers. After your return, you should be more than ready to rejoin the tribe."

Dreda tried once more. "Please—"

"No." Quiz cut her off. "And I will discuss this no more. You will guide them to Lonyi. I will write to a shapeshifter there to ensure you did your job, so don't even think of skipping out. After the completion of this task, you will be welcomed back into the tribe."

Dreda glared at him, her anger palpable. "Like I would want anything to do with this tribe now! You're no better than my other group. I can live on my own; I don't need anybody!"

She stormed out of the tent and walked over to the strange travelers.

"Come on," she yelled, giving each of them an angry glare. "We're moving out."

The travelers stood and gathered their bags. They followed a very unhappy Dreda as she marched across the hot, rocky surface. She was walking faster than was necessary, but they had to follow her. She was their only hope of surviving Suta.

After an hour and a half of walking, she finally stopped at a grouping of large boulders that provided a good deal of shade. She had been seated about three minutes before the rest of the group finally caught up.

"Umm," Genevia said, a bit out of breath. "Could you slow down a bit? It's hard enough on me, but we have children and an older man, no offence Traynord, traveling with us."

Dreda gave her a hard look. "Who are you exactly?"

"I'm Genevia, and your name is…?"

"Dreda. We will travel at my pace, but I *might* slow down. What is your destination?"

"We're not really sure…" Frelati began.

"Callum Cove," Genevia interrupted. She was going to do this for her father.

Frelati groaned as he grabbed her arm to make her look at him. They had gone over this when she first mentioned it. Trusting in dreams was never a good idea. "Genevia, you just came up with that out of the blue. For all we know it's in the opposite direction of where we're going."

Dreda looked up at them. "Where are you headed?"

"Azol," Genevia and Frelati said simultaneously without shifting their gazes from one another.

"So you're planning on stopping in Lonyi, right?"

"Yeah," Frelati answered, still battling Genevia quietly with his eyes. She was determined to go against him on this, and he did not want to back down.

"Well, Callum Cove is in that direction. I wasn't planning on heading there, but we can."

Genevia smiled in triumph, her eyes sparkling as they looked into Frelati's.

"See," she said. "It's right on the way, so we can go there."

Frelati's jaw tightened. He didn't feel right about the whole situation, but he knew he didn't have a good enough argument to sway her.

He sighed and broke eye contact, which made Genevia's smile grow wider.

"Fine," he conceded then met her gaze again. "But if we even sense any soldiers at that cove, we're going to the next one we come across."

The fire crackled happily, throwing light against the surrounding trees that danced and twisted as the flames chased each other in the night. The light also played on Dreda's face. It was a pretty face, but she always wore a scowl to make her seem very uninviting. Her deep black hair reflected the orange light, and her dark eyes took in everything around her. She was in her late twenties but looked younger than that. She was slender, a hunter, her tan outfit completing that image.

She hadn't had an easy life. Her parents had dumped her in the desert when she was old enough to understand what they were doing but still young enough to need someone to take care of her. She had wandered until she finally stumbled upon an oasis. That had saved her life. She stayed there a few months until a nomad tribe had picked her up. She was ten and became their slave. Quiz told her later that she had been found by the worst group of traveling nomads she could have possibly encountered.

She lived with them for three years before she finally ran away. Unfortunately, they caught her a week later. She lived with them another five years before they traded her to another tribe. She had no desire to stay with this group either and took her escape two years later. She lived on her own from oasis to oasis for six years. That's how she knew Suta like the back of her hand, maybe better.

Then she met Quiz. His group was peaceful, relatively speaking. Quiz convinced her to stay with them, giving her the freedom to leave any time she wanted, and she wouldn't be a slave. She took the offer, and seven months later he makes her guide these strangers across Suta. She knew she never should've trusted him. She should never trust anyone, but she had caved. Sure, he told her she could come back, but he wouldn't really let her. She would be on her own again, but she liked it better that way anyway.

She looked around the group. They seemed like nice people, but she was going to be very careful. In her experience, it didn't pay to trust people. However, the least she could do was warn them about the dangers that the nights in Suta held.

"All right, all of you listen," Dreda said, still looking into the flames. "There are a few things you need to know before you go to sleep. First, Suta isn't safe unless you're in a huge tribe. There are dangers to avoid both night and day.

"At night, you need to watch out for huge spiders; they can paralyze you and eat you in one hour. The only way to avoid them is to scream and have a partner kill them. The paralysis is temporary, and you'll be fine after it wears off. You need to stay close to the fire to avoid the desert foxes. They blend in with their surroundings, and they're smart. They don't attack whole groups; they pick one out at a time, so it's better to sleep in pairs or threes.

"Another problem is other nomad tribes. You need to look out for them at all times, but at night they'll snag travelers one by one and enslave them. Believe me, you don't want to be a nomad's slave.

"You also want to look out for the mosquitoes. They aren't like those tiny ones every other continent has. They thrive out here for some reason. One bite from them looks like you were bitten by a viper, and when it swells, you have a lump the size of a small stone… about this big." She picked up a rock by her foot; it was about two inches in diameter. "You don't want to get bitten. They suck out like two cupfuls of blood."

"I'm really glad the kids are asleep," Jezzie whispered to Asben. "This would give 'em nightmares."

Dreda heard. "The real thing is worse than any nightmare."

"I'm going to lay down with the girls," Genevia said worriedly.

"Bring them closer to the fire," Frelati ordered.

Genevia nodded. She woke the girls gently, spread out the blanket closer to the fire, Frelati, and herself, and they instantly went back to sleep. Genevia sat between them and Frelati, leaning against the same boulder he was.

Dreda continued. "As to daytime dangers, you need to watch for nomads and the desert foxes. The foxes come out mainly at night, but watching during the day is helpful. You need to avoid soft patches of sand because more than likely they're quicksand. If you see any moving boulders, tell me quickly. Those aren't boulders, even though they look just like them; they're yuldos, very dangerous animals that can easily crush you. They usually lay out under the sun, they travel alone, and if they even sense anything near them, they run at it. They run fast, but only for short distances. They're very heavy, so it tires them out to move, but if you get close to one, they will trample you, and you will die.

"Other than that, Suta is pretty safe. It's in the middle of nowhere, so you don't have to worry about soldiers, and in the day, you can see for miles, so no one can sneak up on you. Because you have a guide, you won't die of thirst," Dreda finished with a smug smile. "Now, I'm planning on starting early, so you might want to go to bed."

She stepped over to where her blanket was spread out on the ground and lay down, ignoring her own advice of sleeping in pairs.

Genevia turned to Frelati worriedly. "What if those things come tonight? I don't want the girls to get bitten or anything."

"Don't worry about it," Frelati said as he looked around them. "I'll stay up for a while."

"Okay," Genevia said with a nod. "I'll keep you company."

"You don't need to do that."

"I know, but I couldn't go to sleep now if I tried, not after hearing all that."

"You'd be surprised how quickly you'll fall asleep," Frelati said.

He felt a soft weight on his shoulder and realized that Genevia had laid her head against him.

"Genevia?" he asked with no answer. "You couldn't have fallen asleep that fast."

He turned his head as best he could to look at her. She appeared to be fast asleep, and her breathing was even.

"Genevia?" he asked in confusion.

Still no answer.

Frelati sighed and shook his head. He put his arm around her shoulders, shifting her and himself into a more comfortable position. Hopefully, she would wake up and lay down with the girls. It would certainly be more comfortable for her, but he didn't want her to wake too soon because despite himself, he really liked the feel of her in his arms.

"Have you left the nomads yet?"

"Yes, we actually just left them. We have a nomad guide too. She's taking us to Callum Cove."

"So you are traveling there?"

"Of course. That's what you told me to do."

"Good. I have to go. Keep to the course. I probably won't speak with you for a few days. I just wanted to check up on you."

"All right, but can you stay longer next time?"

"I'll see what I can do. I love you, sweetheart. Follow your heart and…go to Callum Cove."

"Why is that so important?"

"It's…you should go to Callum Cove. I have to go now."

"Wait, I want to…"

Nalofré stepped through the door, and Genevia awoke.

She sat bolt upright and looked around her.

"Are you okay, Genevia?"

"Frelati?" Genevia was a bit disoriented. "I fell asleep? But I wasn't tired."

Frelati nodded, but it was clear that he didn't like it one bit. "You've been falling asleep a lot lately, really quickly. Are you feeling all right?"

"Yes, I feel fine. I guess I'm just more tired than I thought."

Frelati stared at her, searching her face for any sign of illness and finding none. "All right, but if you start feeling sick, I want you to tell me. Okay?"

"Fine."

"Go back to sleep. I can tell you're still tired."

Genevia shook her head as she leaned back against him. "I'm all right. If I feel sleepy, I'll lie down."

They watched the fire as it slowly died to embers. The others were all stretched out around it fast asleep. The darkness was draped on the air like a cape, and the tree branches seemed menacing in the night. But as the wind rushed through the night air, it caressed the surface of the small pond of water nearby and created a peaceful sound to dispel a bit of the gloom, and the few stars that twinkled through the tree tops gave a comforting light to those in the clearing below. It wasn't long before the sun began to peek over the horizon and replace the darkness with its radiant light, waking the sleepers from a pleasant slumber.

Jezzie and Asben woke first to glory in the beautiful splash of colors. The sunrise was breathtaking, and soon Traynord awoke to see it too.

"Beau'iful, ain' i'?" he said with a yawn.

"Absolutely gorgeous," Jezzie breathed, viewing it with a smile before turning away. "Well, I'm goin' ta start gatherin' our things together. Dreda said we were gettin' an early start."

She turned to roll up the sleeping bags and glanced over to where Genevia and Frelati were propped against the boulder.

"Ahh, look at the young'uns," she gushed. "At least in sleep they can't deny they like each other."

The two men turned around, and Traynord chuckled. "They sure do pu' up a figh' durin' the day, though."

Genevia was lying against Frelati's chest. His arm was around her, and his head was rested against the top of hers.

"They look so sweet ta'gether," Jezzie said. "I just wish they'd realize it and do somethin' about it."

"Well, a' one poin' in time, they starte' gettin' closer," Traynord said. "I' was on'y after tha' inscription thingy tha' Frelati starte' backin' away."

"Oh, yes," Asben exclaimed. "That reminds me. I'm supposed to be looking something up for Genevia."

He rushed over to his books.

"Asben," Jezzie scolded as she rushed over. "I just packed that up. Don't you go rippin' everythin' out again."

"Jezzie, I have to get my books out to look up…"

Jezzie shook a finger at him. "You can do that later once everythin's unpacked."

"But…"

"Asben, please don't make me pack all a that up again."

Their voices had risen a bit higher, and Frelati and Genevia woke up a bit sleepily. When they realized how close they were, they both moved away a bit, Genevia rather reluctantly and Frelati with a firm determination.

Genevia smiled sheepishly at him in a sort of apology before moving over to the girls, waking them gently to get them ready for the journey. Frelati stood and began to walk around.

"Where's Dreda?" he asked suddenly.

Everyone looked to where she had fallen asleep as if they expected her to suddenly materialize right there.

"I didn't even realize she wasn't here," Jezzie said.

"Do you think she just left us here?" Genevia asked worriedly.

"No," Frelati said, trying to be the voice of reason. "She probably just went for a walk and will be back soon. Don't worry. We'll get ready to leave, and when she gets back we'll head out."

"Okay," Genevia said, her voice still carrying a hint of worry.

The others weren't so sure of that either, but they all began rolling up blankets and packing up the pans they'd used the night before. When they were almost finished packing, Dreda walked into the clearing, tossing a nut into her mouth.

"So you all finally woke up," she said. "Are you ready to get moving?"

Frelati walked over to her and accused softly, "Where were you?"

"Shut off the anger, lover boy." She held up a fairly large sack that was half filled with nuts. "I was gathering food in case anyone gets hungry while we walk. Is that a crime or something?"

"No." Frelati scowled, stared at her for a bit as if judging the truth of her words, and began walking back over to where Genevia was rolling up the last blanket. Before reaching her, he turned back with an order. "Stop calling me that."

Dreda ignored him. "Last I checked, you two were the fugitives. Shouldn't I be more afraid of you running away than you should be of me running?"

Frelati grimaced. "Point taken."

"All right then, lover boy," she said before looking around the group. "You all look ready. Let's go."

Chapter Twenty-Seven

After the first few days of walking, everyone was dead tired by the time nightfall arrived. By the end of the week, though, they were all beginning to get used to the endless activity. They were still a week away from Callum Cove, but according to Dreda, they were making great time.

"The landscape doesn't change, does it?" Genevia complained to Frelati as they walked along.

"No, it pretty much stays the same no matter where you go," Frelati answered as he glanced over to where the girls were running around with Quinsnap. "I don't know how they can do that in this heat."

The sun was high, and there was no shade along their route, although off in the distance there were some large boulders that had very tantalizing dark patches stretching out behind them where the sun couldn't reach.

"It's pretty bor—" Genevia's word was cut off by a yawn. "Boring."

Frelati glanced her way and smirked. "Tired, are we?"

Genevia shook her head in confusion. "I don't feel tired. It's weird, though. I feel like I have to go to sleep, but I'm not tired."

That put Frelati on instant alert. She had said that twice before. As Frelati watched, her eyes glazed over.

"I don't feel..." she murmured softly.

Her words were lost as her head fell back. Her body grew limp, and she collapsed, Frelati just barely managing to catch her before she hit the ground.

"Genevia! Genevia!" Frelati yelled in growing intensity, his anxiety increasing with the volume. "Asben, come over here now!"

That brought an immediate response from everyone. They all rushed over, except for Dreda.

"Mama! Dseg'h fimt?" Lela asked worriedly, trying to shake Genevia awake.

"Girls, come with me. We don't need ta crowd 'em," Jezzie ordered as she hustled them away.

"Asben, what's wrong with her?" Frelati asked as he cradled her in his arms. "She keeps doing this; it isn't normal."

Asben shook his head. "If this had not occurred previously, I would diagnose overheating. However, beyond that, I can't tell; she appears to be sleeping. What was she doing before she fell?"

Frelati looked anxiously at Genevia's face. "She was just talking, and then she yawned. She said she didn't feel tired but that she had to go to sleep. Then, her eyes glazed over, and she just melted. She's all right, isn't she? This isn't serious?"

Asben studied her closely. "I'll check my books; I believe I have a medicinal one."

He rushed to his bags and pulled out his books. He found the lone medical one and flipped through but didn't find anything that corroborated with Genevia's symptoms.

He shouted over to the group. "I don't have anything in here about that."

He scanned through once more before returning to Genevia. "I think we should let her rest. When she wakes up, we can move on. We should construct a tent to get her out of the sun."

Traynord nodded and moved to do his bidding.

"Do you think she could have any internal injuries?" Frelati asked to no one in particular.

"That's highly unlikely, but I can be more certain once she awakens," Asben replied. He looked around with an impressed smile at the quickly constructed tent. "I believe I will congratulate Traynord on his tent-building prowess. Let me know when she wakes up."

"Come on, Genevia," Frelati said as he brushed her hair. "Wake up."

"Don't go!" she yelled, startling Frelati, as she sat bolt upright.

She stared straight ahead for a few moments, arm outstretched, before blinking several times and trying to figure out where she was. Her arm dropped slowly as she looked around, but her body remained tense and rigid.

When her gaze landed on Frelati, she visibly relaxed. "Frelati? Where am I?"

Frelati scrutinized her closely. "Are you okay?"

"I think so. Why?"

"You collapsed. One minute you were up, the next you were down."

"What?"

"You passed out."

Genevia was confused and a bit worried. "Why did I do that?"

Frelati shrugged and shook his head. "Do you think you'll be okay to walk? We still have to make it to the oasis."

"Yea, yea," Genevia nodded. "I'll be fine."

"Okay, but if you feel tired or weak, I want you to tell me."

The tent was taken down and packed up, and everyone started walking again. It was late when they finally reached the oasis, and after a quick dinner everyone immediately went to bed.

One day before they reached Callum Cove, Genevia had another episode.

"Asben!" Frelati shouted. "Genevia passed out again!"

"Put up a tent," Asben said. "We'll wait it out."

He walked over to his bags. While he had the time, he might as well see if he could find the information he promised himself he would find for Genevia. He pulled out the book with her prophesy and began skimming through. He still found it odd that the sixth essence of Kiem was not listed with the others here. He momentarily puzzled over it when a pattern clicked into place. "Earth and air, water and fire, light and darkness. The sixth is darkness…the Dark King." His head reeled. Their evil overlord, Fezam, was endowed with Kiem's essence as well. He was just as powerful as Genevia. Where she could control the ground or grow plants, he could…

what? Could he possibly control dreams, have power over the mind? It was a terrifying thought, but unfortunately, entirely possible.

He walked over to Genevia as she began to wake. "Genevia, I need you to tell me what you're dreaming."

"Um, okay, why?" she asked a bit drowsily.

"I think I know the problem, but, to be certain, I need you to tell me your dreams."

"All right," Genevia said. "In every dream, I'm talking to my father. I don't think it's a dream, though; it's too real."

"What does he say?"

"He's checking on me, making sure we're going to Callum Cove, asking questions. I think the dreams are part of his gift."

Frelati's head snapped up. "Wait, you're talking about your real father?" Genevia nodded in confusion. "I thought you were talking about Drisgal."

"No, it's my real father. I think he's using his gift to contact me."

Frelati shook his head. "That's not his gift. He controls moonlight, like the direction of the beam, and he can regulate tides when the moon is full. He can't talk to someone through their dreams."

Genevia looked from Frelati to Asben. "So how's he contacting me?"

Asben closed his eyes. "Fezam."

"What?" Frelati asked.

"I hope I'm wrong, but I highly suspect he is Kiem's essence of darkness, the unknown sixth essence. If that is the case, it is not much of a stretch to believe him capable of mind control through our dreams."

Neither Genevia nor Frelati responded.

"What exactly does your father tell you?" Asben pushed.

"He asks how far I am from Callum Cove, and he always tells me how much he loves me and how much I look like my mother," Genevia said with a smile.

"We don't need to go to Callum Cove," Frelati said suddenly and fiercely. "Fezam could be using your father to lead us into a trap."

"But why would my father help him?" Genevia argued.

"He may not have a choice."

Genevia rubbed her head. Things seemed to be getting worse every day. "He always looks sad."

"Does he ever seem to be telling you something without actually saying it? Maybe pausing or staring intently or...anything like that?" Frelati asked.

"I don't know; it's not easy to remember dreams. He always seems sad, like he doesn't really want to be there, but he does want to see me." Genevia paused to think. "Actually, now that I think about it, almost every time Callum Cove comes up, he pauses, and he always says, 'You know that I love you' or something similar before asking my location."

Asben looked at Frelati in concern. "I believe you're right; we shouldn't continue on this course. Genevia, if your father contacts you again, do not tell him our plans. Let him think we were temporarily prevented from traveling to Callum Cove. We need to find another route. I'll talk to Dreda."

He hurried away, and soon after everything was gathered up again, they were heading off to the north, parallel to the ocean.

"It will probably take another week to reach the next cove," Dreda yelled back at them as she led the group.

She was right. It took exactly a week. Genevia had three sleeping spells throughout the journey, and she did exactly as Asben suggested. She told her father that the girls were sick and couldn't travel. He seemed relieved to hear that.

Once they reached the cove, it finally registered that they didn't have a boat and were stuck on Suta's coast. They had gathered several yards from the ocean and watched the waves as they lapped at the sand.

"What now?" Genevia asked.

Dreda, who had been pacing the sand closer to shore, rolled her eyes. She was the only one among the group that had no worries about travel arrangements. "None of you know anything about nomads, do you?"

They looked at each other, then back at her blankly, although Asben was slightly offended.

Dreda sighed. "We always have hidden boats around coves. Any nomad is allowed to use them as long as the boat is returned once the job is finished, if at all possible. If it can't be returned, the nomad has to leave a group of rocks where the boat once was so that passing nomads know to replace it. That's what we'll do, because Kiem knows how long this is going to take."

She walked over to a patch of soft sand and started stomping. When she heard a hollow, wooden sound, she motioned to the others.

"Dig here. The boat's underneath."

They brushed off all the sand and uncovered one boat. It wasn't large enough to hold them all comfortably.

"We're going to have to take two." Dreda grimaced as she began stomping again.

Soon, a second boat was resting beside the first. The oars were tied to the bottom of each.

"That's not goin' to be very comfortable," Jezzie said, eyeing the boats with distaste.

"We only have to be in them about a week, maybe less," Dreda said. "This is the closest cove to Lonyi, which is your destination. Right, lover boy?"

Regardless of his countless demands, she still managed to interject the frustrating nickname at the most aggravating moments.

"Yes," Frelati said, trying to hide his frustration. "We need a good boat, and these will not get us to Azol, so a stop there is mandatory."

"Well, why don't we push off," Dreda said. "The sooner we leave, the sooner we get off these things."

Everyone picked a boat. Genevia, Frelati, the girls, and Quinsnap were on one boat. Jezzie, Asben, Traynord, and Dreda were in the other. They pushed off and began a voyage that would be remembered as one of the worst parts of the entire journey.

Genevia felt the now familiar sleepy sense weave around her.

"Frelati," she said. "I'm about to fall asleep."

"Pull in your oars," he said, "and lay back."

She did as he said and soon was fast asleep. She was in the white area once again for a short while before the door appeared and her father stepped through.

"Where are you now, baby?" her father asked.

"Still in the same place. The girls are better, but we want to make sure they're well enough for travel," she said.

Nalofré nodded, his face showing relief before he hid it. "All right, I was…"

He looked over his shoulder as another man stepped through the door. He was terrifying with blood red eyes and a malicious smile. His pasty white skin, nearly the same hue as the colorless room, had obviously not seen sun for a while, and his black hair made him seem all the more pale.

"Hello, Alernoa," he said in an oily voice. "I have heard much about you. It is a pleasure to finally speak with you. I hope we can soon meet in person."

"You are Fezam, I presume?" Genevia stated icily, though her heartbeat increased at the menacing aura that pulsed around the man.

Nalofré's eyes narrowed to slits as he glared at the intruder. Unconsciously, he pushed Genevia behind him, shielding her with his body from the evil man.

"What are you doing?" he asked icily.

"Temper, temper." The man clucked. "For someone who depends on my good humor to save his wife, you certainly are trying it. Just remember Lenaia; perhaps that will cool you down."

Nalofré didn't answer, but his anger noticeably intensified.

"Now, Alernoa," the man said, turning to her. "I know that you are up to something, and I would like to know what it is."

Genevia shook her head. "I don't know what you're talking about."

His eyes glittered dangerously. "I think you do. I also think that you are aware of my identity, and the power I have over your parents. As it is, your mother has a knife to her throat. She will live if this meeting ends well.

"Somehow, you discovered me. For your father's sake, I hope it wasn't his doing."

"It wasn't," Genevia said hotly. "I'm not stupid, and neither are the people I'm traveling with. When I started falling asleep in the middle of the day, we did some research and figured out what you were up to."

"Then your father is safe, unless you refuse to give me the information I want," he said coldly. "Where are you?"

"If I answer that question, both of my parents stay safe, alive, and they aren't to be punished in any way. Do you agree?"

"Why would I agree?"

"Because you need to know where I am if you wish to capture me, and you need to capture me because I'm your biggest threat. I can defeat you, and that scares you."

At that moment, the temper of Fezam could be described with no milder term than livid. The air around him began to turn dark, and the room practically hummed with dread at the anger he exuded. She had hit a nerve.

"I do *not* make *deals*." He bit out the words icily.

"Then I guess you do *not* get *answers*," Genevia mimicked his enunciation without even a hint of fear, which heightened his anger. "If my parents die, you will not hear a word from me. If they are harmed in any way, your chances of getting information will be very slim. I want to see my father and mother again in three days. If they are still alive, then I will give you a hint at my location. It's up to you to solve the puzzle, but remember I am constantly moving. If you want to keep track of me, my parents will stay alive and unharmed." She was angry but in complete control, as her slight, humorless smile made readily apparent. "Good-bye."

With that word, everything rushed away: the door, her father, and the evil tyrant. In an instant, she awakened, completely surprised that she had the control to do so. She didn't seem able to avoid falling asleep when Fezam wished, but apparently she wasn't completely at his mercy. She was breathing heavily, but she was not nearly as disoriented as she usually was after one of those episodes. Genevia was proud of herself; she had found a way to keep her parents alive, and she had found a way to manipulate Fezam. It was beginning to look like she could beat him, and she would.

Chapter Twenty-Eight

The canopy of trees was a welcome sight after a week of endless water. The foliage was large and thick. It was a true forest, but everyone could tell that the shapeshifters took great care in keeping undergrowth at bay.

After storing the boats, they walked inland for a while before finding a good place to stay the night. It was a small clearing with pine straw as its floor, and the branches and leaves above created a sense of security that had long been missed at sea.

"Okay," Dreda said, tossing down her bags. "This looks like a good place to bed down."

The others agreed as they dropped their things and began to unpack the necessities.

"I'll fix us up some supper," Jezzie said cheerfully despite her exhaustion.

"I'll buil' the fire," Traynord offered. He had been gathering sticks as he saw them while they walked.

Genevia looked at the girls. "Why don't you roll out our blankets?"

They did so and went to play with Quinsnap, who was sniffing around curiously. He kept returning to one particular stump that looked a lot like a chair. It had broken off to provide a high back and smooth seat. Dreda noticed it and sat down, watching all the activity around her as if she were a queen. Frelati thought about saying something but decided against it. She was a disagreeable sort, best to avoid an argument.

When everyone was settled and the food was cooking, things calmed down. Everyone relaxed around the fire, suddenly feeling the effect of their travel. Dreda was a bit apart from the group, still sitting on the stump, and watched everyone closely, listening to their easy conversations and envying the close relationship between them. As caught up as she was in this survey, it was some time before she realized that vines were growing around her.

"Whoa," she shouted, gaining everyone's attention. She tried to hop up, but the vines held her firmly in place.

Frelati turned to Genevia, not sure whether to be pleased or give a reprimand. "Genevia."

"I'm not doing it," she protested; her eyes on the growing vines were wide. She looked at her hands, then back at the vines, wondering if her gift had grown a mind of its own.

"Well, if you are doing it, stop it," Dreda said as she struggled. "And if you aren't, do that nature thing to stop it."

Genevia didn't have time to try anything though. As everyone watched, the stump started changing. The back was becoming a torso, the bottom was changing into legs, and the vines looked suspiciously like arms. Dreda noticed too, and she wasn't taking it too well. Her eyes were wide as saucers, and she was twisting madly, trying to get away.

Finally, after an entirely human form emerged from the stump, a face could be seen. The eyes were laughing, and the grin was playful and a bit mischievous. He nuzzled her neck before she finally broke away, drawing a knife from a hip pocket quickly and holding it out in front of her.

Then laughter spread throughout the clearing, coming from directly behind Genevia, who gasped and jumped over to Frelati. Right behind her, what she thought was a log had turned into another person, who was rolling around in laughter. He finally got up and walked over to the other one, but he was still chuckling.

"Man, that was good," he said, laughing and clapping the other one on the back. "None of them saw it coming, even with the lefnode sniffing you every five minutes. I was sure that creature would give you away."

The other man laughed. "I know, me too, but I got a sweet one to sit on me."

"Lucky," came the muttered reply. "I had a nice looking one, but she was next to Mr. Tall, Grim, and Handsome. Figured I shouldn't mess with her."

Frelati stood abruptly, and the two eyed him while finishing their conversation in softer tones.

"You should have gone for it anyway. I would have."

"Yeah, maybe, but…"

"Excuse me," Frelati interjected as he walked over to them, his no-nonsense look catching their attention. "Would you mind telling us what you are doing? Why are you here anyway?"

They both looked over at him. They were tall and thin; identical versions of each other, except for the hair color. One was a dirty blond; the other was a rusty red-head. They both had brown eyes and slender faces, and both were looking at Frelati with humor etched in every line.

"We live on Lonyi, traveler," the red head said.

"And we were just walking through when we noticed your group traipsing through the woods," the blond continued.

"So we decided…"

"…that having a little fun with you…"

"…would be the perfect end to our day."

They looked at each other with identical wide grins, finishing in unison. "And we were right."

"Who are you?" Genevia asked, walking forward tentatively and stopping just behind Frelati.

They both smiled.

"Well, cutie, we…" the red head began, changing into a large letter Q and then a T rapidly as he gave the endearment.

"…are shapeshifters," the blond finished, changing into a large letter R. The transition was so smooth between the two that the sentence flowed as if only one was speaking.

"It's nice to…" the other started while turning into the number two.

"…meet you," his brother completed, shifting into a large U.

Then they both changed back into themselves and glanced at one another with smiles before continuing with their fun.

"Do you..." the red head turned into a U.

"...wish to see more?" the blond transformed into a large C.

Once again, they returned to normal, grinning from ear to ear to ear to ear. Frelati put his hands on his hips and scowled.

"We're good. Are you working for anyone? Did someone hire you as scouts?"

They looked at each other, confusion clearly written on their faces. "No, why would..."

"...someone be looking for you?"

Genevia was fascinated when they spoke. If she closed her eyes, it would sound like only one person speaking.

Frelati scrutinized the shapeshifters, looking for any sign that they might be hiding something. He didn't exactly feel threatened by them, they seemed like simple immature mischief makers, but he also didn't want to take any chances by giving them too much information.

Genevia didn't have that reserve. Before Frelati could stop her, she answered. "Fezam is looking for us. Well, he's looking for me and Frelati."

Frelati glanced at her in annoyance. *Why was she so trusting? That was going to get her into serious trouble one of these days.*

"Why is he after you?" the red head asked, curiosity clear in his tone.

Frelati cut her off. "That is not your concern, but we aren't dangerous unless forced to be. So, are you or are you not here to discover our whereabouts and report them to Fezam?"

"We don't associate with that scumbag," the blond answered.

"Yeah, he killed our best friend and our older brother."

"So you don't know who we are, why we're here, or anything?" Frelati pressed.

"No," they said with perfectly synchronized shrugs.

"All right then." Frelati turned and settled in the place he had previously been sitting. That's all he needed to know.

There was a period of awkward silence before Traynord walked over and offered his hand to the redhead.

"Traynord's me name, and wha's urs?" he said as they shook hands.

"Sizzle," said the red head.

"Slice," said the blond.

Jezzie chuckled. "That's like sugar an' spice an' everythin' nice."

Both shapeshifters grimaced.

"Yea, our mother thought it was catchy too," Sizzle said.

"She didn't realize how miserable it would make us," Slice elaborated.

"Or maybe she did," they both laughed as they shot glances at each other. It was obviously an inside joke.

Lela had walked over to Slice and was looking at him intently. Finally, she poked his leg and realized that it was firm.

She looked up at him. "How? You are…hard. You…look like…lots…of things, but you are…hard."

Slice raised an eyebrow, and a slight grin played at the edges of his lips. "I'm a shapeshifter. Anything I change into is solid; it's only while I'm changing that I'm not."

"Oh," Lela said thoughtfully. "Like me?"

The twins frowned, looking at each other before saying anything.

"Like you…"

"…how?"

Lela tilted her head, studying Slice closely before changing into a mirror image of him.

The twins were startled, as was everyone except Traynord, Frelati, and Genevia. Then they started laughing.

"Now, we're triplets," Sizzle said cheerfully. "Can you change into me?"

"Okay," Lela said in Slice's voice, which brought out another bout of laughter from the twins.

Only Lela's hair color changed.

Slice examined Lela closely. "Wow, I never realized we look so much alike. She didn't change at all."

"Huh. It's weird that we can't tell when we shift into each other."

"Could be because we liquefy between forms."

"Yeah, probably."

Lela changed back and walked over to Genevia, laying her head in Genevia's lap. Genevia ran her fingers through Lela's hair and looked over to the shapeshifters.

"Why are you here?" she asked. "I mean, what were you doing walking through the woods?"

Both shrugged and answered. "Looking for something to do."

"We were bored…"

"…and decided to look here for some adventure."

The red head winked at Dreda. "And I found me an adventure."

Dreda scowled. "Is there a village around here somewhere?"

"Umm…" Sizzle thought. "Our village is about…"

He turned to his brother. "…about a day and a half travel from here."

Sizzle grinned. "Mom's gonna flip when we don't come home tonight."

"Maybe we should have told her before we left. You know the last time we did this she sent the whole village out looking for us."

"Ooo, yeah, she wasn't too happy when we just popped in asking what was up."

"But it's too late now to tell her."

"It wouldn't have been as much fun if she had known."

"Shoot, she wouldn't have let us leave is she knew we were going this far."

Asben looked up from his books. "How old are you two?"

"Too old for her to worry about us."

"Not that it stops her."

They saw that Asben was still looking for an age, so they gave it to him.

"Twenty-two," they answered together.

"But I'm two minutes older," Sizzle said with a grin.

"And two times more annoying," Slice added, punching Sizzle on the arm.

Dreda rolled her eyes. "Does your village have a large ship we can use to sail to Azol?"

"Wait," Frelati said suddenly. "'We'? As in you're coming too?"

Dreda glared at him, but she was clearly uncomfortable.

"Frelati," Genevia scolded quietly. "Stop being mean."

"I'm not," he argued. "She just up and decided to join us."

"And we need to welcome her, not push her away," Genevia whispered before addressing Dreda. "Frelati didn't mean anything by that, Dreda. Ignore him."

Frelati scowled, but Genevia continued. "You are welcome to travel with us. He was just surprised, as was I, because we thought you'd want to get back to your group."

Dreda crossed her arms. "I don't need them. If they don't want me there, I won't bother them by going back."

Sizzle sidled over to her and slung his arm around her waist, pulling her against him with a smile. "Well, you are welcome to stay here with us. You will get absolutely no complaints from me."

He winked, and she punched him in the stomach, backing away. That brought laughter out of Slice.

"You so deserved that, man."

"Oh, shut up," Sizzle gasped, his arms crossed over his stomach.

"Don't touch me again," Dreda warned. "I have a knife, and next time I'll use it. Now, one of you answer my question. Does your village have any large ships?"

"No," Slice answered. "Our village is inland, but there is a village on the shore that has boats."

"Could you take us there?" Frelati asked before Dreda could.

The two looked at each other. Everyone could swear they were having a silent debate without saying a word. Finally, they came to a decision without a sound and answered.

"Sure." They nodded.

"But we have to stop by and tell our mother what we're doing," Sizzle said.

"If she starts worrying, she'll track us down, and when she sees all of you, she will lash out. She has a fear of kidnapping."

"The fun never ends," Frelati said sarcastically with a slight smile. These twins actually amused him.

Two brown glares focused on him before they transferred back to Dreda.

"If you just stay here…"

"…for a short while only…"

"…probably just three days, maybe four…"

"...we can travel to the village..."

"...tell ma what we're doing..."

"...and be back before you can miss me, sweetheart," Sizzle finally finished with a huge smile and wink for Dreda.

"No need to worry about that," she said with a sneer, crossing her arms.

"So, do you want to wait..."

"...so that we can be your guides?"

The group exchanged glances. Genevia was the one who finally spoke up.

"We would really appreciate that. With you two for guides, not only will we be entertained, but we won't get lost."

The twins shared a grin. This was just the type of adventure they had been searching for.

"We're back, Ma!"

"You can stop worrying!"

A middle-aged woman ran to the door of the small hut.

"My boys!" she cried, hugging them fiercely before pulling back and scolding. "Where have you been? You almost gave me a heart attack. I cannot believe you would do this to your poor mother."

Sizzle and Slice grinned sheepishly and apologized simultaneously. "Sorry, Ma."

"We were just walking through the woods..."

"...when we came across these travelers and..."

"...we couldn't help but have some fun with them."

"Strangers! Travelers!" Their mother gasped. "Have I taught you boys nothing? You could've been killed!"

"But we weren't," Sizzle pointed out.

"And we're here now, where we're safe."

Their mother looked them over, checking for any sign of bruises or bumps. "You're both really okay?"

"Yes, Ma," they both answered, rolling their eyes.

"Don't you roll your eyes at your mother," she scolded, hitting them both with her towel. "Now, dinner is almost ready. Wash up, quickly."

The twins looked at each other, and their mother sighed in anticipation.

"Well, Ma, we were kinda…"

"…we were kinda hoping you would understand if we…"

"…if we went back to help the travelers find their way to the village at the coast."

"They need a boat."

"It would be the right thing to do…"

"…and you're always telling us to help others."

"No, no." Their mother wagged her finger at them. "I told you to help people you knew, not complete strangers."

They looked at each other again before trying another tactic.

"Well, you know how we're always bugging you…"

"…about how we want to have a really great adventure?"

After their mother's nod, they continued.

"We think we found it…"

"…if you would just let us go with these travelers."

Their mother looked at the ground and sighed. She knew they would leave anyway, but at least they would leave knowing she wasn't too angry if she gave her consent. "How long will you be gone?"

"We don't know," they said together with twinkling eyes.

"My precious boys," she said, rubbing each of their cheeks lovingly. "If anything happens to either of you, I'll never forgive you. Both of you had better come back. Do we have an understanding?"

"Yes, Ma," they said again.

"Then…" She sighed and closed her eyes. "I suppose you have my blessing, but you two promise me you'll stay safe and watch out for each other." She watched for their nods. "Now, go pack your things, and I'll be getting some food together for you. Don't forget to pack the medicine bag."

As she turned, the boys saw her wiping tears from her eyes. One glance ensured that they shared the same thought. They grabbed her from behind in a great bear hug, literally.

Their mother rewarded them with a laugh before shifting into a larger version of herself and pushing her cubs away. "Get going; you have an adventure to catch."

They grinned and took off to their rooms.

"You think we'll regret this?"

"More than likely."

"Should we just take them to the village and go back home?"

"Do you want to do that?"

"Not really."

"My feelings exactly."

"Okay, so we go all the way. Are we going to face Fezam?"

"Do you think that will be necessary?"

"Yeah, probably."

"And I agree."

"Man, I really don't want to meet that crazy guy."

"Who does?"

"Good point."

"Of course it is."

"Feeling a little sure of yourself, are you?"

"Doubting about this trip a little too much, are you?"

"Touché."

"I did rather well."

"So, what are the plans with that nomad girl?"

"Oh, I'll win her over eventually."

"Meaning you're going to get me to help." Slice grimaced.

"Of course you're going to help."

"What do you have in mind?"

"The usual."

"Which usual? We always use different usuals."

"You know which usual I'm talking about; you always know."

"Elaborate."

"No."

"Then I can't help."

Sizzle sighed. "You cover for me. It's simple. Just say I'm gathering wood, going for a walk, anything. I shift into something natural, get close to her, maybe twine some vines around her so I can sweet talk her, who knows?"

"I hoped it wasn't that one."

"Why hope? You knew it was."

"Yeah, well, I hate your plans. You're worse than I am."

"I have two minutes more practice."

"Funny. Wouldn't it be easier to be nice to her, get her to like you that way?"

"That's not as much fun."

"It's more efficient and gives you a better chance than your way does."

"So you're saying that if you were me, you wouldn't try my way?"

"No. If I was in your position, I would be just as blinded by what I called love as you are. Now, I am clearheaded and can clearly see a better option."

Sizzle weighed that for a minute. "You have a point, but…"

"…you're so blinded right now, you can't possibly listen to reason?"

"You took the words right out of my mouth."

"Don't I always?"

It didn't take long to reach the boating village, and it didn't take long to find a good ship for rent. Unfortunately, it was taking Sizzle a very long time to win over Dreda, and he was getting frustrated. Other than Slice and Dreda, no one else in the group really noticed.

They all got on board, and Frelati counted them off. "Three elves, three humans, one nomad, one dreamer, one lefnode, two shapeshifters, that's everyone. Okay, Traynord, cast off."

"Aye, aye, Cap'n." Traynord saluted with a laugh, and they sailed off. "Nex' stop, Azol."

Fezam was angry. He had done what she wanted. As requested, she had seen her precious mother and father three days after making her emotional demands. Then, he had let her see them after the following three days. And what did he have for his trouble? Nothing. The vague hints she gave him were useless. She could be describing so many places there was no way he could pinpoint her exact location.

First, it was grayish-blue water. Then, it was large, beautiful trees surrounding a small clearing. So she had been somewhere in the ocean and then somewhere on land. How specific. She was playing him. She had the upper hand, and she knew it. She used her location like a lure in an attempt to keep her parents alive until…until what?

Fezam gave a small, evil grin of victory. Until she came to rescue them. Eventually, she was going to come to him. She could be on her way now. He knew she had been on Suta. He had led her to Callum Cove, but she had discovered his plot and moved to another cove, which was probably the next one over.

He walked to his map and studied it. She had played with him for around a week with her sick children. The cove used had to be close enough for them to reach it in a week. That narrowed it down to three coves: Rafe, Larsa, and Yoleem. Those coves led to three possible continents: Reyulicos, Lonyi, and Yima Olem. Based on the time period, she would have been at sea during both exchanges if Reyulicos was her destination. His men had chased them from Yima Olem, so it was quite unlikely that she would go back.

That left Lonyi. But where would she go from there? Would she honestly try to attack him now, without an army? No, she would certainly gather an army, a large one. She must be traveling to Lonyi to recruit shapeshifters. Then she would travel to other continents to recruit others. She probably already had several nomads on her side.

He was sure she had a signal or had set a time for all of them to storm his land, but she wouldn't make her move until everything was in place, so he had some time.

In case he was wrong, though, he would have some of his worthless, unreliable soldiers on lookout while he came up with another threat to keep the little princess worried about her mommy and daddy, which might just lead to a slip-up. Eventually, he would have her pinpointed.

She thought she was smart, but she didn't know who she was up against. He was going to destroy her. No one got the upper hand over him, no one controlled him. It was an unforgivable offense, and it infuriated him that, even for a short time, she had been holding the reins. But he had turned things around; she had lost her leverage, and she would finally realize the magnitude of the consequences for trying to control what she didn't understand.

Chapter Twenty-Nine

"Water again," Genevia stated sourly as she stood at the bow of the ship. "When will we learn that staying on land is better than traveling in a boat?"

"I don't know," Frelati answered with a smile as he leaned against the railing near her. He still didn't like it when she stood that close to the rocking ship's edge. "Maybe when we find a way to fly over the water."

Genevia laughed. "Creative, Frelati. How on Tiweln did *you* of all people manage to come up with that?"

Frelati shrugged. "It's not that farfetched. Pixies fly, dragons fly, birds fly…"

"But we can't, so yea, it's farfetched," Genevia chuckled and leaned farther over the railing to watch the water below as the prow sliced its surface.

Frelati shook his head and grimaced. "Will you stop that? You're making me nervous."

"Overprotective," Genevia muttered just loud enough for him to hear.

"I think a better word is careful. I prefer safety over what you're doing."

"Fine," Genevia sighed, moving minutely away from the bow.

Frelati raised a brow. "You call that moving?"

"Yes, I do." Genevia smiled in an extremely annoying way. "Now, stop bugging me and go play with your daughters."

Frelati turned to look at the girls, who were playing with Quinsnap. "They look like they're having plenty of fun without me. Will you please step back some?"

"You are so paranoid," Genevia said just before yawning. She was feeling Fezam's influence again. "Frelati?"

He crossed his arms as he saw her weave. "If you're trying to trick me into thinking you're going to fall overboard, you might as well forget it. I'm not falling for it again."

Genevia gripped the bars and said on a yawn, "I'm not kidding, Frelati. Fezam is…"

Her knees buckled, and Frelati reached her just as she hit the floor, somehow managing to stop her head from hitting the deck. Guilt flooded him, but after her first trick, could she really blame him for his disbelief?

"Someone bring me a pillow," he shouted over his shoulder.

Jezzie hurried it over to him.

"The poor girl. Why can't he just leave her alone?" Jezzie tut-tutted.

Frelati shrugged and leaned against the side of the boat, helping Jezzie position Genevia more comfortably. They were afraid to move her much in case it woke her from her important "chats." Frelati put the pillow in his lap and lay Genevia's head gently on it, stroking her hair with his fingers once before letting his hand fall. Now they just had to wait until she awoke.

Genevia ran to give her parents a hug. It seemed that ever since she had first met her mother three dreams ago, she couldn't get enough of their affection. "You're both all right?"

They smiled, but it was strained.

"We're okay, sweetheart," Lenaia answered. "It's not ideal, of course, but as far as prisoners go, we're doing just fine."

Fezam was impatient. "You've seen them and spoken to them; I think it's time for my 'hint,' as you so eloquently put it."

Genevia's eyes burned with annoyance. "I think you need to learn patience."

She turned back to her parents. "You're sure he hasn't done anything to you? You're given everything you need?"

Nalofré smiled, and Genevia wished she could see him in nice clothes, shaven and clean. She was sure he would be a very handsome elf.

"Don't worry about us, Alernoa. We'll be fine. We just want you to stay safe."

Genevia nodded. "I'll do my best."

"Give me my information, now," Fezam ordered. "Or I'll have one of your parents killed."

"Then, I guess you would lose your leverage, wouldn't you?" Genevia shot back. "I won't tell you a thing if you harm them."

"I said nothing about harming *them*. One will die unless you tell me what I want."

Genevia's lips tightened as she glared at the evil man.

"Tell me what I want to know," Fezam said coldly.

Genevia smiled. "Water is everywhere. That's all I can tell you."

"You are lying," Fezam accused.

Genevia crossed her arms. "Actually, I'm not, but believe whatever you want. Your paranoia works in my favor, so you won't catch me complaining."

She smiled at her parents. "Stay safe. I've got to wake up now."

"Give me better information next time or your parents will die," Fezam threatened.

"Wait two weeks before you contact me. By that time, I will probably be able to give you a wonderful hint," Genevia said with just a touch of sarcasm in her voice.

Then she awoke to the welcome feeling of a rocking boat and the worried, but sweet, blue eyes of Frelati. That had to be the best part of waking up.

Days had become mundane aboard ship. Everything stayed the same. The shapeshifters were constantly trying to surprise people, which allowed for some momentary excitement, but once land was seen on the horizon, everyone breathed a sigh of relief…even if it didn't look too inviting.

Smoke curled into the air from the active volcanoes that were part of the dismal, ominous landscape. Unlike other continents, there wasn't a friendly ridge of green foliage to welcome them. It was all black rock—unfriendly, unwelcoming, black rock. No one was looking forward to setting foot on that evil-looking land.

It would still take them a few days to reach it, but they would get there sooner than anyone wished.

"That's Azol?" Genevia asked sadly. "We have to travel across that?"

"Unfortunately," Frelati answered.

"There's not a lot we can shift into…"

"…that won't stick out like a sore thumb…"

"…on this continent."

"It's a little depressing." Slice grimaced.

"Well, on the bright side, we'll learn ta appreshate colors," Jezzie tried unsuccessfully to be chipper, but she knew that the effort had fallen flat.

"I'll probably get my books sooty," Asben pointed out. "I don't remember it being this bad the last time I visited."

Traynord shook his head. "This can' be goo' for me health."

The girls looked scared of the place, and Quinsnap wasn't even on deck. The smell of ash and smoke on his very sensitive nose was enough to drive him below.

The days following went by fast. None wanted to get too close to Azol, and it took a lot of willpower to keep sailing forward. They continued, and eventually they landed, however reluctantly, upon Azol's shores.

They secured the boat and began to walk. The ground was hard, the smell was strong and disagreeable, and everyone's eyes stung from the soot.

"How can anyone stand to live here?" Genevia asked rhetorically.

"A better question, honey, is why anyone would *choose* to live here," Jezzie said.

They walked on in silence. The land demanded that of them. With every step they took, it felt like they were being watched, and for all they knew, that could have been the case. The land was free of all vegetation. Only the thorns that pushed through the vicious cracks sprinkled on the ground testified to the fact that life could indeed survive there.

When night fell, Azol was even more forbidding and uncomfortable. The rocks poked into their backs as they slept. The soot got into their noses and throats, causing them to cough, which woke them often. Everyone was exhausted in the morning and completely dreaded the trek before them.

After traveling for half of the next day, they could barely lift their feet. By unspoken consent, they all stopped and took a nap inside a cave that was secluded and relatively cool. After they woke, they decided to stay put until the next morning. More than likely, they wouldn't run across a spot as good as this by nightfall.

They gathered together and ate bread and cold meat for their dinner, but they remained subdued, unlike with all previous meals on the journey.

"So, what's the plan after we reach Fezam's castle?" the twins asked.

Everyone looked to Genevia and Frelati.

"Um, well..." Genevia faltered and sent a glance at Frelati.

He had been staring at the ground and reluctantly lifted his eyes. "We haven't figured that out yet. I guess we'll just wing it."

"Wing it?" several people asked in unison.

"Nice plan, lover boy. You don't actually think that will work, right?" Dreda scoffed.

"I mean, we're going..."

"...against Fezam."

"You have to have..."

"...something more than that."

Silence followed the twins' statements before Traynord softly broke it. "I have faith in ye, la', bu' I'm hopin' ye have a bi' mor'n a wingin' i' plan."

"Well, I don't," Frelati stated flatly.

"Statistically speaking, we don't have much of a chance in the first place," Asben pointed out. "But without a course of action, we don't really have one at all."

"That's pretty dismal, hun," Jezzie scolded lightly.

Frelati looked around the group in annoyance. "Do any of you have an idea? I'm just a servant who was held prisoner here for sixteen years, but now everyone looks to me for guidance? What in my life has ever prepared me to make these decisions? Why doesn't someone else come up with something for a change?"

Genevia laid a hand on his arm. "Frelati, you've done a great job taking charge. Don't degrade what you've done."

Frelati said nothing and looked at no one.

"Let's look at our advantages," Genevia said. "The first and most important, the one that will work the best in our favor, is that he doesn't know we're here. Whatever we do will be a surprise.

"Then, if you look at our group, it's fairly small, which most people would count as a disadvantage, but really it can be used to our advantage. We can slip in unseen if we break apart, and we can blend in. If we had a large army, we would instantly be spotted, but with us being small, they may not realize we're here.

"Also, Fezam's army is not nearly as diverse as we are. They're just humans...no offense," she said, looking to Jezzie, Asben, and Traynord.

"None taken," Asben answered for them all.

Frelati finally spoke up rather reluctantly. "Actually, Genevia, even though the soldiers he has sent out so far are humans, around his castle he has his shadow beings. Hundreds of them; all like wraiths." He shivered unconsciously at the memory. "It will be hard to see them, if you even manage to before they attack, and if they manage to inject their venom...trust me, you won't be fighting after that."

"Hundreds?" Genevia repeated in dismay. "Why didn't you tell me?"

Frelati scoffed at the question. "And scare you half to death? Yeah, that would've convinced you to come with me."

"I deserved to know. I was eventually going to have to fight those things, and a warning would have been nice."

"You have your warning now."

"That's not exactly enough time to prepare. What if one of those things bites me? I don't want to be a shadow bear."

"It's a shadow being, not a bear, and you'll probably be perfectly fine."

"Probably, prob-ab-ly." Genevia drew out the word. "That is the key word. It allows a bite to come into the picture without you being at fault for giving me false information."

"Listen, Genevia, I'm going to be right by you. If one starts to attack, I'll deal with it."

"Who says you'll always be there?"

"I just will, and you're going to have to trust me on that," Frelati said. "Haven't I been with you throughout this whole trip?"

"Just about," Genevia said as she thought of those terrifying moments after she found out he'd been thrown in jail on Rom. She didn't want to remember that.

Frelati had instantly thought of that too, but he pushed his point forward. "Exactly, I've been there, and I'll do the same now."

"But what if you get bitten?" Genevia protested.

"I'm not going to play a what-if game with you. If it happens, it happens, and we can figure it out from there."

"You still should have told me."

Frelati sighed. "Yes, I should have, but I didn't, and it's too late to go back and fix it now. Can we drop it?"

Genevia didn't answer, and the others were pretending to be preoccupied with other things to give them a bit of privacy, although every word was heard.

"Genevia," Frelati pushed on softly. "You know I'm going to do everything in my power to keep you safe, right?"

"I guess," Genevia whispered with a shrug.

Frelati brought her chin up with a finger to look her in the eyes. "I will."

Genevia stared into his intense blue eyes and nodded. That brought a slight smile from Frelati, who tried to pull her from her melancholy. "Now, what was that last point of yours?"

Genevia shrugged. "Just that we're a widely diversified group. We have shapeshifters, elves, humans, a nomad, and a lefnode. We can do almost anything with everyone we've got."

"She makes a good point," Frelati continued for her, realizing she didn't feel like talking anymore. "I think we may have more of an advantage than we originally thought. We can use our individual gifts to break the prisoners out, and any of those who are capable of fighting can help us after. Here's what we can do."

Chapter Thirty

The guards to the prison were going to be relieved in two hours, but right now, they were bored stiff. They didn't have a thing to do except stand there. No one ever visited Azol, or even traveled through it. If they didn't have to be there, they would avoid it. It was dark, gloomy, sooty, rocky, bleak, frightening, and the smell was terrible. You never got used to it, no matter how long you stayed there.

To make matters worse, they weren't allowed to talk, unless it was directly associated to work, so that made the time go by even slower. All four would have given anything for a little excitement. They were about to get it. A swarm of hornets was flying their way.

"What is that?" one guard asked as he squinted at the indistinct mass flying closer and closer.

"It looks like hornets," another answered worriedly. "I'm allergic."

"What are they doing here? They aren't supposed to be on Azol," a third said.

"Are they coming toward us?" asked the fourth.

"It looks like it," replied the first guard.

They looked at each other nervously and backed up to the wall of the building. This wasn't just a small cloud; it was massive, dangerous, and the hornets kept coming.

"I can't stay here. If I get stung by even one, I'm gone," one guard said just before turning to run.

"Fezam will kill you," a guard yelled after him, but he got no response. Either he wasn't heard or he was ignored. Regardless, that guard had better get himself off Azol and hidden as quickly as possible. Fezam's wrath was not one to be tested.

The other guards pressed tightly against the wall, watching as the hornets got closer and closer. That was a cloud of death, painful death, certain death. They at least had a chance if they ran—Fezam might not catch them. Eyes wide in silent agreement, all turned tail and ran as fast as possible, following the path of the first fleeing guard. Fezam would not be happy with them.

They did not see the hornets reach the wall, but they would not have understood their eyes if they had. The cloud seemed to disappear; where once hornets flew, now stood Sizzle and Slice.

"Did you see…"

"…their faces!"

"That was by far…"

"…the best prank ever!"

They high-fived and motioned the others over. One by one the group ran to the wall and pressed their backs against it.

"Good job." Frelati encouraged quickly before kneeling down to Lela's level. "All right, Lela, change into one of the soldiers."

"I didn't see them good enough," she said quietly.

Frelati's forehead creased in thought, and he turned to the twins. "Can one of you shift into a guard?"

"Sure," they answered together, while one shifted into one guard and the other shifted into another. Then, a split second later, each shifted into one of the other two. "Take your pick." Lela studied them and picked the one who looked the easiest—short, thin, and bald. She shifted into him slowly.

"How…do I…talk?" she asked. The tiny voice coming from a man's body sounded quite unusual, but without hearing the guard speak, she had no way to mimic it.

"Just use my voice, Lela," Sizzle said.

"Like this?"

"That definitely sounds more normal," Slice murmured.

"Good job, Lela," Frelati said quickly. "Now, you all remember what to do next?"

Dayze answered first. "I stay out here and hide behind those rocks so that in case anyone comes I can make them see three guards, other than Sizzle, out front."

"The rest of us stay outside 'til you tell us it's okay to go in," Jezzie said next.

The twins shifted to their normal selves but kept the uniforms.

"I stay out here as a functioning guard in case some busybody comes along," Sizzle said.

"While I help Lela convince whatever guards are in there that we have to get Genevia's parents out of the cell," Slice recited.

"Good, now let's go," Frelati said with a nod. "Dayze, the rest of us are staying by the building, so you have to cover us. Don't let anyone realize we're here."

Dayze nodded and ran over to the group of boulders several feet away. Sizzle positioned himself military-like before the door as Lela and Slice slipped inside the dark building.

"It's...dark," Lela said, grabbing Slice's arm closely.

He smiled a bit uncomfortably. "Lela, not that I don't want to help you, but it's a little awkward for me having a grown man clinging to my arm like that."

She reluctantly let go but stayed close, a little too close.

"Try not to be scared. You need to act like you've been here before; be confident."

Lela nodded and straightened up a little bit.

"That's it." Slice gave her an encouraging smile.

They walked down the hall until they came upon a guard. He stood up quickly at their approach.

"What is your business here?" he demanded.

Slice spoke up. "We're here to escort Nalofré and Lenaia to Fezam."

The guard looked at each of them closely, then he stared at Lela. "Aren't you supposed to be guarding outside?"

Slice hurriedly explained. "Yes, but I needed one more escort. He was chosen. After I'm finished with him, he'll go back to his post."

"Does Fezam know about this?"

Slice laughed. "Of course he knows. If he didn't, do you think I would have told this soldier to leave his post? I'd lose my head!"

The guard smiled. "You're right about that. All right, you can go."

They had started to walk off when Slice turned back. "Oh, yeah, I forgot to tell you. The guards out front need your help, something about random hornets."

The guard grunted and walked off, muttering under his breath.

"Well, that takes care of one guard," Slice said, and they continued down the hall. "Now to find the cell."

"Papa said it has…a captain," Lela pointed out.

"Well, there's a lot of cells here, so we might as well start searching."

The outside door opened to reveal a soldier. Frelati could see the guard, but, thanks to Dayze, the guard couldn't see him. The moment the soldier stepped away from the building, Frelati knocked him out and, with the help of Traynord, hid him behind the boulders with Dayze. Then Frelati called to Asben, who rushed over with a small green leaf in his hand. "Here it is. This should keep him out for several hours."

They got him to swallow it and moved back to the wall.

"Now we just have to wait for any more guards coming through the door," Frelati whispered to Genevia.

"I hope this works."

"Of course it will."

"What do we do if it doesn't?"

"I don't think we'll get a chance to try anything else."

"Well, there was no captain down that hallway," Slice whispered with a sigh. "Maybe this third one will have what we're looking for."

They slowly peered around the corner, and Slice grinned.

"Found it. You ready?"

Lela nodded, but she was biting her lip.

"You'll be fine. Just let me do the talking."

With that, Slice straightened and rounded the corner, Lela on his heels. As before, the guard stood up from his chair quickly to confront them.

"What is your business here?"

Slice pushed authority into his voice. "We're here to take Nalofré and Lenaia to Fezam."

The guard looked at them closely, just as the first had done.

"I don't remember Fezam mentioning that," the guard said as he scrutinized Slice.

"You know he changes his mind on the spot. There is no itinerary for Fezam," Slice replied with a roll of his eyes.

The guard watched him a bit longer before nodding. "I'll unlock the door."

Out of habit, Slice opened his mouth to thank him but managed to reel the words in just in time.

"Just open the door," Slice demanded instead. "You know how Fezam likes to wait."

"I'll get to it in my own good time," the guard retorted angrily.

"Fezam will love to hear that when we arrive late with the prisoners." Slice smirked. "I hear he's come up with another form of torture that he's been dying to try out."

The guard shot them an angry look, but he did speed up. Apparently, threats weren't taken lightly here. After the door was open, Slice jumped in with the same comment as before.

"Oh, I forgot to tell you, the front guards need some help outside, something about hornets. You might want to hurry."

"Do you not realize I am a captain? I do not take orders from underlings like you."

"Fine, I'm not the allergic one who's battling hornets outside; I don't care."

The guard's face showed a little worry, proving that at least one guard at the front was a buddy.

"What are hornets doing on Azol?"

Slice shrugged. "Who knows? It isn't my job to keep up with local wildlife. I just deliver prisoners to their respective places." He paused and looked over his shoulder. "Your buddy's probably seriously wishing for your help right now."

The guard's worry overcame him, and he ran down the hallway. Slice breathed a sigh of relief. "Glad that's over with. Good job, Lela."

She gave him a small smile.

"Now, let's get Genevia's parents."

They walked through the door and saw the couple sitting on the floor against the wall. They didn't look too good. Lela hurried in.

"Biu'fa nene'h kefamgh!" she exclaimed, but it sounded strange coming out in a man's voice, and from a human no less.

Nalofré and Lenaia looked at Lela in confusion, understanding the words if not the meaning.

Nalofré cleared his throat and spoke in Welnish. "Excuse me? Whose parents?"

Regardless of his haggard appearance, he still sounded regal. Slice couldn't help but be impressed.

"Lela, you're in disguise," Slice said softly.

Her face fell. "Oh, I...forgot."

"What's going on here?" Nalofré demanded.

Slice grinned. "We're busting you out of here. Genevia's right outside."

"Genevia?" Lenaia asked in her beautiful, melodic voice.

"Your daughter," Slice said slowly in confusion before remembering Genevia's birth name. "Alernoa."

"Alernoa? She's outside! Take me to her!" Lenaia exclaimed. "Take me to my daughter!"

She was on her feet quickly but then had to lean against the wall. Lack of food had made her dizzy, and Nalofré, regardless of his own frailty, stood to support her.

"I want to see my daughter," Lenaia demanded.

"Follow us," Slice said, leaving the room.

Once in the hall, though, he stopped them. "I forgot about the other prisoners. Lela, take Genevia's parents outside and be sure to warn Frelati about who you are. Then send my brother in to help me get everyone else out."

"Frelati's here too?" Lenaia said happily. "Take me to them, please!"

Lela nodded and started down the hall with Lenaia, but Nalofré hung back.

"Do you have keys?"

"I don't need them," Slice said. "My brother and I are shapeshifters."

Nalofré paused. "Do you need my help?"

Despite the question, it was clear he really wanted to see his daughter, so Slice gave him the answer he wanted. "I'm fine; go see your daughter."

He grinned. "Thank you."

With that, he went to catch up with Lela and his wife. Slice watched him go and waited just a few minutes before his brother joined him. With a nod, they moved to the first door, and Sizzle shifted into a key. As Slice inserted him into the lock, he changed minutely to fit the tumblers. No lock could keep them out. Once unlocked, Sizzle shifted to stand beside Slice again, and they opened the door to release the first of the unknown prisoners.

"Two down..." Slice muttered.

"...entirely too many to go."

They shared a glance and grin. "Let's get a move on."

When the door had opened for a third time, Frelati had been about to hit the guard that walked through, but the soldier changed before Frelati was given the chance. Lela stood where the guard had, and she gave him a hug before turning to Sizzle to send him inside. Then she turned back to her papa.

"Ie deh hefaw om gsafa, keke," she said.

He knelt down and brushed her hair behind her ear. "I know you were scared, and I'm sorry, honey, but you're out now. You did a great job. I'm really proud of you."

She smiled, wrapping her small arms around his neck, and Frelati swung her up as he straightened. It was then that Frelati realized that two people were standing behind her, and they couldn't see anyone. They could hear them, though, and he could clearly see the confusion on their faces. Dayze must have allowed only Lela into the invisible group. He yelled over to Dayze.

"Drop the illusion, Dayze."

It took just a moment before Lenaia and Nalofré were able to see them. They saw Frelati with a little girl in his arms and behind him a long line of people, one of them Alernoa. After the guard had walked through the door, he'd disappeared, and he wasn't in this group either. One look at Alernoa and all thought of the guard evaporated.

Lenaia ran over to her daughter and hugged her tight, showering her in kisses. "Oh, my sweet, beautiful girl! It's been so long. Let me look at you."

She held her back at arm's length and tears glistened in her eyes. "You're so beautiful and so grown up."

She ran a hand down her daughter's cheek. "I'm so sorry I didn't get to see you grow up. You had a good childhood?"

Genevia managed a nod before she was pulled into another tight hug. Then Lenaia backed away to allow Nalofré to embrace her. The Queen went over to Frelati and started fussing over him, glancing momentarily at little Lela in his arms and giving her a smile, but her focus was on Frelati.

"Frelati." She kissed him on the cheek and looked him over. "Have you been taking care of yourself?"

He looked a bit uncomfortable, but he smiled. "I'm fine."

"I'm so glad you got away, but I missed you so much." She gave him a hug and then looked around her in confusion. Now that everyone had been greeted, she had an unanswered question. "But, tell me, where did that soldier go, the one that led us out here?"

Frelati smiled and bounced Lela. "That would be Lela."

Lenaia looked at him in confusion.

His smile widened slightly. "Her gift is to change into anyone she sees."

"Oh," Lenaia said, finally taking in the small girl. "And how did you come to find the child?"

"On the trip here, Genevia and I picked her up. She was an orphan." He smiled at the girl, and Lenaia could instantly tell Lela had wormed her way into his heart.

Genevia walked over and explained further. "She's our adopted daughter, along with Dayze over there behind the boulders. She's a dreamer."

Lenaia grinned. "Oh, you're getting along so well. It's better than we could have ever expected, Nalofré!"

Nalofré put his arm around his wife, smiling.

Frelati's brows knitted together. What did that mean? However, he wanted to make sure they didn't misconstrue the situation, to think he was overstepping his bounds. In Elven, he tried to reassure them and keep from upsetting Genevia. "You don't need to worry; I don't expect this to go anywhere. She can still marry whomever you've chosen. I'm going to leave once you're all safe. This was just temporary."

The smiles faded. Lela whimpered a bit, a crease in her brow, but otherwise she stayed silent.

"You don't want to get married?" Lenaia asked, keeping to the Elven language.

"No, we didn't…um, we kept things distant. I knew you wouldn't like it."

"I don't think you understand, Frelati," Nalofré said. "We…"

He cut off as the door opened to reveal around one hundred prisoners. The majority of them were elves; all of them were disheveled and malnourished, blinking in the bright sunlight as they huddled together just outside the door in uncertainty. Frelati turned to face them before realizing that they couldn't see him.

"Dayze, you can join us over here now," he called, motioning toward her. "And you don't have to hide us anymore."

The prisoners had been frightened when they heard the voice without seeing a source, but fortunately, no one had run. When they saw the small group of people, they calmed down a bit, but, as was the way with prison life, they remained wary. This reserve was obliterated and they very visibly relaxed after Nalofré stepped forward.

Their King smiled and began to explain the situation as best he could. "As you may or may not know, Frelati left a while back to search for my daughter, Alernoa."

There was murmuring in the crowd, and Nalofré turned to bring Genevia to the front beside him.

"This is my daughter, Alernoa. I'm sure most of you remember her as a baby."

More murmuring followed with nodding heads.

"She's here to help us, but I want everyone to try to keep her safe. She's the only heir to the Elfin throne and my only daughter. Please, try to protect her," he entreated while still maintaining a noble bearing. "This is the group that helped bring her to us. They need our help. So, from this point forward, I am one of you, and we will all listen to Frelati and Alernoa. They have been planning this, and they know what to do."

He walked over to his wife, and hand in hand they joined the other prisoners, awaiting their instructions. Frelati stepped forward to stand beside Genevia.

He was clearly uncomfortable, but nevertheless he came across confident, as usual. "I'll quickly introduce our group and explain what little piece of a plan we have. If anyone has any ideas beyond that, we'll be happy to hear them." Frelati paused a moment and took a deep breath. "You already know me, even though I probably look really different from the last time you saw me. As King Nalofré said, I'm Frelati. You all know of Alernoa, and she is…powerful." He turned to Genevia with a nod. "Show them something."

Genevia nodded and bent to touch the ground with her forefinger. As she lifted it, a green sprout followed and grew into a rose. The crowd pushed forward a bit to see then stared at Genevia in excitement and admiration.

"She can do more than that, grow trees and vines; she caused an earthquake once. Anything involving the earth, that's her domain," Frelati continued. "So we have that major asset. Then we have Lela." He set her down between himself and Genevia. "She can change into people she sees, a mirror image, so it's not quite exact, and talk like them as well. Will you show them, Lela?"

She nodded, picked someone from the crowd, and changed. The crowd drew in a breath and compared the replica to the original. Then Lela changed back and moved to hug Genevia. The large crowd made her nervous.

Frelati motioned behind him, calling Dayze forward. "This is Dayze. You can all tell she's a dreamer, and probably most of you have an idea as to what she can do, but for any who don't...Dayze, hide us really quick."

The crowd watched as Frelati's group disappeared before their eyes and then reappeared.

"Thank you, Dayze," Frelati said as she moved to Genevia's other side for reassurance. "We have the best cook we could ask for, Jezzie, and her husband, Asben, who knows almost everything. What he doesn't know, he can look up in one of his numerous books. He's great at puzzle solving and numbers. So he'll be a great strategist."

Jezzie and Asben stepped back so Dreda could come forward.

"This is Dreda. She hasn't traveled with us too long. She's a nomad, great with her hands. She led us through Suta without any mishaps, and I'm sure she'll be a great help to us now."

"We also have a lefnode with us, and you all know how good their sense of smell is, so he'll be an alarm if guards show up. His name's Quinsnap," Frelati said. "Also, inside are the two shapeshifters that released you. They're still letting prisoners out, right?"

Several nods confirmed his statement, and he continued. "They're twins; names are Sizzle and Slice." Several chuckles followed as he continued. "Because they're shapeshifters, they'll help tremendously. That's a brief run down. Any questions?"

No one spoke, and Frelati continued. "If we can, we'd like to get to Fezam and get him out of the picture before a huge battle breaks out. More than likely, once he's gone, his soldiers will run, and we won't have to fight at all. Does anyone know where Fezam stays specifically?"

Nalofré spoke up.

"Lenaia and I have paid him several visits." He paused and glanced sorrowfully at Genevia. "I'm terribly sorry, sweetheart, about the reason behind those visits."

She smiled her forgiveness.

"Will you take us to the place once we're ready?" Frelati asked.

"Certainly, but I have a question for you. Where are we all to stay? If we stand clear out in the open, we'll be spotted, and there isn't much coverage out here, certainly not enough to hide us all."

Frelati thought a bit, but it was Genevia who spoke up. "What if we used this building as our headquarters of sorts? Everyone could stay in there, and we could post guards at the door in case someone stopped by."

Several people started to protest loudly, but the king silenced them.

"While I, as does everyone else, loathe to be kept in that building again, we really have no choice, so I suppose that will do," Nalofré spoke for them all.

"We should go ahead and get inside, then. We don't want anyone to come across us," Frelati said, and they all proceeded grudgingly inside.

As they entered, another group of prisoners was on its way out. They explained quickly what the prisoners needed to know. There was only one hallway of cells left for Sizzle and Slice to open. Frelati left Traynord and Lela, in guard form, at the door to stand watch as he and Genevia went down the last remaining hallway to see if there was any way they could help. The twins had just opened a cell door as they walked up.

"It would move faster…"

"…if we both could change into keys."

"Both of you could unlock the cells," they said together.

"Just insert us into the locks…"

"…and we'll shift to fit the tumblers."

They changed into keys, and Genevia and Frelati bent to pick them up from the ground. They each went to different doors and did as they were told. Soon the cells were open, and the prisoners went to join the others.

"By the time we have all the prisoners out, we'll have a small army," Genevia pointed out to Frelati.

"Yes, but they are all weak, so I hope we won't have to use them for any fighting," Frelati said.

Two more doors opened, and more prisoners came filing out. Frelati and Genevia explained the situation, and they too went to join the others. It didn't take long before all the doors were open and all the prisoners were free.

After they opened the last door, Frelati voiced his worry. "It's been awhile. I hope no one at the castle knows we're here. We need the element of surprise."

Genevia rushed to reassure him. "Of course they don't know we're here. Who would tell them?"

With all the bustle of everyone in the prison building, it was easy to slip out unnoticed. It also wasn't all that hard to figure out which building Fezam inhabited—the big, black castle was a safe bet—but getting past the guards posed a bit of a problem. Of course, after mentioning that the whereabouts of Alernoa could be learned if they would just allow an audience with Fezam, it didn't take long to get past that obstacle as well.

Fezam didn't bother with a greeting. "What are you doing here?"

"I can tell you where you can find Alernoa."

Fezam narrowed his eyes. "How do you know her location?"

"I'm traveling with her."

The edge of Fezam's lips twitched in an almost-smile. "Then why would you give away her position?"

"I have a feeling you will make it worth my while. What do you plan on giving me as a reward for this information?"

"What do you expect?"

"Nothing less than two thousand in gold."

"You drive a hard bargain," Fezam said, impressed. "But what makes you think your information is worth that?"

"Isn't it?" the informant quipped with a raised brow. "My information, I'm sure, is worth much more than that. But because you don't, as of yet, know that for yourself, I feel my expectations are accurate."

Fezam studied the person before him closely. "You are very sure of your information."

"Well, I have great reason to be. In fact, I think you should go beyond the two thousand gold for the information I will soon give. After you hear my information, if it pleases you, which it certainly will, you should offer me an additional two thousand pieces."

"Or I could refrain from killing you now, and after I hear your information, if it pleases me, I could only give you two thousand in gold," Fezam said in mock pleasantry.

"You won't kill me. You want my information. That's why you didn't kill Alernoa's parents. Promise me the money, and I'll give you what you want."

"I promise nothing. Tell me the information, and I may give you the ridiculous amount of compensation you are requesting," Fezam said testily; his patience was beginning to run out.

The informant could tell that Fezam meant business.

"What would you say if I told you that Alernoa was close enough that with just a little walking she could be in your grasp?"

"I would ask just how much of an imbecile you believe me to be."

"None at all, I'm just stating facts. Right now, Alernoa is hiding in your prison."

Fezam decided to humor the traitor. "How did she enter Azol without my knowledge?"

"By boat, or ship rather, and after docking she walked here."

"Yet my guards did not capture her?"

"Obviously they weren't doing a very good job. As you can see, they didn't capture me either."

"Clever girl, a worthy adversary. I am very pleased with this information. You will get your money, and I will get my quarry." Fezam shouted for a guard. "Take several men, and I mean several, to the prison and bring back Alernoa and her group."

"You might want to take more men than you originally planned," the informant spoke up.

"Why is that?" Fezam asked.

"Because all the prisoners have been released."

Chapter Thirty-One

"Let go of me!" a struggling Genevia yelled at the guards before they broke through double doors and entered a large chamber. At the very front of the room sat Fezam on his black throne. Beside him stood Dreda.

Genevia had wondered how the soldiers knew to burst into that particular building with such great numbers. Now she knew. She glared at the traitorous nomad.

"How could you? We trusted you," she shouted at the girl.

Dreda smiled. "Rule number one, Princess, look out for yourself. It doesn't matter what you have to do or who you have to hurt to accomplish that."

Genevia said nothing more as she struggled against the two guards that held her and glared at the woman to whom she had forced Frelati to be kind.

"Alernoa, at long last we meet," Fezam said, drawing her gaze away from Dreda and onto his horrifying image. "And the timing is perfect. I am almost ready to completely rule this planet, and having your help would be a most wonderful development."

"I'll never help you!"

"Oh, I think you will."

"And why would I do a stupid thing like that?"

"Because if you don't, I will kill you."

"Go ahead and do it. I'm never going to help scum like you."

The Dark King was unfazed with the adamant denial. "I'll give you a night to...dream on it. In the morning, if you continue to be stubborn, I will kill you in front of everyone. I hope you make the wise choice."

"Nothing you do or say will make me change my mind."

"I'm sure all those you love will miss you and honor this misplaced determination, but you, my dear, will still be dead. Keep that in mind as you decide." He turned to the guards. "Take her to our best chamber and put it under heavy surveillance." His gaze locked onto hers as he sneered. "Just a small taste of the riches that could be yours should you choose to join me."

They did as ordered, and she struggled until they finally threw her alone into the solitude of her luxurious chamber.

Frelati slammed against the door. "I promised myself I'd never get locked up here again!"

"Well, there are some promises we can't keep because of outside forces we cannot control," Asben pointed out.

He was using a lamp to read his books; how he had managed to secure one, Frelati would never know. Asben had almost solved Genevia's problem; he could feel it.

"I feel so helpless," Frelati moaned. "Genevia's in that castle having to confront Fezam on her own. He could have killed her, and I wouldn't even know. I promised her I would protect her. I promised her parents that I would protect her. But where am I? I'm stuck in a cell while she's in danger."

"Once again, Frelati, I must point out that, because of circumstances you cannot control, the promise you made to Genevia cannot be fulfilled at the moment. That is no reason to berate yourself. Although, I realize that won't stop you."

"I just...I need to be over there."

"You can't be over there," Asben said. "Besides, you don't even like the girl. Why do you care what happens to her?"

Asben was reading like a maniac. The information was strongly pointing to something that could help. If he could simply figure out what it was talking about.

"I do care about her," Frelati argued. "I just…can't let anyone know that. It would mess up everything."

"How?"

"Because she's royal."

"Son, her family is the only Elfin royal family," Asben said absently. "Who exactly do you think she's supposed to marry?"

Frelati opened his mouth to answer but paused. "Someone… with influence and wealth." He shook his head. "At the very least, they would be higher up than I am."

"What makes you think that? Do you know that for a fact?"

"No, but…she deserves someone better."

"Seems to me she deserves to be with whoever she wants to be with," Asben said, but his mind still wasn't really on the conversation. He had a tendency to ignore his surroundings when he focused on his reading; it drove Jezzie crazy.

"Well, she has Kiem's essence. Can she even get married?"

Asben didn't answer. Finally, he had found what he was looking for. He beamed up at Frelati.

"That's not a problem anymore."

Frelati stared at him. "What are you talking about?"

"Listen to this…'In time of trouble, Kiem's essence will choose one to inhabit until trouble has passed. Then, it will return to shroud the planet until trouble begins again.' That makes it sound like Kiem's essence is in her only as long as Tiweln is in danger. Once everything rights itself, the essence returns to its origin, which is surrounding Tiweln," Asben explained. "At least, that's one reading of it."

"But what happens to the one who was chosen once the essence leaves?" Frelati asked, not sure if he wanted to hear the answer.

Asben scanned the page. "It doesn't say. Presumably, they go on to live a normal life. That would be the hope."

Frelati nodded. "Hope. The one thing that seems to be missing in this place."

Genevia was terrified. Today was the day. She had to face Fezam. She had to die.

"I guess the prophecy was right after all," she whispered.

The guards banged on the door before filing in, which seemed unnecessary if they were going to barge in anyway.

"You are to go to Fezam at once."

Genevia sighed and nodded, and they escorted her downstairs. She stood before Fezam, but unlike the day before, Dreda wasn't in the room.

"What is your decision?"

Genevia lifted her chin and met his red gaze. "Unchanged."

"I'm sorry to hear that."

"I'm sure you are," Genevia said sarcastically.

Fezam ignored her and spoke to the guards. "Gather everyone outside. They are to witness the punishment of those who rebel against me. Go quickly!"

It was done as ordered, which was too quickly for Genevia's taste. After a soldier informed Fezam that everyone was outside and waiting, she was dragged outside as well.

The soldier didn't exaggerate when he said everyone was outside. There were huge masses of prisoners and soldiers alike, as well as some frightening looking shadow creatures that had to be the dreaded shadow beings Frelati had described.

"And they're all here to see me die," Genevia said quietly. "How comforting."

Fezam stood alone a short ways from the crowd, and he had a large black bow but no arrows. The soldiers walked her to a place one or two hundred yards from Fezam. The two formed a line parallel to the crowd.

"If you try to run, you will be shot down. Not killed but harmed. We have several arrows trained on you," a soldier warned just before backing off to join the crowd.

Genevia faced Fezam, trying not to let her fear show. She took slow, deep breaths to calm herself; unfortunately, the endeavor brought no results.

Fezam grinned. "I've been looking forward to this, Alernoa."

"That doesn't surprise me."

Fezam wanted to rant a bit before he killed her, although he wasn't certain why. Usually, he preferred brevity, but this was special. He had hunted her far too long and having her die without knowing his plans just did not seem right. It was too easy that way, and he enjoyed long, agonizing torture. That was what gave him immeasurable pleasure; she would not escape without a bit of torment.

"I have waited entirely too many, long years for the moment when finally I would own this planet. It isn't as beautiful as my own Ashneer, but it is essential for me to have in my possession. You see, I have plans to own all of Imaemaroza, and, with this planet behind me, I will control it. I will be the ultimate dictator, and these people will be my slaves from birth until death. And after you're gone, no one will stand in my way. I will be free to reign, century after century, and no one will stop me. You were Tiweln's only hope, a pathetic hope, an empty hope, and now, Alernoa, you shall die."

Genevia watched as he lifted his bow. Still he had no arrow. A flicker of hope surfaced until she saw him trail his hand from the arced wood to the string, beginning to draw the thin, flexible cord to its farthest extension. He didn't need an arrow apparently. He could make his own.

Darkness trailed from his fingers as he created a deathly arrow. Black, wavy, and lethal, it was long and probably would pierce entirely too well. From the corner of her eye, Genevia could see several guards having to force Frelati to stay in the crowd. He was fighting like crazy, trying to stop Fezam's shadowy weapon from piercing her heart. She loved that he was fighting so hard to save her but hated to put him through that pain.

Her gaze traveled away from him, over her parents and the two girls she'd come to love as her own; her eyes glanced over the crowd, and then she stared Fezam in the eyes. She wouldn't go down without a fight. As he released the string, he wasn't rewarded with a flicker of fear in those beautiful green orbs, only stubborn confidence and fortitude.

Before the arrow hit, a circle of earth blocked its path. Fezam roared in anger, drawing another dark arrow. The earth beneath his feet began to shift, and he quickly shot the arrow before sliding to another position. Genevia dodged, momentarily distracted and allowing him to get his footing.

"You can't defeat me!" Fezam called.

As Genevia began growing vines to encircle Fezam's legs, she murmured, "I can try."

The vines tightened, and Fezam's red eyes glowed his hatred. "Let's see how you fare in the dark."

Instantly, the area around her began to grow dim until nothing but blackness surrounded her. Her breathing grew choppy as she was transported back to her childhood, facing every fear she had ever encountered. Where were these images coming from? They felt so real, but they couldn't be.

Spiders started crawling up her legs, snakes reared up at her ready to strike, bats were swooping overhead, their screeching loud in her ears. This was more than darkness…Fezam was doing something in her mind. She tried to calm her panic and think of a way to escape, but her only thought was "run." Crippling panic swept through her as she began trying to beat the spiders off her and block the attack of snakes from below and bats from above. She had to get away from these creatures. When she tried to run, they kept pace with her, the darkness a continuous shroud around her. She couldn't get away…maybe if she went up, up out of the dark, away from spiders and snakes.

Barely had she formed the thought than an earthen mound shot her upward, higher and higher as the bats became a thick cloud around her. She threw her arms around her head protectively, eyes squeezed tightly shut until the flutter of wings was no longer felt. Cautiously, she peaked through her arms and saw the dark cloud far below her. Looking out, her gaze focused on Fezam, a small figure from this height. Angrily, she brought her arms down to retaliate, but Fezam had been waiting. His aim was true when he shot a third dark arrow.

In shock, Genevia felt the arrow meet its mark and watched as it melted into her chest, feeling its inky fingers sweep throughout every corner of her body. The darkness was overwhelming, all-consuming. Her sight grew dim, and she stumbled back, forgetting she was high above the earth on a small platform. She was vaguely aware of the sweep of air as she fell and the deep pain as she landed, her column of earth dissolving with her fall. She managed to take one last, short breath, and then the world went black.

A slow smile spread across Fezam's face. He had won. Alernoa, carrier of Kiem's earthen essence, was dead. In triumph, he turned to the crowd.

"This has been a demonstration of what happens to anyone who attempts to defeat me. No one can overcome me. I am unstoppable." He swelled with pride. "If I can defeat your best, the prophesied earth essence, how can you think you have a chance? You all witnessed what happens when my wrath is provoked. You all saw…"

His voice faded in Frelati's ears. He stood in shock, staring at Genevia's limp body, until his legs could support him no longer and he fell to his knees. It was over; Genevia was gone. He had no feeling, no thought as he stared at her, but as he watched, a green mist lifted from her. It took on the shape of an elf, but it was obviously not even close to being that lowly.

The mist bent over and grew flowers of all shapes, sizes, and colors to cover Genevia's body. Then, it slowly straightened and turned to Fezam, who still raved over his prowess, completely oblivious to the threat that awaited him.

It took a few moments, but soon Fezam noticed that every eye had left him to look toward the place Genevia's body had fallen. He turned quickly, his body growing rigid at the sight before him.

"It's not possible," he breathed. "How? You're dead. I killed her. You're dead."

A booming, thunderous voice answered him. "You know as well as I that you cannot kill me in this way."

"I own this planet! Tiweln is mine!"

"No. It belongs to me. Leave this place."

"I refuse. I won this planet," Fezam yelled. "Alernoa is dead, and so are you."

"I cannot be bound in a mortal carcass, regardless of its longevity," the voice boomed. "Neither can I be killed within one."

"You are one, just as I am one with the essence of Ashneer."

A loud bark of laughter escaped the green, shining essence.

"Yes, you are bound," he scoffed. "You are bound through corruption. Your chosen has warped you, Kiem-hox, but I have no such limitations. You can be destroyed much easier than I for that very reason. You are as fragile as your bond, as corrupt as your bond, and may never separate. You have lost the secrets."

"No, that's not true!"

"It is. Search yourself, and you will find the truth in my words."

"I won!"

"No. You will need more than your simple power to defeat one of the essence now."

"This can't be possible!"

The green essence merely nodded.

Fezam searched for an advantage, any advantage. "You can't make me leave."

The mist nodded. "You have a key. I can do nothing to prevent your travel."

Fezam smiled maliciously.

"However, I can make it very uncomfortable for you here."

The mist took several steps forward with raised arms. Huge vines with long thorns grew up around Fezam, lashing at him brutally.

"Where there are thorns, there can be no peace."

"No, no!" Fezam yelled, too busy shielding himself to fight back.

The pain intensified, the lashing vegetation grew more violent.

"No!" Fezam's yell grew louder and more agonizing. The pain was unbearable.

He reached out a hand, upon which he wore his onyx ring. At sight of the trinket, the earthen essence halted the thrashing plants, watching Fezam raise the key and chant unknown words. Then, a portal opened.

"I'm not finished here!" Fezam yelled as he turned toward his escape. "This planet will be mine!"

He disappeared through the floating orb, and it closed behind him. Every shadow being fled as he left Tiweln, and many soldiers seemed to wake, looking around in confusion. The green essence slowly dissipated, simply vanishing as quickly as it had appeared, but Frelati did not notice this as he broke away from the crowd and ran to where Genevia lay. He fell to his knees before her flower covered body, afraid to disturb the precious blooms despite his wish to be close to her. He bowed his head and covered his face as racking sobs shook his body.

Lenaia and Nalofré walked forward slowly, crying silently.

"I didn't get to tell her how much I loved her," Lenaia said softly. "She didn't get a chance to live."

Nalofré pulled her close for a moment, but Lenaia broke away to kneel next to Frelati. She hugged him, resting her head against his shoulder, but he gave no response.

"We always knew you would be perfect for each other," she said quietly. "You did a wonderful job keeping her safe while she traveled here. I wish I could have seen your union. She was taken too soon, my baby."

"What?" Frelati managed to ask through his haze. "What union?"

"You were betrothed," Lenaia said softly as she looked down upon the flowers. "It may not help, but I know that she loved you. I could see it in her eyes when she looked at you."

Frelati turned from her to stare at the colorful arrangement of flowers. It seemed a mockery to the lifeless body it hid. The King and Queen took one last look at where their daughter lay before turning to leave Frelati alone with her. He had known her longer than they had, and he needed time. Time to grieve, time alone.

That's irony, Frelati thought to himself. *I've just been given permission to marry her, and she's lost to me forever.*

His life seemed to be full of perpetual irony, but this was the worst hand life had ever dealt. The pain he felt at that moment was so intense he had no doubt that his heart had split in two.

Chapter Thirty-Two

"He hasn't moved in three days," Lenaia said to Jezzie. "He refuses to eat, he's sleeping fitfully...I'm worried about him. I don't know how much longer he can go on like this."

Jezzie shook her head sadly. "Poor dear, I knew all along that he loved her, but he never told her, and he constantly denied it."

"Why? Why would he do such a thing?"

"He said ya wouldn' like it," Jezzie answered. "He said that he didn't have a chance because he wasn't good enough."

Lenaia sighed a soul-deep, sorrowful sigh. "We should have told him. I didn't think he would fight it if he loved her; we wanted to see if they felt any affection on their own."

"Affection is a mild term for what they felt, but he fought it; the boy fought it somethin' fierce."

"I told him the wrong thing," Lenaia muttered as she closed her eyes tightly.

"What are ya talkin' about?"

"I told him they were betrothed," Lenaia said remorsefully. "I thought that would give him some comfort, let him know that we would be there for him in his pain, but it must have simply made things worse. I didn't realize...I didn't want him to keep anything more bottled up inside. He's so quiet already..."

Jezzie looked at the woebegone face of the Queen. "Go talk ta him. You can make it better. Besides, we need to break through somehow. We can't stay here too long. We need ta go home an' try to put this behind us."

Lenaia nodded and stumbled toward Frelati. He didn't hear her approach. He didn't seem aware of anything. She looked down at his hunched form. He had suffered greatly for one so young. Her eyes traveled to her daughter's flower-covered body. The wind was playing with the blooms so that they began to dance. It looked so peaceful and beautiful, a mockery of the tragedy that had taken place as the flowers bobbed with the breeze.

"But I don't feel any wind," Lenaia whispered as the thought registered.

Frelati's head came up as he looked at her. His eyes were expressionless, almost dead. It was as if he was merely going through the motions, giving the response he knew was expected of him. Then he saw her eyes glued to the flowers covering Genevia, and he slowly turned to look at the spot as well. The flowers were moving, but as Lenaia had said, there was nothing to make them move. There was no wind.

Frelati stared, gradually coming back to life as he waited for some answer to the strange phenomenon. The flowers rustled more and more. Then a soft sigh was heard though the blooms.

"Genevia?" Frelati said tentatively as he leaned nearer.

There was no answer, and he began to wonder if his mind had finally gone when the flowers began to part. Slowly, an arm rose from between the colorful, bobbing flower faces, stretching fully as if the fingers hoped to brush the sky. Frelati's heart beat faster and disbelief shined in his eyes when he heard another soft sigh issue from within the foliage.

"Genevia...." His whisper made barely a sound.

The arm disappeared again, but in its place, Genevia's head popped up, her eyes glazed with tiredness and confusion. She brushed a hand across her eyes with a yawn, finally taking in the awestruck assembly around her.

"What's going on? Where am I?" she murmured, looking all around her in hopes of finding something familiar about the landscape.

Frelati's breathing quickened. "You're…you're alive! Genevia, you're alive!"

He grabbed her quickly, pulling her into a tight hug.

"I thought I'd lost you," he said, tears pulling at his eyes, but he refused to shed them. "I'm so sorry for everything. I was wrong, so wrong."

Genevia hugged him back through her confusion. "What were you wrong about?"

"Genevia." Frelati pulled back to look at her face. "I…I love you."

Genevia stared at him. "What?"

Frelati glanced down and took a deep breath. "I said…I love you."

Genevia reached up to place her hand on his cheek.

"I didn't think I'd ever hear you admit that," she said quietly. "I waited because I loved you and I knew you loved me…but you were so determined."

Frelati finally looked into her eyes. "I'm sorry. I was wrong."

"You've made it right; that's what counts," Genevia said with a small smile, and her eyes lifted to see her mother, who was patiently waiting for her turn with her daughter. "Mother?"

Lenaia nodded, tears rolling down her cheek. "My baby."

She knelt down and pulled Genevia into a hug.

"My sweet, sweet baby girl, I've waited so long to hold you again."

Genevia closed her eyes and hugged her mother tight.

"I'll be around, and you can hug me anytime you want."

A sob broke free from Lenaia's throat at hearing those words of acceptance.

Jezzie turned from her perch at the top of the hill to see how the heart to heart was going down below. It took awhile for her to realize that Genevia was the third person in the group, but even then she wasn't sure if she believed it.

"Genevia," she whispered before raising her voice to yell the good news to the others. "Genevia, she's alive!"

Everyone from the group turned to look and then ran en masse toward Genevia.

"How is this possible?" Nalofré exclaimed.

Asben stared at Genevia as he worked it all out. "'In three days, all will mend.' That's what it was talking about. She mended in three days."

He knelt to examine the flowers, then gave a startled laugh. "These are all healing plants! They've been healing her wound."

Nalofré knelt to hug Genevia. "You're alive. Alernoa, you're alive!"

"What's been going on? Where's Fezam?"

Frelati answered. "He's gone. You did it. You saved Tiweln, just like I always knew you would."

It had been several months since that terrible day when everyone had thought Genevia was dead, and everything seemed to be working out beautifully now that Fezam was gone…however long that would be.

Asben and Jezzie had opened another bakery and a library. Genevia and Frelati visited them from time to time, and they always got free bread and a berating from Jezzie about how thin they were. This admonishment had them leaving the shop with entirely too much food, but the happy Jezzie that remained inside made it all worthwhile.

Sizzle and Slice had gone home to a fierce scolding from their mother, who made sure to shift into an extremely tall version of herself to overwhelm them. They had eventually calmed her down, but she wouldn't let them out of her sight for a while. That was fine with the twins, for a few weeks. They began making trouble soon after, but it was local trouble. Sizzle transferred his affection from Dreda to another shapeshifter. The thought of betrayal didn't sit very well with him.

Dreda had very humbly walked up to Genevia to ask for forgiveness. Genevia had given it to her, but she knew that the apology was just for self-preservation. She ended up rejoining her nomad tribe. It turned out that Quiz did a lot of good for her, and she eventually really did repent of her traitorous deed to Quiz.

Traynord went back to his perfect life, and his happiness was complete. Genevia had given him a brand new boat, and he was sailing the seas. He popped in now and then to say hello and give the girls little gifts he had picked up in his travels, always with a smile and stories full of adventure.

The girls were perfectly happy. They lived in the palace on Meufa and never ran out of things to do, especially with Dayze creating new worlds for them to explore. They finally had two parents that loved them, and they felt secure. They always had enough food, and they were treated kindly. Even their grandparents spoiled them, and Lela was thrilled at being a little princess.

Quinsnap, of course, lived on Meufa as well and trailed Genevia everywhere. Nothing was ever lost for long because Quinsnap would find it. He loved playing with the girls, who gave him plenty of attention and entirely too many treats, regardless of how often Genevia warned against it.

As for Genevia and Frelati, they were floating on clouds. They were getting married…today. The only thing that could possibly make Genevia happier was if Drisgal was there to walk her down the aisle to meet her groom. As she closed the clasp of her locket around her neck, she gazed at the portrait of herself and Drisgal. She had found the perfect place for the portrait that had been done so long ago and that had somehow managed to survive through the grueling travel she had put it through. It hung just to the side of her dressing table. She saw it every morning and evening.

With a smile filled with both joy and sadness, she rose, brushing out any creases that might have found their way into the folds of her wedding gown. She glanced in the mirror to check her hair, done up beautifully by her lady's maid, and heard the door open behind her.

"You need to hurry," Lenaia said with a smile as she moved to place a kiss on Genevia's cheek. "I love you, Alernoa. You're beautiful."

She hurried to the front of the crowd. The wedding was outside, beneath the most beautiful oak tree. Flowers were in bloom all around, but none could rival the beauty of the bride as she awaited her turn to walk to the front. All attention was focused on her as the music changed to signal her arrival, her debut into married life.

With a happy heart, Princess Alernoa, once simply Genevia, prepared for her first step into her new life.

A world away, Fezam too was making a new beginning.

As Genevia took her first step down the aisle, Fezam began his first phase in the downfall of Randor.